OXFORD WORLD'S CLASSICS

THE QUEEN OF SPADES

AND OTHER STORIES

ALEXANDER SERGEEVICH PUSHKIN was born in Moscow in 1799 and as a schoolboy was recognized as a poetic prodigy. In 1817 he received a nominal appointment in the government service, but for the most part he led a dissipated life in the capital producing much highly polished light verse. His narrative poem, *Ruslan and Lyudmila* (publ. 1820), secured his place as the leading figure in Russian poetry. At about the same time a few seditious verses led to his banishment from the capital. During this so-called 'southern exile', he began his novel in verse, *Eugene Onegin*. As a result of further conflicts with state authorities he was condemned to a new period of exile at his family's estate of Mikhailovskoe. There he wrote some of his finest lyric poetry, and completed his verse drama *Boris Godunov*. In 1825 he was still in enforced absence from the capital when the Decembrist Revolt took place. Despite close friendships with some of the conspirators he was not implicated in the affair. In 1826 Nicholas I finally permitted him to return to Moscow, ending seven years of exile. By the end of the decade, he had turned increasingly to prose composition. In 1830, while stranded at his estate of Boldino, he completed *Eugene Onegin*, wrote a major collection of prose stories (*The Tales of Belkin*), and composed his experimental 'Little Tragedies'. In 1831 he married Natalya Goncharova. The rest of his life was plagued by financial and marital woes, by the hostility of literary and political enemies, and by the younger generation's dismissal of his recent work. His literary productivity diminished, but in 1833, he produced both his greatest prose tale, *The Queen of Spades*, and a last poetic masterpiece, *The Bronze Horseman*. In 1836 he completed his only novel-length work in prose, *The Captain's Daughter*. Enraged by anonymous letters containing attacks on his honour, he was driven in 1837 to challenge an importunate admirer of his wife to a duel. The contest took place on 27 January and two days later the poet died from his wounds.

ANDREW KAHN is Reader in Russian Literature, University of Oxford, and Fellow and Tutor, St Edmund Hall. He is the editor of *The Cambridge Companion to Pushkin*, and his books include *Pushkin's 'The Bronze Horseman'* (1998) and *Pushkin's Lyric Intelligence* (2008). He has also edited Montesquieu's *Persian Letters* for Oxford World's Classics.

ALAN MYERS has translated a wide variety of contemporary Russian prose and poetry, including poems, essays, and plays by Joseph Brodsky, and *An Age Ago*, a volume of facsimile versions from the golden age of Russian poetry. His translations of Dostoevsky's *The Idiot* and *A Gentle Creature and Other Stories* are also in Oxford World's Classics.

OXFORD WORLD'S CLASSICS

*For over 100 years Oxford World's Classics have brought
readers closer to the world's great literature. Now with over 700
titles—from the 4,000-year-old myths of Mesopotamia to the
twentieth century's greatest novels—the series makes available
lesser-known as well as celebrated writing.*

*The pocket-sized hardbacks of the early years contained
introductions by Virginia Woolf, T. S. Eliot, Graham Greene,
and other literary figures which enriched the experience of reading.
Today the series is recognized for its fine scholarship and
reliability in texts that span world literature, drama and poetry,
religion, philosophy and politics. Each edition includes perceptive
commentary and essential background information to meet the
changing needs of readers.*

CONTENTS

Introduction   vii

Select Bibliography   xlix

A Chronology of Alexander Pushkin   lii

A Short Chronology of the Pugachev Uprising   lv

TALES OF THE LATE IVAN
PETROVICH BELKIN   1

    The Shot   7
    The Snowstorm   19
    The Undertaker   31
    The Stationmaster   38
    The Lady Peasant   50

THE QUEEN OF SPADES   69

THE CAPTAIN'S DAUGHTER   101

PETER THE GREAT'S BLACKAMOOR   209

Explanatory Notes   246

INTRODUCTION

In his late imitation of a poem by Horace, Alexander Pushkin predicted that his own verse would come to be widely read. In the 1820s he had enjoyed extraordinary fame as a poet. With his turn to prose in the 1830s not only had Pushkin's celebrity suffered, but he became the focus of hostile criticism. Confident as he was about the verdict of posterity, he could not have foreseen the universality of his appeal as poet and prose-writer in modern Russian culture—nor the complexity of his status. For the masses of Soviet Russia he became a set text in school and a visible presence: there is scarcely a town without its statue of Pushkin and a street bearing his name. For the Soviet authorities, particularly in the period leading up to the 1937 centenary of his death on the eve of the Stalinist Terror, the study of Pushkin's life and art became an act of cultural appropriation and means of self-legitimation for a political regime quick to capitalize on the writer's uneasy relation with his own ruler. The next step was to claim him as a truly democratic writer, and ignore the fact that he was an aristocrat proud of his class and heritage. For the Russian poetic tradition he represents what Harold Bloom calls a 'strong poet' whose verse has set a standard to imitate or to react against through a range of intertextual devices like allusion and quotation. In Russian literature his life has come to embody the tragic fate of the poet in a country where, at least until now, the moral authority of the writer carried weight and personal risk. Consciously or unconsciously, Russian poets, from Lermontov in the early nineteenth century to Mandelshtam a century later, seem to have assimilated parts of Pushkin's life into their own *cursus honorum*. It is hard to think of a great Russian poet who has not expressed an autobiographical anxiety of influence about living under the spell or shadow of Pushkin's life.

Pushkin's career from 1820 till his death in 1837 spans what is widely known as the Golden Age of Russian Literature. Of the older generation of pre-Romantic poets, Konstantin Batyushkov (1787–1855) and Vasily Zhukovsky (1783–1852) stand out, the former for his elegies in the Italian style and imitations of the Greek Anthology, the latter for his famous translations of Gray's 'Elegy written in a Country Churchyard', quasi-mystical Ossianic lyrics, and rousing ballads. From Pushkin's immediate contemporaries the idylls and pastoral verse of Anton Delvig (1798–1831), the philosophical and narrative poems of Evgeny Baratynsky (1800–44), and the songs of Nikolai Yazykov (1803–47) all still deserve to be read. Against this constellation of major and minor poetic talents, most of them little known to Western readers, Pushkin's star shone brightest. From almost the moment when Pushkin fell in a duel in January 1837 he became a mythic figure in Russian culture. His own contemporaries referred to him as the 'sun' of Russian poetry. It is true that his immediate posthumous reputation suffered as literature with a more overtly ideological tone enjoyed a vogue, but the conscious repudiation of Pushkin that occurs from time to time by writers of various political and literary inclinations in itself testifies to his canonical position: the utilitarian critics of the 1860s could not forgive his aestheticism, and in the early twentieth century the Futurists coped best with their predecessor by denying his value altogether.

Pushkin had declared that prose demands 'thought, thought, and more thought', but even before he turned to prose his diverse accomplishments gave ample evidence of a keen intellect. For his contemporaries he was above all the master of the lyric poem, verse that is famous for its formal perfection and its reticent lyric persona, and infamous for its resistance to translation. The English-language equivalent of his lyric talent exists only in a desert-island dream of the technical brilliance, wit, and incisiveness of a Ben Jonson combined with a Keatsian sensuous apprehension of the physical world. In the 1820s his lyric genius was in full spate and earned him a loyal audience even at a distance. The poet had been sent into exile in 1820 for writing politically incautious verse and for incendiary comments in public. The immediate cause of his punishment was the 'Ode. Liberty' (1817), which circulated anonymously and caused an enormous stir. In the best tradition of Enlightenment political philosophy, but with the menacing example of the French Revolution as a backdrop, it reminded Alexander I that he too was subject to the law, and that tyrants could expect to meet the fate of his father, Paul I, who had been assassinated in 1801. Initially Alexander wished to exile Pushkin to Siberia, but in the end, owing to the intercession of friends at court, the poet was sent to southern Russia for a period of four years, beginning in Kishinev and Odessa. Although never directly involved in any plots against the government, Pushkin liked to live dangerously and continued to maintain links with men of liberal political sympathies. In 1824, as punishment for a blasphemous correspondence, he was sent to his family's estate at Mikhailovskoye where he lived in isolation until the new Tsar, Nicholas I, pardoned him and recalled him to the capital in 1826. Their initial interview after Pushkin's return marked the beginning of an uneasy relationship, in which the Tsar acted as the poet's personal censor. In the narrative poems of his southern exile Pushkin had reduced with elegant economy the Byronic narrative to its bare essentials: exotic scenic description and characterization were pared away, laying bare stark emotional and philosophical contrasts. In *The Gypsies* (1824), drama and psychology make a riveting vehicle for Pushkin's deconstruction of the romantic reception of Rousseau and his idealized vision of man in a state of nature. *Boris Godunov* (1825), modelled on the example of Shakespeare's historical plays, is a technical *tour de force*, drawing the reader into the very pell-mell of history through a kaleidoscopic succession of scenes and superb study of the psychology of the ruler; it also embodies Pushkin's early thoughts on his philosophy of history, thoughts that would eventually seek expression in the prose works of his final years. By the late 1820s he had also demonstrated a superb gift for realism and social satire in *Eugene Onegin*, a novel, but one composed in verse. As he pointed out to a friend, 'there's a diabolical difference'.

By the late 1820s, out of economic necessity and a natural inventiveness—he is often described as Protean—Pushkin began to turn to fiction and history. With the rise of the reading public and growing circulation of newspapers and journals, the demand for fiction increased in the first decades of the nineteenth century. The notion of the professional writer became conceptually viable for the first time in Russia, even if it still was

economically tenuous.[1] But the public that had lionized his
poetic creations cold-shouldered his prose. Their preferences
lay with the work of writers such as Faddei Bulgarin, who inter-
larded a verbose style with tendentious patriotic sentiment years
after the Napoleonic campaigns. Pushkin's inability to achieve a
commerical success on the scale of his rivals only aggravated the
wound that his financial reliance on the Tsar caused his sense of
professionalism and personal pride. Far from repudiating verse,
Pushkin wrote many of his greatest poems in the last years of his
life, but he desisted from publishing works that were written in
something like the private language of a man beset by problems
who found an outlet in the pure and independent realm of
language and art. When Evgeny Baratynsky, another great poet
of the age, read through these poems in manuscript not long
after Pushkin's death he was stunned by the compression of a
whole range of philosophical argument and ideas that Pushkin
had only hinted at in his earlier poems.

It would be strained to counterpose Pushkin the poet and
Pushkin the prose-writer. In both spheres Pushkin is one of the
great artists of literary transformation who assimilates, parodies,
reduces, and reinvents. Great writers are great readers, and
Pushkin's originality begins in his appropriation and recombination of literature. The energies and traits that characterize his
lyric gift also define his performance as a writer of prose. While
clarity and sparseness are the terms most often applied to his
descriptive style, part of Pushkin's great talent as a stylist was
his chameleon-like powers of imitation. Leaving aside their formal differences, what sets the lyric and prosaic branches of his
creation apart is the observation that while a single impulse to
refine his models animated both the poet and the prose-writer,
great separate themes can be traced through each aspect. Poems
begin in feeling, and his lyric talent was a nuanced instrument of
intense yet elegant expression that examined the poetic speaker's
inner state and his relation to the world. In his fiction the same
impulse to rework literary conventions and genres combines
with a talent for elaborating plots out of ancedote that regularly

[1] See William Mills Todd, III, *Fiction and Society in the Age of Pushkin:
Ideology, Institutions, and Narrative* (Cambridge, Mass., 1986).

dramatizes the force that engages his wit and curiosity, and makes Pushkin's world go round—namely, chance.

Tales of the Late Ivan Petrovich Belkin

Pushkin spent the autum of 1830 on his family's estate at Boldino near Moscow. This period, often called the first Autumn at Boldino, saw a creative outpouring of spectacular versatility. Lyric poems, narrative poems, dramas, and prose flowed unstintingly from his pen, among them *The Tales of the Late Ivan Petrovich Belkin*. In the late 1820s Prince Peter Vyazemsky (1792–1878), a critic of impeccable taste and rare humour (at least when compared to the more celebrated but dour Vissarion Belinsky) had lamented that 'Mirth, genuine and infectious cheerfulness very rarely are to be met with in our literature'. As Vyazemsky but few others recognized at the time, *The Tales of Belkin* marked a singular advance for these very qualities in Russian literature. Their critical reception was unenthusiastic; and at least initially in some cases spectacularly literal-minded, as numerous readers fell for the ruse of the publisher's letters and believed in the actual existence of Belkin. Belinsky, of course, was not taken in by a device that had been widely popular since the eighteenth century, but he none the less found the stories frivolous and too artificial to satisfy his growing conviction that the purpose of literature was not to comment on literature, but to explore life. Pushkin, on the other hand, saw parody as a challenge to both the writer and the reader, and in a note written shortly before he composed *The Tales of Belkin* made its appreciation a measure of cultural achievement:

The art of imitating the style of famous writers has in England been brought to perfection. Walter Scott was once shown verses, supposedly written by him. 'I think these are my verses,' he said laughing, 'I have been writing so many for so long that I daren't disclaim even this nonsense!' I do not think that any of our famous writers could mistake a parody . . . for his own work. This type of jest demands rare flexibility of style; a good parodist has every style at his command, and ours has barely one.

Through the great age of Russian Realism the cycle of stories, excepting the more overtly humanitarian 'The Stationmaster',

frustrated critics who saw satire as the vehicle of social instruction and political criticism, whilst having little patience for caricature and parody. Beginning in the early twentieth century, the
Formalist school of criticism spearheaded a new approach to the
study of literature by concentrating on its factitious quality outside its historical context. It investigated not only the relation of
literature to life, but of literature to literature in texts that simultaneously cast the illusion of reality while destabilizing that
reality through a complex set of devices that acknowledged the
artificiality of the text. It was in that climate that the critical
reception of *The Tales of Belkin* came into its own. Each of the
tales can be related to distinct movements in Russian romantic
and sentimental fiction. *The Tales of Belkin* are woven from a
tissue of earlier works, devices, motifs, and themes, and keep history at a distance while all the same trying teasingly to pass off
their story-telling as true to life.

It will be appropriate to examine in greater depth Pushkin's
debt to the novels of Sir Walter Scott in the context of his historical fiction, where this influence is most apparent and significant. However, in organizing *The Tales of Belkin* Pushkin
appropriated Scott's standard device of introducing his works
with a fictitious history of their author, including an explanation
of how they came to be published. While the topos of the adventitious manuscript long precedes Scott, he exploited it as a way
of protecting his own anonymity as the author of *Waverley*.
The usual preface, of which the introduction to *Old Mortality*
(1816) is the classic example, establishes a hierarchy of relations
between the text and a number of figures responsible for its
publication. Typically, the stories, presented as historical fact,
originate with a narrator who passes them on to an intermediary
figure who dies before he can publish the stories he has collected. These tales in turn come into the hands of a publisher
who testifies to the integrity of their collector and claims to
publish them as he desired. While Pushkin borrows this structure, his version involves further complications. He inserts two
more links in the chain, so that there are four stages of transmis-
sion from the original stories collected by Belkin, who passes
them on to his good neighbour in Nenaradovo (needless to say,

an invented place), who in turn sends them to his relation and heir Maria Alexeyevna Trafilina. Unable to provide information on Belkin, she refers the editor to an anonymous neighbour, through whom they become the possession of the publisher A.P. Pushkin diverges from Scott in two important ways. Whereas Scott's narrator normally purports to have collected his material from a single source, Belkin identifies separate narrators for each story, giving their rank or status and initials. In shoring up their realistic effect Scott usually gives ample factual evidence concerning the publisher. Here little is said about A.P., whose identity most readers had no trouble guessing, as the clear intention is to limit his role as the mere agent of their publication. The fun of the literary mystification lay in persuading the reader of Belkin's existence, and this was best corroborated by an independent figure who supplies much biographical information:

Ivan Petrovich left a good many manuscripts behind him, some of which are in my possession, though some have been put by his housekeeper to sundry domestic uses. For example, last winter all the windows in her wing of the house were sealed up with the first part of an unfinished novel of his. The tales mentioned above were his first efforts, I do believe. They are, as Ivan Petrovich used to say, for the most part true, and heard from various people. The proper names, however, are almost all invented, and the names of villages and hamlets borrowed from those hereabouts, which is why my village gets mentioned somewhere too. There was no sort of malice intended, it was just lack of imagination. (pp. 5–6)

Readers nowadays are all-too familiar with legal disclaimers that head works of fiction, typically reminding one that characters, names, and events bear no resemblance to real persons and incidents. Although he is writing to the publisher, his criticism of Belkin is intended for Pushkin's audience, presenting precisely the type of naïve reader the work so easily runs rings around. Belkin's neighbour has not acquired the modern reader's almost instinctive wariness of unreliable authors and narrators. For her the author's comments on his own fiction are entirely believable, but she never makes clear precisely what he meant in denigrating his own imagination. What proportion of truth and fiction are mixed together? Are the stories no more than gossip ('malicious ulterior motive'), second-hand tales lightly disguised? Did Belkin transcribe his sources more or less verbatim, applying no artifice of his own? Or is it more likely that 'heard from varous people' refers only to the germ of each tale, and that Belkin's neighbour lacked the imagination to mistrust the playful author's modest pose and grasp his sophisticated talent for parody?

The impossibility of answering these questions with absolute certainly is what makes this work so beguiling. There have been critics who, taking Belkin at his word when he purports to be reproducing five true stories of individual narrators, have attempted through close textual analysis to filter out Belkin's own narrative voice and show its distinctness from the original teller of the tale. But in the end the entire text belongs to Belkin, and efforts to discriminate between an original account and Belkin's reworking becomes a hopelessly subjective and unreliable operation. Its results are unreliable above all because we lack the information and authorial sanction that are necessary to resolve the fundamental question before the reader: is Belkin an intentional parodist? Three possibilities confront us: whether (1) Belkin retells closely what he has heard, in which case his original narrators reveal a wide range of talent; or (2) fashions a story out of the original tale by clumsily applying techniques from contemporary fiction, sometimes with loss of control of his material; or (3) knowingly mimics a style because he is good at playing at being a 'bad' writer. *The Tales of Belkin* keep the reader perpetually guessing at the relative status of fiction and truth, sincerity and mockery in the text, and engaged by the possibility that a story is enjoyable because it is clever at being an inferior work, or because the failed pretension at literariness offers its own amusements. In the end, therefore, the point of the two extra-literary 'documents' at the beginning is that they raise the problem of how difficult it is without external guidance to judge the intention and effect of skilful pastiche. In 1834 the more discerning recognized that Belkin's endearing ambiguity was A.P.'s ruse, designed to give enjoyment to that small portion of the reading public equipped with the knowledge and irony and sense of play of the Pushkinian reader. Those readers who failed to see A.P. as a password for Pushkinian irony and spiritedness took it all literally, and felt empowered as story-tellers while they had in fact been entirely gulled. If anyone with experiences akin to Belkin's could become an author, not everyone, however, was a worthy Pushkinian reader. In matters of sensibility Pushkin was not a democrat, but his challenges to the reading public use wit and delicacy. It would only be a decade before Lermontov, energized by the romantic cult of the writer, angered by the unappreciation and envy that in his view led to Pushkin's death, lashed out at his readership's literary unsophistication in the preface to his novel *A Hero of our Time*. And yet, for all the limitations of her letter, Trafilina reminds us that while Belkin is not exactly a realist, there is the microcosm of Russian country life behind his fiction whose true function, like all entertainment, is to relieve boredom. Where the reader faces risk is above all in deciding whether Belkin really lacked imagination or in fact let his imagination get carried away with him as he dissipated boredom by converting simple anecdotes into fictions. In these tales chance determines individual fates. But the mystification surrounding Belkin makes it difficult to know whether the strangeness of reality outdoes fiction (as Pushkin firmly believed it often did), disrupting the use of chance merely as a traditional device; or whether Belkin lets himself down as a craftsman and mismanages his plots, and thereby increases the effect of parody. Ultimately the effect is to make the truth of any interpretation the reader wishes to venture also a matter of chance.

The ambiguity is visible in 'The Shot', which may well be Pushkin's most amusing debunking of Romantic stereotypes and devices, whatever Belkin's aims. Knowingly or not, the narrator casts events according to the pattern of an unreconstructed romantic model, but it is the mismatch of plot and literary design that catches the reader's eye. Authorial irony lies in the narrator's unself-conscious approach, and in the number of clichés strewn acros his narrative. The surprising thing about 'The Shot' is that it is high on melodrama but low on action. Events and characters continually overturn the expectations of the narrator. Despite the strict code of honour, Silvio does not fight his assailant; the sang-froid of the Count unnerves him and he does not kill him; and in their final encounter he once again loses his nerve and departs, honour unavenged, and content merely to have spoiled his opponent's newly wedded bliss. Commentators have identified keys to irony in 'The Shot' in the numerous references to the prose of Alexander Bestuzhev (1797–1837). A treasury of romantic plotting, characterization, and phraseology, his novels and stories enjoyed enormous popularity in the 1820s. Lavish description of exotic locations set the scene for lurid erotic intrigue and brave exploits, and the usual unexpected outcomes. The style of his prose is as lush as Pushkin's is sparing. Double and triple adjectives and long periodic sentences achieved amplification and exaggeration. And while the style of narration in 'The Shot' is only sporadically like Bestuzhev, it strikingly diverges from the more neutral stylistic norm Pushkin prefers. The narrator's description of Silvio, with his gloomy pallor, strange name, morose manner, air of mystery, and waspish tongue reproduces in a toned-down version the standard features of Bestvzhev's Byronic hero.

The theme of vengeance, sudden, unexpected, and bloody, was another Bestuzhev specialty. 'My revenge will be every bit as remarkable as my passion is unlimited!' declares Edwin, the hero of 'The Tournament at Reval'. In the tales 'Wenden Castle', 'The Traitor', and 'Eisen Castle', all from the 1820s, the thirst for satisfaction is linked to a treacherous love-affair. In the story 'Gedeon' the vengeful hero appears in the house of his enemy on the eve of his son's marriage; there is a clear parallel with the final meeting of Silvio and the Count soon after the latter marries. When the Countess, having turned paler than her own handkerchief, throws herself on her husband's neck and faints dead away before the final duel, her histrionics have nothing in common with Pushkin's preferred sort of heroine who, like Tatyana in *Eugene Onegin*, bears unhappiness with a certain reserve or, like Zemfira in *The Gypsies*, shows reckless bravery. And what does one make of the final shot, when bloodthirsty Silvio, his opponent at his mercy, fires at a painting instead? In their excellent analysis of the story, David Bethea and Sergei Davydov interpret this as delibering the *coup de grâce* to Romanticism, the ultimate self-reflexive act of self-destruction, not only by the Romantic hero, but of the character type. The painting is a last in a series of objects, including a playing-card and an officer's cap, all of which emblematize various aspects of Romanticism. As they observe, '[i]f in the epigraph Pushkin pulls the hammer back, then in the concluding paragraph he pulls the trigger. Thus in addition to the prop, costume, and setting of fading romantic art, the central cliché—the protagonist—is shot through and down by the author's ironic marksmanship.'[2] And yet while the flat report of Silvio's death in Byronic circumstances, fighting on behalf of the Greek patriots, finishes off this Romantic type, even here irony reigns. For the reported death as the coda to a tale reproduces yet one more topos favoured by Bestuzhev.

While the interplay between literary models and the 'reality' of the characters' lives can be detected throughout *The Tales of Belkin*, it is most pronounced in the cluster of tales where the style, feelings, and postures of Sentimentalism are displayed and played with. Calqued on English and French models, Russian Sentimentalists fashioned a new language of sensibility and gentility that concentrated the mind and soul on individual feeling and private virtues. The Sentimentalist movement proved to be a reaction against the more public style of neoclassicism by placing its emphasis squarely on the direct communication, the heart-to-heart relationship, linking poet and reader whose moral universes flow one into another. The writer no longer cultivated the monarch, but looked inward to self-perfection while also looking outward in a show of democratic feeling to his fellow man of any status. Sincerity tinged with melancholy, ease of communication, and facile joy suffuse both sentimental poetry and prose. Like parallel movements in Britain and France, the Russian cult of sensibility finds sincerity in the lachrymose and revels in the belief that happiness is the experience of another's misfortune. As one scholar has put it, 'the Sentimental tribute of a tear exacted by the spectacle of virtue in distress was an acknowledgement at once of man's inherent goodness and of the impossibilty of his ever being able to demonstrate his goodness effectively'.[3] Foremost among the Russian Sentimentalists was the mid-career Nicholas Karamzin, who was a complex source

---

[2] David Bethea, and Sergei Davydov, 'Pushkin's Saturnine Cupid: The Poetics of Parody in *The Tales of Belkin*', *Proceedings of the Modern Language Association*, 96: 1 (1981), 8–21.

[3] R. F. Brissenden, *Virtue in Distress* (London, 1974), 29.

of inspiration to Pushkin, but a literary father to be celebrated and ultimately overcome.

Having made his mark as the author of exquisite idylls and elegies, his belief in gentle progress shattered by the French Revolution, Karamzin summed up the Sentimental movement (and delivered its death-blow) in his famous story *Poor Liza*. Written in the smooth middle style, in a syntax based on French, this tale surprised his élite readership by establishing the democracy of sensibility. Virtue, as chronicled in the love of a peasant girl for an ignoble aristocrat, depends on purity of emotions and motive rather than class. If this was news to Karamzin's readers, so was the Russian writer's expression of pessimism and disenchantment. After all, the hero, transplanted to the countryside from the city, seduces and then abandons Liza in a display of less than fine feeling. The story ends in her tragic suicide.

Parody is flexible because it encompasses any purposeful incorporation of earlier literary material in a new text, always presupposing an ironical distance on the predecessor but not necessarily implying humorous caricature. In drawing on the Sentimentalist movement's conventions of characterization and plotting, 'The Snowstorm', 'The Lady Peasant', and 'The Stationmaster' create ironic rereadings that employ a wide emotional and stylistic range. Both Maria Gavrilovna, the heroine of 'The Snowstorm', and Liza in 'The Lady Peasant' learn to experience love through their understanding of the heroines of Sentimental fiction, but the difference between them is pointed. In 'The Snowstorm' the codes of the romantic tale, with its sudden reversals and abrupt coincidences, clash with the sentimental self-image of the characters, even as history—the year is 1812—breaks in and disrupts their own plotting. Maria Gavrilovna is a literal reader who fails to distinguish between life and art. In sentimental fiction expression of feeling vouchsafes moral excellence. The heroines display their sensibility by swooning in distress and dissolving into tears. She sees herself as a heroine from Rousseau's great novel of sensibility, *Julie, ou la nouvelle Héloïse* (1761), and treats her fiancée Burmin as a St-Preux, ready to sweep her off her feet. Events overtake the literary projection she has of her life by first undoing her plans, and then magically restoring her happiness. In this tale constancy maintained is love restored through accident and accidental displays of virtue. Is it a send-up, or does Belkin believe that fate rewards a true love?

In 'The Lady Peasant' true love begins in falsity. Like 'The Snowstorm', this tale combines elements from different modes, bringing together the theme of mistress-into-maid of comic provenance with the idealized heroine of the sentimental tale. All the wit lies in the deliberateness with which the new figures self-consciously fashion their behaviour according to literary stereotypes. Rustic virtue rewarded by marital bliss was a familiar motif in eighteenth-century culture. Liza need have looked no further than Ablesimov's popular libretto for his opera *The Miller* for an example of a peasant girl who gets her man through cunning. While it is not made clear whether Liza knew Marivaux, Pushkin certainly did, and the antics he contrives for his heroine recall Marivaux's plays, *Le Jeu de l'amour et du hasard* (The Game of Love and Chance) in particular. While these models provide the amusing conceit for this tale, it is also clear that the specific intertext invoked by Pushkin, and knowingly or unknowingly parodied by Belkin, is *Poor Liza*. Both hero and heroine of 'The Lady Peasant' function as mirror-images of their prototypes. The Liza of Karamzin's seminal tale is reborn as the minxish young lady who disguises herself as a peasant. Alexey Berestov, while sharing Erast's charms, reverses Karamzin's cynical portrait by possessing a truly noble heart, and demonstrating the sincerity and good feeling of the true sentimental hero who can feel genuine affection for a peasant girl. Pushkin adds a twist to the class barrier that separates them by invoking the theme of family discord reminiscent of *Romeo and Juliet*:

The thought of an indissoluble bond quite often flashed through their minds, but they never spoke about that to each other. The reason was plain: Alexey, however much he might be attached to his sweet Akulina, was ever conscious of the distance which existed between him and the poor peasant girl; Liza, aware of the profound animosity between their fathers, did not dare to hope for their reconciliation, and besides, her vanity was secretly stirred by an obscure romantic hope of eventually seeing the Tugilovo squire at the feet of the daughter of the Priluchino blacksmith.

When Liza and Berestov assume their peasant guises, their dress
and diction adhere not to observed life but rather to their literary image, glamorized and sentimentalized. Like their counter-
parts in the earlier story, Liza and Berestov first meet in a grove
in the early morning. All the features of the landscape, from the
clear sky to the singing of the birds, replicate that of the sentimental idyll. But Pushkin's narrator disrupts the comparison:
while poor Liza dreams of her future lover, her *faux-naïf* imita-
tor provokes a reticence typical of the fastidious sentimental narrator: 'She thought . . . but can anyone identify precisely what a
17-year-old lady is thinking about, alone, before six on a spring
morning?' In the sentimental novel decorum requires an immediate attraction: heart speaks to heart without affectation, but
with vows of eternal love. Here Alexey, while out hunting, unexpectedly comes upon Liza and surprises her. He is unaware
that in point of fact he is being hunted by her. Liza repays
Alexey's initial surprise by turning the tables on her suitor and
reversing Karamzin's ending. Parody, once again, converts tragedy into comedy.

'The Lady Peasant' lightly mocks Karamzin's dictum that
good fiction normally praises virtue and points a moral. 'The
Stationmaster' with its overt pathos struck readers as more con-
sistent with the tone and philosophy of Sentimentalism. While
parody of the narrator once again forms part of the literary game
it does not distract or detract from the power of the story to move
the reader. The narrator's ostensibly humane tone and position
—it is the only one of the Belkin tales to have an introduction—
became a classic statement of philanthropy in Russian literature,
imitated by Gogol in 'The Overcoat' and *Dead Souls*, and by
Dostoevsky beyond him. 'The Stationmaster' is also the only
tale of the collection to present, in the figure of the Prodigal
Daughter, a morally problematic character whose elopement and
final return have provoked and divided readers' sympathies.

Pushkin was not the first writer to treat the figure of the
stationmaster. Once again his narrator takes a cue from earlier
writers. Early in his celebrated *Journey from St Petersburg to
Moscow*, the eighteenth-century radical writer A. N. Radishchev
recorded the venality and indolence of stationmasters. In his
'The Stationmaster' (1826), the now-obscure Wilhelm Karlgof

(1799–1841) produced a picture of domestic happiness akin to the
bliss in which Dunya and Samson Vyrin initially live. For that
matter, the opening paragraph ironizes the source of its epigraph,
Prince Vyazemsky's poem 'The Station' (1828), where mockery
outdoes sympathy. While it was commonplace to grumble about
their inadequacies, the sentimental narrator can find good even
in an unfashionable subject and extend democratic benevolence
despite the stereotype:

Is there anyone who has not cursed all stationmasters, or never had
occasion to wrangle with them? Anyone who, in a moment of anger, has
not demanded the fateful book in order to inscribe his useless complaint at high-handed treatment, rudeness, and inefficiency? Who does
not regard them as outcasts from the human race, the equivalent of the
pettifogging quill-drivers of yore, or Murom brigands at the very least?
Let us be fair, however, let us try and put ourselves in their shoes
and then, it may be, we will judge them much less severely. What is a
stationmaster? A veritable martyr of the fourteenth grade, protected by
his rank only from actual beating, and then not invariably (I refer that
to my reader's conscience). . . . I will just say that the stationmaster
rank has been presented to public opinion in a most misleading light.
These much-maligned officials are peaceable folk, by nature accommodating, inclined to sociability, modest in their ambitions, and not over-
mercenary. One can extract much that is curious and instructive from
their conversation (which the travelling public is wrong to ignore). As
for myself, I admit to preferring their talk to the discourse of some
sixth-rank official travelling on government business. (pp. 38–9)

While the narrator may claim to enjoy the speech of the stationmaster, he only gives Vyrin a brief opportunity to recount his
own story before pre-empting him, often resuming the highly
affective language of the introduction. Tears, heartache, sorrow,
and warm-hearted friendship come easily to the narrator, well-
packaged in tried and true cliché. But despite the overt appeal of
A.G.N.'s rhetoric, 'The Stationmaster' is hardly a work filled
with comforting Karamzinian sentiment. In 'The Shot' the events
of the narrative and the manner of narrative reveal a mismatch
between fact and fiction, opening a gap for Pushkin's irony.
Similarly, the intrusive, retrospective narrator of 'The Stationmaster' appears to be determined to shape his anecdote according to the conventions and tone of sentimental fiction. Consider,

for example, the central image of the parable of the Prodigal Son, which has several symbolic functions. The series of prints displayed in Vyrin's home are meant to serve as emblems of Dunya's good upbringing and filial piety, and to express Vyrin's attachment as a father. More importantly, they also signal to the reader a positive ending to the story. In the end, of course, the plot reverses the expectations set up by the parable: the son is a daughter; chance rather than fraternal jealousy motivates an only child; the prodigal prospers instead of almost perishing; the parent dies, the reunion occurs at the graveside, and the tears finally shed may be expression either of remorse or grief. Allusions and resemblances in the plot to *Poor Liza* invoke another parallel to this account of the betrayal of parent by child, but there is no case to be made for poor Dunya, who is one of the first Russian heroines to violate a standard convention and not perish after her seduction. In 'The Stationmaster' Vyrin's cry of 'Oh, Dunya, Dunya' expresses paternal grief, while Karamzin's 'Oh, Liza, Liza!' is a lament for virtue and sensibility. The question is whether, in imitating Karamzin's manner, A.G.N. hears the difference. After Karamzin's narrator experienced disillusion and grief, the revival of his style of speech and sensibility would have automatically provoked suspicions of naïveté or irony. The reader enjoys the ambivalence between pastiche (where an author's style is admiringly imitated) and parody (where an author's style is invoked satirically). And ultimately it is for the reader to determine whether the mismatch of sentiment and plot represents the deliberate irony of A.G.N. or whether the irony belongs to Belkin, who enjoys exposing the clumsiness of yet another amateur writer devoid of the self-consciousness that good writers possess if they are not to become unwitting caricatures rather than able parodists.

Yet the *Tales of Belkin* are not merely a series of send-ups and jokes. It is a tribute to the charm of the cycle that while these stories may be read most profitably as distillations and parodies of literary modes and clichés, they also inspire deliberate naïveté and delight as stories, retaining the capacity to charm as individual narrative performances. Exuberant parody, together with the device of the found manuscript, only partly obscure from view another layer of sentiment and romance that can safely be said to belong to Pushkin. If you read the *Tales of Belkin* not only for its send-up of hackneyed plots, forced coincidences, and melodramatic characters, it is possible to see Belkin's cycle as a celebration of the rather enchanted world of the gentry, and a comment on the relation between experience and literature. Nostalgia for a lost paradise of the gentry idyll is offset in Pushkin by the distancing effects of irony, but the mirage of this patriarchal world would come to enchant Gogol in *Tales on a Farm Near Dikhanka*, Turgenev in *The Hunter's Sketches* and *Nest of the Gentry*, and Slavophiles like Aksakov. Pushkin deeply regretted the lost world of the late eighteenth century, when the gentry enjoyed freedom from service to the monarch and life on the country estate brought relief from the European trappings of urban life. Through its tissue of parody and complicated structure we glimpse a lost world of fumbling but endearing gentility, of good-feeling and modest domesticity. It is a world of, in the phrase of the poet Anna Akhmatova, 'toylike dénouements', where the laws of real life are no longer valid. Death is either present only through rumour, gossip, or anecdote, or in the case of 'The Undertaker' in a dream. Bretter does not kill his enemy, Silvio vanishes, a bride abandoned at the altar finds her husband, Dunya's seduction turns into family happiness, and only now and again does history intrude. Pushkin's affection for this world, part invention, part memory of his youth and the years of exile in Mikhailovskoye, lovingly reappears in *The Captain's Daughter*, again refracted through the nostalgic vision of an elderly narrator.

The Queen of Spades

The Queen of Spades, the shortest separate work in the collection, is the only one of Pushkin's prose works to have enjoyed immediate acclaim at home and abroad from its publication in 1834. In 1836 the Russian writer A. A. Shakhovskoy, whose dramas were firmly stuck in the moralizing style of neoclassical drama, responded with a play clumsily entitled *Chrysomania, or the Passion of Money*. It is unlikely that any of its viewers were persuaded to shun the evils of the card-table. In Paris the composer Fromental Halévy and librettist Eugène Scribe, the former now remembered solely for his grand opera *La Juive*, produced their opéra-comique *La Dame de pique* (1850). Tchaikovsky's far more celebrated opera (1890) with the same title interpreted the tale in the spirit of his own *fin-de siècle* gloom. Irony and detachment, intrinsic to Pushkin, were perhaps too subdued for the theatre and alien to the composer's streak of melancholy. In the Russia of the 1890s a heady brew of Nietzschean philosophy, revolutionary activity, and doctrines of free love had elevated passion and obsession to a philosophy of personal conduct. When Hermann shoots himself on stage, Liza having thrown herself into the Neva, Pushkin's protagonists are made to act like characters out of the pages of Dostoevsky. They live, love, and die very much in the style of the period, reinvented by Tchaikovsky for an age that reveled in sex, scandal, and suicide.

Whatever the period, with and without operatic trappings, *The Queen of Spades* remains unsurpassed in all of Russian fiction for its fusion of psychological complexity and symbolic density; and for its deadpan exposition. It is constructed with consummate artistry; and while it raises tragic questions concerning the nature of chance and the power of passion, the remorseless self-effacement of the narrator, relieved only by momentary flashes of irony, bleeds it of melodrama and even the power to provoke sympathy. Its narrative is as taut, clear, and inevitable as its use of numerological symbols, weather patterning, and stark binary oppositions is subtle and suggestive. So suggestive in fact that an improbable mass of scholarship, reflecting the influence of a wide range of critical schools, has amassed around it.[4]

Its tantalizing epigraphs left to one side, *The Queen of Spades* has none of the extrovert literary play of *The Tales of Belkin* where literature is woven from literature, and Pushkin's implied reader negotiates the conventions and registers that are subtly mixed, mocked, and parodied. Belkin's ideal readers will second-guess themselves even as they give the narrator's intentions a second guess. In this work the source of irony is the gap between the editor's assurances of sincerity and the reader's superior grasp of the literary material that Belkin charmingly and unknowingly mishandles in refashioning or embellishing the ancedotes

---

[4] For a survey of interpretations of the tale, see Neil Cornwell, *Pushkin's The Queen of Spades* (Bristol, 1993).

at the base of each story. By contrast, in *The Queen of Spades* it is the impassive fatality of the narrator that is the source of irony, suggesting that everything is inevitable and known when in fact the questioning reader will find much unexplained and perhaps inexplicable. Whatever certainty the narrator projects, the reader will find that speculation is the only interpretative recourse.

In the event, then, while parody constitutes the interpretative game in reading *The Tales of Belkin*, guessing at the unknown makes up the gamesmanship of solving the many questions implied in *The Queen of Spades*: Was the story of Saint-German true? When precisely does Hermann go mad? Or does the story credit an occult explanation? The 'real' events of the story are entwined with elements of the fantastic supplied in part by the gloomy setting in wintry St Petersburg—in Dostoyevsky's famous phrase, 'the most invented city in the world'—but have also been explained as the product of Hermann's hallucination and final madness. In the literature of the fantastic the uncanny defies straightforward explanation. Is this a study in obsession or a meditation on fate? Entire schools of interpretation have evolved around answers to these and other questions. In essence, as Caryl Emerson has pointed out, *The Queen of Spades* asks the reader to take a chance by impelling us to find a single interpretative code, provoking an obsession to explain without providing authority for any one model.[5] The playful reader will recognize the situation of an open text which at times offers multiple explanations, and at times refuses all certainty of meaning. To the reader, however, who bets his hand on only one explanatory model, let Hermann's be a cautionary tale on the dangers of seeing only what you believe rather than believing what you see. Much of the pleasure of the work is concentrated in the gamble of interpretation, and much of its understated portentousness lies in the implicit connection between reading fiction as though it were life, and the other way round.

The hermeneutic gamble begins with a typical piece of baiting. 'The queen of spades indicates some covert malice',

[5] See Caryl Emerson, '"The Queen of Spades" and the Open End', in David Bethea (ed.), *Pushkin Today* (Indiana, 1993), 31–7.

announces an epigraph, thus provoking a number of questions.
Who or what is this figure? Who is the object of her malevolence?
Why is it secret? Eventually the plot will supply answers of a
kind to these particular queries. Less easy to discern, however,
are the authorial intentions of the narrator. The source of this
pronouncement—'The latest fortune-telling manual' is the given
title—itself produces mystification. Like all works of the supernatural and of the Gothic, *The Queen of Spades* tantalizes by
suggesting a a potential naturalistic explanation of the fantastic,
and winks now and then at the pseudo-scientific. We are in a
fiction where Mesmer and Galvani are on the tips of the beau
monde's tongues almost as often as references to the devil and
Casanova. While a pedantic reader will find the attribution of
the epigraph inadequate, its title bears clues and irony with
respect to the themes and events of the story. The status of
knowledge—what the characters can reliably say about one
another, what the reader knows about the characters—is continually called into question in the text. Did the Countess trick
Hermann? Did Hermann really see a vision or was the apparition a hallucination? Did Lizaveta truly love him or was she,
too, scheming? This process of questioning, of considering and
reconsidering, of even divining intentions, begins with the epigraph. 'Latest', says the title, without offering a date for guidance.
Such vagueness anticipates one curious feature of the text, namely,
that despite its careful plotting of narrative time, its setting cannot be dated accurately. Furthermore, and ironically, given the
usual Gothic association of occult knowledge with antiquity, it is
to be wondered why 'the latest' work would be more authoritative. Finally, and relatedly, if the dictum refers to a card-game,
why is it not drawn from a manual on card-playing? Here the
epigraph anticipates the confusion between winning at cards
and mastering chance through an occult power that possesses
Hermann.

Even an examination of Pushkin's sources reveals that all is
far from clear-cut. Obverse strategies of frankness organize the
prose in these two works. Just as the Belkin stories advertise
their sources and subtexts because the work's message depends
on the recognition of parody, in *The Queen of Spades* obfuscation
hides the origins of Pushkin's inspiration and makes its enigmas

reader-proof. The indeterminacy principle permeates every layer of the work and bedevils scholarly attempts to ascertain sources and their interrelation. No one story can be singled out as the source; various details and themes were common to a number of works known to him.[6] But whatever elements each contributed, Pushkin's story exceeds a mere recombination. His literary models are 'so many tiny building blocks, whose individual shape could not influence the eventual configuration'.[7] His fascination with gambling expressed more than an idiosyncratic passion. Consider, if only briefly, characterization. It is a tenet of modern literary criticism that the pursuit of real-life models for characters and episodes in literary works is only partially instructive. The genetic material of literary personages is complex, blending prototype, literary type, and then the writer's own vision. But it is also true that blurring the boundaries between fact and fiction is a topos of the Romantic period. To this the creation of the Old Countess bears witness. Pushkin confessed that he modelled her on the Princess Natalia Golitsyna. Born in 1741, she was a fixture at court, but in fact, unlike her fictional incarnation, had never been celebrated for her beauty. Indeed, her nickname was 'Princesse Moustache', and her reputation was as a living codex of manners and etiquette. It was in fact one of her daughters who had enjoyed a reputation for her beauty. Already the historical prototype has been complicated by the conflation of two figures. Yet the Countess's curmudgeonly character, her sniping at her servants, seemed to owe much more to another

---

[6] It is likely that the title is taken from the short novel *Spader Dame* by the Swedish writer Clas Johan Livijn; it was published in a German translation by Baron de La Motte-Fouqué as *Pique-Dame: Berichte aus dem Irrenhause in Briefen* in 1826. E. T. A. Hoffman's novel *Die Elixiere des Teufels* features a hero who hallucinates about a queen of hearts that looks like his lady-love, while his story 'Spielerglück' (1820) shares a number of details with Pushkin's story. In Karl Gottlieb Samuel Huen's novella 'Der Hollandische Jude', the hero discovers a sure way of winning at card-games, and bets on the trey and the seven. References to Napoleon, to Mephistopheles, Mesmerism, and Swedenborg occur in Balzac's story 'La Peau de chagrin', another tale of gambling that probably only served as an anti-model. Finally, the calculating attitude that Hermann and Liza display toward love may owe something to Stendhal's *The Red and the Black*, which Pushkin was known to admire.

[7] Paul Debreczeny, *The Other Pushkin* (Stanford, 1983), 209.

famous dowager who captivated Pushkin with tales of life at court in the eighteenth century, Natalia Kirillovna Zagrizhskaya. But none of these figures is known to have supplied Pushkin with the anecdote of St Germain that injects the uncanny into this tale.

Pushkin had an acute sense for the arbitrariness of fate, and the story is possibly his most powerful treatment of the hazards of chance. Having staked and lost the copyright to more than one of his works at the card-table, Pushkin was well acquainted with the mentality of the gambler. 'The passion for playing is the strongest of passions', he commented to a friend. Reality fed the attraction of gambling as the subject for a plot. When Pushkin wrote *The Queen of Spades* in 1833, card-playing had achieved a status and significance that is well-described by his friend Prince P. A. Vyazemsky:

There is nowhere else that cards have entered into such usage: in Russian life cards are one of the unavoidable and indisputable elements . . . Passionate gamblers were everywhere all the time. Writers of drama displayed this passion on the stage with all its fatal consequences. The most intelligent people got caught up in it . . . Such gaming, a sort of battle for life and death, has its turbulence, its drama, its poetry. Whether this passion, this poetry is good and beneficial is another question.

Turbulence, drama, and poetry were precisely what was missing from life in Russia of this period. Inspired by their travels during the Napoleonic campaigns and fired by victory, the gentry élite conceived a vision of a new Russia ruled on the English model, where legislature and monarch heeded a consitution and code of laws. A more radical element also envisioned agrarian reform leading to the emancipation of the serfs. Fired by these ideals, several hundred men conspired to unseat Nicholas I during his coronation on 14 December 1825; the rebellion ended in a fiasco, and set the repressive tone that would endure till the end of Nicholas I's reign in 1855. The failure of the Decembrists blotted out hopes for reform. Russia entered what one of Pushkin's contemporaries called an Iron Age, where everything became subjected to the stultifying official policy of Nicholas I's state: Autocracy, Nation, and Orthodoxy. The world of Nicholas I's Russia, where the liberal élite were quickly superfluous after the failed Decembrist revolution, left nothing to chance; for aristocrats deprived of political influence, with nothing to lose but their hearts and fortunes (witness the behaviour of Pavel Petrovich Kirsanov in Turgenev's *Fathers and Sons*), the notion of risk and tempting fate becomes much more exciting. In essence, gambling, as Vyazemsky makes clear, represented a type of counter-culture, an emancipation of spirit. The Russian aristocracy inherited from the French aristocracy the attitude toward gambling not only as an aristocratic *jeu d'esprit* but also as an expression of Enlightenment confidence in reason's power to demystify and conquer chance. In his book on the duel, another aristocratic pastime dedicated to tempting fate, V. G. Kiernan noted that 'A man had to be able to hazard his fortune on a turn of the cards as coolly as his forefather risked their lives on the field of battle. Card-tables at Versailles, where millions of livres were yearly staked, offered a new tournament ground for blood to show its quality.'[8]

This spirit of defiant recklessness comes through in the banter and anecdotes of Tomsky, Narumov, and the others in the brilliant first chapter where the quick pace of the dialogue confers drama and speed. Gossip and conversation also provide an elegant economy of characterization. Pushkin is indirect about the story's hero, who seems the odd man out in this company. He begins to establish Hermann's character through juxtaposition of his values with those of the other gamblers. In fact, Tomsky makes a point of establishing Hermann's alienness by chalking up the oddness of Hermann's conduct to his Germanic ancestry (although we later learn that Hermann is at the very least a first-generation Russian). The fact that he is an engineer rather than an officer also sets him apart socially from the company he keeps. Underlying the organization of the scene is a mood of contrast: between the values of the eighteenth century and those of the present; the brilliant Parisian salon of the anecdote and the gloomy Petersburg night; the passion of the beautiful Countess and Hermann's reason; her rank in society and Hermann's status as an outsider. While the reader will have to account for several motivations on Hermann's part, at least at the outset the link between social ambition and gambling as a means of moving

---

[8] V. G. Kiernan, *The Duel in European History* (Oxford, 1988), 154.

upwards—utility contravening the aristocratic ethos of the salon—is implicit. In a recent study of the culture of gambling in France and its literary representations, Thomas Kavanagh has noted that the hero of the eighteenth-century novel typically espouses two positions: on the one hand, his vocabulary is that of determinism, espousing confidence in the determinism of much Enlightenment thought; on the other hand, he recognizes that within that predictability 'the chance event may at any moment redefine the individual's place within the world's apparently ordered sequences of cause and effect'.[9]

At least initially, Hermann resists the temptation to gamble. The rule he has set himself—'Not to sacrifice the necessary in the hope of acquiring the superfluous'—has neither the *élan* of the aristocrat nor the willingness of the eighteenth-century hero to hazard chance in the confidence that a measure of predictability is discernible in the world. What makes Hermann gamble? In the second chapter, the narrator's potted biography of Hermann not only refines Tomsky's remark but gives the key to Hermann's character:

Hermann was the son of a Russianized German, who had left him a small sum of money. Firmly convinced of the necessity of consolidating his independence, Hermann had not laid a finger even on the interest, preferring to live solely on his pay, and denying himself the smallest extravagance. As he was reserved and keenly ambitious, however, his comrades rarely had an opportunity to make fun of his excessive thrift. He was a man of strong emotions and possessed an ardent imagination, but his steadiness preserved him from the usual errors of youth. For example, though he had the soul of a gambler, he never picked up a card, calculating that his finances did not permit him (as he used to put it) 'to sacrifice the necessary in the hope of acquiring the superfluous'— and yet he would sit up all night at the card tables, trembling feverishly, as he followed the shifting fortunes of the play.

The story of the three cards played on his imagination . . . (p. 80)

Shortly thereafter Tomsky once again provides further clues to Hermann's character when he calls him 'a genuinely Romantic personality [who] has the profile of Napoleon, and the soul of

[9] Thomas M. Kavanagh, *Enlightenment and the Shadows of Chance: The Novel and the Culture of Gambling in Eighteenth-Century France* (Baltimore: 1993), 108.

Mephistopheles.' Tomsky speaks here in terms of literary cliché, although the remark is calculated to appeal to Liza's sense of danger, fed no doubt by her appetite for fiction of the period where the dangerous criminal hero, like Julien Sorel of Stendhal's *The Red and the Black* (one putative model for Hermann), took on the world. Like Tatyana in *Eugene Onegin*, the sensibility of the Pushkinian heroine can be deciphered on the basis of her reading: the novels of Richardson and the poems of Byron had encouraged a dangerous fascination with the 'man without values and religion', to quote the epigraph to Chapter 4. The narrator confirms this when he notes that 'thanks to the latest novels, her imagination was both daunted and enchanted by this type—actually quite hackneyed by now'.

Yet Tomsky's remark is also aimed at the reader. For Pushkin, and for his entire generation, Napoleon represented the magnificent success of an upstart who combined calculation, a belief in his own star, and a willingness to take risk to the limit. He is an engineer who believes that it is possible to make life conform to one's will by pronouncing a magic formula. In the end, of course, fate mocked Napoleon and his own ambition subverted him. Both Napoleon and Hermann, therefore, enjoy Pyrrhic victories: Napoleon found himself the conqueror of a devastated Moscow, just as Hermann possesses a magical combination of the cards that no longer works. Tomsky likens Hermann to Mephistopheles for superficial reasons: his dark, brooding appearance, his gloomy silences and predatory skulking have a diabolical aura. But for the reader the comparison introduces an occult element in the story that begins with the tale of the three cards. What seizes Hermann's imagination is his conviction that, like Mephistopheles, he can penetrate the secrets of nature and thus overpower chance as embodied in the card-game.

The impossibility of reviving the secret is symbolized in the physical contrast of his own youthful passion and the decay of the Countess. There is method to his madness, of course. He wishes to gain the secret at any cost, and therefore if he can win the Countess's heart he will win the secret, and what could be more flattering to an old lady than a proposal of marriage from a young man? When he finds himself in the Countess's mansion he faces two doors, one leading to her boudoir, the other to

Liza's room, symbols of the choices he must make in life between fortune and love. But this house of cards rests on the false
premiss that Saint Germain's success—was it just an anecdote?
Was it accident? Did the Countess blurt out any three cards to
placate Chaplitsky?—could be repeated. For Tomsky, the eighteenth century, the period of reckless abandon, is a source of
fascination that survives only in an anecdote. It would be simp-
listic to contend that Pushkin condemns Hermann to failure
merely because he is an outsider socially and culturally. Hermann
is doomed because his obsession blinds him to the obvious fact
that the secret of the cards belongs to an era that cannot be
revived, and to the fact that the Parisian Venus of yesteryear is
now an old, yellowed woman.

It is no ordinary zeal that fires Hermann's resolutions. His
ambition, his controlled imagination, his self-discipline reflect
a determination not just to lead a rational life, but to eradicate
chance altogether. Behind Hermann's attitude to fate stands
Pushkin's own sense of mystery. Whether or not it was possible
to predict the course of events, to impose one's will on life, and
make it conform to one's own ambition, as Napoleon did, was a
philosophical question that intrigued Pushkin. In a famous poem
of 1828 he interrogated fate by asking why it had given him 'the
accidental gift of life'. In the end Pushkin found in the study
of history the most satisfactory mode for such inquiry, and his
sense of the arbitrariness of events and the role of accident
rather than providence in individual lives as well as the lives of
nations became a principle.

In Hermann he provided one set of answers to these questions. Upon hearing the anecdote of the three cards Hermann,
quite irrationally, believes that he has hit upon a foolproof method
of securing his fortune. That Hermann overhears the anecdote
in the first place is ironical and indicative, since no amount of
planning can totally predetermine the course of a life. What
interests Pushkin is less the psychology of the gambler than the
snares and delusions that, set entirely by chance, obliterate will
and self-awareness. Writing in the early twentieth century, the
critic and philosopher M. O. Gershenzon saw the *The Queen of
Spades* as a study in the sudden, irreversible advent of a destruc-
tive passion:

Tomsky's portrayal, the situation in which he relates his anecdote, and the very nature of his story, all of these, as it were, strip away one layer after another from reality in order to leave only the shadow of reality. And this shadow turned out to be sufficient to act on Hermann like a spark thrown into a powder-keg. It is as though Pushkin wanted to say: we all go about prepared any minute for a drama; our soul, saturated with passion, greedily seeks in this world some food for its passion—so greedily that even the shadow of a thing is capable of tempting it; and then it instantaneously flares up and burns out in tortured happiness, one soul more slowly, another straightaway like Hermann. Such is the law of the human spirit.

Peter the Great's Blackamoor and The Captain's Daughter

From the late 1820s until his death in 1837 Pushkin continually pondered the figure of Peter the Great and the consequences of his programme of Westernization for Russian history. Having been pardoned by Nicholas I in 1827, Pushkin composed the poem 'Stanzas', in which Peter serves as an exemplary figure as much for his clemency toward his enemies as for the revolution in statecraft that he achieved. Because Nicholas I had taken a hard line with the Decembrists, in some circles the poem was read as a statement of capitulating and even toadying. But its message is much more ambivalent, and a correct reading, while acknowledging the poet's attempt to flatter Nicholas I by a comparison with his great-grandfather, recognizes that Pushkin is in fact setting up Peter as a model for emulation and thus issuing a challenge to the Tsar. In the narrative poem *Poltava* (1828), commemorating Peter's decisive victory over Charles XII of Sweden in 1709, the poet accords Peter the treatment of an Olympian and creates out of him a mythic figure. There is an arc stretching from this vision of Peter to Pushkin's final treatment of him in his great narrative poem *The Bronze Horseman* (1836). While the narrator in this last work pays tribute to the beauty of St Petersburg, the famous equestrian statue of the Emperor that comes to life, terrorizing a pathetic clerk, embodies the abstract power of the state and the ineluctable and even crushing force of History. In 1832 Pushkin had told his friend the lexicographer Vladimir Dal of his intention to devote himself to the study of the Petrine period, commenting on the vast amount of archival material requiring mastery. At his death

Pushkin left behind his notes and a preliminary outline for what is now called *The History of Peter*.

Although unfinished, the *Blackamoor* merits attention because of its novel presentation of Peter the Great, and as a key stage in Pushkin's evolving conceptualization of the relation between fact and invention in historical literature. Nicholas Karamzin's *History of the Russian State* had elevated Russian historiography on to a new level. It combined massive archival research with insightful psychological portraiture. Once fascinated by the revolutionary oratory of Robespierre and a proponent of greater liberties, Karamzin's account of the development of medieval Russia till the beginning of the Romanov dynasty in 1613 reflected his later traditionalism and was read as a justification of the monarchy. While its historical message caused a storm of controversy, admiration for the work's method was virtually unanimous and led to renewed interest in other periods. In 1824 A. O. Kornilovich, a future member of the Decembrist movement and translator of Latin historians, produced three well-researched sketches of life in the Petrine period devoted to topics that, unusually for his day, would currently be the standard stuff of social history: the feasts and festivals of the Russian court; the first Russian balls; the private lives of Russians during the reign of Peter the Great. These sketches not only served as factual sources in the writing of *Peter the Great's Blackamoor*, but also suggested to Pushkin the particular emphasis he might give his work.

The subject of this historical fiction is Abram Petrovich Hannibal (1696?–1781), Pushkin's great-grandfather on his mother's side. Legend had it that he was the son of an African prince who had been sold into slavery. In 1705 or 1706 Count Savva Raguzinsky purchased him in Constantinople as a gift for Peter the Great whose love of curiosities was boundless. Hannibal, who soon became a great favourite with the Emperor, converted to Orthodoxy. In 1716 he joined Peter's retinue on his tour of Europe, and remained behind in France in order to complete his education as an engineer. He served in the Spanish War, earning the rank of captain. After Peter's death Hannibal's fortunes waxed and waned: opposition to the powerful courtier, Prince Menshikov brought him a period of exile to Siberia. In 1731,

contrary to the details of Pushkin's *Blackamoor*, he was engaged
to a Greek woman who bridled at the match, then cuckolded
him. Hannibal resorted to the traditional right of the Russian
husband to torture his wife in such cases. In the end a court
interceded and saved her life by imprisoning her for eleven
years, during which time Hannibal married a second time. His
wife bore him six children, including a son Osip who fathered
Pushkin's mother Nadezhda. During the early years in the reign
of Peter's daughter, Elizabeth I, Hannibal once again enjoyed
favour. He retired from service in 1762, the year of Catherine
II's accession. Documentary evidence for the biography of this
colourful figure was fragmentary. Critics have justifiably treated
the *Blackamoor* mainly as an experiment with the genre of the
historical novel, as a stepping-stone on the path to *The Captain's
Daughter*. But the *Blackamoor*, fragmentary though it is, deserves
renewed consideration as a single artistic structure in which characterization, historical detail, and development of plot function
together in conveying the dynamic changes of the Petrine world.
It is this design that limits Pushkin's ambition in the work's
characterizations. Commentators have explained the differences
between the heroes of the *Blackamoor* and *The Captain's Daughter*
in terms of Pushkin's increasing maturity, but another extensive
fragment of a novel written at this time period, *Dubrovsky*, clearly
demonstrates that Pushkin was fully capable of developing psy-
chologically complex portraits at this stage in his career as a
novelist. Through the biography of his ancestor Pushkin concentrates on changes in social trends and customs; he captures
the making of history through the perceptions of his characters
as they experience its impact on their lives.

The portrayal of Peter, however, reveals a new facet to
Pushkin's approach to his subject. Whereas the Peter of the two
narrative poems remains remote and mythic, aloof from history
while being intrinsic to it, in *Peter the Great's Blackamoor* attention focuses not on the Emperor or even on the title-character;
rather, it is the age in all its contradictory tensions that forms
the subject. As the epigraph suggests, the work will aim to
capture the transformation of Russia and the consequences of
Peter's reforms on all levels of society—the effects at court, in
domestic affairs, on Russians abroad and newly returned home.

Whereas images of France are concentrated in the world of the salon, Russia is seen more positively as a great workshop. Somewhat tangential, the love plot only partly disguises the schematic structure of the work; for it may be said to break down into a series of antitheses capturing the differences between the old and new Russia. The differences between the position of an extreme Westernizer like Korsakov and the conservative posture of the boyars is reflected across a wide spectrum of cultural artefacts, including dancing and clothing (French costume versus the traditional bears and caftans). Pushkin is also attentive to variations in the characters' speech, as Gallicisms come fast and furious in Korsakov's dialogue by contrast with the old-fashioned Slavonic idiom of a character like Ekimovna.

Through the biography of his ancestor Pushkin concentrates on changes in social trends and customs; he captures the making of history through the perceptions of his characters as they experience its impact on their lives. Over the course of the ensuing decade Pushkin would hone his historiographical skills, aspiring to a level of accuracy and command of sources worthy of the professional. In so far as the goal of his fiction was, however, not a documentary account of the past, Pushkin let other criteria guide him. The reality of the events of the narrative are in part a useful and probable historical fantasy. In his wish to capture the mentality of the period Pushkin admits the use of anachronism and invention as long as they remain plausible. Peter the Great's efforts to integrate Ibrahim into Russian society by betrothing him to a young noblewoman never happened. Once again, as in the portrayal of the old Countess, Pushkin found it expedient to graft events from one biography on to another: Peter took the initiative in arranging a match between his orderly Rumyantsev and the daughter of Count Matveyev. For Pushkin an anecdote was an essential means of capturing the spirit of the time, but in his fiction he deliberately refashions his sources and recombines certain facts, conforming to the demands of external probability. In this case the altered details once again help Pushkin to emphasize Hannibal's place as a mediator between two civilizations in this panorama of transformation. Steeped in French culture, but untarnished by it, unlike Korsakov, he represents the happy mean between the parodied Westernizer and the reactionary noble. His entire appearance embodies this spirit of compromise and justifies Peter's affection for him: while his attire is European dress, he wears no wig; his movements are steady while Korsakov is positively frenetic; his adherence to the new customs is sure yet not offensive to the boyars. Hannibal is the new man of Petrine Russia. But the underside to his exemplary facility in accommodating the alien is the implication that it was much easier for a foreigner to adopt the new ways since he had so little to cast off. In doubt is the success with which the indigenous élite could successfully merge the native and foreign.

Fiction anticipated Pushkin's historical study of the reign of Peter the Great. Conversely, it was his interest in the history of the Pugachev rebellion that generated *The Captain's Daughter*. The legendary Pugachev, about whom little was known owing to an official ban on his name in force since the eighteenth century, none the less captured Pushkin's interest in the early 1820s. In 1830 cholera and famine broke out in Russia, prompting popular unrest. Nicholas I showed considerable bravery in confronting more than one provincial mob; the confrontation between the people and the sovereign reawakened Pushkin's interest in the extraordinary rebellion that from 1772 to 1775 swept southern and central Russia like wildfire. With the Tsar's permission Pushkin began archival research in 1832 and 1833, and the idea of writing a novel on the subject seems to have occurred to him immediately. Yet, as he explained in a letter, 'I was thinking at one point of writing a historical novel relating to the times of Pugachev, but upon discovering masses of material, I abandoned this idea and wrote *The History of the Pugachev Rebellion*.' In 1833 he travelled to Kazan and the fortress town of Orenburg in search of further documentary material, when possible interviewing eyewitnesses to the rebellion, and put the finishing touches on his historical work in the autumn of 1833. The sheer magnitude of Pushkin's labour is visible in the collection of documents and notes he made for the history, which occupy two folio volumes in the Academy edition of his works, and take up more than 1,100 pages. The Tsar, Pushkin's personal censor, demanded a number of, mainly minor, changes

before the work could appear in late 1834, including a change of
title from *The History of Pugachev* to *The History of the Pugachev
Rebellion*, since he deemed it unfitting to dignify a brigand by
naming a literary work after him. The study failed to enjoy
popular success. To Pushkin's terse, documentary style the public
preferred narrative continuity and psychological portraiture, what
Pushkin had criticized in the historian N. Polevoy's writings
as 'the artless simplicity of a chronicle that has the vivid quality
of fiction'. Exceptionally, Belinsky, having earlier proclaimed
Pushkin's prose the sure sign of his decline, commented that the
history was written 'with the pen of a Tacitus on bronze and
marble'. Stung by the criticism, and eager for a popular success
that would aid his precarious finances, Pushkin resumed writing
the short historical novel he began in 1833. *The Captain's Daughter*
was published in November 1836 in the fourth issue of *The
Contemporary*, the journal that Pushkin had founded a year
earlier.

It would be a fruitless exercise here to do more than touch on
the disparities between the two treatments. Generally speaking,
in turning fact into fiction Pushkin barely cannibalized his own
historical work. And while the events of the novel approximate
the course of the rebellion of 1772, the incorporation of historical detail is highly selective, and—lest one forget that the novel
is Grinyov's memoir—highly subjective too. A number of historical figures appear in secondary roles as a way of lending
verisimilitude. If several of the novel's protagonists descend
from historical figures, as with *The Queen of Spades*, it is not
without having undergone significant change. Captain Mironov,
for instance, owes his genesis to a memoirist's description of her
grandfather who, like Mironov, commanded a fort although he
was not active during the Pugachev rebellion. In her account
Pushkin found the raw material for a portrait that corresponded
to his own sense of the eighteenth century as an age when
men combined good-hearted bluffness and bravery with decent
sensibility. Yet as we have already seen, recombination of biography and events typifies the interchange of fact and fiction in
much of Pushkin's prose. The execution of Captain Mironov,
one of the few moments of naked violence in the novel, is based
on fact, but the victim there otherwise made no contribution to

the biography of the fictional character. Ultimately the most instructive discrepancy occurs between the historical Pugachov and his fictional other; it is this transformation that explains the sharp contrast in tone between the two works. Possibly because he was constrained by the censorship's official view, in his historical work Pushkin created a two-dimensional Pugachev. Less charismatic and commanding than Grinyov's 'guide', he is on the one hand hardly more than a figurehead for the disgruntled rebels who manipulate him; and on the other hand, he is considerably more brutal and arbitrary than the figure who winks charmingly and loyally to Grinyov from the scaffold. The 'real' Pugachev is as merciless as his re-creation is merciful. It has been sometimes supposed that Pushkin reconceptualized his understanding of Pugachev on the basis of documents to which he gained access after the completion of the *History*. But in his autobiographical narrator Pushkin has not created a spokesman for a revisionist history of the Pugachev rebellion. So patent and copious is the imaginary in the novel, whether read on its own or in comparison with the *History of Pugachev*, that Pushkin appears to have built in a refutation for critics who interpret the work mainly as a whitewashing of the Cossack hero. To interrogate the novel for clues to a political change of heart is to misunderstand the special opportunities fiction gave Pushkin to create a world in which the perpetual irruption of the improbable becomes the single identifiable principle of causality in the narrator's personal history. Pushkin's double treatment of the Pugachev rebellion has its roots in a long-standing ambivalence in his historical thought. As if to polarize these positions, Pushkin required two modes of presentation of related events. His romance with history led, in *The Captain's Daughter*, to a masterpiece of historical romance.

In the 1820s Pushkin was moved to consider questions concerning the style of historical writing and the extent of the historian's knowledge. He never produced a systematic philosophy of history, but in the 1830s the opposition between these two approaches crystallized into a coherent position as he sharpened his views in reponse to the influential and popular historical writings of the French Romantic school. In his pioneering *History of the Russian State*, Karamzin had deeply absorbed the

premiss of writers such as Guizot and Thierry that the hand of
Providence gives shape and purpose to the course of events; and
that it is the task of the historian, through unusual powers of
insight, to discern in the welter of disconnected happenings the
patterns and goal of this moving force. Pushkin made a first
effort to express this view in his play *Boris Godunov*. Although
attention focuses on the tortured title-character, Pushkin placed
the monk Pimen at the centre of the historical drama. It is
Pimen, engaged in writing for posterity an account of his era,
who embodies the objective distance of the historian. But while
Pushkin confers moral authority on him through his *gravitas*
and the solemnity of his diction, the play captures the unpre-
dictable course of events surrounding him and destabilizes the
reliability of his chronicle. *Boris Godunov* continually calls into
question the nature of historical writing by juxtaposing Pimen's
view of history, a view based on the monk's conviction that
providence guides events to their just end, and the sheer randomness of the story as it unfolds. Underlying this contrast is
the opposition between Pushkin and Karamzin.

For Pushkin the cyclical patterning of Karamzin's work did
violence to the unpredictability that he saw as the only know-
able law of Russian history. It is not for nothing that in all his
historical works Pushkin concentrates on turning-points in Russian history where the will of a strong individual is pitted against
a bewildering confluence of forces and accidents. It is in the
moments of revolution and radical rupture with the past, the
vast scale on which the accidental occurs, that Pushkin identifies
the historical in Russia; and while individuals continually try to
gain control of these forces, their complexity makes a mockery
of attempts, by the heroic leader and in due course by the historian, to turn this into what might be called a historical process.
In this connection, if the notion that the purpose of history was
intractable to rational analysis was acceptable to Pushkin, his
intellect was too sceptical and empirical to endow the historian
with special powers of divination. At best the historian was an
educated guesser. He made this clear in his review of Nicholas
Polevoy's multi-volume *History of the Russian People*, another
work written under the spell of French historiography: 'Foresight
is not algebra. The human mind, to use a colloquial expression,

is not a prophet, but a guesser; it sees the general course of things, and can deduce from that deep propositions that are often justified by time; but it cannot foresee chance—the poweful, sudden weapon of providence.'

The rise in the professional study of history in Russia coincided with an increasing appetite for historical fiction. Walter Scott, in Russian and French translation or even in the original English, enjoyed great popularity.[10] In 1829 editions of *The Legend of Montrose*, *The Pirate*, *The Fair Maid of Perth*, *The Monastery*, *The Fortunes of Nigel*, and two versions each of *Rob Roy* and *Woodstock* appeared in Russia. He begat a flock of imitators, each eager to assume the mantle of 'national genius', as Scott had, at a time when the strangeness and individuality of peoples and nations was a staple of the cultural discourse of Romanticism. The fault-line between Pushkin and the reigning school of historiography emerges in their attitude to Scott's fiction; it is significant that for each of these admirers the same aspects of his fiction served diametrically opposed views of the nature of history. Guizot, Thierry, and Michelet, among others, lauded Scott because he brought to bear a powerful imagination that gave life to an unusually wide range of sources, including oral folklore, songs, and documents. In the eyes of these theorists, it was this combination of historicity and imagination that allowed Scott to understand the links between events, and it was this apprehension of the connectedness of the apparently random that formed his gift of historical divination. Where Scott's technique and imagination subserved the French creation of a sublimely percipient historian, their value was of a different kind for Pushkin. Imagination generated the advantages fiction had over history in approximating the spirit of the time and in re-creating the mentality of its protagonists, but could not be equated with the duty of the historian to seek out truth and record it in an objective narrative based on research. Where historical fiction appealed to Pushkin was in the licence it gave to invention in converting and expanding the historical record. Historical fiction

---

[10] James West, 'Walter Scott and the Style of Russian Historical Novels of the 1830s and 1840s', *American Contributions to the Eighth International Congress of Slavists at Zagreb* (Columbus, Ohio, 1978), i. 757–72.

owed fidelity to probability rather than strict fact, and the success of a work in this genre was in direct proportion to the conviction its characters carried as situated in a believable milieu rather than their correspondence to an established documentary account of events.

In this earlier work the adaptation of Scott's approach to historical fiction is already incipient, visible mainly in the way Pushkin treats the historical in its domestic manner and the domestic as historical. To be sure, it is in *The Captain's Daughter* that Pushkin reveals to the full extent the lessons he learned from Walter Scott. Pushkin was captivated by Scott's demonstration that the historical novel not only charted turning-points in national politics, but also presented a family chronicle, dividing the fiction between domestic space and the public arena of warfare and lavishing realistic detail on both. In this connection, Pushkin found in *Rob Roy* an appropriate narrative model, as he had previously found one in *Old Mortality* when writing *The Tales of Belkin*. History comes packaged in the form of a memoir, written for the sake of the author's descendants. In a fragment of an incompleted article Pushkin remarked:

The chief charm of W. Scott's novels consists in the fact that we become acquainted with the past not with the *enflure* of French tragedy—and not with the primness of Sentimental novels—not with the *dignité* of history, but in a contemporary fashion, in a domestic manner—that which charms us in the historical novel is the fact that what is historical is absolutely what we see. Goethe, W. S. [William Shakespeare] do not have a servile passion for kings and heroes. They do not resemble (like French heroes) flunkies who mimic *la dignité et la noblesse*. They are familiar with the ordinary circumstances of life, their speech has nothing affected about it, or of the theatrical even in solemn circumstances—because they are accustomed to great occasions.

On a purely formal level, Pushkin recalls Scott by appropriating devices and structures that Scott had perfected. Footnotes and documents, epigraphs, chapter labels, even the memoir structure, all standard features of the repertory, contribute to Pushkin's novel and run variations on their usual function: the presence of footnotes, for example, permitted the writer to stand outside the narrative and comment on the status of history in the fiction or to bolster its realism. Even as a sequence of improbable occurrences takes *The Captain's Daughter* from the realm of history into the world of fairy tale, it is important to remember that as a memoirist Grinyov gives every evidence of being reliable. Apart from citing his own literary efforts, he adduces numerous documents from his copious scrapbook, including four letters (Zurin's note, A. P. Grinyov's moral instruction, Savelich's to A. P. Grinyov, Masha Mironova's to Grinyov), and a military communiqué. In keeping with the high value Scott set on folkloric material, Grinyov also quotes Pugachev's folk-tale and a folk-song. The reader will note independently a host of other documents which are paraphrased or reworded by characters, although not given in direct citation. In *The Captain's Daughter* Pushkin did not intend to transplant the massive evidence he had compiled for his history to the world of his fiction. In part this is because the extensive nature- and architectural descriptions, the elaborate monologues, and vast choreography of battle scences that filled Scott's novels and those of his Russian imitators went against Pushkin's inclination to prize economy. The first-person narrator permitted Pushkin to avoid the demands of Scott's historical realism while remaining recognizably within the conventions he established.

Pushkin's epigraphs signal literary models, anticipate themes to be treated in the individual chapters, and suggest tone or, by creating false expectations, irony. Consider the quotations from Fonvizin's *The Minor*, an important intertext in the chapters treating Grinyov's early youth. This great comedy exposes the pretensions and misguided intentions of the provincial gentry. The Skotinin family wish to educate their son Mitrofan, not for the sake of enlightenment, but to satisfy their ambitions for social advancement; Fonvizin mocks their mindless aping of Western ways and the hopeless incompetence of the foreign tutors whom they hire. The epigraphs convey the patriarchal atmosphere of gentry life of the period, but also imply unsettling parallels between the younger Grinyov and Mitrofan. In the event, none of these are borne out in the narrative, and long before its end the reader will recognize that Grinyov's tale of loyalty and honour provides an antidote to Fonvizin's corrosive satire.

Pushkin's innovation in *The Captain's Daughter* lies in the

work's unusual combination of novelistic modes: it brings together features of the historical novel, the *Bildungsroman*, the
memoir-novel, the adventure novel, and the fairy-tale. As in *The
Tales of Belkin*, the structure isolates the author from the performance of the fictive narrator. And once again, the task of the
reader is to recognize the literary styles from which the narrators
fashion their stories. Here, as in 'The Shot', we have a narrator
whose approach to his own narrative shows fluency but inexpert
command of styles. When Shvabrin mocks Grinyov's verse as
pastiche of the outmoded Tredyakovsky, Pushkin draws attention
to the fictional author's archaizing and untutored sense of style.

  In evaluating these codes we can move on to the plane of
intentionality and consider the relation between these features of
the text and the real author's message. Why is *The Captain's
Daughter* not a historical novel? The answer lies in the balance
between the background and biography. In the Waverley novels
the hero interests the omniscient narrator in so far as he is a
participant in historical events; there is no hero where there is
no history. While we know that the problem of historical writing
interests the author, in *The Captain's Daughter* history interests
the autobiographical narrator only as the setting for the chain of
incidents and accidents that act upon his character and bring
him happiness. Novels in the manner of Scott cannot be written
as first-person histories, where the key criterion is the extent to
which the hero influences history rather than the converse.
Whereas the historical novel firmly embeds the hero in historical
time, the *Bildungsroman* places the hero in biographical time as
presented realistically. And while the panoply of devices derived
from Scott indicates that it is Grinyov's invention to give his
memoir the shape and structure of a novel by Scott, in the
manner of the memoir-novel so popular in eighteenth-century
France, Grinyov's biography leads rather than follows the historical account.[11]

---

[11] The memoir-novel is a form of pseudo-autobiography in which the real
author pretends to be only an 'editor' of a true account, a feature that Pushkin
eliminated by discarding Grinyov's preface. 'This term could cover all novels in
which a character tells his or her life-story, but in practice it is applied almost
exclusively to works up to the early 19th c.' (P. France (ed.), *The New Oxford
Companion to Literature in French* (Oxford, 1995), 518). In England John Cleland's

Is *The Captain's Daughter* a *Bildungsroman*? In a brilliant (but sadly incomplete) essay, the literary historian and theorist Mikhail Bakhtin identified four necessary features of this mode.[12] First, the usual plot of the 'biographical novel' (his term for the *Bildungsroman*) will chart a predictable pattern of biological and conventional actions, encompassing birth, childhood, school, marriage, and so on. Secondly, despite the interaction between the hero and the world, the biographical novel presents the hero's image as essentially static: 'the hero's life and fate change, they assume structure and evolve, but the hero himself remains essentially unchanged.' Third, in the biographical novel representation of time will respect laws of nature (so conspicuously violated in the fairy-tale), and locate events and smaller units of time in the larger framework of a period in the subject's life. Moreover, while for obvious reasons the biographical novel cannot directly incorporate its subject into the future and thus into the larger flow of historical time, indirect access to 'historical duration' is gained with reference to future and past generations. Fourth, and perhaps most important, is the close connection between the hero and the surrounding world. The novel now sets its task in observing the hero exercise his will, attempt to realize his aims, and shape and affect his environment. The world of the novel no longer exists merely to test the hero. In the realistic novel, as Bakhtin points out, the world itself is an object of interest to the hero, and the way in which he engages it and lives in it is from the reader's point of view as important a part of the biographical narrative as where he ends up, whereas in the adventure novel, one variant of the *Bildungsroman*, the relation between the hero and the world is characterized by 'the random and unexpected meetings on the high road'. The ways in which features of the historical novel both suggest and disrupt

Memoirs of a Lady of Pleasure (1748–9) and Defoe's *Moll Flanders* (1722) are classical examples, while the most famous French versions are Prévost's *Histoire du chevalier des Grieux et de Manon Lescaut* (1731) and Lesage's *Histoire de Gil Blas de Santillane* (1715–35). For a full discussion of this mode of fiction, see Philip R. Stewart, *Imitation and Illusion in the French Memoir-Novel, 1700–1750* (New Haven, 1969).

[12] M. M. Bakhtin, 'The *Bildungsroman* and its Significance in the History of Realism (Toward a Historical Typology of the Novel)', in *Speech Genres and Other Late Essays*, trans. Vern W. McGee (Austin, Texas, 1986), 10–59.

the affiliation with the memoir-novel emerge at the very beginning of Grinyov's account when he gives details of his birth and the expected course of his life:

My father, Andrei Petrovich Grinyov, served in his youth under Count Minikh and retired with the rank of sergeant-major in 17—. From then on, he lived in his Simbirsk village, where he married the spinster Avdotya Vasilyevna Yu***, the daughter of an impoverished local nobleman. There were nine of us children. All my brothers and sisters died in infancy.

Mama was still pregnant with me when I was entered as a sergeant in the Semyonovsky regiment, through the good offices of Guards Major Prince B., our close relative. If, against expectations, mama had produced a girl, then papa would have notified the proper authorities of the death of the non-reporting sergeant, and that would have been the end of the matter. I was considered to be on leave until the completion of my studies. (p. 103)

Only an oblique reference to the events of 1762 that enthroned Princess Catherine hints at historical time. Where the historical novel would as a matter of course elaborate the scenario, set out before the reader a background of conflict based on faction or political principle, Grinyov situates his biography in family history. It is true, as a number of scholars have observed, that the first words of the novel, in laying emphasis on Grinyov's father, point to the important theme of paternal identity in the novel as Grinyov must gain the approval of a whole sequence of father-like figures, from Captain Mironov to Pugachev, before he passes the ultimate test of vindicating his honour and establishing his independence before his own father. But on a broader plane the details of the novel's opening belong more to the genre of the biographical novel, hinting at but finally supplanting the expectations of a narrative that will give equal space and emphasis to historical questions. In chronicling family mores, describing Grinyov's early education, taking a long view of his youth as an entire period to be compressed in a few pages and key episodes, the first chapter indeed satisfies the criteria which Bakhtin spelled out—until expectations are overturned.

All the details given in the first two paragraphs appear to predetermine the course of Grinyov's life and the military cursus that he will undergo. In fact, we are told that nothing—not even the contingency of gender—is left to chance even before the child's birth. Yet the elder Grinyov, probably out of abiding pique over the incident with M. Beaupré, changes plan by sending his son to serve in Orenburg rather than in St Petersburg. The new pattern that emerges from this fateful decision returns us to the world of the adventure novel where laws of history appear suspended and randomness determines the obligatory course of obstacles that the hero must face before achieving the prize. The late decision to name the novel for Masha Mironov was an inspired stroke, clarifying and yet paradoxical. On the one hand, Grinyov prompts the reader to keep Masha in view even though she does not play a decisive role in the action until the eleventh hour. On the other hand, if we read the novel as an adventure tale the title reveals a discrepancy. All adventure novels, especially those where devices of folklore are active, posit a goal of a kind, and normally the prize is a bride. Despite adhering to the structure of the historical novel, Grinyov's memoir as the history of his moral growth remains closer to the biographical novel: the injunction he received in setting out in the world was to preserve his honour, and this is precisely what Grinyov does. Like the hero of the adventure tale and the biographical novel, his character is fixed at the beginning and scarcely changes. Yet the title does not give 'honour' top billing, but rather 'the Captain's daughter', who combines in herself all the functions of the beautiful princess from the Russian fairy-tale even while being a plucky but plain country girl: Masha secures Grinyov his honour, the goal of the *Bildungsroman*, but also satisfies the aim of the quest by bringing him happiness. And because we know that Grinyov writes his memoir for the benefit of his descendants, it is clear that she has also given Grinyov children, and thus continued the sequence of generations that is the bedrock of the historical and biographical genres.

Two themes dominate the evaluation of Pushkin's place in Russian fiction, both of them misleading. The first, purveyed in standard literary histories, speaks of his prose in terms of the invention of a tradition *ex nihilo*. But Pushkin did not invent Russian prose or the Russian literary language, and he would have been shocked rather than flattered at the distortion of these widespread claims. In fact, fiction of many styles, Gothic, historical, and sentimental, had flourished in Russia since the 1780s. If Russia's prose literature of the period rarely achieved a memorable standard, it none the less shaped the sensibilities of a readership and acquired a market. The extent to which Pushkin recalls and parodies home-grown fiction refutes this proposition. The second approach has been to see Pushkin as the founder of one tradition of Russian realism leading directly to Dostoevsky and Tolstoy. This is equally misguided. Whatever their reverence for his work, and the occasional inspiration they found in Pushkin, the novelists of the late nineteenth century saw in fiction the reordering and re-creation of a realistically depicted life, often on an epic scale, and open to a far wider socio-linguistic range than Pushkin envisaged for his own work.[13] While there have been claims that Pushkin set down syntactic patterns and rules of diction that underlie modern Russian prose, 'there are levels of the language that Pushkin did not explore (mercantile, urban clerical jargons and the developing language of Russia's German-influenced metaphysics); his syntax has a spare Voltairian quality that has hardly become a norm for Russian expository writing.'[14] In so far as Pushkin's prose self-consciously creates literature out of other texts, it draws on the traditions of eighteenth-century European fiction, and the great 'anti-novelists' Diderot and Sterne. If Pushkin looks forward, it is to twentieth-century modernism rather than to nineteenth-century realism. Perhaps it is not surprising that Pushkin's true Russian heirs are few, numbering writers like Mikhail Zoshchenko in the 1930s, the Nabokov of *Pale Fire*, or, more hyperbolically, Andrei Bitov in his *The Pushkin House*. Russia's most classical writer is paradoxically Russia's first great modernist.

Andrew Kahn

[13] On this topic, see briefly Victor Terras, 'Pushkin's Prose Fiction in a Historical Context', in *Pushkin Today*, 214–19.

[14] William Mills Todd III, 'Alexander Sergeevich Pushkin', in V. Terras (ed.), *Handbook of Russian Literature* (New Haven, 1985), 357.

SELECT BIBLIOGRAPHY

While the critical literature on Pushkin in Russian is vast, there is a substantial corpus of work in English on most aspects of his life and work.

General Studies

Bayley, John, *Pushkin: A Comparative Commentary* (Cambridge, 1971).

Binyon, T. J., *Pushkin: A Biography* (London, 2002; New York, 2003).

Bloom, Harold (ed.), *Alexander Pushkin: Modern Critical Views* (New York, 1987).

Briggs, A. D. P., *Alexander Pushkin: A Critical Study* (London, 1983).

Budgen, David, 'Pushkin and the Novel', in A. McMillin (ed.), *From Pushkin to 'Palisandria* (Basingstoke and London, 1990), 3–38.

Debreczeny, Paul, *The Other Pushkin: A Study of Alexander Pushkin's Prose Fiction* (Stanford, 1983).

Golburt, Luba, 'Catherine's Retinue: Old Age, Fashion and Historicism in the Nineteenth Century', *Slavic Review* 68: 4 (Winter 2009), 782–803.

Greenleaf, Monika, *Pushkin and Romantic Fashion: Fragment, Elegy, Orient, Irony* (Stanford, 1994)

Gregg, Richard, 'Pushkin's Novelistic Prose: A Dead End?', *Slavic Review*, 57: 1 (Spring 1998), 1–27.

Kahn, Andrew (ed.), *The Cambridge Companion to Pushkin* (Cambridge, 2007).

Mirsky, D. S., *Pushkin* (London, 1926).

Sandler, Stephanie, *Distant Pleasures: Alexander Pushkin and the Writing of Exile* (Stanford, 1989)

Steiner, Lina, 'Pushkin's Parable of the Prodigal Daughter: The Evolution of the Prose Tale from Aestheticism to Historicism', *Comparative Literature*, 56: 2 (Spring 2004), 130–46.

Vickery, Walter, *Alexander Pushkin* (New York, 1970).

Wolff, Tatiana, *Pushkin on Literature* (London, 1971).

The Tales of Belkin

Debreczeny, Paul, 'Pushkin's Use of his Narrator in "The Stationmaster"', *Russian Literature*, 4: 2 (1976), 149–66.

Gregg, Richard, 'A Scapegoat for All Seasons: The Unity and the Shape of *The Tales of Belkin*', *Slavic Review*, 30: 4 (1971), 748–61.

Kodjak, Andrej, *Pushkin's I. P. Belkin* (Columbus, Ohio, 1979).

Shaw, J. Thomas, 'Pushkin's "The Stationmaster" and the New Testament Parable', *Slavic and East European Journal*, 21: 1 (1977), 3–29.

Unbegaun, B. O., 'Introduction', in A. S. Pushkin, *The Tales of the Late Ivan Petrovich Belkin* (Oxford, 1947), pp. xi–xxxiii.

The Captain's Daughter

Anderson, Roger, 'A Study of Petr Grinev as the Hero of Pushkin's *Kapitanskaia dochka*', *Canadian Slavic Studies*, 5 (1971), 477–86.

Davie, Donald, '*The Captain's Daughter*: Pushkin's Prose and Russian Realism', in (ed.), *The Heyday of Sir Walter Scott* (New York, 1961), 7–20.

Dolinin, Alexander, 'Historicism or Providentialism? Pushkin's History of Pugachev in the Context of French Romantic Historiography', *Slavic Review*, 58: 2, Special Issue: *Aleksandr Pushkin 1799–1999* (Summer 1999), 291–308.

Emerson, Caryl, 'Grinev's Dream: *The Captain's Daughter* and a Father's Blessing', *Slavic Review*, 40: 1 (1981), 60–76.

Greene, M., 'Pushkin and Sir Walter Scott', *Forum for Modern Language Studies*, 1: 3 (1965), 207–15.

Mikkelson, Gerald, 'The Mythopoetic Element in Pushkin's Historical Novel *The Captain's Daughter*', *Canadian–American Slavic Studies*, 7 (1973), 296–313.

—— 'Pushkin's *History of Pugachev*: The Littérateur as Historian', in G. J. Gutsche (ed.), *New Perspectives on Nineteenth-Century Prose* (Columbus, 1982), 26–37.

Reyfman, Irina, 'Poetic Justice and Injustice: Autobiographical Echoes in Pushkin's *The Captain's Daughter*', *Slavic and East European Journal*, 38: 3 (1994), 463–78.

Sandler, Stephanie, 'The Problem of History in Pushkin: Poet, Pretender, Tsar', Ph.D. Dissertation, Yale University, 1981.

Stenbock-Fermor, E. 'Some Neglected Features of the Epigraphs in *The Captain's Daughter* and Other Stories of Pushkin', *International Journal of Slavic Linguistics and Poetics*, 8 (1964), 110–23.

Tsvetaeva, Marina, 'Pushkin and Pugachev', in *A Captive Spirit*, trans. J. Marin King (Ann Arbor, 1980), 372–403.

The Queen of Spades

Barker, Adele, 'Pushkin's *Queen of Spades*: A Displaced Mother Figure', *American Imago*, 41: 2 (1984), 201–9.

Bocharov, S. G., ' "The Queen of Spades" ', *New Literary History*, 9 (1978), 315–32.

Burgin, Diana, 'The Mystery of "Pikovaja Dama": A New Interpretation', in J. T. Baer and N. Ingham (eds.), *Mnemozina: Studia litteraria russica in honorem Vsevolod Setchkarev* (Munich, 1974), 46–56.

Clayton, J. Douglas, '*Spadar Dame, Pique Dame*, and *Pikovaia dama*: A German Source for Pushkin?', *Germano-Slavica*, 4 (1974), 5–10.

Doherty, Justin, 'Fictional Paradigms in Pushkin's "Pikovaya dama" ',

Essays in Poetics, 17: 1 (1992), 49–66.

Faletti, Heidi, 'Remarks on Style as Manifestation of Narrative Technique in "The Queen of Spades"', *Canadian–American Slavic Studies*, 11: 1 (1977), 114–33.

Gregg, Richard, 'Balzac and the Women in *The Queen of Spades*', *Slavic and East European Journal*, 10: 3 (1966), 279–82.

Helfant, Ian M., 'Pushkin's Ironic Performances as a Gambler', *Slavic Review*, 58: 2, Special Issue: *Aleksandr Pushkin 1799–1999* (Summer 1999), 371–92.

Kodjak, Andrej, '"The Queen of Spades" in the Context of the Faust Legend' in Andrej Kodjak and K. Taranovsky (eds.), *Alexander Pushkin: A Symposium on the 175th Anniversary of his Birth* (New York, 1976), 87–118.

Leighton, Lauren, 'Numbers and Numerology in "The Queen of Spades"', *Canadian–Slavonic Papers*, 19 (1977), 417–43.

—— 'Pushkin and Freemasonry: "The Queen of Spades"', in G. J. Gutsche (ed.), *New Perspectives on Nineteenth-Century Prose* (Columbus, 1982).

Lotman, Jurij, 'Theme and Plot: The Theme of Cards and the Card Game in Russian Literature of the Nineteenth Century', trans. C. R. Pike, *PTL* (1978), 455–92.

Reeder, Roberta, 'The Queen of Spades: A parody of the Hoffmannian tale', in G. Gutsche and L. Leighton (eds.), *New Perspectives on Nineteenth-Century Russian Prose* (Columbus, Ohio, 1982), 73–98.

Rosen, Nathan, 'The Magic Cards in "The Queen of Spades"', *Slavic and East European Journal*, 19: 3 (1975), 255–75.

Schwartz, Murray and Schwartz, Albert, '"The Queen of Spades": A Psychoanalytic Interpretation', *Texas Studies in Literature and Language*, 17 (1975), 275–88.

Shklovsky, V., 'Notes on Pushkin's Prose. A Society Tale: *The Queen of Spades*', in *Russian Views of Pushkin*, trans. D. J. Richards and C. R. S. Cockrell (Oxford, 1976), 187–95.

Shrayer, Maxim, 'Rethinking Romantic Irony: Pushkin, Byron, Schlegel and *The Queen of Spades*', *Slavic and East European Journal*, 36: 4 (1992), 397–414.

Thomas, Alfred, 'A Russian Oedipus: Lacan and Pushkin's "The Queen of Spades"', *Wiener Slawistischer Almanach*, 31 (1992), 47–59.

Williams, Gareth, 'Conventions and Play in *Pikovaja dama*', *Russian Literature*, 26 (1989), 523–38.

A CHRONOLOGY OF
ALEXANDER PUSHKIN

All dates are given in the Old Style. Russia switched from the Julian to Gregorian Calendar only after the 1917 Revolution.

1799   (26 May), Alexander Pushkin born in Moscow to Major Sergei Lvovich Pushkin (1771–1848) and Nadezhda Osipovna (neé Hannibal) (1775–1836).

1811   Enters the prestigious Lyceum at Tsarskoe Selo as a member of its first class.

1814   (20 June), makes his debut in print with the publication of two poems in the literary journal *The Herald of Europe*.

1815   (Winter), Pushkin's lyric poem 'Remembrances in Tsarskoe Selo', published in April, in manuscript, gains the attention of Vasily Zhukovsky and other poets. Zhukovsky visits Pushkin at the Lyceum in Tsarskoye Selo, thus initiating one of the most important friendships and literary associations in Pushkin's life (May). After this meeting Zhukovsky predicts that Pushkin will be 'a future giant who will outgrow us all'.

1816   (March), meets historian and writer Nicholas Karamzin and Prince P. A. Vyazemsky, poet and critic and soon to be one of Pushkin's closest friends and literary allies. Pushkin joins Arzamas, the most innovative of the St Petersburg literary societies.

1817   (June), is graduated from the Lyceum. Lives in the Kolomna District in St Petersburg, where he secures an appointment in the Ministry of Foreign Affairs. Initial stages of the Decembrist conspiracy, calling for the abolition of serfdom and the establishment of a constitution in Russia.

1818   First eight volumes of Karamzin's *History of the Russian State* (February) published to great popular success.

1820   (April), at the order of Alexander I, Pushkin investigated and arrested for subversive behaviour linked to the politically inflammatory ode 'Liberty' that circulated anonymously.

1820–4 Exile begins under military supervision with a period of travel in the Crimea; from the autumn of 1820 based in Kishinev until June 1823, followed by spells in Odessa from July 1823 till July 1824.

1820 (July), publication of long poem *Ruslan and Lyudmila* to considerable (if not unanimous) acclaim. Rebellion in the élite Semyonovsky regiment in St Petersburg (October).

1821 First of Pushkin's long 'Byronic' poems published, *The Caucasian Captive*. Rebellion of Ypsilanti in Greece, and unrest in Piedmont inspire Decembrists.

1824 (December), *The Fountain of Bakhchisaray* published. End of exile in the south. Pushkin is now confined to the family estate at Mikhailovskoe.

1825 Chapter 1 of *Eugene Onegin* published. Death of Alexander I. Coronation of Nicholas I disrupted by the Decembrists (14 December). *Boris Godunov* written.

1826 *Poems of Alexander Pushkin, Part I* published. Nicholas I ends Pushkin's exile. At an interview he makes himself the poet's personal censor.

1827 *Brothers-Brigands* (July), and *The Gypsies* (written 1824) published. (31 July), *The Blackamoor of Peter the Great* begun.

1828 (February), chapters 4 and 5 of *Eugene Onegin* published. Second edition of *Ruslan and Lyudmila*. Renting rooms at the Hotel Demuth, St Petersburg. (July), placed under surveillance after the dissemination in manuscript of the poem 'Andrei Cheniér'. At the same time, although Pushkin denies authorship in a letter to the Tsar, he is investigated in conjunction with the blasphemous poem 'Gavriiliada'. (September), *Poltava* begun.

1829 (March), publication of *Poltava; Poems of Alexander Pushkin, Part II*. (May–September), Pushkin travels to Georgia and the Caucasus; he records the experience in *A Journey to Erzurum*. Elected to membership in the Society of Lovers of Russian Literature on 23 December.

1830 Chapter 7 of *Eugene Onegin* published. Pushkin becomes engaged to Natalya Nikolaevna Goncharova of a once-prosperous but impoverished family of paper manufacturers (April). (September–December), 'First Autumn at Boldino': Pushkin writes *Tales of Belkin, Little House in Kolomna*, Chapter 8 of *Eugene Onegin*, the *Little Tragedies*, i.e., *The Stone Guest, Mozart and Salieri, The Covetous Knight, The Tale of the Priest and his Worker Balda*, and over thirty lyric poems.

1831 (January), death of Baron A. Delvig, Pushkin's oldest friend, publisher, and literary ally. (18 February), marries. *Tale of Tsar*

Sultan written (August–September), *Tales of Belkin* published. (November), by order of the Tsar, Pushkin readmitted to a nominal position in the Foreign Office with an annual stipend. Chapter 8 of *Eugene Onegin* published. *Boris Godunov* published.

1832   (March), *Poems of Alexander Pushkin, Part III* published. (18 May), birth of daughter Mariya. (November), *Dubrovsky* begun (abandoned January 1833, and published incomplete in 1837). Election to membership in the Russian Academy.

1833   (March), *Eugene Onegin* published in book form. First sketches of *Captain's Daughter* penned. (6 July), birth of son Alexander. (August–September), travels to the Orenburg and Kazan districts in connection with his research on the *History of the Pugachev Rebellion. Tale of the Fisherman and the Fish* written (October). (6–31 October), composition of *The Bronze Horseman.* The finances of the Pushkin family, including the poet's father, are in a critical state; they nearly lose the family estate to creditors.

1834   (1 January), to his consternation, the Tsar appoints Pushkin Gentleman of the Chamber. (March), *Queen of Spades* published. *Andzhelo,* based on Shakespeare's *Measure for Measure,* published (April). Writes 'Kirdzhali' (short story). Researching the history of the reign of Peter the Great. *History of the Pugachev Rebellion* published with the Tsar's express approval (December). *Tale of the Golden Cockerel* begun. His financial position remains precarious.

1835   (April), *Poems of Alexander Pushkin, Parts III and IV* published. (14 May), birth of son Grigory. (September), the story *Egyptian Nights* begun.

1836   (April), first volume of the journal *The Contemporary* published under Pushkin's editorship. Three more volumes appear during the course of the year, with *The Captain's Daughter* published in volume 4 (November). (29 March), death of Pushkin's mother. (23 May), birth of daughter, Natalya. (19 October), final lyric in the cycle of six poems commemorating the friendships formed at the Lyceum.

1837   (26 January), fights duel with the French officer George d'Anthès, who courted his wife in vain and then married Natalya's sister. (29 January) Pushkin dies of his wounds. By the order of the Tsar, who feared disruptions in the capital, his body is removed under darkness to its final resting-place in Trigorsk, near Pushkin's family estate.

A SHORT CHRONOLOGY OF
THE PUGACHEV UPRISING

Sept. 1773 After menacing the fortress at Yaik, Pugachev gains strength and heads toward Tatishchev and then on to Orenburg. He appeals for support to the non-Russian peoples of the enormous area between the Volga, the Yaik, and Western Siberia. The government offers a reward of 500 rubles for his capture alive, 250 for him dead.

Oct. 1773 Catherine II appoints Major General Carr to deal with the renegade. At this time Pugachev overwhelms a Russian detachment and hangs the commander and officers. 25,000 Cossacks are said to join his forces.

Nov.–Dec. 1773 Bashkirs begin causing unrest in Ufa, which spreads to the Kalmyks. Pugachev places Ufa under siege, which is now cut off from Kazan, the largest town in the Samara region. Ilinskaya Fortress is taken. General A. I. Bibikov is appointed to put down the rebellion and to investigate the causes of the revolt.

Jan.–Feb. 1774 Mansurov and Bibikov in action near Stavropol and Ufa. Pugachev in the area of Orenburg. Skirmishes continue throughout the month as General Major Freiman enters the action. The government increases its reward for Pugachev's capture to 10,000 rubles. Pugachev has been ejected from Samara and begins terrorizing the area around Ekaterinburg, stirring up the native populations.

Mar. 1774 Pugachev sustains heavy losses in a battle near Tatishchev against General P. M. Golitsyn.

Apr.–May 1774 Pugachev's wife and other leaders of the rebellion taken into captivity. The seige of Orenburg is broken. General Bibikov dies; his command passes to Lieutenant-General Prince F. F. Shcherbatov. Mikhelson restores order in Ufa. After lying low in the steppe Pugachev attacks Orenburg, and then proceeds to take a string of fortresses before circling back to the city. As one Russian general reported in a despatch, 'Pugachev is like the wind, rushing everywhere, controlling his forces even when they are dispersed.' Beloborodov attacks Pugachev near Magnitnaya Fortress; the latter is wounded in the hand.

late June 1774 Mikhelson is alarmed that Pugachev may head to Penza and then on to the Don region. General Beloborodov is taken captive.

July 1774 Pugachev is in the area of Nizhny-Novgorod where he is initially repulsed by Mikhelson. By mid-July Pugachev has taken Kazan, freeing his wife and children, whereupon he crosses the

Volga, raising fears that he may be heading toward Moscow. He issues a manifesto promising freedom to the local peasantry. According to Russian intelligence, 'it is not only the local folk that are well-disposed to him where he happens to be, but even those at a distance are willing to sacrifice their property to him'. In Kazan, Pugachev leaves behind 129 dead, 486 missing, and twenty-five churches, three monasteries, and 1,772 houses destroyed before heading for Penza. His mob suffers a decisive defeat at the hands of Mikhelson, who kills 4,000 and takes captive 6,000 men. In the Saransk region he is greeted as Peter III by the local clergy and nobility. He rewards a local widow who entertains him by having her hanged.

Aug. 1774 Pugachev attacks Saratov, where he opens the prisons and hangs numbers of the gentry indiscriminately. His next move is to march south, and to foment uprising among the peasantry and Old Believers. To his consternation the Don Cossacks remain loyal to the government and refuse to follow the so-called Pretender. Late in the month he withdraws from his siege of Tsaritsyn, whereupon he is pursued by Mikhelson who breaks the centre of his army, leaving Pugachev with the bare remnants of his army.

mid-Sept. 1774 Pugachev flees with his wife and a small band of conspirators who eventually disarm him, ending the revolt.

TALES OF THE LATE
IVAN PETROVICH BELKIN

TALES OF THE LATE
IVAN PETROVICH BELKIN

MRS PROSTAKOVA: That's right, my dear sir, he's been a
rare one for histories since he was little.
SKOTININ: Mitrofan takes after me.

(*The Minor*)*

FROM THE PUBLISHER

In undertaking the publication of I. P. Belkin's *Tales*, now placed
before the reader, we had hoped to include a biography of the
late author, however brief, thus satisfying to some extent the
legitimate curiosity of lovers of our native letters. To this end,
we were minded to approach Maria Alexeyevna Trafilina, the
heiress and next-of-kin of Ivan Petrovich Belkin; she was unable, however, to furnish any information, since she had not
known the deceased at all. She advised us to address our enquiries on the matter to a certain worthy gentleman, a former friend
of Ivan Petrovich. We followed this advice, and in answer to our
letter, received the desired response, which we print below. We
are publishing it without alteration or commentary, as a precious
memento of a noble cast of mind and a touching friendship, as
well as being in itself a perfectly adequate biographical sketch.

My Dear Sir,
    On the 23rd of this month I had the honour of receiving your
most esteemed letter of the 15th, in which you advise me of your
desire to have detailed information concerning the dates of birth
and death, military service, domestic circumstances, pursuits,
and habits of the late Ivan Petrovich Belkin, my erstwhile true
friend and neighbour. It is with great pleasure that I comply
with your wish and herewith convey to you, my dear sir, everything I can remember from his conversations, as well as recalling
my own observations as best I can.

Ivan Petrovich Belkin was born of honourable and noble parents in 1798 in the village of Goryukhino. His late father, Major Pyotr Ivanovich Belkin, had married the spinster Pelageya Gavrilovna of the Trafilin family. He wasn't rich, but he was a sober fellow and had a good head on him as regards estate management. Their son received his elementary education from the parish clerk. It was this worthy man, it seems, he had to thank for his fondness for reading and his studies in the field of Russian literature. In 1815 he enlisted in a chasseur infantry regiment (I don't recall the number) in which he remained right up till 1823. When his parents died almost simultaneously he was forced to retire and come to Goryukhino village, his patrimony.

Having assumed control of his estate, Ivan Petrovich, from lack of experience and soft-heartedness, very soon let his affairs drift and relaxed the strict discipline which his late father had established. Replacing the meticulously efficient village elder, with whom his peasants (as usual) were discontented, he entrusted the management of the village to his old housekeeper who had gained his confidence through her skill in story-telling. This foolish old woman could never tell a twenty-rouble note from a fifty; the peasants, who were all her boon companions, had not the least fear of her; the elder they had chosen indulged them to such an extent, cheating along with them, that Ivan Petrovich was compelled to abolish the *barshchina* and introduce instead a very moderate quit-rent;* but even then they took advantage of his weakness and got a considerable concession out of him the first year; in the following years they paid more than two-thirds of the quit-rent in the form of nuts, bilberries, and suchlike, and even then there were arrears.

As a friend of Ivan Petrovich Belkin's late father, I regarded it as my duty to offer my advice to the son also, and on several occasions volunteered to restore the former system of discipline which he had allowed to lapse. To this end, I once came to him requesting to see the account books, summoned that rascally elder, and in the presence of Ivan Petrovich, began to examine them. The young squire at first followed me, all attention and assiduity, but as soon as it emerged that over the last two years the number of peasants had risen, while that of poultry and cattle had gone down, Ivan Petrovich contented himself with these initial findings and listened to me no more. At the very moment when I had driven that rogue of an elder into utter confusion by my inquiries and stern interrogation, reducing him to complete silence, I heard, to my great annoyance, Ivan Petrovich snoring away in his chair. After that I consigned his affairs (as indeed did he) to the Almighty, and ceased meddling in his business arrangements.

This incident, by the way, in no way affected our amicable relations; for though I deplored his weakness and the ruinous negligence so common among our young noblemen, I was genuinely fond of him; indeed it would have been hard not to love so mild and honest a young man. For his part, Ivan Petrovich evinced a proper respect for my years and was warmly attached to me. He saw me practically every day until his passing, valuing my straightforward conversation, although to a great extent we were dissimilar in our habits, ways of thinking, and general disposition.

Ivan Petrovich led a most temperate existence, avoiding any sort of excess; I never had occasion to see him tipsy (which in these parts may be regarded as an incredible miracle); he had a great fondness for the female sex, but his modesty was truly maidenly.[1]

In addition to the tales you were pleased to mention in your letter, Ivan Petrovich left a good many manuscripts behind him, some of which are in my possession, though some have been put by his housekeeper to sundry domestic uses. For example, last winter all the windows in her wing of the house were sealed up with the first part of an unfinished novel of his. The tales mentioned above were his first efforts, I do believe. They are, as Ivan Petrovich used to say, for the most part true, and heard from various people.[2] The proper names, however, are almost all

[1] There follows an anecdote which we are omitting, deeming it superfluous; we do assure the reader that it contains nothing prejudicial to the memory of Ivan Petrovich Belkin. (*Note by A. S. Pushkin.*)

[2] Indeed, in Mr Belkin's manuscript there is a note above each tale in the author's handwriting: 'heard by me from such and such a person' (followed by rank, title, and initials). We copy them here for inquisitive researchers: 'The Stationmaster' was related to him by Titular Councillor A.G.N., 'The Shot' by

invented, and the names of villages and hamlets borrowed from those hereabouts, which is why my village gets mentioned somewhere too. There was no sort of malice intended, it was just lack of imagination.

In the autumn of 1828 Ivan Petrovich contracted a cold which developed into a high fever, and he died, despite the tireless efforts of our district doctor, a man of exceptional skill, especially in the treatment of deep-seated conditions, such as corns and so forth. He passed away in my arms in the thirtieth year of his life, and was buried at Goryukhino Church, close to his deceased parents.

Ivan Petrovich was of middling height, with grey eyes, lightish brown hair, straight nose; his face was pale and lean.

There it is, my dear sir, all I could bring to mind concerning the mode of life, pursuits, disposition, and appearance of my late neighbour and friend. If you should see fit to make use of this, my letter, I most humbly request you not to mention my name. Although I greatly respect and like authors, I regard it as unnecessary and, at my age, improper to assume this calling. With sincere respect, etc.

16 November 1830.
Nenaradovo Village'

Considering it our duty to respect the wish of our author's worthy friend, we express our most profound gratitude for the information he has furnished, and trust that the public will appreciate its sincerity and good-natured intent.

A. P.

Lieutenant-Colonel I.L.P., 'The Undertaker' by the steward B.V., and 'The Lady Peasant' by spinster K.I.T. (*Note by A. S. Pushkin.*)

THE SHOT

We exchanged fire.

(Baratynsky)

I vowed to shoot him according to
the duello (I still had my turn to come).

('An Evening on Bivouac')*

I

We were stationed in the township of N. Everyone knows the
life of an army officer. In the morning, drill and horsemanship;
dinner with the regimental commander or at the Jew's tavern; in
the evening, punch and cards. In N. there wasn't a single house
open to us, not a single marriageable girl; we congregated in one-
another's quarters, where we saw nothing but our own uniforms.

There was only one individual belonging to our circle who
wasn't with the military. He was about thirty-five years old,
which made him an old man in our estimation. Experience gave
him a good many advantages over us; in addition to which, his
habitual morose manner, brusque temper, and waspish tongue
exercised a considerable influence on our young minds. A kind
of mystery surrounded him. He appeared to be Russian, but had
a foreign name. At one time he had served in the hussars, with
some distinction indeed; nobody knew the reason which had
prompted him to retire and take up residence in a miserable
township, where he led an existence that was at once poverty-
stricken and extravagant: he went everywhere on foot, dressed
in a threadbare black frock-coat, but kept open house for all
the officers of our regiment. True, his dinners consisted of two
or three courses, cooked by a retired soldier, but the champagne
flowed without stint. Nobody knew the extent of his fortune,
nor whence he drew his income, and nobody had the courage to
ask him about it. He had books, military for the most part, but
also novels. He readily loaned them out and never asked for

them back; on the other hand, he never returned any that he
borrowed. His chief pursuit consisted in pistol-shooting. The
walls of his room were all riddled with bullets, fairly honey-
combed. A considerable collection of pistols was the sole item of
luxury in the miserable, mud-plastered hut in which he lived.
He had attained an incredible level of skill, and if he had offered
to shoot a pear off anyone's cap, nobody in our regiment would
have hesitated to risk his head. Our talk frequently turned to
duelling; Silvio (as I shall call him) never involved himself. If
asked whether he had ever had occasion to fight, he would reply
stiffly that he had, but never divulged any details, and it was
plain that he found questions of this sort distasteful. We assumed that some luckless victim of his fearful skill lay on his
conscience. At any rate, it never occurred to us to suspect him
of anything like timidity. There are people whose mere appearance is enough to banish any suspicions of that nature. An unexpected incident left us all astounded.

One evening, about ten of our officers were dining at Silvio's.
We were drinking as usual, that is to say, a considerable amount;
after the meal we began persuading our host to hold the bank for
us. He refused for a long time, as he practically never gambled;
at length he sent for the cards, poured out some fifty gold pieces
on to the table, and sat down to deal. We sat down around him
and play commenced. It was Silvio's custom to maintain absolute silence during play, never arguing and never explaining.
If a player happened to miscalculate, Silvio immediately either
paid the difference or jotted down the extra staked. We knew
this by now and just let him run things in his own way; there
was, however, an officer among us who had only recently been
transferred. As he played, he absently turned down the corner
of a card.* Silvio picked up the chalk and adjusted the stakes
as was his wont. The officer, thinking a mistake had been made,
launched into explanations. Silvio went on dealing without a
word. The officer, losing patience, took up the brush and erased
what he thought had been wrongly written down. Silvio took
the chalk and wrote it again. The officer, overwrought by the
wine, the play, and the laughter of his comrades, took strong
offence and in his fury snatched up a brass candlestick from the
table and hurled it at Silvio, who barely managed to evade the

impact. We were utterly taken aback. Silvio rose, pale with rage, and with eyes blazing said:

'Dear sir, be good enough to leave, and give thanks to God that this took place in my house.'

We had no doubt of the consequences and assumed that our new comrade was now a dead man. The officer departed, saying that he was ready to answer for the insult in whatever fashion the gentleman-banker thought fit. The game proceeded for several more minutes, but we could see that our host's heart was not in it and we left one by one and wandered back to our quarters, discussing the imminent vacancy.

The next day, during riding exercises, we were already asking whether the poor lieutenant was still alive when he appeared among us in person; we addressed our question to him. He replied that he had not yet had any news of Silvio. We were amazed. We went to Silvio's and found him outside, planting bullet after bullet into an ace stuck to the gate. He received us as normal, saying not a word about the previous evening's events. Three days went by and the lieutenant was still alive. We asked one another in surprise: could it be that Silvio was not going to fight? Silvio did not fight. He contented himself with an offhand explanation and was reconciled with the lieutenant.

This might have done him great harm in the eyes of the young men. Lack of courage is the thing found least excusable by the young, who usually see valour as the acme of human virtue and an excuse for all manner of vicious behaviour. Little by little, however, all was forgotten, and Silvio recovered his former authority.

I alone could no longer warm to him. Having an inborn romantic imagination, I had formerly been attracted more strongly than any of them to a man whose life was a riddle and who seemed like the hero of some mysterious tale. He was fond of me; at least it was only with me that he put aside his usual acerbic, scoffing manner and spoke of this and that in an unaffected and vastly agreeable fashion. But after that unfortunate evening the thought that his honour had been besmirched and left uncleansed through his own inaction never quitted me, and prevented me from treating him as before; I felt ashamed to look at him. Silvio was too intelligent and experienced not to be

aware of this and guess the reason behind it. It seemed to distress him; at all events, I detected on one or two occasions a
desire on his part to explain matters, but I evaded the opportunities, and Silvio withdrew from me. Since that day I saw him
only when I was in company, and our former frank conversations came to an end.

The distracted denizens of the capital have no conception of
the myriad emotions so familiar to the inhabitants of villages or
small towns, for example, the suspense of waiting for the mail:
on Tuesday and Friday our orderly office used to be filled with
officers: some were expecting money, some letters, some newspapers. The packages were usually unsealed on the spot and
news given out. The office always presented a most animated
scene. Silvio used to receive his letters addressed via our regiment, and was usually there along with us. One day he was
handed a package from which he tore the seal with an air of the
utmost impatience. As he skimmed through the letter his eyes
flashed. The officers, each occupied with his own letters, took
no notice. 'Gentlemen,' Silvio said, 'circumstances demand my
immediate departure; I leave tonight; I hope you will not refuse
to dine with me one last time. I expect you also,' he went on,
addressing me, 'without fail.' So saying, he quickly left; after
agreeing to meet at Silvio's, we all went our different ways.

I arrived at Silvio's at the appointed hour and found virtually
the whole regiment there. All his belongings had already been
packed; only the bare, bullet-riddled walls remained. We sat down
at table; our host was on extremely good form, and his high spirits
were infectious; corks popped by the minute, glasses foamed and
hissed incessantly, as we wished the departing host all the best and
God speed. It was late in the evening by the time we rose from
the table. While caps were being sorted out, Silvio took me by
the arm as he said his goodbyes to the rest, and detained me as I
was about to leave. 'I have to talk to you,' he said softly. I stayed.

The guests departed; now left alone, we sat down opposite
one another and silently lit our pipes. Silvio was preoccupied;
there was no trace now of his febrile gaiety. His grim pallor and
glittering eyes, together with the dense smoke issuing from his
mouth, gave him a genuinely diabolic appearance. Some minutes
passed before Silvio broke the silence.

'It may be that we shall never see one another again,' he said to me. 'Before parting, I wanted to explain matters to you. You may have noticed that I pay little heed to the opinion of others; but I am fond of you and it worries me; I would find it hard to leave an unfair impression of me in your mind.'

He stopped and began filling his extinguished pipe; I said nothing, my eyes lowered.

'You found it strange', he went on, 'that I did not seek satisfaction from that drunken hothead R***. As I had choice of weapons, you will agree that his life was in my hands and my own virtually safe: I could ascribe my moderation to magnanimity alone, but I have no wish to lie. If I could have punished R*** with absolutely no risk to my own life, I would not have pardoned him for anything.'

I looked at Silvio in amazement. A confession of this nature utterly staggered me. Silvio continued.

'Just so: I haven't the right to risk my own life. Six years ago I received a slap in the face, and my enemy still lives.'

My curiosity was powerfully aroused.

'You didn't fight him?' I asked. 'Circumstances kept you apart, no doubt?'

'I did fight him,' replied Silvio, 'and I have here a memento of our duel.'

He got up and from a box took out a braided red cap with a gold tassel (what the French call a *bonnet de police*); he put it on; it had been shot through an inch above his forehead.

'You know', Silvio went on, 'that I used to serve in a hussar regiment. Everyone is aware of the sort of man I am: I am used to being the best, but as a young man it was my ruling passion. Back then, hell-raising was the fashion: I was the worst troublemaker in the whole army. Getting drunk was a bragging matter: I could outdrink the famous Burtsov, the one celebrated in Denis Davydov's poems.* In our regiment duels were taking place all the time: I attended every one, either as a witness or a participant. My comrades adored me, though my regimental commanders, who were constantly being replaced, looked on me as an unavoidable evil.

'I was enjoying my celebrity quietly (or not so quietly), when a young man from a wealthy and distinguished family (I would rather not give him a name) took service in our regiment. Never in my life had I encountered so brilliant a favourite of fortune! Picture it—youth, intelligence, good looks, the wildest of humour, the most casual courage, a noble name, money beyond the counting and always available, and imagine the impression he was bound to make on us. My pre-eminence was in jeopardy. Attracted by my reputation, he would have sought my friendship; but I received his overtures coldly, and he withdrew without the least regret. I began to cherish a hatred for him. His success in the regiment and in the society of women was driving me to utter despair. I began to look for ways of picking a quarrel with him; he capped my witty remarks with witty remarks of his own, which always seemed to me more original and pointed than mine, as well as being, of course, incomparably more amusing: he was joking, while I was consumed with spite. At length, at a ball given by a Polish landowner, seeing him singled out for attention by all the ladies, especially the hostess herself, with whom I had a liaison, I whispered some feeble coarseness in his ear. He flared up and slapped my face. We went for our sabres; ladies fainted; we were dragged apart, and set off to fight a duel that very night.

'It was at dawn. I stood on the appointed spot with my three seconds. I awaited my opponent with indescribable impatience. The spring sun came up and the heat began to build. I caught sight of him in the distance. He was on foot, accompanied by a second; he was carrying his coat on the point of his sabre. We advanced to meet him. He approached, holding his cap, which was full of cherries. The seconds measured out our twelve paces. I was supposed to fire first, but so intense was the nervous rage inside me that I could not rely on the steadiness of my arm; in order to give myself time to cool down, I conceded the first shot to him: my antagonist would not agree. We decided to draw lots; the first number fell to him, always fortune's favourite. He took aim and sent a bullet through my cap. Now it was my turn. At last his life was in my hands; I gazed at him hungrily, trying to detect at least a trace of unease . . . He stood there under the pistol, selecting the ripe cherries from his hat, and spitting out the stones which came flying towards me. His indifference infuriated me. What was the point, I thought, of depriving him of

life when he set no store by it at all. A savage notion flashed
through my mind. I lowered my pistol.

'"It seems you are in no mood to die at the moment," I told
him. "Do please carry on with your breakfast: I wouldn't wish to
disturb you."

'"You aren't disturbing me in the least," he rejoined. "By all
means take your shot; however, just as you please; you have one
shot to come; I am always at your service." I turned to the
seconds, announcing that I did not intend to shoot for the moment, and that was the end of the duel.

'I retired from the service and withdrew to this little township. Since then, not a day has passed without thoughts of
revenge. Now my hour has come round . . .'

Silvio took from his pocket the letter he had received that
morning and gave it to me to read. Someone (his agent evidently) had written to him from Moscow, that *a certain person* was
soon to be married to a young and beautiful girl.

'You realize', said Silvio, 'who this *certain person* is. I am
going to Moscow. We shall see whether he will accept death
with as much indifference before his wedding, as once he did
over his bowl of cherries!'

With these words Silvio got up, hurled his cap on the floor,
and began pacing up and down like a caged tiger. I listened to
him without moving, a prey to strange, conflicting emotions.

The servant came in and announced that the horses were
ready. Silvio shook my hand firmly; we kissed. He mounted the
cart which contained two suitcases, one holding his pistols, the
other his belongings. We said goodbye again, and the horses
galloped away.

II

Several years went by and domestic circumstances compelled
me to move to a miserable little village in the N*** district.
Busy as I was with my estate, I never ceased to hanker secretly
after my former boisterous and carefree existence. The hardest
thing of all to bear was getting used to spending the autumn and
winter evenings in complete solitude. I somehow managed to
drag the time out before dinner in discussing matters with the

village elder, riding round supervising the working of the place, or walking about the new building projects; but as soon as it began getting dark I had absolutely no idea what to do with myself. I knew by heart the small number of books which I had found under cupboards or in the store-room. All the fairy tales my housekeeper Kirilovna could remember had been told over and over again; the songs of the peasant women made me depressed. I would have set about the fruit liqueur, but it gave me a headache; I must confess, too, that I was somewhat afraid of turning into that most sorry of drunkards, the one who drowns his sorrows, of which I saw a good many examples in our district. I had no near neighbours, apart from two or three of these sorry types, whose conversation consisted for the most part of sighs and hiccups. Solitude was preferable.

About five miles from me there was a prosperous estate belonging to the Countess B***, but only the manager lived there, and the Countess had visited her estate just once, during the first year of her marriage, and even then had stayed less than a month. In the second spring of my reclusive existence, however, word got about that the Countess and her husband would be coming to her village for the summer. And indeed they did arrive at the beginning of June.

The advent of a rich neighbour is a historical event in the life of country-dwellers. Landowners and their domestics discuss it for two months before and three years afterwards. As far as I was concerned, I have to admit that the tidings concerning the arrival of a young and beautiful neighbour affected me considerably; I burned with impatience to set eyes on her, and so, on the first Sunday after she came, I set off after lunch to her village to make the acquaintance of their excellencies and pay my respects as their closest neighbour and most humble servant.

A footman conducted me into the Count's study, then went off to announce me. The spacious study was furnished with all possible lavishness; book-cases stood by the walls, each one surmounted by a bronze bust; a wide mirror hung over the marble fireplace; the floor was carpeted in green and strewn with rugs. By now unaccustomed to luxury in my poor abode, and not having set eyes on another's wealth for long enough, I quailed inwardly and awaited the Count with a certain flutter of anxiety, like a provincial petitioner waiting for the minister's appearance. The door opened and a handsome man of about thirty-two came in. The Count approached me with an expansive and cordial air; I tried to rally and was about to introduce myself, when he forestalled me. We sat down. His easy and graceful conversation swiftly dispelled my boorish shyness, and I was beginning to feel my usual self when the Countess entered and shyness overwhelmed me worse than before. She was indeed a beauty. The Count introduced me; I wanted to seem at ease, but the more I tried to appear relaxed, the more awkward I felt. So as to allow me to recover myself and get used to my new acquaintances, they began talking to one another, treating me without formality, just like a good neighbour. Meanwhile, I began pacing back and forth, examining the books and pictures. I am no connoisseur of paintings, but one caught my eye. It was some sort of Swiss landscape, but what struck me about it was not the actual painting, but the fact that the picture had been pierced by two bullets, one on top of the other.

'That's a good shot,' I said, turning to the Count.

'Yes', he replied. 'A very fine shot indeed. Are you a marksman?' he went on.

'Tolerable,' I said, glad that the talk had at last got round to something congenial. 'I don't miss a card from thirty paces, using pistols I know, naturally.'

'Really?' said the Countess, apparently all attention. 'And can you hit a card at thirty paces, my dear?'

'We'll have a try sometime,' responded the Count. 'In my younger days I wasn't a bad shot, but it's been four years since I last handled a pistol.'

'Ah,' I remarked, 'in that case, I'll wager your excellency won't hit a card even at twenty paces: pistol-shooting requires daily practice. I know this from experience. In our regiment I was considered one of the best shots. It happened once that I didn't pick up a pistol for a good month: mine were off being repaired; and what do you think, your excellency? The first time I fired after that, I missed a bottle four times at twenty-five paces. We had a captain in our regiment, a wag, a joker, who chanced to be close by and said: "I can see your hand refuses to aim at a bottle." No, your excellency, it doesn't do to neglect practice, otherwise you lose the knack immediately. The finest marksman I ever met fired every day, at least three times before dinner. It was his custom, like his glass of vodka.'

The Count and Countess were glad that I had started talking freely.

'And what sort of a shot was he?' the Count enquired.

'It was like this, your excellency: he would see a fly settle on the wall: you laugh, Countess? I swear it's true. He would see the fly and shout: "Kuzka, the pistol!" Kuzka would bring him a loaded pistol. Bang! And the fly would be drilled into the wall!'

'That's amazing,' said the Count. 'And what was his name?'

'Silvio, your excellency.'

'Silvio!' The Count exclaimed, leaping up from his chair. 'You knew Silvio?'

'Indeed I did, your excellency; we were friends; he was like a brother to us in the regiment; it's five years now since I had any news of him. It seems your excellency knew him?'

'I did, I certainly did. Didn't he tell you . . . but no, I shouldn't think so; he didn't tell you of a certain very curious incident?'

'You mean about the slap he received at a ball from some scallywag?'

'And did he tell you the name of that scallywag?'

'No, your excellency, he never told me . . . Ah! Your excellency,' I went on, guessing at the truth, 'Forgive me . . . I did not know . . . Could it have been yourself? . . .'

'It was I,' returned the Count, looking utterly distraught. 'And that shattered picture is a memento of our last encounter . . .'

'Ah, my sweet,' said the Countess, 'for heaven's sake don't go over it; it frightens me to listen to it.'

'No,' demurred the Count, 'I will tell it all; he knows how I insulted his friend: let him hear how Silvio paid me out.'

The Count shifted his chair nearer to me, and it was with the keenest curiosity that I heard the following tale.

'Five years ago I got married. The first month, the honeymoon, I spent here in this village. I am indebted to this house for the best moments of my life and one of the grimmest memories.

'One evening we were out riding together; my wife's horse was in a stubborn mood; she got frightened and, handing me the reins, made her way home on foot; I went on ahead. In the yard I saw a travelling-wagon; I was informed that a man was sitting in my study who had not wished to give his name, saying only that he had business with me. I came into this room and in the darkness saw a man, covered in dust and with an unkempt beard; he was standing here by the fireplace. I went up to him, trying to recall his features.

'"You don't recognize me, Count?" he said in a tremulous voice. "Silvio!" I cried, and I admit I could feel the hair rise on my head. "Just so," he went on. "I have my shot to come; I am here to discharge my pistol; are you prepared?"

'The pistol was protruding from his side pocket. I measured out the twelve paces and stood over there in the corner, begging him to shoot quickly before my wife got back. He delayed matters, asking for light. Candles were brought. I locked the door and forbade anyone to enter, then once again asked him to fire. He drew out his pistol and took aim . . . I counted the seconds . . . I was thinking of her . . . a terrible minute passed! Silvio lowered his arm.

' "I regret that the pistol is not loaded with cherry-stones . . . a bullet is heavy. I keep thinking that this is not a duel, but murder; I am not used to taking aim against an unarmed man. Let's start all over again; we'll draw lots for who fires first."

'My head was reeling . . . I think I objected . . . At length we loaded a second pistol and rolled up two pieces of paper; he put them into the cap I had shot through that time; I again drew the first number. "You, Count, have the devil's own luck," he said, with a grin I shall never forget. I cannot understand what came over me or how he managed to force me to do it, but I fired and hit that picture.' (The Count pointed to the perforated painting; his face burned like fire; the Countess was paler than her handkerchief; I could not hold back an exclamation.)

'I fired,' the Count went on, 'and, thank God, I missed; then Silvio . . . (he was truly dreadful at that moment) took aim at me. Suddenly the door opened, Masha ran in and shrieked as she threw herself on my neck. Her presence gave me back my strength of mind.

'"Darling," I said to her, "can't you see we're just having a joke? There's no need to be so alarmed! Off you go and have a drink of water, then come back and I'll introduce my old friend and comrade from days gone by. Masha still couldn't believe it.

'"Tell me, is my husband speaking the truth?" she said, addressing the grim Silvio. "Is it true that it's all a joke between you?" "He is always the one for a joke, Countess," Silvio replied. "He once slapped my face as a joke, he shot a hole in this cap of mine for fun, he missed me just now for fun; now I'm in the mood for a little joke myself . . ."

'So saying, he was going to take aim at me again . . . with her there! Masha threw herself at his feet.

'"Get up, Masha, this is shameful!" I cried in a frenzy. "And you, sirrah, are you going to leave off tormenting the poor woman? Are you going to fire or not?"

'"I won't," said Silvio. "I am satisfied: I have seen your agitation, your fear; I have forced you to fire at me, I am content. You will remember me. I give you over to your conscience."

'At this he made to leave, but halted in the doorway, glanced back at the picture I had hit, and barely taking aim, shot at it, and disappeared. My wife lay in a faint; people did not dare to stop him and just stared at him in terror; he walked out on to the porch, called his driver, and had made his departure before I had time to recover myself.'

The Count fell silent. In this fashion I learned the ending of a story whose beginning had so astonished me. I never encountered its hero again. The story goes that Silvio, during Alexander Ypsilanti's rebellion,* had commanded a detachment of Hetairists and was killed at the Battle of Skulyani.

THE SNOWSTORM

Across the hillocks, deep in snow,
Horses speeding lightly . . .
A church is glimpsed as on we go,
Alone and shining brightly.

Soon snow, obscuring everything,
Across the road comes sifting;
The hissing of a raven's wing
Above our sleigh goes drifting;
The grief-presaging, moaning wind
Spurs horses with its whistling;
They peer into the murk, half-blind,
Every mane a-bristling . . .

(Zhukovsky)*

Towards the end of 1811, an epoch so memorable for us all,
kindly Gavrila Gavrilovich R*** was living on his estate at
Nenaradovo. He was renowned throughout the district for his
cordial hospitality; his neighbours would be forever arriving to
have a bit to eat or drink, or stake five kopeks on a game of
Boston* with his wife, Praskovia Petrovna—and some to gaze
upon his daughter, Maria Gavrilovna, a pale, slender girl of
seventeen. She was considered a wealthy match, and many a
man had designs on her, either for himself or one of his sons.

Maria Gavrilovna had been brought up on French novels
and, consequently, was in love. The chosen object of her affections was a penurious army ensign, on leave in the village. It
goes without saying that the young man was consumed with an
equal passion, and that the parents of his beloved, noticing their
mutual partiality, had forbidden their daughter to so much as
think of him, and treated him worse than a retired assessor.*

Our lovers corresponded and saw one another every day in the
pine spinney or by the old chapel. There they pledged eternal
love, lamented their fate, and made various plans. Writing and
conversing in this manner, they (as was only natural) came to

the following conclusion: if we cannot breathe without one another, and the will of our cruel parents is standing in the way
of our happiness, why cannot we disregard it? It goes without
saying that this happy idea occurred first to the young man, and
that it appealed enormously to Maria's romantic imagination.

The arrival of winter brought their trysts to an end, but
made their correspondence all the livelier. Vladimir Nikolayevich
besought her in every letter to entrust herself to him, to get
married secretly, hide for a time, then throw themselves on the
mercy of the parents, who would finally, of course, be moved by
the constancy and unhappiness of the lovers and would assuredly
say to them: 'Children! Come to our arms.'

Maria Gavrilovna hesitated for a long time; many plans to run
away were rejected. At length she assented. On the appointed
day she was supposed to miss supper and retire to her room on
the pretext of having a headache. Her maid was in on the plot;
they were both to go out into the garden by way of the back
porch and find a sleigh in readiness beyond the garden, get
aboard the sleigh, and travel the three miles from Nenaradovo to
the village of Zhadrino, directly to the church, where Vladimir
was supposed to be waiting for them.

On the eve of the day of decision Maria was unable to sleep
all night; she packed her belongings, bundled up her linen and
clothes, and wrote a long letter to a certain sentimental young
lady, her girl-friend, and another to her parents. She bid farewell to them in the most touching terms, justified her action by
the overpowering strength of her passion, and concluded by
saying that she would count it the most blissful moment of her
life when she might be permitted to throw herself at the feet
of her very dear parents. Sealing both letters with a Tula seal
on which were depicted two flaming hearts and a decorous cap-
tion, she threw herself on the bed as dawn was breaking and
began to doze; but even then frightful imaginings kept waking
her up. She pictured that at the very moment when she was
stepping into the sleigh, on her way to be married, her father
would prevent her, and with agonizing swiftness drag her through
the snow and hurl her into a dark, bottomless pit . . . and she
hurtled headlong down with an indescribable sinking of the
heart; then she saw Vladimir lying on the grass, pale, bloodied.

As he was dying, he beseeched her in a piercing voice to make haste to marry him ... other hideous, senseless visions floated before her one after another. At length she got up, paler than usual and with an unfeigned headache. Her father and mother noticed her agitation; their tender concern and ceaseless questions—'What's the matter, Masha?* You're not ill, are you, Masha?'—cut her to the quick. She tried to reassure them, to appear cheerful, but was unable to do so. Evening drew on. The thought that she was spending her last day among her family made her heart sink. She felt barely alive; she was secretly bidding farewell to all the people, all the objects around her. Supper was served; her heart began to beat violently. In a quavering voice she announced that she did not feel like any supper and began saying good-night to her father and mother. They kissed her and, as usual, blessed her: she almost wept. On getting to her room, she threw herself into a chair and dissolved into tears. The maid persuaded her to calm herself and take heart. All was ready. Within half an hour Masha would have to leave her parents' house for ever, her room, the tranquil life of an unmarried daughter ... Outside, a snowstorm was in progress; the wind howled, the shutters shook and clattered; everything seemed to be a threat and a dismal omen. Soon the household had settled down and was asleep. Masha wrapped herself in a shawl, donned her warm hood, picked up her case, and went out on to the back porch. The servant carried out the two bundles after her. They descended into the garden. The storm had not abated; the wind blew directly into their faces, as if trying to stop the young transgressor by main force. It cost her an effort to reach the end of the garden. The sleigh was waiting for them on the road. The horses were chilled and restless; Vladimir's coachman was pacing about in front of the shafts, restraining the restless animals. He assisted the young lady and her maid to get into the sleigh and stow away the bundles and case, then took up the reins and the horses sped away. Consigning the young lady to the care of providence and the skill of Tereshka the coachman, let us turn to our young paramour.

Vladimir had been out and about all day. In the morning he had been with the Zhadrino priest, and had with difficulty come to an understanding; then he had gone in search of witnesses

among the surrounding landowners. The first he had visited, a
retired forty-year-old cornet of horse, one Dravin, agreed with
alacrity. This adventure, he kept assuring Vladimir, reminded
him of former days and his pranks in the hussars. He persuaded
Vladimir to stay to dinner and assured him that there would be
no difficulty in finding the other two witnesses. Indeed, a land-
surveyor named Shmitt, moustachioed and spurred, and the son
of a police-chief, a boy of some sixteen years who had recently
enlisted in the uhlans, presented themselves immediately after
dinner. They not only fell in with Vladimir's proposal, they
positively pledged their readiness to sacrifice their lives for him.
Vladimir embraced them rapturously and went home to make
his preparations.

It had been getting dark for a long time. He sent off his trusty
Tereshka to Nenaradovo with the troika, and instructions which
were thorough and detailed. For his own use he had a small,
one-horse sleigh, and set out alone, without a driver, for Zhadrino,
where Maria Gavrilovna was due to arrive in some two hours
time. He knew the road and it was only a twenty-minute drive.

But no sooner had Vladimir got out of the village and into the
fields when the wind got up and such a snowstorm developed
that he couldn't make out a thing. In a matter of minutes the
road was covered; his surroundings disappeared into a thick,
yellowish murk, through which the white snowflakes came flying;
the sky merged with the earth. Vladimir found himself in a field
and sought in vain to reach the road again; his horse stepped
aimlessly, now heading into a snow-drift, now falling into a hole;
the sleigh kept on overturning; Vladimir strove at least not to
lose the right direction. He seemed to have been travelling for
over half an hour, however, without even reaching Zhadrino
woods. Another ten minutes or so went by; the woods were still
nowhere to be seen. Vladimir was traversing a field intersected
by deep gulleys. The snowstorm was not abating, the skies failed
to clear. The horse was beginning to tire, while sweat fairly
rolled off Vladimir, despite his being constantly up to his waist
in snow.

At length he realized that he was going in the wrong direction. Vladimir halted: he began to think, recall, consider, and
became convinced that he should have turned to the right. He

headed right. The horse could barely stir. He had been on the
road more than an hour. Zhadrino could not be far off. But on
and on he went across the endless field. Nothing but drifts and
gulleys; the sleigh kept on overturning, he kept on having to
right it. Time was passing; Vladimir was starting to get seriously
worried.

At last something dark began to take shape away to one side.
Vladimir turned in that direction. As he drew nearer he saw the
woods. Thank God, he thought, not far now. He went by the
trees, hoping to come across a familiar road, or pass right round
the wood: Zhadrino lay directly behind it. He soon discovered
the road and drove on into a dark mass of trees stripped bare by
winter. The wind could no longer rage in there; the road was
smooth; the horse bucked up and Vladimir relaxed.

But on and on he went with no glimpse of Zhadrino; the
wood had no end to it. Vladimir realized with horror that he had
driven into an unfamiliar forest. Despair overwhelmed him. He
struck his horse and the poor animal made as if to trot, but soon
wearied and in a quarter of an hour was back to walking pace,
despite all the efforts of the hapless Vladimir.

Little by little the trees began to thin out, and Vladimir
emerged from the forest; Zhadrino was nowhere to be seen. It
must have been close to midnight. Tears burst from his eyes;
he pushed on aimlessly. The weather had subsided, the clouds
were breaking, and before him lay a level expanse, spread with
a white, undulating carpet. The night was fairly clear. Not far
off he could see a hamlet, made up of four or five houses.
Vladimir headed towards it. At the first hut he leapt from his
sleigh, ran up to the window, and began knocking. In a few
minutes the wooden shutters opened and an old man stuck out
his grey beard.

'What d'ye want?'

'Is it far to Zhadrino?'

'Is Zhadrino far from here?'

'Yes, yes! Is it far?'

'Not so far; it'll be around seven miles.'

At this response Vladimir clutched his hair and stood stock-
still, like a man condemned to death.

'And where would you be coming from?' the old man pursued.

Vladimir was in no mood to answer questions.

'Old man,' he said, 'can you get hold of some horses to take me to Zhadrino?'

'You'll get no horses here,' responded the peasant.

'Can't I at least get a guide? I'll pay him whatever he wants.'

"Wait a minute,' said the old man, lowering the shutter. 'I'll send you my son out, he'll show you the way.'

Vladimir waited. Less than a minute later he was knocking again. The shutter went up and the beard came in sight.

'What d'ye want?'

'Where on earth's your son?'

'He'll be out directly, he's getting his boots on. Ye'll be frozen stiff, come in and get a bit of a warm.'

'Thanks, but just send your son out quick.'

The gate creaked; the lad emerged carrying an oak cudgel and went on ahead, either indicating the road or searching for it among the snow-drifts. 'What time is it?' Vladimir asked him. 'Soon be dawning,' replied the young peasant. Vladimir said not a word more.

The cocks were crowing and it was already light when they reached Zhadrino. The church was locked. Vladimir paid his guide and drove round to the priest's yard. His troika was missing. And what news awaited him!

But let us return to the good proprietors of Nenaradovo and see what is happening there.

Nothing at all.

The old folk got up and went into the living-room. Gavrila Gavrilovich was in his night-cap and flannel jacket, Praskovia Petrovna in her quilted dressing-gown. The samovar was brought in and Gavrila Gavrilovich sent the girl to see how Maria Gavrilovna was and how she had slept. The girl came back and announced that the lady said she had slept poorly, but was feeling better now and would be in to breakfast presently. And indeed, the door opened and Maria Gavrilovna approached to greet her dear papa and mama.

'How is your headache, Masha?' asked Gavrila Gavrilovich. 'Better, papa,' replied Masha. 'It must have been the smoke from the stove,' said Praskovia Petrovna. 'Perhaps that's it', replied Masha.

The day passed off uneventfully, but that night Masha fell ill. The doctor was sent for from the town. He arrived towards evening and found the patient delirious. A high fever had set in and the poor girl was at death's door for two weeks.

Nobody in the house knew of the proposed elopement. The letters which Masha had written on the previous evening were burned; her maid told no one, fearing the wrath of her employers. The priest, the retired cornet of horse, the moustachioed land-surveyor, and the young uhlan were all discreet, and for good reason. Tereshka the driver never said a word too much to anyone, even when he was drunk. Thus the secret was preserved by more than half-a-dozen conspirators. But Maria Gavrilovna herself came out with it during her unceasing delirium. However, her words were so absurd that her mother, who never stirred from her bedside, could only make out that her daughter was madly in love with Vladimir Nikolayevich and that, in all probability, this love was the cause of her illness. She consulted her husband, several neighbours, and at length it was unanimously resolved that such was evidently Maria Gavrilovna's fate, that love is blind, poverty was no sin, it was a man you lived with, not his money, and so forth. Moral maxims come in surprisingly useful in situations where we cannot think up very much in the way of self-justification.

Meanwhile the young lady was on the mend. Vladimir had not been seen in Gavrila Gavrilovich's house for a long time. He had been frightened off by the reception he usually got. They decided to send for him and advise him of his unexpected good fortune: their consent to the marriage. But imagine the astonishment of the Nenaradovo folk when, in response to their invitation, they received a half-demented letter! He declared that his foot would never cross their threshold again, and begged them to forget an unhappy man for whom death remained as the only hope. A few days later they learned that Vladimir had gone off to join the army. This was in 1812.

For a long time they did not dare to break the news to the convalescent Masha. She never mentioned Vladimir. Some months later, when she found his name among those badly wounded at Borodino,* she fainted away and there were fears that her fever might return. However, thank heavens, the fit had no consequences.

Another cause for sadness was visited upon her: Gavrila Gavrilovich passed away, leaving his entire estate to her as his heiress. The legacy was no consolation, however; she sincerely shared poor Praskovia Petrovna's grief and vowed never to part from her; they both left Nenaradovo, the scene of so many sad memories, and went to live on the *** estate.

Here too suitors danced attendance upon so sweet and wealthy a prospective bride; she, however, gave none of them the least encouragement. Her mother sometimes tried to persuade her to choose a partner; Maria Gavrilovna would shake her head and become lost in thought. Vladimir no longer existed: he had died in Moscow, on the eve of the French entry into the city. His memory seemed sacred to Masha; at all events, she kept everything that might remind her of him: books he had once read, his drawings, the music and poetry he had copied out for her. The neighbours, who had learned the full story, marvelled at her constancy and awaited with curiosity the hero who should finally triumph over the melancholy fidelity of the chaste Artemis.

Meanwhile, the war had ended gloriously. Our regiments were returning from abroad. The people ran out to meet them. Bands played appropriated songs: 'Vive Henri Quatre',* Tyrolean waltzes, and arias from *Gioconda*.* Officers who had left for the war almost as adolescents were returning as men hardened in battle, festooned with medals. The soldiers talked among themselves cheerily, constantly interpolating French or German words into their speech. Unforgettable time! A time of glory and rapture! How strongly beat the Russian heart at the word *Fatherland*! How sweet were the tears of reunion! With what unanimity we linked our national pride with our love for the Tsar! And what a time it was for him!

Women, Russian women, were incomparable then. Their habitual cool demeanour vanished. Their delight was genuinely intoxicating as they welcomed the conquerors with shouts of 'hurrah!'

> And threw their bonnets in the air.*

Who of the officers of those days will not admit that it was to the women of Russia that he owed his best and most precious reward? . . .

At that glittering time Maria Gavrilovna was living with her mother in *** province and never saw the two capitals celebrating the return of the armies. But the general euphoria was possibly even greater in the outlying districts and country villages. The appearance of an officer in these parts was truly a triumph and things went badly for a frock-coated lover in his vicinity.

We have already related that, despite her coldness, Maria Gavrilovna was surrounded as before by suitors. But they all had to withdraw when a wounded hussar colonel named Burmin, with the Saint George Cross in his buttonhole and sporting *an interesting pallor*, as the young ladies of the time used to say, presented himself at the manor house. He was about 26 years of age. He had come home on leave to his estates, which adjoined Maria Gavrilovna's village. She singled him out for special attention. In his presence her habitual pensive mood brightened. It could not be said that she flirted with him, but a poet observing her behaviour might have said:

S'amor non è, che dunque?*

Burmin was in fact an extremely amiable young man. He had just the kind of mind which appeals to women: one of delicacy and observation, devoid of the slightest pretension and with a gift for light-hearted badinage. His manner with Maria Gavrilovna was easy and straightforward, but whatever she said or did, his heart and glance followed her. To all appearances he was of a peaceable and modest disposition, but rumour insisted that at one time he had been a terrible scallywag. Nor did this do him any harm in the eyes of Maria Gavrilovna, who, like the generality of young ladies, readily excused any devilment which revealed a daring and ardent disposition.

But what fired her curiosity and imagination above all (more than his gentleness, his agreeable conversation, his interesting pallor, or his bandaged arm) was the young officer's reticence. She could not fail to be aware that he was greatly attracted to her; he too, most probably, with his intelligence and experience, might well have noticed that she had singled him out: so how could it be that she had not yet seen him at her feet, not heard his declarations of love? What was holding him back—the diffidence inseparable from true love, pride, or the teasing of an artful philanderer? It was a mystery to her. After a good deal of thought, she decided that shyness was the sole reason behind it, and resolved to encourage him with a greater show of attention and even, depending on the circumstances, tenderness. She was setting the stage for a most surprising denouement and waited impatiently for the moment of romantic declaration. A secret of whatever nature is hard for the female heart to bear. Her military operations had the desired effect: at least Burmin was so plunged in thought, and his dark eyes rested with such ardour on Maria Gavrilovna, that the decisive moment seemed close at hand. The neighbours talked about the wedding as of something already settled, and kindly old Praskovia Petrovna was gladdened that her daughter had at last found herself a worthy suitor.

The old woman was sitting by herself in the living-room one day, playing patience, when Burmin came in and asked the whereabouts of Maria Gavrilovna. 'She's in the garden', answered the old woman. 'Go out to her, I'll wait for you both here.' Burmin went off, as the old woman crossed herself, thinking: perhaps the business will be settled today!

Burmin found Maria Gavrilovna by the pond, under the willow; she was wearing a white dress and had a book in her hand, like a true heroine of a romantic novel. After his first enquiries, Maria Gavrilovna deliberately refrained from keeping up her end of the conversation, thus intensifying a mutual embarrassment which could only be escaped by way of a sudden and decisive declaration. And so it turned out: Burmin, sensing the awkwardness of his situation, announced that he had long been seeking an opportunity to open his heart to her, and requested a moment of her attention. Maria Gavrilovna closed her book and lowered her eyes as a sign of permission.

'I love you,' said Burmin. 'I love you passionately . . .' (Maria Gavrilovna blushed and lowered her head still further). 'I have acted imprudently in indulging a delightful habit, the habit of seeing and hearing you every day . . .' (Maria Gavrilovna remembered St Preux's first letter*). 'Now it is too late to resist my fate; the remembrance of you, your sweet incomparable image will be for me henceforth the torment and joy of my life; but it still remains for me to perform one painful duty, to reveal to you a terrible secret and place between us an insurmountable barrier . . .'

'It was always there,' Maria broke in quickly. 'I could never be your wife . . .'

'I know,' he replied softly. 'I know that once you loved, but death and three years of mourning . . . Kind, sweet Maria Gavrilovna! Do not try to take away my last consolation: the thought that you would have agreed to bring about my happiness, if . . . say no more, I beg you, say no more. You are torturing me. Yes, I know, I feel it, that you would have been mine, but I am a most unhappy creature . . . I am married!'

Maria Gavrilovna stared at him in astonishment.

'I have been a married man', Burmin went on, 'for over three years and I don't know who my wife is, or where she is, or whether I am ever to see her!'

'What do you mean?' exclaimed Maria Gavrilovna. 'How strange! Do go on; I'll explain later . . . but please, do go on.'

'At the beginning of 1812,' said Burmin, 'I was hurrying on to Vilna, where our regiment was stationed. Arriving at one post-station late at night, I was about to order the horses to be harnessed up quickly, when a fearful blizzard set in, and both the stationmaster and the driver advised me to wait it out. I assented, but an unaccountable sense of unease gripped me; it was as if someone was positively urging me on. Meanwhile the snowstorm continued unabated; I couldn't bear it. I had the horses harnessed again and headed out into the teeth of the blizzard. The driver took it into his head to go along the frozen river, which would supposedly shorten the journey by five miles. The banks were covered in snow, and, missing the spot where we were to regain the road, we found ourselves in an unfamiliar area. The storm was still raging; I glimpsed a light and ordered the driver to head that way. We arrived in a village; there was a light in the wooden church. It was open, and several sleighs stood behind the fence; people were moving about the porch.

'"Over here! Over here!" cried several voices. I ordered the driver to approach. "For God's sake, where did you get yourself to?" someone said. "The bride's fainted; the priest doesn't know what to do; we were ready to go back. Get out, quick!"

'I jumped out of the sleigh without a word and went into the church, feebly lit by two or three candles. The girl was sitting on a bench in a dark corner of the building; another girl was rubbing her temples.

'"Thank heaven you've got here at long last," said this one. "You've practically done for the young lady." The old priest came up to me and asked: "Shall we make a start?" "Yes, yes, do start, father," I replied unthinkingly.

'The girl was lifted up. She seemed to me quite pretty... Incredible, unforgiveable foolishness... I took my place next to her before the lectern; the priest was in a hurry; three men and the maid were holding up the bride and concerned solely with her. We were married.

'"Now kiss," we were told. My wife turned her pale face towards me... She screamed "Oh, it's not him, it's not him!" and fell down senseless. The witnesses stared at me in alarm. I turned, left the church without hindrance, flung myself into the sleigh, and shouted: "Go!"'

'Good heavens!' cried Maria Gavrilovna. 'And you don't know what happened to your poor wife?'

'No, I don't,' replied Burmin. 'I don't know the name of the village where I was married; I don't remember the post-station I started from. At the time I attached so little significance to my criminal prank that I fell asleep as we drove away from the church and didn't wake up until next morning, when we were already at the third station. The servant I used to have then died on campaign, so I have no hope of finding the girl on whom I played such a cruel joke, and who is now so cruelly avenged.'

'Good God, Good God!' cried Maria Gavrilovna, seizing his hand. 'So it was you! And you don't recognize me?'

Burmin turned pale... and threw himself at her feet...

THE UNDERTAKER

See we not coffins every day,
The grey hairs of a world decaying?

(Derzhavin)*

The last belongings of the undertaker Adrian Prokhorov were
loaded up on to the hearse, and the gaunt pair of horses plodded
round for the fourth time from Basmannaya to Nikitskaya,
whither the undertaker was removing, along with his entire
household. Before setting out on foot for his new abode, he
locked the premises and nailed a notice to the gate announcing
that the place was for sale or rent. As he neared the little yellow
house which had tantalized his imagination for so long, and
which he had finally purchased for a tidy sum, the old undertaker sensed with astonishment that his heart did not rejoice. As
he stepped across the unfamiliar threshold and found turmoil in
his new habitation, he sighed for the decrepit hovel where for
eighteen years everything had been strictly ordered; he began to
scold both his daughters and the housemaid for their slowness,
and set about assisting them himself. Soon order had been established; the icon-case, the crockery-cupboard, the table, the sofa,
and the bed occupied their allotted positions in the back room;
the kitchen and the living-room were filled with the master's
stock in trade: coffins of all colours and sizes, cupboards full of
mourning hats, capes, and torches. A sign was hung up outside
the gate, depicting a stout cherub with a downturned torch in
his hand and bearing the inscription: 'Coffins plain and painted
sold and upholstered here, also for rent and old ones repaired.'
The girls went off to their front room. Adrian did the rounds of
his dwelling, sat down by the window, and ordered the samovar
to be got going.

The cultivated reader is aware that both Shakespeare and
Walter Scott portrayed their grave-diggers as cheery, facetious
individuals, so that our imagination might be the more affected
by the antithesis. Out of respect for the truth, we are unable to

follow their example and are compelled to admit that the demeanour of our undertaker was wholly appropriate to his gloomy profession. Adrian Prokhorov was, as a rule, lugubrious and moody. He broke silence only to tick off his daughters when he caught them idly gaping through the window at people passing by, or in order to demand exorbitant prices for his wares from folk who had the misfortune (and sometimes the pleasure) of needing them. So it was that Adrian, sitting by the window drinking his seventh cup of tea, was, as usual, absorbed in cheerless reflection. He thought of the torrential rain of the previous week, which had descended upon the funeral procession of a retired brigadier just as it reached the city gate. Many a cape had shrunk, many a hat gone out of shape. He foresaw inevitable expense, since his ancient stock of funeral garments was getting into a wretched state. He was hoping to recoup his losses on the old merchant's wife Tryukhina, who had been at death's door for nearly a year. But she was dying over in Razgulyai, and Prokhorov was afraid that the heirs, despite their promise, would employ the nearest undertaker rather than take the trouble to send for him at that distance.

These musings were abruptly curtailed by three masonic knocks at the door. 'Who's there?' enquired the undertaker. The door opened and an individual, who at first glance might have been taken for a German craftsman, came in and approached the undertaker with an expression of high good humour.

'Forgive me, dear neighbour,' said he, with the kind of Russian accent we cannot hear to this day without a smile. 'Forgive the interruption . . . but I wished to make your acquaintance without delay. I am a shoemaker and my name is Gottlieb Shultz, I live across the street in the little house opposite your windows. Tomorrow I am celebrating my silver wedding, and I am asking you and your daughters to have dinner with me as a friend.' The invitation was graciously accepted. The undertaker asked the shoemaker to be seated and have a cup of tea, and thanks to Gottlieb Shultz's expansive manner, they were soon conversing amicably.

'How's business, your honour?' Adrian inquired.

'Eh-eh-eh,' responded Shultz. 'So-so, mustn't grumble, although my trade isn't the same as yours: a living man can do without shoes, but a dead one can't live without a coffin.'

'Very true,' remarked Adrian. 'On the other hand, though, if a living man can't afford shoes, he can, if you'll pardon the expression, still walk about barefoot; a dead pauper gets himself a coffin free.'

So the talk proceeded in this fashion for some little while; at length the shoemaker stood up and said goodbye to the undertaker, renewing his invitation.

Next day, at exactly twelve o'clock, the undertaker and his daughters went out through the wicket gate of his newly acquired house and set off for his neighbour's. Deviating in this instance from the custom of modern-day novelists, I will refrain from describing Adrian Prokhorov's caftan, or the European attire of Akulina and Darya. I consider it relevant, however, to point out that both girls had put on yellow hats and red shoes, which they only did on festive occasions.

The shoemaker's cramped quarters were crowded with guests, German artisans for the most part, with their wives and apprentices. The sole Russian official there was a Finnish watchman called Yurko, who had managed to obtain, despite his humble occupation, the special favour of the host. He had served for about twenty-five years, faithful and true, like Pogorelsky's postman.* The fire of 1812, which had razed Russia's ancient capital, had also destroyed his yellow sentry-box. But as soon as the enemy had been driven out, a new one appeared, greyish in colour, with white Doric columns, and Yurko began pacing about it *with pole-axe and armoured in coarse cloth*.* He knew most of the Germans living near the Nikitsky Gate: one or two of them had even had occasion to spend their Sunday night with Yurko. Adrian at once made his acquaintance as a man of whom, sooner or later, he might have need, and as the guests made their way to the table, the two sat down together. Mr and Mrs Shultz and their seventeen-year-old daughter Lotchen, as they dined with the guests, also passed dishes around and helped the cook with the serving. The beer flowed. Yurko ate enough for four; Adrian kept up with him; his daughters held back; the German conversation grew noisier as time went by. All at once the host requested silence, and, as he unstoppered a pitch-sealed bottle, announced loudly in Russian: 'To the health of my good Louisa!' The near-champagne foamed. The host tenderly kissed the rosy face of his forty-year-old partner, and the guests noisily drank the health of good Louisa. 'The health of my dear guests!' proclaimed the host, unstoppering a second bottle—and his grateful guests emptied their glasses once again. Then the toasts began to follow one after another: every guest's health was drunk separately; they toasted Moscow and a good dozen German towns; they toasted all guilds in general and each in particular; they drank the health of masters and apprentices. Adrian drank assiduously, and cheered up to the extent of proposing a facetious toast himself. Suddenly one of the guests, a stout baker, raised his glass and exclaimed: 'To the health of those we work for, *unserer Kundleute!*'* This suggestion, like all the others, was accepted with joyous unanimity. The guests began bowing to one another, the tailor to the shoemaker, the shoemaker to the tailor, the baker to them both, all to the baker, and so it went. In the midst of this reciprocal bowing Yurko turned to his neighbour, shouting 'Well then, brother, drink to the health of your corpses.' Everyone roared with laughter, but the undertaker took offence at this and frowned. Nobody noticed. The guests went on drinking and the bells were ringing for vespers by the time they got up from the table.

The guests dispersed late, most of them tipsy. Observing the Russian saying: 'one good turn deserves another', the stout baker and a bookbinder, whose face seemed bound in reddish morocco, led Yurko off to his sentry-box, supporting him under each arm. The undertaker came home drunk and angry. 'Well, what a state of affairs,' he reasoned aloud. 'Is my profession less honourable than the others? Is an undertaker akin to a hangman? What have those infidels got to laugh at? Is an undertaker a Christmas clown or what? I was going to invite them to my housewarming, a feast fit for a king: not now! I'll invite those for whom I work: Russian Orthodox corpses.'

'What do you mean, master?' said the housemaid, who was taking his boots off at that moment. 'What sort of talk is that? Cross yourself! Inviting corpses to a housewarming! Don't say such things!'

'I'll invite them, so I will,' Adrian pursued. 'And for tomorrow at that. I bid you welcome, my benefactors, tomorrow evening at my house, to wine and dine; I will treat you to what the Lord has sent me.' With this, the undertaker headed for bed and was soon snoring.

Outside it was still dark when Adrian was woken up. The merchant's widow, Tryukhina, had passed away that very night and a special messenger on horseback, dispatched by her steward, had galloped over with the news. The undertaker gave him ten kopeks for vodka, dressed quickly, and went over to Razgulyai. The police were already standing by the gate and merchants were hovering about like crows, sensing a carcase. The deceased was lying on a table, yellow as wax, but as yet undefiled by decay. Relatives, neighbours, and domestics jostled about her. All the windows stood open; candles burned; priests were saying prayers. Adrian went up to the nephew, a young merchant in a fashionable frock-coat, and announced to him that the coffin, candles, shroud, and other funeral trappings would be delivered at once in good condition. The heir thanked him absently, saying that he wouldn't haggle over the price, but would leave everything to his conscience. The undertaker, as was his wont, swore that he would charge nothing more than was standard; he exchanged a meaningful glance with the steward and went off to set things in motion. He spent all day travelling back and forth between Razgulyai and Nikitsky Gate; by evening everything had been organized and he walked home after dismissing his driver. It was a moonlit night. The undertaker got safely as far as Nikitsky Gate. Near the Ascension church our acquaintance Yurko hailed him, and recognizing the undertaker, bade him good-night. It was late. The undertaker was nearing his house when he seemed to see someone approach his gate, open the wicket, and disappear inside.

'What might this mean?' thought Adrian. 'Who else wants me? Not a thief creeping in there, is it? Not suitors after my silly girls? Who knows?'

It occurred to the undertaker to shout to his friend Yurko for assistance. At that moment someone else approached the wicket and made to enter, but seeing the master of the house running up, halted and took off a tricorn hat. His face seemed familiar, but in his haste Adrian couldn't get a good look at him.

'You have honoured me with a visit,' said the panting Adrian, 'so do please be good enough to come in.'

'Don't worry about the niceties, friend,' came the indistinct reply. 'You go on ahead; show your guests the way!'

Indeed, Adrian had no time to observe the niceties. The wicket gate was open; he ascended the steps with the other close behind. Adrian fancied there were people moving about his rooms. 'What in the devil's name!' he thought, and hurried inside . . . whereupon his legs turned to jelly. The room was crowded with corpses. The moon, shining through the windows, lit up their yellow and blue faces, their sunken mouths, their dull, half-closed eyes, projecting noses . . . To his horror, Adrian recognized them as people who had been interred as a result of his efforts, and the guest who had come in with him as the brigadier who had been buried during the cloudburst. All of them, ladies and gentlemen, surrounded him, bowing and offering greetings, apart from one poor man, recently buried free of charge, who stayed humbly in a corner, ashamed of his rags. The others were all attired decently: the deceased ladies in bonnets and ribbons, the high-ranking men in uniform, though unshaven, the merchants in festive caftans.

'You see, Prokhorov,' said the brigadier on behalf of the whole honourable company, 'we have all risen at your invitation; the only ones to stay at home are those who are too far gone, those who have fallen apart completely, or who are just bones and no skin—and even one of those just had to come, he so wanted to be here . . .'

At that moment a small skeleton squeezed his way through the crowd and came up to Adrian. His skull was smiling warmly at the undertaker. Shreds of cloth, light-green and red, and old linen hung on him, as if from a pole, while his leg-bones rattled in his big jack-boots, like a pestle in a mortar.

'You didn't recognize me, Prokhorov,' said the skeleton. 'Do you recall a retired sergeant of the Guards, Pyotr Petrovich Kurilkin, the one you sold your first coffin to in 1799—pine, when you said it was oak?'

So saying, the corpse offered a bony embrace—but Adrian summoned up all his strength and, with a shout, repulsed him. Pyotr Petrovich staggered, fell over, and disintegrated completely. A murmur of indignation sprang up among the corpses; all of them were for defending the honour of their comrade, and advanced upon Adrian with abuse and threats. Their poor host, deafened by the shouting and almost crushed, lost his presence of mind and fell over in turn on to the bones of the retired Guards sergeant, before fainting away.

The sun had long been shining across the bed where the undertaker lay. At length he opened his eyes and saw the housemaid in front of him, fiddling with the samovar. Adrian recalled with horror all the events of the previous day. Tryukhina, the brigadier, and Sergeant Kurilkin came nebulously to mind. He waited in silence for the housemaid to start talking to him and reveal the upshot of his nocturnal adventures.

'You've really overslept, master Adrian Prokhorovich,' said Aksinia, handing him his dressing-gown. 'Your neighbour the tailor dropped by, and the local watchman came in with a message that today is the police-chief's name-day, but you were pleased to sleep and we didn't want to wake you.'

'Has anyone been here from the late Tryukhina?'

'Late? Has she died then?'

'Fool! Didn't you give me a hand with her funeral arrangements yesterday?'

'What do you mean, sir? You haven't lost your wits have you? Or haven't you got over yesterday's drinking yet? What funeral yesterday? You spent the whole day feasting at the German's, came back drunk; collapsed on to the bed, and slept until now, when the bells have already rung for mass.'

'Is that so?' said the undertaker, overjoyed.

'Course it is,' replied the maid.

'Well in that case, hurry up with that tea and call my daughters.'

THE STATIONMASTER

Low in the administration,
Dictator of the posting station.

(Prince Vyazemsky)*

Is there anyone who has not cursed all stationmasters, or never had occasion to wrangle with them? Anyone who, in a moment of anger, has not demanded the fateful book, in order to inscribe his useless complaint at high-handed treatment, rudeness, and inefficiency? Who does not regard them as outcasts from the human race, the equivalent of the pettifogging quill-drivers of yore, or Murom brigands* at the very least? Let us be fair, however, let us try and put ourselves in their shoes and then, it may be, we will judge them much less severely. What is a stationmaster? A veritable martyr of the fourteenth grade,* protected by his rank only from actual beating, and then not invariably (I refer that to my reader's conscience). What does the job of this dictator, as Prince Vyazemsky jokingly calls him, actually amount to? Is it not out-and-out hard labour? He has no peace day or night. All the annoyance accumulated by the traveller during a tedious journey is taken out on the stationmaster. The weather is intolerable, the roads awful, the driver pig-headed, the horses sluggish—it's all the stationmaster's fault. On entering his poverty-stricken dwelling, the traveller treats him as an enemy; he's in luck if he contrives to be quickly rid of his uninvited visitor; but if there are no horses . . . Heavens! What language, what threats shower down on his head! In rain and sleet he has to run about the village yards; come storm or Epiphany frost, he goes out into the passage to catch at least a moment's respite from the shouting and jostling of his splenetic customer. A general arrives; the trembling stationmaster lets him have the two last troikas, including the government courier's. The general goes off without a word of thanks. Five minutes pass—a jingle of bells! . . . and the government courier throws his travel warrant on to the table! . . . If we really looked into the matter, our hearts would fill with genuine sympathy rather than indignation. A word or two more: over twenty years I have travelled across Russia in all directions; I know almost all the post-roads, and several generations of drivers. It's a rare stationmaster I don't know by sight, or have not had dealings with; I hope to publish, in the not-too-distant future, a curious collection of my travel reflections. In the meantime, I will just say that the stationmaster rank has been presented to public opinion in a most misleading light. These much-maligned officials are peaceable folk, by nature accommodating, inclined to sociability, modest in their ambitions, and not over-mercenary. One can extract much that is curious and instructive from their conversation (which the travelling public is wrong to ignore). As for myself, I admit to preferring their talk to the discourse of some sixth-rank official travelling on government business.

It is not difficult to guess that I have friends among the worthy stationmaster estate. Indeed, the memory of one of them is precious to me. Circumstances once brought us together, and it is about him that I wish to converse with my gentle readers.

In May 1816 I chanced to be travelling through N. province, by a post-road which has since disappeared. Being of lowly rank, I was travelling by post-chaise in relays, my allowance covering only two horses. As a consequence, the stationmasters treated me with scant ceremony, and I often had to fight for what I felt was mine by rights. Being young and hot-headed, I resented the baseness and cowardice of the stationmaster when he harnessed a troika meant for me to the carriage of some high-ranking gentleman. It took me a similarly long time to get used to servants arbitrarily missing me out when serving at governors' dinners. Nowadays I see nothing out of the way in either. Indeed, what would become of us if, in place of the generally convenient principle: 'rank defers to rank', a different notion were to be introduced, for example: 'intelligence defers to intelligence'? What arguments there would be! Who would get served first at table? But I return to my narrative.

The day was hot. Two miles from a certain posting-station it came on to rain, and in a moment a cloudburst had soaked me to the skin. On arriving at the station, my first priority was a quick change of clothing, the second to ask for tea.

'Hey, Dunya!' cried the stationmaster. 'Put the samovar on and go and fetch some cream.'

At these words, a girl of about fourteen emerged from behind a partition and ran into the passage. I was struck by her beauty.

'Is that your daughter?' I asked the stationmaster. 'My daughter, sir,' he replied with an air of contented pride. 'And so sensible and quick, just like her late mother.'

At this, he began copying my travel warrant and I fell to examining the little pictures which adorned his humble but neat abode. They depicted the story of the prodigal son:* in the first, a venerable old man in dressing-gown and cap is taking leave of a restless youth, in a hurry to receive his blessing and a bag of money. In another, the dissipated behaviour of the young man is portrayed in vivid strokes: he is sitting at a table, surrounded by false friends and shameless women. In subsequent pictures the ruined youth, in rags and a tricorn hat, is shown herding swine and sharing their meal; his face expresses profound sorrow and remorse. Finally, his return to his father is shown; the good old man, in the same dressing-gown and cap, is running out to meet him: the prodigal son falls to his knees; in the background a cook is slaughtering the fatted calf and the elder brother is questioning the servants as to the reason for all this rejoicing. Under each picture I read the relevant German verses. I have preserved it all in my memory to this day, along with the pots of balsam, the bed with its colourful curtain, and the other objects around me at the time. I see as if it were now the host himself, a man of about fifty, hale and hearty, and his long green frock-coat bearing three medals on faded ribbons.

I had barely paid off my previous driver before Dunya was back with the samovar. Two glances were enough for the little flirt to notice the impression she had made on me; she lowered her big blue eyes. I began talking to her and she responded without the least shyness, like a girl experienced in the ways of the world. I offered her father a glass of punch, and handed a cup of tea to Dunya; the three of us began talking as if we had known one another for ages.

The horses had been ready long ago, but I was disinclined to part from the stationmaster and his little daughter. At length I bade them farewell; the father wished me Godspeed and his daughter saw me to the cart. In the passage I halted and asked permission to kiss her. Dunya consented . . . I can reckon up many a kiss,

Since I took up that sort of thing,

but not one has left so lasting or so pleasant a recollection.

Several years passed before chance brought me once again to those same places along that road. I recalled the daughter of the old stationmaster and was gladdened by the thought of setting eyes on her again. On the other hand, I thought, perhaps the former master had been replaced; Dunya was no doubt married by now. The notion that one or other might have died also flashed through my mind, and I drew near to the posting-station with gloomy forebodings.

The horses came to a halt by the stationmaster's little house. Entering the room, I at once recognized the pictures depicting the story of the prodigal son; the table and bed stood in their former places, but there were no longer any flowers on the window-sills, and everything about the place spoke of dilapidation and neglect. The stationmaster was asleep beneath a sheepskin coat; my arrival woke him and he sat up . . . It really was Samson Vyrin, but how he had aged! While he was copying my travel warrant I gazed at his grey hairs, at the deep furrows in his long unshaven face, his bent back, marvelling at how three or four years could have transformed such a robust individual into a feeble old man.

'Do you recognize me?' I asked him. 'You and I are old acquaintances.'

'That may well be,' he responded cheerlessly. 'It's a busy road here; I get lots of travellers passing through.'

'Is your Dunya keeping well?' The old man frowned.

'God only knows,' came the reply.

'She must be married then?' I asked. The old man feigned not to have heard my question and went on reading my travel document in an audible whisper. I ceased my questioning and asked for the kettle to be put on. Curiosity was beginning to get the better of me, and I trusted that the punch would loosen the tongue of my old acquaintance.

I was not mistaken: the old man did not refuse the proffered glass. I noted that the rum lightened his gloomy mood. At the second glass he became talkative; he remembered me, or pretended to do so, and I listened to a story which at the time I found absorbing and deeply touching.

'You knew my Dunya then?' he began. 'Still, who didn't know her? Ah, Dunya, Dunya! What a lass she was! Nobody passed through without praising her, no one had a harsh word to say of her. The ladies would give her presents, a handkerchief, earrings. Gentlemen would halt deliberately, supposedly for dinner or supper, but really it was just to have a good look at her. It used to be that no matter how bad-tempered a gentleman might be, he would calm down if she was there, and speak politely to me. Believe it or not, sir, but couriers, government messengers, would chat with her for half an hour on end. The house depended on her: tidying up, cooking, she coped with it all. And I, old fool that I was, never tired of just looking at her and rejoicing in it all; didn't I love my Dunya? Didn't I cherish the dear child; didn't she have a good life? Still, you can't swear trouble away; what must be must be.' At this, he began a detailed account of his misfortune. Three years previously, one winter evening, while the stationmaster was ruling a new entry-book and his daughter was sewing herself a dress behind the partition, a troika drew up and a traveller in a Circassian fur hat and military greatcoat, swathed in a shawl, came into the room, demanding horses. All the horses were out. At this news the traveller was about to raise his voice and his whip when Dunya, used to scenes like this, ran out from behind the partition and coaxingly asked the traveller whether he wouldn't care to have a bite to eat? Dunya's appearance produced its usual effect. The traveller's rage subsided; he agreed to wait for horses and ordered supper. Doffing his wet, shaggy cap, disentangling the shawl, and shrugging off his greatcoat, the traveller stood revealed as a slim young hussar with a small, dark moustache. He made himself at home in the stationmaster's room, and struck up a cheery conversation with him and his daughter. Supper was served. Meanwhile the horses arrived and the stationmaster ordered them to be harnessed at once, unfed, to the traveller's wagon. On returning to his room, however, he discovered the young man lying almost unconscious on a bench; he had felt unwell and developed a splitting headache. It was impossible for him to go on . . . There was nothing for it, the stationmaster gave up his own bed, and it was decided that if the sick man made no improvement by morning, they would send to S*** for the doctor.

Next day the hussar felt worse. His batman rode to town to fetch the doctor. Dunya wrapped a handkerchief soaked in vinegar round his head, and sat by his bed with her sewing. In the stationmaster's presence the sick man groaned and uttered barely a word, nevertheless, he did drink two cups of coffee and, still groaning, ordered dinner. Dunya never left him. He kept asking for something to drink and Dunya would bring him a jug of lemonade she had made herself. The patient would moisten his lips and, each time he returned the jug, feebly squeeze Dunya's hand with his own as a token of thanks. The doctor arrived towards dinner-time. He felt the patient's pulse and spoke with him in German before announcing in Russian that the only thing he needed was rest and that he would be able to resume his journey in a couple of days. The hussar handed him twenty-five roubles for the visit and invited him to dine with him. The doctor assented and both ate with a hearty appetite, shared a bottle of wine, and parted well satisfied with one another.

Another day passed and the hussar made a complete recovery. He was exceedingly cheerful and joked incessantly, now with Dunya, now with her father. He whistled songs, chatted to the travellers, entered their travel documents in the posting-ledger, and so endeared himself to the good stationmaster that he was sorry to part from his amiable guest. It was a Sunday, and Dunya was getting ready to go to mass. The hussar's wagon was brought round and he bade farewell to the stationmaster, generously rewarding him for his room and board; he said goodbye to Dunya too and offered to take her as far as the church, which lay on the edge of the village. Dunya stood there in perplexity . . .

'What on earth are you afraid of?' said her father. 'His honour isn't a wolf, you know, he won't eat you; ride along as far as the church.'

Dunya took her seat in the wagon next to the hussar, the servant jumped up on to the box, the driver whistled, and the horses galloped off.

The poor stationmaster could not understand how, of his own accord, he could have allowed his Dunya to go off with the hussar, how this blindness had descended upon him, and why his reason had deserted him. Within half an hour his heart had become increasingly uneasy, and anxiety overwhelmed him to the point where he could stand it no longer and set off himself to the church. As he drew near he saw the people already dispersing, but there was no sign of Dunya either in the churchyard or the porch. He hastened into the church: the priest was emerging from the chancel, the sexton was snuffing the candles, and two old ladies were still praying in a corner, but Dunya was not in the building. The poor father forced himself to ask the sexton if she had attended mass. The sexton replied that she had not. The stationmaster went home in a state of profound disquiet. He had only one hope left: Dunya, with the impulsiveness of youth might have taken it into her head to go on to the next station, where her godmother lived. In an agony of perturbation he awaited the return of the troika on which he had let her leave. The driver did not return. At length he did arrive towards evening, alone and drunk, bearing the appalling news: 'Dunya went on from the next station with the hussar.'

The old man sank under his misfortune; he at once took to the very same bed in which the young deceiver had lain the day before. Now the stationmaster, reviewing all the circumstances, realized that the illness had been a sham. The poor old man developed a high fever and was taken to the town of S***, being replaced by another on a temporary basis. There he was treated by the same doctor who had attended the hussar. He assured the stationmaster that the young man had been perfectly well and that he had suspected his wicked intentions at the time, but had kept quiet, fearing his whip. Whether the German was telling the truth, or merely wished to boast of his foresight, he supplied no consolation to his poor patient. Barely recovered from his illness, he elicited from the S*** postmaster a two-month leave of absence, and, without saying a word to anyone of his plans, set out on foot after his daughter. He knew from the travel warrant that Captain Minsky had been *en route* from Smolensk to Petersburg. The driver of the sleigh told him that Dunya had cried all the way, although it appeared that she was travelling of her own free will. 'Perhaps,' thought the stationmaster, 'I shall bring my strayed lamb back home.' With this thought in mind he arrived in Petersburg and took up residence in the Izmailovsky Regiment district, in the home of a retired NCO, an old fellow-soldier. He then commenced his search. Before long, he discovered that Captain Minsky was in Petersburg and living at Demuth's Hotel.* The stationmaster made up his mind to present himself.

He arrived in the entrance hall early in the morning and asked that his honour be informed that an old soldier wished to see him. The batman, who was polishing a boot on its tree, declared that his master was asleep and received no one before eleven. The stationmaster went away and returned at the appointed time. Minsky himself came out in a dressing-gown and red skullcap.

'What is it you want, friend?' he enquired.

The old man's heart overflowed, tears sprang to his eyes and all he could bring out in a trembling voice was: 'Your Honour! . . . Have the Christian goodness! . . .'

Minsky shot a swift glance at him, flushed, and led him by the arm into the study, closing the door behind him.

'Your Honour,' the old man pursued, 'it's no use crying over spilt milk; at least give me back my poor Dunya. You've had your fun with her; don't ruin her for nothing.'

'What's done can't be undone', said the young man, overcome with embarrassment. 'I am sorry for what I have done to you and am glad to ask your forgiveness, but please don't think I could abandon Dunya; she will be happy, you have my word of honour. What do you want with her? She loves me, and has grown out of her former condition. Neither you nor she could forget what has happened.' Then, tucking something into his sleeve, he opened the door and the stationmaster found himself unaccountably outside.

He stood motionless for a long time, then his eye lit on the bundle of papers in his cuff; he retrieved them and unfolded a number of five- and ten-rouble notes. Tears once more sprang to his eyes, tears of resentment! He crumpled the notes into a ball and flung them to the ground, grinding them with his heel. He set off, but after walking a few yards he halted, considered . . . and went back . . . but the banknotes had already disappeared.

A well–dressed young man, on seeing him, ran over to a cab, got in hurriedly, and shouted: 'Let's go! . . .' The stationmaster did not pursue him. He made up his mind to go back to his posting-station, but first he wanted to see his poor Dunya at least once more. To this end, a couple of days later, he went back to Minsky's. The orderly, however, told him roughly that his master wasn't receiving anyone, shouldered him out of the hallway, and slammed the door in his face. The stationmaster stayed standing there—and then left.

That same evening, he was walking along Liteinaya,* after saying a 'Te Deum' at the Church of our Lady of Sorrows. All at once an elegant carriage tore past him, and the stationmaster recognized Minsky. The carriage drew up immediately before the entrance to a three-storey house, and the hussar ran up on to the porch. A happy thought occurred to the stationmaster. He walked back and, as he drew level with the coachman, he asked:

'Whose horse is this, friend? Isn't it Minsky's?'

'Yes it is,' responded the coachman. 'Why, what do you want?'

'Well, it's like this: your master asked me to take a note to that Dunya of his, and I've clean forgotten where she lives.'

'It's here she lives, on the first floor. You're behindhand, friend, with your note; he's there with her now himself.'

'Never mind,' returned the stationmaster, with an inexplicable lurch of the heart. 'Thanks for setting me right, I'll still do what I was told.' And with that, he set off up the stairs.

The door was locked; he rang and spent several seconds in anguished suspense. The key rattled and the door opened. 'Does Avdotya Samsonovna reside here?' he asked.

'Yes,' answered a young servant girl. 'What do you want with her?' The stationmaster, without replying, entered the hall.

'You can't! You can't!' cried the servant girl after him. 'Avdotya Samsonovna has visitors.'

But the stationmaster paid no heed and went on. The first two rooms were dark, but there was a light on in the third. He went up to the open door and halted. Inside the beautifully furnished room sat Minsky, plunged in thought. Dunya, dressed in the height of fashion, was sitting on the arm of his chair, like a horsewoman on her English side-saddle. She was gazing tenderly at Minsky, twisting his dark curls round her glittering fingers. Poor stationmaster! Never had his daughter seemed so lovely; against his will, he feasted his eyes upon her.

'Who is it?' she asked, without raising her head. He remained silent. Getting no answer, Dunya looked up and . . . screamed as she fell to the carpet. Minsky, alarmed, hastened to pick her up, and suddenly catching sight of the old stationmaster standing in the doorway, abandoned Dunya and strode over to him, quivering with rage.

'What is it you want?' he gritted through clenched teeth. 'Why are you creeping round after me like some robber? Do you want to murder me? Get out of here.' And, grabbing him by the collar with a powerful hand, he thrust him out on to the stairs.

The old man returned to his quarters. His friend advised him to lodge a complaint, but the stationmaster, on reflection, waved this away and resolved to let the matter drop. Two days later he set off from Petersburg back to his station and resumed his post.

'It's over two years now,' he concluded, 'since I've been without Dunya, and I haven't heard a whisper about her. God alone knows whether she's alive or dead. Anything might have happened. She's not the first or the last to be lured away by some passing rogue, to be kept for a while and then dropped. There's plenty of them in Petersburg, silly little fools, today in satins and velvet, tomorrow sweeping the streets alongside the tavern riff-raff. When I think sometimes that Dunya may have gone to the bad like that, I can't help being sinful enough to wish her in her grave . . .'

Such was the narrative of my friend the old stationmaster, the story more than once punctuated by tears, which he wiped away picturesquely with the hem of his coat, like the loyal Terentich in Dmitriev's beautiful ballad.* These tears were partly prompted by the punch, of which he had got through five glasses in the course of his narration; but for all that they touched my heart. After we parted, the old stationmaster stayed long in my mind, and I kept thinking of poor Dunya . . .

Quite recently, passing through the *** township, I remembered my old friend. I knew that the posting-station he had supervised had been done away with. In answer to my question 'Is the old stationmaster alive?', no one was able to give a satisfactory answer. I decided to pay a visit to those old, familiar places, hired horses, and set off for N. village.

This was in the autumn. Greyish cloud obscured the heavens; a cold wind blew across the stubble-fields, bearing off the red and yellow leaves from the trees. I arrived in the village at sunset and stopped at the posting-house. In the passage (where once poor Dunya had kissed me) a stout peasant woman came out, and in answer to my questioning, replied that the old station-master had died a year since, that a brewer had taken over residence, and that she was the brewer's wife. I began to regret my pointless journey and the seven roubles I had wasted on it.

'What did he die of, then?' I inquired of the brewer's wife.

'Drank himself to death, master,' she replied.

'And where was he buried?'

'Outside the village next to his wife.'

'Could someone take me there?'

'Why ever not? Hey, Vanka! Stop fooling about with the cat. Take the gentleman to the cemetery, and show him the station-master's grave.'

At these words, a ragged, one-eyed boy with ginger hair came running out to me and led me at once out beyond the village.

'Did you know the deceased?' I asked him as we went.

'Of course I did! He taught me to whittle pipes. He used to come out of the tavern (may his soul rest in peace!) with us behind him: "Grandad, grandad! Give us some nuts!" and he would hand them out. He was forever playing with us.'

'And do the travellers remember him?'

'There's not many of them nowadays, apart from the court assessor, and he's not bothered about the dead. A lady did come last summer, and she asked about the old stationmaster and went over to his grave.'

'What sort of a lady?' I asked, intrigued.

'A beautiful lady,' replied the boy. 'She had a coach and six, with three little lords, a wet nurse, and a black pug-dog; and when they told her the old stationmaster was dead, she started crying and told the children: "sit quietly, while I go to the cemetery." And I offered to take her there. But the lady said: "I know the way myself." And gave me five silver kopeks—a really kind lady, she was . . .'

We arrived at the graveyard, a desolate place, unfenced, with
a sprinkling of wooden crosses and unshaded by a single tree. I
had never seen such a dismal cemetery in my life.

'Here's the old stationmaster's grave,' the boy said, leaping on
to a pile of sand into which a black cross with a copper icon had
been driven.

'And the lady came here?' I asked.

'Yes, she did', Vanka replied. 'I watched her from a distance.
She lay down down here and stayed like that for a long time.
And then she walked into the village, called the priest, gave him
some money, and drove away; and she gave me five silver kopeks
—a really nice lady!'

I too gave the urchin five kopeks and no longer regretted
either my trip, or the seven roubles I had spent.

THE LADY PEASANT

You're pretty, Dushenka, whatever clothes you wear.

(Bogdanovich)*

The estate of Ivan Petrovich Berestov was situated in one of our remote provinces. As a young man he had served in the Guards; on retiring at the beginning of 1797 he had set off for his village and thereafter never left it. He married an impoverished noble-woman, who died in childbirth when he was far afield. Managing the estate soon consoled him. He designed and built his own house, started up a textile mill, tripled his income, and began to look on himself as the cleverest man in the entire neighbour-hood, an opinion not disputed by the neighbours who came to stay with him, accompanied by their families and dogs. On weekdays he affected a short velveteen jacket, while for holidays he donned a coat made out of estate cloth; he kept his own accounts and read nothing apart from the *Senate Record*.* He was generally liked, though considered a haughty individual. The only person who didn't get on with him was his nearest neighbour, Grigory Ivanovich Muromsky. He was a true Rus-sian gentleman. Having got through the greater part of his for-tune in Moscow, and being widowed at that time, he went off to the last village he owned, where he continued his follies, though now in a different vein. He laid out an English garden,* on which he spent most of what remained of his wealth. His grooms were dressed like English jockeys. His daughter had an English governess. He used the English method in working his fields.

But Russian grain won't grow in foreign ways,*

and despite a significant reduction in his outgoings, Grigory Ivanovich's income did not increase; even in the country he had contrived to accumulate new debts. For all that, he was consid-ered no man's fool, as he had been the first in his province to mortgage his estate through the Board of Trustees,* which seemed at that time an extraordinarily complicated and risky venture. Of those who condemned the move, Berestov had been the most severe. Hatred of new-fangled notions was a distinguishing mark of his character. He could not speak of his neighbour's Anglomania with detachment and was forever finding some occasion to pick fault. If he was showing a visitor round the estate, he would respond to any praise of his managerial arrangements by saying, with a crafty smile:

'Yes, sir! It's different from the way my neighbour Grigory Ivanovich goes on. We can't manage to ruin ourselves the English way, so we have to stay well-fed the Russian way.'

These and similar pleasantries were conveyed, thanks to the assiduity of the neighbours, to the ears of Grigory Ivanovich, replete with additions and explanations. The Anglomane reacted to criticism as impatiently as our journalists do. He was furious and called his critic a bear and a provincial.

So matters stood between these two proprietors when Berestov's son came to see him in the country. He had been educated at *** university and was minded to enter military service, but his father was opposed to the idea. The young man felt himself to be wholly unsuited to a civilian career. Neither would give way, and young Alexey took up the life of a squire for the time being, letting his moustache grow, just in case.

Alexey was in truth a splendid fellow. It would really have been a pity if a military uniform had never hugged his slender frame, or if, instead of cutting a figure on a horse, he had spent his youth hunched over papers in an office. Watching him always galloping ahead of the field when out hunting, regardless of the terrain, the neighbours were of one voice in saying that he would never make a decent head of department. The young ladies would eye him, some of them positively couldn't take their eyes off him, but Alexey paid them little heed. They put his indifference down to some romantic attachment. Indeed, an address copied from one of his letters was going the rounds: 'Akulina Petrovna Kurochkina, Moscow, opposite the Alexeyevsky Monastery, house of coppersmith Savelyev, I humbly request you to forward this letter to ANR.'

Those of my readers who have never lived in rural parts cannot imagine how delightful these provincial young ladies are! Brought up on fresh air, in the shade of their apple orchards, they draw their knowledge of life and the world at large from books. Solitude, freedom, and reading are quick to develop in them emotions and passions unknown to our light-minded beauties. For a country miss, the jingle of a coach-bell is an adventure, a trip to the nearest town marks a stage in life, and a guest's visit leaves a lingering, even permanent memory. Of course, anyone is at liberty to laugh at some of their oddities, but the gibes of a superficial observer cannot efface their essential virtues, of which the chief is: *distinction of character, originality (individualité)*, without which, in the opinion of Jean Paul,* human greatness cannot exist. In the capital cities women receive a better education, perhaps, but the ways of society soon iron out their character and render their minds as indistinguishable as their hats. The above is not meant as a judgement, nor yet a censure, however, *nota nostra manet*,* as one ancient commentator puts it.

It is easy to imagine the effect Alexey was bound to create among our young ladies. He was the first to appear among them sombre and disillusioned, the first to talk to them of lost joys and the fading of his youth; on top of that he wore a black ring carved with a death's head. This was all terribly novel in that province. The young ladies lost their heads over him.

But it was the daughter of our Anglomane, Liza (or Betsy, as Grigory Ivanovich was in the habit of calling her), who was taken with him most of all. The fathers did not call on one another, so she had not set eyes on Alexey; meanwhile he was the sole topic of conversation among the neighbouring girls. She was seventeen years old. Dark eyes lit up her dusky and most attractive face. She was an only child and therefore spoiled. Her high spirits and constant mischief captivated her father and drove to distraction her governess, Miss Jackson, a prim, forty-year-old maiden lady, who whitened her face, blackened her eyebrows, reread *Pamela** twice a year, got 2,000 roubles for it, and was dying of boredom in *this barbarous Russia*.

Liza had a companion, Nastya; she was a little older, but just as giddy as her mistress. Liza doted on her, made her privy to all her secrets, planned her doings with her; in a nutshell, Nastya was a much more important personage in Priluchino village than any confidante in a French tragedy.

'Please let me go visiting today,' said Nastya one day, as she was dressing her young lady.

'By all means; where are you going?'

'Tugilovo, to the Berestovs'. Their cook's wife is celebrating her name day and she came over yesterday to invite us to the dinner.'

'I see!' said Liza. 'The masters have fallen out, but the servants play host to one another.'

'What the masters do is none of our business!' returned Nastya. 'Besides, I'm yours not your papa's. You haven't had words with the young Berestov, after all; let the old folk fight among themselves, if it keeps them happy.'

'Nastya, do try and get a look at Alexey Berestov, then tell me all about him, what he looks like and what sort of person he is.'

Nastya promised, and all day Liza waited impatiently for her return. In the evening she presented herself.

'Well, Lizaveta Grigorievna,' she said, as she came into the room, 'I've seen young Berestov; looked my fill; we were together all day.'

'How do you mean? Tell me, tell me it all in order.'

'As you please, miss; off we went, me, Anisya Egorovna, Nenila, Dunka . . .'

'All right, I know. Well, and then?'

'Please, miss, I'll tell it all in order. So we arrived just in time for dinner. The room was full of people. From Kolbino, Zakharevo, the steward's wife and daughters were there, the Khlupino people . . .'

'Well, what about Berestov?'

'Do wait a minute, miss. So we sat up to the table, the steward's wife in the place of honour, me next to her . . . Her daughters took the huff, but I didn't care a straw about that.'

'Ah, Nastya, what a bore you are with your never-ending details!'

'It's you who are the impatient one! So then, we got up from the table . . . we'd sat there about three hours, and the dinner was marvellous; the sweet was blancmange, blue, red, and striped . . . So we got up from the table and went into the garden to play catch, and that was when the young master turned up.'

'Well then? Is he really good-looking?'

'Amazingly handsome. An Adonis, you might say. Tall, slim, roses in his cheeks . . .'

'Really? And I was thinking he had a pale face. Well then, how did he strike you? Dreary was he, moody?'

'Of course not! I've never seen such a boisterous man in my life. He only ups and plays tag with us!'

'Plays tag with you? Impossible!'

'Very possible! And what else do you think he got up to? If he caught you he kissed you!'

'Say what you like, Nastya, but you're fibbing.'

'Say what you like, I'm not fibbing. I had a hard job getting away from him. He spent the whole day fooling around with us like that.'

'So why do they say he's in love and has eyes for nobody?'

'I don't know, miss, but he looked plenty at me, and Tanya the steward's daughter as well; and Pasha from Kolbino, honestly, nobody got left out, the naughty boy!'

'That's amazing! And what's the gossip around the house?'

'They say he's a wonderful master: so kind and cheery. There's only one drawback: he likes chasing the girls too much. That's all right by me: he'll settle down by and by.'

'Ah, how I'd love to see him!' sighed Liza.

'What's so hard about that? Tugilovo's not far, only five miles: take a walk over there or ride over; you're sure to come across him. He's out early every morning with his gun.'

'No, that wouldn't do. He might think I was chasing after him. Besides, our fathers are on bad terms so I won't be able to get to know him in any case . . . Ah, Nastya! You know what? I'll dress up as a peasant girl!'

'That's it! Put on a thick shirt and sarafan* and march over to Tugilovo; I'll guarantee Berestov won't miss you.'

'And I can talk just like a local girl. Oh, Nastya, dear Nastya! What a marvellous idea!' And Liza went to bed resolved on putting her jolly scheme into action.

Next day she proceeded to carry out her plan; she sent to market for some coarse linen, blue nankeen, and brass buttons, cut out a shirt and sarafan with Nastya's help, set all the servant girls sewing, and by evening all was ready. As she tried on her new garments, she acknowledged, in front of the mirror, that she had never looked prettier. She rehearsed her role, bowing low as she went, then rocked her head several times from side to

side like an earthenware cat, spoke in the peasant dialect, and
covered her mouth with her sleeve when she laughed, thus earning Nastya's full approval. Only one thing bothered her: she had
tried to run across the yard barefoot, but the the turf prickled
her tender feet, and the sand and the pebbles seemed intolerable. Here too Nastya helped her out: she measured Liza's foot
and ran off to the fields to Trofim, the shepherd, and ordered
a pair of bast shoes to fit. The next day Liza awoke before sun-
up. The whole house was still asleep. Nastya was waiting for
the shepherd by the gate. There came the toot of a horn and
the village herd came straggling past the manor-house. As he
came level with Nastya, Trofim handed her a pair of small, gaily
coloured bast shoes, and received fifty kopeks from her as reward.
Liza quietly donned her peasant finery, whispered her instructions with regard to Miss Jackson, went out on to the rear porch,
and ran through the kitchen-garden into the fields.

Dawn glowed in the east and golden ranks of clouds seemed
to be awaiting the sun, like courtiers their sovereign; the clear
sky, the morning freshness, the dew, the light breeze, and the
song of the birds filled Liza's heart with childlike gaiety; fearing
to encounter someone she knew, she seemed to fly rather than
walk. As she neared the wood which marked the boundary of
her father's estate, Liza slackened her pace. This was where she
was supposed to expect Alexey. Her heart was unaccountably
thumping; but the trepidation which accompanies our youthful
pranks is also their chief delight. Liza entered the sombre grove
to be greeted by its deep, rumbling noises. Her high spirits
subsided. Little by little, she abandoned herself to sweet reverie.
She thought . . . but can one identify precisely what a seventeen-
year-old young lady is thinking about, alone, before six on a spring
morning? So then, she was making her way along the path, deep
in thought, shaded on both sides by tall trees, when all of a
sudden a splendid pointer barked at her. Liza cried out in fright.
At that moment, a voice rang out:

'*Tout beau, Sbogar ici . . .*' and a young hunter appeared from
behind a thicket. 'Don't be scared, my dear,' said he to Liza,
'My dog won't bite.'

Liza had already managed to recover from her fright and
contrived to take immediate advantage of the situation. 'No, sir,'

she said, pretending to be half-afraid and half-bashful. 'But I am scared: look how vicious it is; it's jumping at me again.'

Alexey (the reader has already recognized him) was meanwhile staring hard at the young peasant girl.

'I'll keep you company if you're afraid,' he said to her. 'Will you let me walk by your side?'

'Who's stopping you?' responded Liza. 'Our wills are free and the road belongs to everybody.'

'Where are you from?'

'Priluchino; I'm the blacksmith Vasily's daughter. I'm off to pick mushrooms.' (She was carrying a basket on a string.) 'And you, sir? Tugilovo is it?'

'That's right,' Alexey answered. 'I'm the young master's valet.' He was minded to equalize their social status. But Liza shot a glance at him and burst out laughing.

'That's a fib,' she said, 'but you don't fool me. I can see you're the squire himself.'

'Whatever makes you think that?'

'Just everything.'

'What though?'

'How could I not tell a master from a servant? You're dressed different, you talk different, you call your dog different from what we do.'

Alexey felt more attracted to Liza with every minute that passed. Not being accustomed to stand on ceremony with pretty peasant girls. He made to embrace her, but Liza leapt away from him and assumed such a cold and severe expression that, although Alexey found it funny, he refrained from further attempts.

'If you want us to be friends from now on, please don't forget yourself.'

'Where did you learn such wise ways?' asked Alexey, convulsed with laughter. 'Not from my friend Nastenka, was it, not your young lady's maid? So this is the way knowledge spreads!'

Liza sensed that she had been about to act out of character and hastened to correct herself.

'You think I never go to the squire's house? Don't worry: I've heard and seen all sorts there. Still,' she went on, 'I'll get no mushrooms picked chattering to you. You go your way, sir, and I'll go mine. I'm sorry . . .'

Liza wanted to get away, but Alexey kept hold of her hand.

'What's your name, dear heart?'

'Akulina,' replied Liza, trying to free her fingers from Alexey's hand. 'Let me go, sir, it's high time I was getting home.'

'Well, my friend Akulina, I shall certainly be visiting your father, Vasily the blacksmith.'

'The idea!' protested Liza spiritedly. 'For the Lord's sake, don't you come. If they find out at home that I've been chatting away with the squire in the woods on my own, then I'm in trouble. My father, Vasily the blacksmith, will thrash me to within an inch of my life.'

'But I really must see you again.'

'Well, I'll be this way again some time for mushrooms.'

'When though?'

'Tomorrow maybe.'

'Sweet Akulina, I'd smother you with kisses if I dared. So tomorrow, at this time, is that it?'

'Yes, yes.'

'You won't let me down?'

'I won't.'

'Swear.'

'I swear by Good Friday I'll come.'

The young folk parted. Liza left the woods, cut across a field, stole into the garden, and dashed headlong for the farm where Nastya was waiting for her. There she changed her clothes, dreamily responding to the eager questioning of her confidante, before presenting herself in the dining-room. The table was laid, breakfast ready, and wasp-waisted Miss Jackson, face powdered, was cutting wafer-thin slices of bread and butter. Her father praised Liza for her early morning walk.

'Nothing healthier', said he, 'than rising at dawn.'

He then cited a number of examples of human longevity, culled from English magazines, remarking that everybody who lived to be over a hundred abstained from vodka and got up at dawn, winter and summer. Liza paid him no attention. She was reliving in her mind all the circumstances of her morning encounter, all Akulina's talk with the young hunter, and her conscience was beginning to trouble her. In vain did she protest to herself that their conversation had not transgressed the bounds of decorum, that her prank could not possibly have any consequences: the voice of conscience was louder than that of reason. The promise she had given for the morrow worried her most of all. She was on the point of resolving not to keep her solemn vow. But Alexey, after waiting for her in vain, might go off and seek out the real Akulina, a stout, pock-marked lass, in the family of Vasily the blacksmith, and so find out about her flighty behaviour. The thought terrified Liza, and she resolved to appear in the wood again the next morning as Akulina.

For his part, Alexey was enchanted and kept thinking about his new acquaintance the whole day; at night, the image of the dusky beauty haunted his imagination even in dreams. He was already up and dressed before dawn had fairly broken. Without giving himself time to load his gun, he went out into the fields with his faithful Sbogar and ran towards the promised trysting-place. Nearly half an hour passed in unbearable suspense before he caught a glimpse of her blue sarafan through the thickets and rushed to meet his dear Akulina. She smiled at his rapturous gratitude, but Alexey at once noticed traces of despondency and worry on her face. He wanted to learn the reason for this. Liza confessed that her action now seemed light-minded, and that she regretted it, that this time she had not wanted to keep her given word, and that this meeting would be the last; she would ask him to break off an acquaintance which could lead to nothing good. All this, of course, was spoken in peasant dialect; but the thoughts and emotions, unusual in a simple girl, dumbfounded Alexey. He employed all his eloquence in an attempt to divert Akulina from her intention; he protested the innocence of his intentions, promised he would never give her reason for regret, obey her in all things, and besought her not to deprive him of his only joy: to see her alone, if only every other day, even twice a week. He spoke the language of genuine passion, and at that moment was certainly in love. Liza listened to him in silence.

'Give me your word,' said she, 'that you will never seek me out in the village, or go round asking questions about me. Give me your word that you will not ask for meetings with me, aside from those I appoint myself.' Alexey was about to swear by Good Friday, but she stopped him, smiling. 'I don't need you to swear,' she said. 'Your promise is enough for me.'

After that, they talked in friendly fashion, strolling together through the woods, until Liza told him it was time to go. They parted, and Alexey, left on his own, was unable to comprehend how a simple peasant girl had contrived to establish such genuine dominion over him after two meetings. His relations with Akulina held the charm of novelty for him, and although he thought the injunctions laid down by the strange village girl onerous, the thought of breaking his word never even crossed his mind. The fact of the matter was that Alexey, notwithstanding the ominous ring, the mysterious correspondence, and his sombre air of disillusion, was a good-natured, impulsive young fellow, with a pure heart capable of innocent enjoyment.

Were I to follow my own inclinations, I would certainly give a detailed account of how the young people used to meet, their growing mutual affection and trust, what they did and what they said; but I am aware that the majority of my readers would not share my pleasure in doing so. Details of that sort must seem mawkish, and so I will omit them, saying only that before two months had passed my Alexey was head over heels in love, and Liza equally so, though less outspoken. Both were happy with the present and gave no thought to the future.

The thought of an indissoluble bond quite often flashed through their minds, but they never spoke about that to each other. The reason was plain: Alexey, however much he might be attached to his sweet Akulina, was ever conscious of the distance which existed between him and the poor peasant girl; Liza, aware of the profound animosity between their fathers did not dare to hope for their reconciliation. And besides, her vanity was secretly stirred by an obscure romantic hope of eventually seeing the Tugilovo squire at the feet of the daughter of the Priluchino blacksmith. All of a sudden a momentous occurrence bid fair to alter their relationship.

One clear, cold morning (so frequent in our Russian autumns) Ivan Petrovich Berestov went out riding, taking with him three couple of borzois just in case, along with a groom and several of the serf urchins with rattles. At that very moment, Grigory Ivanovich Muromsky, seduced by the fine weather, ordered his bob-tailed filly to be saddled up, and set off for a canter round his Anglicized domains. As he neared the woods he caught sight of his neighbour, in his jacket lined with fox-fur, proudly astride his horse as he waited for a hare which the boys with their rattles and shouting had driven out of a thicket. If Grigory Ivanovich had foreseen this encounter he would have turned aside, of course; but he had come upon Berestov quite unexpectedly, and all at once found himself only a pistol-shot away. There was nothing for it. Muromsky, like a cultivated European, rode up to his adversary and greeted him courteously. Berestov responded with as much enthusiasm as a chained bear that bows to the *ladies and gentlemen* at his master's command. Just at that moment the hare leapt out of the woods and ran across the field. Berestov and his groom yelled out at the top of their voices, released the hounds, and galloped off after them at full tilt. Muromsky's horse, never having hunted before, took fright and bolted. Muromsky, who had proclaimed himself to be an excellent horseman, gave her free rein, inwardly pleased at the opportunity to be rid of a disagreeable companion. The horse, however, reaching a gully hitherto unnoticed, hurtled off to one side, unseating Muromsky. Having fallen rather heavily on the frozen ground, he lay cursing his bob-tailed filly, which, as if bethinking itself, came to a sudden halt as soon as it felt the absence of a rider. Ivan Petrovich came galloping up to find out whether he had hurt himself. The groom meanwhile led up the guilty horse, holding it by the bridle. He helped Muromsky up into the saddle and Berestov invited him to his house. Muromsky could not refuse, feeling himself under an obligation. And so Berestov returned home in pomp, having caught the hare and leading his wounded adversary almost as a prisoner of war.

The neighbours, as they breakfasted, got on talking in fairly amicable fashion. Muromsky, admitting that after his fall he was in no fit state to ride home, requested a droshky. Berestov saw him out on to the porch, and Muromsky left only after securing his neighbour's promise that he (together with Alexey Ivanovich) would come to Priluchino the very next day to dine as friends. Thus the long-standing and deep-rooted hostility, was, it appeared, about to come to an end owing to the nervousness of a dock-tailed filly.

Liza ran out to meet Grigory Ivanovich. 'What's happened,

papa?' she asked, surprised. 'Why are you limping? Where's your horse? Whose droshky is that?'

'Now you'll never guess, *my dear*,' replied Grigory Ivanovich, and recounted all that had happened. Liza couldn't believe her ears. Without giving her time to recover, Grigory Ivanovich announced that both Berestovs were to have dinner with him on the following day.

'What?' she cried, growing pale. 'The Berestovs, father and son! Tomorrow for dinner! No, papa, do as you like, but I won't show myself for anything.'

'Have you taken leave of your senses?' countered her father. 'Since when have you grown so shy—or are you carrying on some hereditary vendetta, like a romantic heroine? Stop being silly, now . . .'

'No, papa, not for anything in the world, not for all the tea in China will I appear in front of the Berestovs.'

Grigory Ivanovich shrugged his shoulders and argued no more, knowing that it was hopeless trying to contradict her. He went off to rest after his remarkable outing.

Lizaveta Ivanovna proceeded to her room and summoned Nastya. They had a long discussion about the forthcoming visit. What would Alexey think if he recognized his Akulina in the well-bred squire's daughter? What would he think of her behaviour and code of conduct, her common sense? On the other hand, Liza very much wanted to see what effect such an unexpected encounter would produce . . . All at once she had an idea. She at once told Nastya; both of them rejoiced at a heaven-sent solution and resolved to implement it without fail.

The next day, at breakfast, Grigory Ivanovich asked his daughter whether she still intended to conceal herself from the Berestovs.

'Papa,' replied Liza, 'I will receive them if you wish it, but with one proviso; whatever guise I appear in, whatever I do, you will not scold me and not give any sign of either surprise or displeasure.'

'Up to some nonsense again!' said Grigory Ivanovich, laughing. 'Well, all right, all right; I agree, do what you like, my dark-eyed bundle of mischief.' So saying, he kissed her on the forehead and Liza ran off to get ready.

At two o'clock exactly a home-constructed carriage, harnessed up with six horses, drove into the courtyard and bowled around the dark-green circle of turf. Old Berestov ascended the porch steps with the assistance of two of Muromsky's liveried servants. Behind him came his son on horseback, who then accompanied him into the dining-room, where the table had already been laid. Muromsky received his guests with the utmost civility; he proposed that they have a look round the garden and menagerie before dinner, and conducted them along paths which had been meticulously swept and sanded. Old Berestov inwardly deplored the time and trouble wasted on such idle whims, but politely held his peace. His son shared neither the displeasure of the thrifty squire, nor the raptures of the self-regarding Anglophile; he was impatiently waiting for the appearance of the host's daughter, of whom he had heard a great deal, and although his heart, as we know, was already engaged, a young beauty always had a claim on his imagination.

On returning to the living-room, all three sat down: the old men recalled times gone by and stories from their service days, while Alexey mused on what his role should be when Liza was present. He decided that an air of cold abstraction would be most appropriate in any event, and prepared himself accordingly. The door opened and he turned his head with such indifference, such negligent hauteur, that the heart of the most inveterate coquette must surely have quailed. Unfortunately, instead of Liza it was old Miss Jackson, white-faced and wasp-waisted, with lowered eyes and a small curtsey, so that Alexey's splendid manœuvre went for nothing. He had no time to collect himself before the door opened again, and this time Liza came in. They all got up; her father began introducing the guests, but suddenly stopped and hastily bit his lip . . . Liza, his dusky Liza, was whitened to the ears, eyebrows even blacker than Miss Jackson's; false ringlets, much lighter than her own hair, were swept up like a Louis XIV wig; her sleeves, *à l'imbécile*,* stuck out like Madame de Pompadour's hooped skirts; her waist was laced-up like the letter X, and all her mother's diamonds which had not yet been pawned sparkled on her fingers, neck, and ears. Alexey could not recognize his Akulina in this ridiculous, glittering lady. His father bent to kiss her hand, and he resentfully followed suit; when he touched her white fingers, he fancied that they trembled. Meanwhile, he did contrive to notice her little foot, shod in the most flirtatious fashion possible and quite deliberately displayed. This reconciled him somewhat to the rest of her attire. As for the ceruse and the eyebrows, it has to be admitted that, in his simplicity of heart, he had not noticed them at first glance, and subsequently did not suspect their presence. Grigory Ivanovich remembered his promise and tried not to show the least hint of surprise; but he thought his daughter's prank so amusing that he could barely restrain himself. The prim and proper Englishwoman was far from amused. She had guessed that the eyebrow-pencil and ceruse had been plundered from her drawer, and a crimson flush of annoyance showed through the artificial pallor of her face. She kept looking daggers at the young mischief-maker who, keeping explanations for later, pretended not to notice them.

They sat down to dinner. Alexey continued to play the brooding and preoccupied role. Liza behaved affectedly, speaking through her teeth, intoning her words and then only in French. Her father kept staring hard at her, not grasping what she was up to, but finding it all extremely diverting. The Englishwoman seethed in silence. Ivan Petrovich was the only one to feel at home: he ate for two, drank his usual amount, laughed at his own jokes, and chatted and guffawed more convivially as the time passed.

At last they rose from the table; the guests departed and Grigory Ivanovich gave free rein to his laughter and questions:

'What gave you the idea of fooling them like that?' he asked Liza. 'And do you know, the whitener suits you; I won't go into the secrets of a lady's toilette, but in your place I'd start using it; not too much, of course, just a bit.'

Liza was thrilled over the success of her scheme. She embraced her father, promised to consider his advice, and ran off to mollify the fuming Miss Jackson, who barely consented to open her door and listen to her explanations. Liza was ashamed to appear before strangers with a complexion so dark; she had not dared to ask . . . she had been sure that dear Miss Jackson would forgive her . . . and so on and so forth. Miss Jackson, once assured that Liza had had no thought of holding her up to ridicule, calmed down, kissed Liza, and, as a pledge of reconciliation, presented her with a jar of English ceruse, which Liza accepted with expressions of sincere gratitude.

The reader will have guessed that on the following day Liza was not slow in turning up for her rendezvous in the woods.

'You were at our master's last night, sir?' she said at once. 'How did our young lady strike you?'

Alexey replied that he had not noticed her.

'Pity,' countered Liza.

'And why is that?'

'Because I wanted to ask you if it's true what they say . . .'

'And what do they say?'

'Whether it's true that I look like the mistress.'

'What nonsense! Compared to you, she's an absolute freak.'

'Oh, sir, you shouldn't say such things; our young lady has such a white complexion, she's such a lady of fashion! How can I be compared to her?'

Alexey swore that she was better than any conceivable pale-skinned young lady, and so as to reassure her completely, began describing her mistress in such an amusing fashion that Liza fairly roared with heartfelt laughter.

'Still,' she sighed, 'although the mistress might be funny and all, I'm an illiterate fool compared to her.'

'Really! Now that is something to worry about! If you like I'll teach you to read and write.'

'Well, yes', said Liza. 'Why not give it a try at that?'

'If you like, sweetheart, we can start now.'

They seated themselves. Alexey produced a pencil and note-book from his pocket and Akulina learned the alphabet with astonishing speed. Alexey couldn't get over her quick-wittedness. The next morning she wanted to try and write; at first the pencil wouldn't obey her, but after a few minutes she began drawing the letters quite decently too.

'It's wonderful!' said Alexey. 'Our study is going better than the Lancaster system.'*

And indeed by the third lesson, Akulina was already reading 'Natalya, the Boyar's Daughter'* syllable by syllable, interrupting her reading with remarks which genuinely amazed Alexey, as well as covering a whole sheet of paper with aphorisms, selected from the same story.

A week went by and a correspondence sprang up between them. The post-box was in a hollow oak tree. Nastya secretly carried out the postal duties. Alexey would bring his letters there, written in his large handwriting, and find in the same spot, on plain blue paper, the scribbles of his beloved. Akulina was evidently getting used to a more refined mode of expression and her mind was perceptibly developing and becoming more cultivated.

Meanwhile, the recent acquaintance between Ivan Petrovich Berestov and Grigory Ivanovich Muromsky was becoming ever firmer and soon turned into friendship under the following circumstances: Muromsky had often thought that, in the event of Ivan Petrovich's death, all of his estate would pass into the hands of Alexey Ivanovich; in that case Alexey would be one of the richest landowners in the province and there would be no reason for him not to marry Liza. Old Berestov, for his part, though acknowledging in his neighbour a certain extravagance (or, as he put it, English foolishness), did not deny him a number of excellent virtues—his exceptional resourcefulness, for example; Grigory Ivanovich was closely related to the Count Pronsky, a powerful and highly placed man: the Count could be very useful to Alexey, while Muromsky (so thought Ivan Petrovich) would no doubt be glad of the opportunity to bestow his daughter advantageously. The old men had so far considered all this individually, but eventually spoke of it to each other; they embraced, and promised one another to prepare the ground properly, and set about the business each from his own side. Muromsky had an obstacle to negotiate: to talk his Betsy into getting more closely acquainted with Alexey, whom she had not seen since that memorable dinner. It appeared that they had not taken to one another; at all events, Alexey had not returned to Priluchino, while Liza had taken to her room every time Ivan Petrovich honoured them with a visit. But, thought Grigory Ivanovich, if Alexey were to be here every day then Betsy was bound to fall in love with him. It was in the nature of things. Time would do its work.

Ivan Petrovich was less troubled about the success of his aims. That same evening he summoned his son into his study, lit his pipe, and said, after a pause:

'Why is it Alyosha,* you haven't said a word about the army all this time? Or does a hussar's uniform no longer hold any attraction for you?'

'No, father,' replied Alexey respectfully. 'I see you don't like the idea of me being a hussar; it is my duty to submit to your wishes.'

'Good,' said Ivan Petrovich. 'I can see you're an obedient son; that's a comfort to me; I don't want to force you into anything either; I'm not going to compel you, for the moment . . . into the civil service; but in the meantime I'm minded to see you married.'

'To whom, father?' enquired Alexey, amazed.

'To Lizaveta Grigoryevna Muromskaya,' replied Ivan Petrovich. 'No better match, am I right?'

'Father, I am not thinking of marriage yet.'

'You aren't, but I'm thinking for you, thinking a lot.'

'As you please. But I don't like Liza Muromskaya at all.'

'You will later. You'll get used to it.'

'I don't think I can make her happy.'

'Her happiness is not your worry. What? Is this how you respect your father's wishes? Very well!'

'As you please, but I don't wish to get married and I shan't get married.'

'You'll get married or I'll curse you, and I'll sell the estate, as God is my witness, and squander the proceeds. I won't leave you a farthing. I'm giving you three days to think it over, and in the meantime don't you dare let me set eyes on you.'

Alexey knew that once his father took something into his head, you couldn't get it out again with a nail, as Taras Skotinin phrased it; but Alexey was a chip off the old block, and he was just as difficult to out-argue. He went off to his room and began to muse about the limits of parental authority, about Liza Grigoryevna, about the solemn promise of his father to reduce him to beggary, and finally about Akulina. For the first time, he could see plainly that he was passionately in love with her; the romantic notion crossed his mind of marrying a peasant girl and living by his labours, and the more he thought of this drastic step, the more sense he saw in it. For some time now, rainy weather had put a stop to the meetings in the woods. He sent a letter to Akulina in his clearest handwriting and most fervent style, informing her of the fate hanging over him, and at once offering her his hand. He took the letter to the hollow oak tree immediately, and went to bed feeling very pleased with himself.

On the following day Alexey, firm in his resolve, rode over to Muromsky early in the morning, to make a clean breast of things. He was hoping to gain his support by appealing to his generosity.

'Is Grigory Ivanovich at home?' he asked, halting his horse by the porch of the Priluchino fortress.

'Oh, no,' replied a servant. 'Grigory Ivanovich was pleased to go out this morning.'

'How annoying!' thought Alexey.

'Is Lizaveta Grigoryevna at home, then?'

'She is, sir.'

And Alexey sprang from his horse, handing the reins to the servant and going in without being announced.

'It'll all be settled,' he thought, heading for the living-room. 'I'll explain matters myself.' He went in . . . and froze! Liza . . . no, Akulina, sweet, dusky Akulina, not in a sarafan, but wearing a white morning frock, was sitting by the window and reading his letter; she was so absorbed, that she did not hear him come in. Alexey could not withhold a joyful exclamation. Liza started, raised her head, cried out, and made to flee. He rushed to hold her back. 'Akulina, Akulina! . . .' Liza tried to escape from him. '*Mais laissez-moi donc, monsieur, mais êtes-vous fou?*'* she repeated, turning away. 'Akulina! My friend Akulina!' he repeated, kissing her hands. Miss Jackson, a witness to this scene, did not know what to think. At that moment the door opened and Grigory Ivanovich came in.

'Aha!' said Muromsky. 'It seems everything is already sorted out . . .'

My readers will excuse me from the unnecessary duty of describing the denouement.

THE QUEEN OF SPADES

The queen of spades indicates some covert malice.
(The latest fortune-telling manual)

THE QUEEN OF SPADES

I

If rain spoiled the day
They would sit down to play
        Gladly;
They wagered their pay
Throwing hundreds away—
        Sadly.
They kept chalky account
Of any amount
        Owing.
So, if rain spoiled the day,
They would still keep the play
        Going.*

One evening, Narumov of the Horse Guards played host to a
card party. The long winter night passed unnoticed, and it was
after four in the morning when they all sat down to supper.
Those who had ended up ahead of the game ate heartily; the rest
sat moodily before their empty plates. But champagne was produced, conversation revived, and everybody joined in.

'How did you get on, Surin?' the host enquired.

'Lost as usual. You must admit I have no luck at all. I play it
straight, I never get carried away or lose concentration, and yet
I just go down and down!'

'Haven't you ever once been tempted? Never backed a sequence? . . . I'm amazed at your will-power.'

'What about Hermann, then?' said one of the company, indicating a young engineer. 'Never handled a card in his life, never
doubled a single stake, yet here he sits up till five watching us
play.'

'I'm very taken with the game,' said Hermann. 'But I'm not
in a position to sacrifice the necessary in the hope of acquiring
the superfluous.'*

'He's German. He counts the pennies, that's all it is,' Tomsky put in. 'If there's anyone I can't fathom it's my grandmother, Countess Anna Fedotovna.'

'What was that? How do you mean?' The guests queried noisily.

'I just can't understand', Tomsky went on, 'how it is that my grandmother never gambles.'

'What's odd about that?' Narumov asked. 'An old lady of eighty not gambling?'

'You mean you really don't know anything about her?'

'No, honestly, nothing!'

'Well, in that case, lend an ear:

'I should tell you that about sixty years ago my grandmother went to Paris and became all the rage. People flocked after her for a glimpse of *la Vénus moscovite*; Richelieu laid siege to her and was on the point of shooting himself because of her cruelty, or so grandmother assures me. In those days the ladies used to play faro.* On one occasion at court she lost a considerable sum to the Duke of Orleans. Back home, as she was peeling off her beauty-spots and undoing her hooped petticoat, she informed grandfather of her losses and instructed him to pay up. My late grandfather, as I recall, was a sort of major-domo to his wife. He was mortally afraid of her; however, when he heard of her appalling losses, he flew into a rage and fetched the accounts to demonstrate to her that she had got through half-a-million in six months, that they had no such estates near Paris as they had at Moscow and Saratov, and flatly refused to pay. Grandmother slapped his face and went to bed by herself, as a mark of her displeasure. Next day she sent for her husband, trusting that this domestic punishment had proved effective, but found him immovable. For the first time in her life she went so far as to argue with him and explain how matters stood; she thought to shame him by pointing out condescendingly that there are debts and debts, and that there was a difference between a prince and a coach-builder. He was having none of it. Grandfather had risen in revolt. No meant no! Grandmother did not know what to do.

'She was intimately acquainted with a most remarkable man. You've heard of the Count de Saint-Germain, the subject of so many weird and wonderful tales. You know he passed himself off as the Wandering Jew, the inventor of the elixir of life and the philosopher's stone, and so forth. People used to ridicule him as a charlatan, and Casanova says in his memoirs* that he was a spy; however that might be, Saint-Germain, for all his air of mystery, was outwardly most respectable, and a model of courtesy in society. Grandmother adores him to this day and gets cross if anyone speaks slightingly of him. She knew that Saint-Germain had a large fortune at his disposal. She resolved to avail herself of his help and wrote him a note asking him to come and see her at once. The singular old man turned up straight away and found her in a dreadful state. She described her husband's barbarous behaviour in the blackest of colours, and concluded by saying that she was reposing all her hopes on his friendship and kindness. Saint-Germain pondered. "I can accommodate you as far as the sum of money goes," he said, "but I know you would not be at ease until you had repaid me, and I would not wish to encumber you with fresh worries. There is another way—you can win it back."

' "But my dear Count," grandmother replied, "I'm telling you, we have no money at all."

' "Money is not necessary in this case," said Saint-Germain, "be good enough to hear me out." It was at this point that he revealed to her a secret which any one of us would give a great deal to possess . . .'

The young gamesters redoubled their attention. Tomsky lit his pipe and got it drawing before he resumed:

'That same evening, grandmother presented herself at Versailles, *au jeu de la Reine*.* The Duke of Orleans was holding the bank; grandmother casually excused herself for not bringing what she owed, spinning some little story as cover, and began staking against him. She selected three cards, betting on them one after the other: all three won and grandmother recouped every bit of her losses.'

'Pure luck!'

'A tall story,' remarked Hermann.

'The cards might have been marked,' pursued a third.

'I don't think so,' Tomsky responded gravely.

'What do you mean?' said Narumov. 'You have a grandmother who can predict three cards in sequence, and you haven't learned the magic formula from her yet?'

'Not much chance of that!' Tomsky replied. 'She had four sons, including my father; all four were desperate gamblers and she hasn't told one of them her secret, though it would have been very much to their advantage, not to mention mine. But this is what my uncle, Count Ivan Ilych, told me, on his word of honour. As a young man, the late Chaplitsky, the one who died penniless after getting through millions, once lost—to Zorich, I think it was—around three hundred thousand. He was in despair. Grandmother always disapproved of youthful frolics, but took pity on Chaplitsky for some reason. She gave him three cards to bet on in succession, and made him give his word of honour never to play again. Chaplitsky went back to his conqueror; they sat down to play. Chaplitsky bet fifty thousand on the first card and won straight off; doubled the stakes, redoubled—and recouped his losses and a bit besides . . .

'Still, time for bed: it's quarter to six already.'

And indeed, day was already dawning. The young men drained their glasses and dispersed.

II

'Il paraît que monsieur est décidément pour les suivantes.'
'Que voulez-vous, madame? Elles sont plus fraîches.'

(Polite conversation)*

The old Countess was sitting in her boudoir in front of the mirror. Three maids surrounded her. One was holding a jar of rouge, the second a box of pins, and the third a tall bonnet with flame-coloured ribbons. The Countess had not the least pretension to beauty, by now long-faded, but had retained all the habits of her youth; she clung rigidly to the fashions of the '70s and was as meticulously long over her toilette as she had been sixty years before. A young lady, her ward, sat by the window at her embroidery.

'Good morning, *grand'maman*!' said a young officer, coming into the room: '*Bonjour, Mademoiselle Lise. Grand'maman*, I have a favour to ask you.'

'What is that, *Paul*?'

'Allow me to introduce one of my friends and bring him to the ball on Friday.'

'Bring him straight to the ball, and you can introduce him to me there. Were you at N.'s yesterday, may I ask?'

'I certainly was! It was very gay; dancing till five. Eletskaya was so pretty!'

'Really, my dear boy! What do you see in her? Her grandmother, the Princess Darya Petrovna, was ten times the woman ... By the way, I expect she's getting on now, Princess Darya Petrovna?'

'What do you mean, getting on?' Tomsky responded unthinkingly. 'She's been dead these seven years.'

The young lady raised her head and made a sign to him. He bit his lip as he remembered that the death of contemporaries was always kept from the old Countess. She, however, received the news with marked indifference.

'Dead!' she said. 'And I didn't even know! We were maids

of honour together, and when we were being presented, the Empress . . .'

And the Countess related the story to her grandson for the hundredth time.

'Well now, *Paul*,' she said presently, 'help me to get up. Lizanka, where is my snuff-box?'

And the Countess went behind the screens with her maids to finish off her toilette. Tomsky was left alone with the young lady.

'Who is it you want to introduce?' Lizaveta Ivanovna inquired softly.

'Narumov. Do you know him?'

'No. Is he a soldier or a civilian?'

'Soldier.'

'An engineer?'

'No, cavalry. Why should you think he was an engineer?'

The young lady laughed and said not a word in answer.

'*Paul*!' cried the Countess from behind the screens. 'Send me some new novel, would you, but please not one of the latest ones.'

'How do you mean, *grand'maman*?'

'I want the sort where the hero doesn't strangle either his father or mother, and there are no drowned bodies. I have a mortal dread of drowned bodies.'

'They don't write that kind nowadays. Unless you'd like some Russian ones.'

'Are there really such things? . . . Send them along, dear boy, by all means!'

'Do excuse me, *grand'maman*: I'm in a hurry . . . Goodbye, Lizaveta Ivanovna. Why on earth did you think Narumov was an engineer?'

And Tomsky left the boudoir.

Lizaveta Ivanovna was now on her own; she abandoned her work and began gazing out of the window. Presently, a young officer emerged from behind the corner-house on the other side of the street. A flush spread across her cheeks; she took up her work again and bent her head close to the design. At that moment the Countess entered, fully dressed.

'Order the carriage, Lizanka,' she said. 'We'll go for a drive.'

Liza rose from her embroidery and began putting her work away.

'What's the matter with you, my girl! Deaf are you?' shouted the Countess. 'Order the carriage this minute.'

'At once,' the young lady answered softly and ran out into the hall.

A servant entered and handed the Countess some books from Prince Pavel Alexandrovich.

'Good! Thank him for me,' said the Countess: 'Lizanka, Lizanka, where are you off to now for heaven's sake?'

'To get dressed.'

'Plenty of time for that, dear. Just stay here. Open the first book now and read aloud . . .'

The young lady took up the book and read several lines.

'Louder!' said the Countess. 'What's the matter with you, my girl? Lost your voice have you? . . . Wait a minute . . . move my footstool; no, nearer . . . well, go on then!'

Lizaveta Ivanovna read another two pages. The Countess yawned.

'Leave off that one,' she said. 'What rubbish! Send it back to Pavel and tell them to thank him . . . Where's that carriage?'

'The carriage is ready,' said Lizaveta Ivanovna, glancing out into the street.

'Why on earth aren't you dressed?' said the Countess. 'Always have to wait for you. It's intolerable, my girl!'

Liza ran off to her room. Within two minutes the Countess had begun to ring with all her might. The three maids ran in at one door and a valet at the other.

'Why is there no getting hold of you?' the Countess demanded. 'Tell Lizaveta Ivanovna I'm waiting.'

Lizaveta Ivanovna entered in her coat and bonnet.

'At last, my girl!' said the Countess. 'Such finery! What are you up to? . . . Who are you out to dazzle? . . . And what's it like outside. Windy, isn't it?'

'No indeed, your highness! Not a breath of wind!' responded the valet.

'You just say the first thing that comes into your head! Open the top pane. Just as I thought: windy! And freezing cold!

Unharness the carriage. Lizanka, we're not going. You needn't
have dolled yourself up.'

'And this is the life I lead!' thought Lizaveta Ivanovna.

Indeed, Lizaveta Ivanovna was a most forlorn creature. The
bread of a stranger is bitter, says Dante, and painful the steps
of a stranger's stair; and who should know the bitterness of
dependency better than the poor ward of a society lady? The
Countess, of course, was not malicious by nature, but she was
wilful, like any lady spoilt by society; she was miserly and sunk
in a cold selfishness, like all old people who have drunk their fill
of love when young and are alienated from the present day. She
involved herself in all the vanities of high society; she would
haul herself along to dances and sit in the corner, heavily rouged
and dressed in antique fashion, for all the world like some gro-
tesque but obligatory ballroom ornament; on arrival, guests would
approach, bowing low according to established ritual, then pay
her no further attention. At home she used to receive the whole
town, observing strict etiquette, though she recognized no one's
face. Her numerous retainers, grown stout and grizzled in her
hall and maid's quarters, did whatever they liked, competing
with one another in robbing the dying old woman. Lizaveta
Ivanovna was a domestic martyr. She poured out the tea and
was berated for using too much sugar; she read novels aloud,
and was to blame for all the author's failings; she accompanied
the Countess on her outings, and was held responsible for the
weather and the state of the roads. She had a fixed salary, but it
was always in arrears; at the same time, she was expected to
dress like other people, or rather like very few other people. In
society, she played a most pitiable role. Everyone knew her, but
no one noticed her; at balls, she would dance only when someone lacked a partner, and ladies would take her arm when they
needed to go to the cloakroom to adjust their clothing. She had
her pride and felt her position keenly; she was ever on the look-
out, impatiently awaiting a deliverer. The young men, however,
calculating in their fickle vanity, did not favour her with their
attention, although Lizaveta Ivanovna was a hundred times nicer
than the cold and haughty maidens on whom they danced attendance. Many a time she had quietly quitted the tedious splend-
ours of the salon and gone off to weep in her own poor little

room, with its papered screen, chest of drawers, small mirror, and painted bedstead, and where a tallow candle burned dimly in its brass holder.

It came to pass—two days after the the evening described at the beginning of this tale, and a week before the scene at which we have just paused—it came to pass that Lizaveta Ivanovna, while seated below the window and busy with her embroidery, happened to glance outside and caught sight of a young engineer standing motionless, staring at her window. She lowered her head and resumed her work; five minutes later she glanced out again—the young officer was standing on the very same spot. Not being in the habit of flirting with passing officers, she stopped looking out and sewed away for two hours with head bent. Dinner was served. She rose and began tidying away her embroidery frame; chancing to look down into the street, she again caught sight of the officer. This struck her as rather odd. After dinner, she approached the window with a certain sense of unease, but the officer was no longer there—and she dismissed him from her mind . . .

Some two days later, as she was coming out with the Countess to get into the carriage, she saw him again. He was standing close by the entrance, his face hidden by a beaver collar; his dark eyes glittered beneath his cap. Lizaveta felt alarmed without knowing why, and sensed an unaccountable flutter as she got into the carriage.

After returning home, she ran over to the window. The officer was positioned as before, his eyes fastened upon her; she turned away in an agony of curiosity, stirred by an emotion entirely new to her.

From that time forth, not a day passed without the young man appearing beneath the windows of the house at a fixed hour. An undefined relationship grew up between them. Seated in her usual work-place, she would sense his approach and lift her head to look at him, a little longer each day. The young man seemed grateful to her for this: she saw with the keen eye of youth how his pale cheeks would flush swiftly whenever their glances met. After a week, she gave him a smile . . .

When Tomsky had asked permission to introduce his friend to the Countess the poor girl's heart had gone pit-a-pat. When she discovered, however, that Narumov was in the Horse Guards and not an engineer, she regretted that by an indiscreet enquiry she had betrayed her secret to the light-minded Tomsky.

Hermann was the son of a Russianized German, who had left him a small sum of money. Firmly convinced of the necessity of consolidating his independence, Hermann had not laid a finger even on the interest, preferring to live solely on his pay, and denying himself the smallest extravagance. As he was reserved and keenly ambitious, however, his comrades rarely had an opportunity to make fun of his excessive thrift. He was a man of strong emotions and possessed an ardent imagination, but his steadiness preserved him from the usual errors of youth. For example, though he had the soul of a gambler, he never picked up a card, calculating that his finances did not permit him (as he used to put it) 'to sacrifice the necessary in the hope of acquiring the superfluous'—and yet he would sit up all night at the card tables, trembling feverishly, as he followed the shifting fortunes of the play.

The story of the three cards played on his imagination and kept running through his head all night. 'What if,' he mused next evening, as he wandered about Petersburg, 'what if the old Countess were to reveal her secret to me? Or named the three winning cards to me? Why shouldn't I try my luck? . . . Get myself presented to her, work my way into her affections; become her lover even; but all that needs time and she's eighty-seven years old: she could die within the week, in two days! . . . And what about the story itself? . . . Is it credible? . . . No! Calculation, moderation, and hard work: those are my three winning cards, they are what will increase my capital three times over, seven times, and provide me with peace of mind and independence!' Reasoning in this fashion, he found himself on one of the main thoroughfares of Petersburg, in front of a house from a bygone architectural era. The street was thronged with carriages, rolling up in succession to the brightly lit entrance. Now the slender ankle of a young beauty would emerge from these carriages, now a clinking jack-boot, or a striped stocking and a diplomatic shoe. Fur coats and capes went flickering past a stately hall porter. Hermann came to a stop.

'Whose house is this?' he asked the watchman.

'Countess ***,' responded the watchman.

Hermann quivered. The amazing story once more rose in his imagination. He began pacing about near the house, thinking of its mistress and her miraculous ability. He came back late to his humble quarters; for long he was unable to drop off, and when sleep did overwhelm him, he dreamed of cards, a green table, heaps of banknotes, and piles of gold coins. He bet on card after card, resolutely doubling his stakes, and kept winning relentlessly, raking the gold towards him and pocketing the banknotes. Waking late, he sighed at losing his fabulous wealth, and set off once more to roam the streets of the city and once more found himself before the house of Countess ***. Some unknown force, it seemed, was drawing him towards it. He stopped and began gazing at the windows. In one, he glimpsed a head of dark hair, bent forward over a book, no doubt, or work of some sort. The head lifted and Hermann caught a glimpse of a fresh young face and dark eyes. That moment decided his fate.

III

Vous m'écrivez, mon ange, des lettres de quatre pages
plus vite que je ne puis les lire.

(A Correspondence)*

No sooner had Lizaveta Ivanovna managed to take off her hat
and coat than the Countess was sending for her and ordering the
carriage again. They went out to take their seats. As the footmen
were lifting up the old woman and passing her through the
doors, Lizaveta Ivanovna caught sight of her engineer right by
the wheel; he seized her arm and, before she could recover from
her fright, he was gone; a note had been left in her hand. She
hid it inside her glove and saw and heard nothing for the entire
journey. The Countess was in the habit of constantly asking
questions when they were in the carriage: who was that person
we passed? What's the name of this bridge? What does that sign
say? This time Lizaveta Ivanovna's responses were random and
irrelevant, incurring the wrath of the Countess.

'What's the matter with you, my girl! Are you in a daze or
something? Can't you hear what I'm saying, or don't you understand me? . . . Thank heaven I've still got my wits and don't
mumble my words!'

Lizaveta Ivanovna ignored her. When they got back home
she ran to her room and took the letter from her glove: it was
unsealed. Lizaveta Ivanovna read it through. The letter contained a confession of love; it was tender, respectful, and translated word for word from a German novel. Lizaveta Ivanovna
did not know German, however, and was very pleased with it.

Nevertheless, the letter troubled her greatly. It was the first
time she had entered into an intimate, clandestine relationship
with a young man. His boldness terrified her. She reproached
herself with her indiscreet behaviour and did not know what
to do: should she stop sitting by the window, and dampen the
young officer's inclination to pursue matters further by ignoring
him? Send his letter back? Answer coldly and firmly? She had

no one to discuss things with: she had neither girl-friend nor mentor. Lizaveta Ivanovna decided to reply.

She sat down at her little writing-table, took up pen and paper—and fell to pondering. She started on her letter several times, then tore it up: the phrases seemed too indulgent, or too heartless. Eventually, she managed to write a few lines that left her satisfied. 'I am sure', she wrote, 'that you have honourable intentions, and that you would not wish to insult me by an ill-considered action, but our acquaintance ought not to begin in this fashion. I am returning your letter and hope that I shall not have cause in the future to complain of an unmerited lack of respect.'

Next day, seeing Hermann walking below, Lizaveta Ivanovna got up from her embroidery-frame, went out into the hall, opened the fanlight, and threw the letter outside, relying on the adroitness of the young officer. Hermann ran up, retrieved the note, and went off into a confectionary shop. Tearing off the seal, he found his letter and Lizaveta Ivanovna's reply. It was no more than he expected, and he returned home much preoccupied with his scheming.

Three days later a pert young miss brought Lizaveta Ivanovna a note from the dress-shop. She opened it with apprehension, anticipating some request for payment, then all at once recognized Hermann's writing.

'You've made a mistake, dear', said she. 'This note is not for me.'

'No, it is really!' replied the audacious girl, not bothering to conceal a sly smile. 'Do read it!'

Lizaveta Ivanovna ran her eye over it. Hermann was asking for a rendezvous.

'Impossible,' said Lizaveta Ivanovna, alarmed both at the speed of the request and its method of delivery. 'Really, this is not for me.'

And tore the letter into small pieces.

'If the letter wasn't to you, why did you tear it up?' said the young miss. 'I would have given it back to the person who sent it.'

'If you please, miss,' said Lizaveta Ivanovna, flaring up at the remark, 'don't bring me notes in future. And tell the person who sent you that he should be ashamed . . .'

But Hermann persisted. Every day Lizaveta Ivanovna received letters from him by one means or another. By now they were no longer translated from the German. Hermann had written them, inspired by his passion, and spoke in his own character: they expressed both the inexorable nature of his desires and the turmoil of his unfettered imagination. Lizaveta Ivanovna thought no more of sending them back: she revelled in them, began to reply to them, and her notes became longer and more affectionate by the day. At length, she threw the following letter through the window:

'Tonight there is a ball at the X embassy. The Countess will be there. We will stay until about two. That will be your opportunity to see me alone. As soon as the Countess goes off, the servants will probably go their different ways; a hall porter will remain in the lobby, but he usually goes off to his cubicle. Come at half-past eleven. Walk straight up the stairs. If you find anyone in the lobby, just ask if the Countess is at home. They'll say no—and there's nothing for it, you'll have to go back. But you probably won't encounter anyone. The maids stay in their room, all together. From the lobby, walk left, then straight ahead till you reach the Countess's bedroom. In the bedroom, behind the screen, you will see two small doors: the one on the right is the study, where the Countess never goes, the left one leads into a corridor and the narrow spiral staircase there leads up to my room.'

Hermann was quivering like a tiger as he awaited the appointed time. At ten o'clock he was already standing before the Countess's house. The weather was dreadful: the wind howled and flakes of wet snow were falling; the street-lights glowed dim; the roads were deserted. Occasionally a cabbie ambled past with his scrawny nag, on the look-out for a late fare. Hermann stood there, clad only in a frock-coat, oblivious to both wind and snow. At long last the Countess's carriage drew up. Hermann watched as the hunched old woman, wrapped in sables, was carried out by flunkeys gripping either arm. Behind flitted her ward in a chilly cloak, her head adorned with fresh flowers. The coach doors slammed, and the carriage moved off ponderously through the damp snow. The hall porter closed the door. The windows darkened. Hermann began to walk nearer the deserted house; he went up to the street-lamp and glanced at his watch: it was twenty-past eleven. He remained under the lamp, staring at the hour hand, and waited out the remaining minutes. At exactly half-past eleven Hermann stepped on to the Countess's porch and went up into the brightly lit vestibule. The hall porter was not there. Hermann ran up the stairs, opened the door into the anteroom, and saw a servant asleep beneath a lamp, in a soiled antique armchair. With light, firm tread, Hermann went by him. The hall and drawing-room were dark but for the feeble lamplight from the anteroom. Hermann entered the bedroom. A golden icon-lamp was burning before a case of antique images. Faded brocade armchairs and sofas with worn gilding and down-filled cushions stood in sad symmetry around the Chinese-papered walls, on which hung two portraits painted in Paris by Madame Lebrun.* One of them depicted a man of about forty, stout and florid, wearing a light-green uniform and star; the other was a young beauty with an aquiline nose, hair combed back from the temples, and a rose in her powdered locks. Every corner was crammed with porcelain shepherdesses, table-clocks by the celebrated Leroy, little boxes, bandalores, fans, and sundry ladies' playthings invented, along with the Montgolfier balloon and Mesmer's magnetism,* at the end of the last century. Hermann went behind the screen. A small iron bed stood here; on the right was the door to the study; on the left, the second door, leading into the passage. Hermann opened it and saw the narrow, spiral staircase which led to the bedroom of the poor ward . . . But he turned back and went into the dark study.

Time passed slowly. All was quiet. The clock in the drawing-room struck twelve; through all the rooms, one after another, the clocks chimed twelve, then all fell silent again. Hermann stood, leaning against the cold stove. He felt calm; his heart beat steadily, like that of a man who had nerved himself to execute some hazardous but necessary enterprise. The clocks struck one, then two—and then he heard the distant rumble of a carriage. An involuntary excitement seized him. The carriage drew up to the house and halted. He heard the sound of a step being lowered. The house began to stir. People ran about, voices were raised, and lights came on. Three aged maids ran into the bedroom, and the Countess, utterly exhausted, entered and collapsed into a Voltaire armchair. Hermann peered through a crack in the door. Lizaveta Ivanovna came past him. Hermann heard her quick steps on the staircase. His heart responded with something like a pang of conscience, then subsided again. He froze.

The Countess began to undress in front of the mirror. Her rose-decked cap was unpinned; her powdered wig was removed from her grizzled, close-cropped head; pins rained down about her. The yellow dress with silver stitching fell to her swollen feet. Hermann witnessed the revolting secrets of her toilette. At length, the Countess was left in her bed-jacket and nightcap: in this garb, more suited to her age, she seemed less dreadful and hideous.

Like all old people, the Countess suffered from insomnia. After undressing, she sat down by the window in her Voltaire armchair and dismissed her maids. The candles were removed; once more the room was lit only by the icon-lamp. The Countess was a study in yellow, mumbling her drooping lips and rocking from side to side. Her dull eyes registered a complete absence of thought. Looking at her, one might have imagined that the fearful old woman's rocking was not something willed, but prompted by some concealed galvanic current.

All at once that dead face changed unutterably. The lips ceased moving, the eyes became animated: before the Countess stood a strange man.

'Don't be afraid, for heaven's sake, don't be afraid!' he said in a low, distinct voice. 'I have no intention of doing you harm; I have come to beg a certain favour of you.'

The old woman looked silently at him, seeming not to have heard. Hermann assumed she was deaf and, bending right down to her ear, repeated his words. The old woman remained mute.

'You can bring about my life's happiness,' Hermann went on, 'without it costing you anything: I know that you can predict three cards in a row . . .'

Hermann stopped. The Countess, it seemed, had realized what he was asking. She appeared to be searching for a reply.

'That was a joke,' she finally brought out: 'I swear to you it was a joke!'

'That was no joking matter,' Hermann protested angrily. 'Remember Chaplitsky, whom you helped to recoup his losses?'

The Countess was evidently disconcerted. Her features registered considerable inward tumult; but she presently lapsed into her former apathy.

'Can you', Hermann pursued, 'name the three infallible cards for me?'

The Countess said nothing. Hermann continued:

'Who are you keeping your secret for? Your grandsons? They are rich as it is; they don't even know the value of money. Your cards won't help a prodigal. A man who can't hold on to his patrimony will end up a pauper whatever happens, no matter what demonic efforts he puts in. I am no spendthrift; I know the value of money. Your three cards won't be wasted on me. Well? . . .'

He stopped and trembled in anticipation of her reply. She said nothing. Hermann knelt before her.

'If your heart has ever known the emotion of love, if you can remember its raptures, if you smiled just once at the cry of a new-born son, if anything human ever throbbed within your breast, I beseech you by the feelings of wife, lover, mother, everything that is sacred in life, do not refuse what I ask! Reveal your secret to me! What do you want with it? . . . Perhaps it is linked to some dreadful sin, the loss of eternal bliss, a pact with the devil . . . Think now, you are old; you have little time to live. I am willing to take your sin on my soul. Just reveal your secret to me. Think, a man's happiness is in your hands; that not only I, but my children, grandsons, and their sons will bless and venerate your memory . . .'

The old woman said not a word in reply.

Hermann rose.

'Old witch!' he said gritting his teeth. 'Then I'll make you answer . . .'

Whereupon he drew a pistol from his pocket. At the sight of it the Countess for a second time betrayed signs of powerful emotion. She began shaking her head and raised her hand, as if shielding herself from the shot . . . then she rolled onto her back . . . and remained motionless.

'Stop being childish,' said Hermann, taking her hand. 'I'm

asking you for the last time: do you want to name me your three cards? Yes, or no?'

The Countess did not answer. Hermann saw that she had died.

IV

7 Mai 18**
Homme sans mœurs et sans religion!
(A correspondence)*

Lizaveta Ivanovna sat in her room, still in her ballroom finery, absorbed in deep reflection. On returning home, she had hastily dismissed the sleepy maid who had reluctantly offered her services, saying that she would undress herself; she went trembling to her room, hoping to find Hermann there and wishing not to. A glance assured her of his absence and she blessed providence for the obstacle which had thwarted their rendezvous. She sat down without undressing and began reviewing all the circumstances which had led her so far in so short a time. It had not been three weeks since she had first seen the young man through the window and she was already corresponding with him—and he had succeeded in obtaining a nocturnal assignation with her! She knew his name only because some of his letters had been signed; she had never spoken to him, never heard his voice, never heard of him indeed . . . until that evening. How strange! That very evening, at the ball, Tomsky had been annoyed at young Princess Polina's uncharacteristic flirting with another, and so put on a show of indifference, hoping to exact revenge: he had invited Lizaveta Ivanovna and danced an endless mazurka with her. He continually teased her about her penchant for engineer officers, assuring her that he knew much more than she might suppose, and some of his witticisms were so close to the mark that Lizaveta Ivanovna thought several times that he was privy to her secret.

'Who told you all this?' she asked, laughing.

'The friend of a person known to you,' replied Tomsky. 'A really capital fellow!'

'And just who is this capital fellow?'

'His name is Hermann.'

Lizaveta Ivanovna made no reply, but her hands and feet turned to ice.

'This Hermann', Tomsky went on, 'is a genuinely romantic personality. He has the profile of Napoleon and the soul of Mephistopheles. I think he has at least three crimes on his conscience. How pale you've turned! . . .'

'I've got a headache . . . What on earth did he say to you, this Hermann . . . or whatever his name is?'

'Hermann is not at all happy with his friend: he says that in his shoes he would have acted quite otherwise . . . I really do think Hermann has his eye on you himself; at any rate, he can't abide his friend's amorous sighs.'

'But where can he have seen me?'

'In church, perhaps, or out walking! . . . Lord alone knows! Perhaps in your room while you were asleep: I wouldn't put it past him . . .'

Three ladies who came up to ask: '*oubli ou regret?*'* interrupted a conversation, which had become agonizingly intriguing for Lizaveta Ivanovna.

The lady Tomsky chose was the very same Princess Polina. She had time to explain her conduct as they danced an extra circuit, making an extra spin in front of her chair. Returning to his place, Tomsky no longer had thoughts of Hermann or Lizaveta Ivanovna. The latter was anxious to resume the disrupted conversation, but the mazurka was over and presently the old Countess took her departure.

Tomsky's words had been nothing more than ballroom banter, but they sank deep into the soul of the young dreamer. The portrait sketched by Tomsky corresponded to the image she herself had formed, and, thanks to the latest novels, this now-hackneyed figure both dismayed and captivated her imagination. She sat, bare arms crossed, as her head, still decked out with flowers, drooped towards her uncovered breast . . . Suddenly the door opened and Hermann came in. She began to tremble . . .

'Where on earth have you been?' she asked in a frightened whisper.

'In the bedroom, with the old Countess,' replied Hermann: 'I've just come from there. The Countess is dead.'

'Heavens! . . . What did you say? . . .'

'And, apparently,' Hermann went on, 'I am the cause of her death.'

Lizaveta Ivanovna shot a glance at him, and Tomsky's words resounded in her heart: *he has at least three crimes on his conscience!* Hermann sat down on the window-sill near her and told her everything.

Lizaveta Ivanovna heard him out with horror. So, those passionate letters, the ardent demands, the audacious, persistent pursuit—all that had not been love! Money! That was what his soul craved! It was not she who could assuage his desires and render him happy! The poor ward had been nothing more than an unwitting accomplice to a bandit, the murderer of her old benefactress . . . She began crying bitterly in an agony of belated remorse. Hermann gazed at her in silence: his heart was also tormented, but neither the tears of the poor girl nor the astonishing charm of her grief touched his grim soul. He did not feel any gnawings of conscience at the thought of the old woman's death. One thing dismayed him: the irretrievable loss of the secret from which he had anticipated enrichment.

'You are a monster!' said Lizaveta Ivanovna at last.

'I did not intend her death,' replied Hermann. 'My pistol is not loaded.'

They fell silent.

Morning was approaching. Lizaveta Ivanovna snuffed out the guttering candle. A pale light suffused her room. She wiped her tearful eyes and raised them to Hermann: he was sitting on the sill, arms folded, grimly frowning. In this pose, he bore an amazing resemblance to a portrait of Napoleon. The likeness struck even Lizaveta Ivanovna.

'How are you going to leave the house?' she said at length. 'I was going to take you down the secret staircase, but that would mean going past the bedroom and I'm frightened.'

'Tell me how to find this hidden staircase and I'll go myself.'

Lizaveta Ivanovna got up and retrieved a key from the chest of drawers, handed it to Hermann, and gave him detailed instructions. Hermann pressed her cold, unresponsive hand, kissed her bowed head, and left.

He went down the spiral staircase and again entered the Countess's bedroom. The dead old woman sat there stonily; her face bore an expression of profound serenity. Hermann halted before her, staring long at her, as if wishing to assure himself of the awful truth. Finally he went into the study, feeling for a door behind the wall-hanging, and began to descend a dark staircase, a prey to strange emotions. 'Perhaps up this very staircase,' he thought, 'sixty years or so ago, into that same bedroom, at the same hour, in his embroidered coat, coiffeured *à l'oiseau royale** and clutching his tricorn hat to his heart, there stole some fortunate young man, now long mouldering in the grave; and to-night the heart of his aged mistress has ceased to beat . . .'

At the bottom of the staircase Hermann discovered a door, opened it with the same key, and found himself in a corridor leading him out into the street.

V

That night the late Baroness von V*** appeared to me.
She was all in white and said to me: 'Good evening,
Mister Councillor!'

(Swedenborg)*

Three days after the fateful night, at nine in the morning,
Hermann set out for the monastery where the funeral service for
the late Countess was to be held. He felt no remorse, yet was
unable to stifle the voice of conscience altogether when it kept
telling him: 'You are the murderer of the old woman!' Though
he possessed little genuine faith, he was a prey to superstition.
He believed that the dead Countess might exercise a pernicious
influence on his life, and had nerved himself to attend her
funeral and beg her forgiveness.

The church was full. Hermann had to force his way through
the crowds of people. The coffin stood on an opulent catafalque
under a velvet canopy. The deceased lay in it, arms crossed
on her breast, wearing a lace cap and a white satin dress. Her
servants stood around and about, holding candles and wearing
black caftans with armorial bearings on their shoulders; the relations wore deep mourning—her children, grandchildren, and
great-grandchildren. No one wept: tears would have been *une
affectation*. The Countess had been so old that her death could
not have been a shock to anyone, and her relatives had long considered her as having outlived her time. A young bishop spoke
the funeral oration. In simple and moving phrases he pictured
the peaceful passing of a righteous woman, for whom the long
years had been a quiet, touching preparation for a Christian end.
'The angel of death found her,' said the orator, 'vigilant in pious
thoughts and in expectation of the midnight bridegroom.'* The
service concluded with mournful formality. The relatives were
the first to go up and take leave of the body. Then came the turn
of the innumerable guests who had come to pay their respects to
one who had for so long been a participant in their frivolous
amusements. After them came all the domestics. Finally an old

housekeeper, the same age as the deceased, approached, supported by two young girls. She was unable to bow to the ground, and she was the only one to shed a few tears as she kissed the cold hand of her mistress. After that, Hermann resolved to approach the coffin. He bowed to the ground and lay for several moments on the cold floor, strewn with fir-twigs. At length he rose, pale as the corpse itself, ascended the steps of the catafalque, and bent down . . . At that moment it seemed to him that the deceased gave him a mocking glance and winked an eye. Hermann, in hastily recoiling, missed his footing and crashed face upwards to the ground. He was helped to his feet. At that same moment Lizaveta Ivanovna was carried out on to the porch in a faint. This episode disturbed the solemnity of the sombre ritual for some minutes. A subdued murmuring started up among the congregation, and a gaunt chamberlain, a close relative of the deceased, whispered in the ear of an Englishman standing close by that the young officer was her illegitimate son, to which the Englishman responded stiffly: 'Oh?'

All that day Hermann was deeply distraught. He had dined at an out-of-the-way inn and uncharacteristically drunk a great deal in the hope of stilling his inner turmoil. The wine, however, stimulated his imagination even more. On getting back home, he hurled himself fully dressed on to the bed and fell soundly asleep.

It was night when he awoke: moonlight flooded his room. He glanced at his watch; it was quarter to three. Sleep having deserted him, he sat on the bed thinking over the old Countess's funeral.

Just then, someone outside glanced at him through the window, and went away at once. Hermann paid no attention. A moment later he heard the door of the outer room being opened. Hermann thought it must be his orderly, drunk as was his habit, returning from a nocturnal outing. But then he heard an unfamiliar step: someone was quietly scuffling their shoes as they walked. The door opened: a woman in a white dress came in. Hermann took her for his old nurse and wondered what could have brought her here at this hour. But the white woman glided right up to him—and Hermann recognized the Countess!

'I have come to you against my will', she said in a steady

voice. 'But I am commanded to gratify your request. The three, the seven, and the ace will win for you in sequence, but with this condition, that you bet on no more than one card each day, and that you gamble no more for the rest of your life. I forgive you my death, on condition that you marry my ward, Lizaveta Ivanovna . . .'

With this, she quietly turned, proceeded to the door, and, with a scuffle of shoes, disappeared from view. Hermann heard the door slam out in the passage and glimpsed someone looking in at him again through the window.

Hermann could not recover himself for a long time. He went out into the other room. His orderly was asleep on the floor; Hermann forced him awake. The orderly was drunk, as usual; there was no getting anything sensible out of him. The door in the passage was locked. Hermann returned to his room, lit a candle, and wrote down what he had seen.

VI

'*Attendez!*'

'How dare you say "*attendez*" to me?'

'Your excellency, I said "*attendez*", sir!'*

Two fixed ideas cannot coexist in the moral sphere, just as two bodies cannot occupy the same space in the physical world. The three, the seven, and the ace soon blotted out the image of the dead Countess from Hermann's imagination. Three, seven, ace never quitted his head, and constantly moved on his lips. If he caught sight of a young girl, he would say: 'Isn't she slender, just like a three of hearts.' If he was asked the time, he would reply: 'five minutes to the seven.' Any pot-bellied gentleman reminded him of an ace. The three, seven, and ace haunted him in dreams, assuming every sort of guise; the three blossomed before him in the shape of a sumptuous grandiflora, the seven took the form of a Gothic gateway, the ace became a giant spider. All his thoughts merged into one—to make use of the secret which had cost him so dear. He began thinking of retirement and travel. In the public casinos of Paris he intended to wrest the treasure from enchanted fate. Chance relieved him of the trouble.

In Moscow, a society of rich gamblers had assembled under the presidency of the famed Chekalinsky, who had spent a lifetime at the card-table and had made millions in his time, winning promissory notes and paying his losses in hard cash. This long experience had earned him the trust of his fellows, and his open house, celebrated chef, his courtesy and affability had won him the respect of the public at large. He had now arrived in Petersburg, and the young men flocked to him, forsaking the ballroom for the card-table, preferring the lure of faro to the fascinations of gallantry. Narumov brought Hermann to see him.

They passed through a series of splendid rooms, crowded with people and well supplied with attentive waiters. A number of generals and privy councillors were playing whist; the young men sat lounging on brocade sofas, eating ice-cream and smoking pipes. In the drawing-room, some twenty gamblers jostled round a long table, where sat the host, who was holding the bank. He was a most respectable-looking man of about sixty; he had a silvery-grey head of hair; his plump, fresh face was a picture of good nature; his eyes shone, animated by a perpetual smile. Narumov introduced Hermann to him. Chekalinsky cordially shook his hand, begged him to make himself at home, and carried on dealing.

Play had been going on a good while and more than thirty cards lay on the table. Chekalinsky would pause after every round to give the players time to make their arrangements, meanwhile noting down their losses, listening politely to their requests, and even more politely straightening the odd corner bent by a distracted hand. At length the round concluded. Chekalinsky shuffled the cards and prepared to deal another.

'Permit me to place a stake,' said Hermann, stretching out an arm from behind a stout gentleman gamester.

Chekalinsky smiled and silently bowed, indicating an accommodating assent. Narumov laughingly congratulated Hermann on breaking his long-maintained abstention and wished him beginner's luck.

'I'm on,' said Hermann, chalking up his large stake above the card.

'How much, sir?' asked the banker, straining his eyes. 'Do excuse me, sir, I can't make it out.'

'Forty-seven thousand,' replied Hermann.

At these words, every head turned instantly and all eyes were fixed on Hermann. 'He's out of his mind!' thought Narumov.

'Permit me to point out', said Chekalinsky with his invariable smile, 'that you are playing for high stakes: no one here has ever staked more than two hundred and seventy-five on a single card.'

'What of it?' countered Hermann. 'Can you beat my card or not?'

Chekalinsky bowed, his air of humble compliance unchanged.

'I merely wished to bring to your attention', he said, 'that, in view of the trust reposed in me by my fellows, I cannot deal otherwise than for ready cash. For my own part, of course, I am confident that your word suffices, but for the conduct of the game and the accounts, I must ask you to place your money on the card.'

Hermann extracted a banknote from his pocket and handed it to Chekalinsky who, after a swift glance, placed it on Hermann's card.

He began to deal. On the right a nine turned up, on the left a three.

'The three wins!' said Hermann, showing his card.

A whispering arose among the punters. Chekalinsky frowned; his smile, however, instantly returned to his face.

'Would you like your money now?' he asked Hermann.

'By all means.'

Chekalinsky took out a number of banknotes and settled on the spot. Hermann took his money and left the table. Narumov was utterly shaken. Hermann drank a glass of lemonade and set off homewards.

On the following evening he again appeared at Chekalinsky's. The host was dealing. Hermann approached the table; the gamesters at once made way for him. Chekalinsky bowed to him courteously.

Hermann waited for the next round, and placed his card with his forty-seven thousand and the previous day's winnings upon it.

Chekalinsky began dealing. A jack fell to the right, a seven to the left.

Hermann uncovered his seven.

Everyone gasped. Chekalinsky was visibly disconcerted. He counted out ninety-four thousand and passed it to Hermann, who accepted it phlegmatically and departed at once.

The next evening Hermann was once more at the table. Everyone was expecting him; the generals and the privy councillors abandoned their whist to watch this extraordinary play. The young officers leapt from their sofas and all the waiters gathered in the drawing-room. Everyone surrounded Hermann. The other punters placed no bets as they waited impatiently for what would befall. Hermann stood by the table, ready to gamble against Chekalinsky, who was pale but still smiling. Each broke the seal on a pack of cards. Chekalinsky shuffled. Hermann drew and placed his card, covering it with a heap of banknotes. It was like a duel. A profound silence reigned.

Chekalinsky's hands shook as he started to deal. On the right lay a queen, on the left an ace.

'My ace wins,' said Hermann, disclosing his card.

'Your queen loses', said Chekalinsky gently.

Hermann gave a start: instead of an ace, the queen of spades was indeed lying there. He could not believe his eyes, unable to comprehend how he could have drawn the wrong card.

Just then it seemed to him that the queen of spades winked at him and grinned. The extraordinary likeness stunned him . . .

'The old woman!' he cried out in horror.

Chekalinsky drew the lost banknotes towards him as Hermann stood there motionless. When he moved away from the table, a hubbub commenced. 'Magnificent play', the gamblers were saying. Chekalinsky shuffled the cards again; the game resumed its course.

CONCLUSION

Hermann went out of his mind. He is in Room 17 at the Obukhov Hospital,* unresponsive to any questioning, merely muttering with extraordinary rapidity: 'The three, the seven and the ace! The three, the seven and the queen! . . .'

Lizaveta Ivanovna married a very pleasant young man; he is in the service somewhere and is possessed of a decent fortune: he is the son of the old Countess's former steward. Lizaveta Ivanovna is bringing up a poor relation.

Tomsky has been promoted to captain and is going to marry Princess Polina.

THE CAPTAIN'S DAUGHTER*

Cherish your honour from a tender age.

(Proverb)*

1

A SERGEANT OF THE GUARDS

'He'd be a captain in the Guards straight off.'
'No need for that; let him see service in the line.'
'Why, that's well said! Hard work will suit him fine.'

. . . .

'But who's his father?'

(Knyazhnin)*

My father, Andrei Petrovich Grinyov, served in his youth under Count Minikh* and retired with the rank of sergeant-major in 17—. From then on, he lived in his Simbirsk village, where he married the spinster Avdotya Vasilyevna Yu***, the daughter of an impoverished local nobleman. There were nine of us children. All my brothers and sisters died in infancy.

Mama was still pregnant with me when I was entered as a sergeant in the Semyonovsky regiment,* through the good offices of Guards Major Prince B., our close relative. If, against expectations, mama had produced a girl, then papa would have notified the proper authorities of the death of the non-reporting sergeant, and that would have been the end of the matter. I was considered to be on leave until the completion of my studies. In those days schooling was different from what it is today. After the age of five, I was entrusted to Savelich, the groom, appointed as my guardian in recognition of his sober conduct. Under his supervision I could read and write in Russian by the time I was twelve and had a very good eye for the finer points of a hound. At this point, papa hired a Frenchman for me, a Monsieur Beaupré,* who had been ordered from Moscow along with our year's supply of wine and olive oil. Savelich took his arrival very badly. 'Praise be,' he grumbled to himself, 'the child is washed, combed and fed. What's the point of laying out needless money on hiring a monsieur, as if they had nobody of their own!'

Beaupré had been a hairdresser in his homeland, then a

soldier in Prussia before arriving in Russia *pour être outchitel,**
without altogether understanding the meaning of that word. He
was a good sort, but light-minded and dissipated to a degree.
His chief failing was a passion for the fair sex; not infrequently
his advances would be rewarded by blows which set him sighing
and complaining for days on end. In addition, he was, to use his
own expression, *no enemy of the bottle*, which meant, translated
into Russian, he was fond of a drop too much. But since we
served wine only at dinner, and then only by the glass, and
usually missing out the teacher, my Beaupré very quickly accustomed himself to Russian home-brew, and came to prefer it to
the wines of his homeland, as an incomparably better specific
for the stomach. We at once arranged matters between us, and
although his contract specified that he was to teach me French,
German, and all other subjects, he preferred learning from me
how to get by in Russian—and after that we each went about
our own affairs. We lived in perfect amity. I wished, indeed, for
no other mentor. Fate, however, was soon to part us, in the
following fashion:

The laundry-maid Palashka, a fat, pock-marked wench, and
the one-eyed dairymaid Akulka somehow agreed between them
one fine day to throw themselves at mother's feet, confessing
their culpable weakness and tearfully complaining about Monsieur, who had taken advantage of their innocence. My mother
did not take such things lightly and complained to father. His
justice was summary. He at once sent for the rascally Frenchman. He was informed that Monsieur was giving me my lesson.
Father came to my room. Meanwhile Beaupré was sleeping the
sleep of the just on my bed. I was busy on a project of my own.
I should mention that a map had been ordered for me from
Moscow. It hung on the wall, unused, and had long tempted me
with its breadth of good-quality paper. I had resolved to make a
kite out of it, and taking advantage of Beaupré's slumbers, set
to work. Father entered at that moment, just as I was sticking
a bast tail on to the Cape of Good Hope. Observing my geo-
graphical exercises, father pulled me sharply by the ear, then ran
across to Beaupré, woke him none too gently, and began heaping
reproaches upon him. Flustered, Beaupré tried to stand up, but
was unable to do so: the wretched Frenchman was dead drunk.

As well be hanged for a sheep as a lamb. Father picked him up from the bed by his collar, thrust him out of the door, and got rid of him that very day, to the indescribable joy of Savelich. So ended my education.

I lived the life of a growing boy, chasing pigeons and playing leapfrog with the house-boys. Meanwhile I turned sixteen, and it was at this point that things changed.

One autumn day mother was making honey preserves in the sitting-room, and I was licking my lips as I stared at the seething froth. Father was by the window reading the *Court Calendar*,* which he received every year. This book always affected him considerably: he could never read it through without becoming exceptionally involved, and perusing it would always stir his ire to a quite astonishing degree. Mother, who knew all his ways and habits by heart, was forever trying to stow the wretched book as far out of sight as possible, so that sometimes it didn't catch his eye for months on end. On the other hand, when he did chance to come across it he wouldn't put it down for hours. So, father was reading the *Court Calendar*, occasionally shrugging and repeating under his breath 'Lieutenant-general! . . . He was a sergeant in my company! . . . Chevalier of both Russian orders! . . . Was it so long ago that we . . .' Eventually, father threw the *Calendar* on to the couch and became plunged in thought, which presaged nothing good.

All at once, he turned to mama: 'Avdotya Vasilyevna, how old is Petrusha, by the way?'

'He's turned sixteen,' replied mama. 'Petrusha was born the same year Nastasya Gerasimovna lost her eye, and when . . .'

'Fine,' father broke in. 'High time he was in the army. Enough of him running around the maids' quarters and climbing into the dovecotes.'

The thought of an imminent parting from me so affected mama that she dropped her spoon into the pan and tears began coursing down her face. By contrast, it would be difficult to describe my elation. The thought of army life was linked in my mind with notions of freedom and the pleasures of Petersburg. I pictured myself as a Guards officer, which was in my opinion the summit of human happiness.

Father did not like either changing his plans or delaying their

execution. The day of my departure was fixed. The evening before, father announced that he was going to send a letter with me
to my future commanding officer, and asked for pen and paper.

'Don't forget, Andrey Petrovich,' said mama, 'to send greetings to Prince B. from me as well; tell him I hope he will
continue to show favour to our Petrusha.'

'What nonsense you do talk!' replied father, frowning. 'What
would be the point of writing to Prince B.?'

'But didn't you say you'd be writing to Petrusha's commanding officer?'

'Well, what of it?'

'But Petrusha's commanding officer is Prince B. Petrusha's
name is down for the Semyonovsky regiment, isn't it?'

'Name down! What do I care if his name's down? Petrusha
won't be going to Petersburg. What's he going to learn if he
serves in Petersburg? How to throw money away and be a rake.
No, let him serve in the army, go through the mill, get a whiff
of gunpowder, then he'll be a soldier, not a fop. Name down for
the Guards! Where's his identity card? Fetch it here.'

Mama looked for my card, kept in a box along with my
christening shirt, and passed it over to father with a trembling
hand. Father read it closely, placed it before him on the desk,
and began his letter.

I was in an agony of curiosity: where on earth were they
sending me, if it was not to be Petersburg? My eyes were glued
to my father's pen, which was moving rather slowly. Eventually
he concluded, sealed it in a packet along with my card, took off
his spectacles, and called me over: 'This is a letter for you to
take to Andrey Karlovich R., my old friend and comrade. You
are going to Orenburg* to serve under his command.'

And so, all my brilliant hopes were dashed! Instead of the
gay Petersburg life, it was boredom that awaited me in some
far-flung backwater. Army service, which I had been looking
forward to with such raptures a moment before, now seemed
a grim misfortune. But there was no arguing! Next morning a
travelling-carriage was brought round to the porch; in it were
loaded my trunk and a hamper with a tea service, along with
bundles containing rolls and pies, the last tokens of a pampered
home existence. My parents blessed me. Father said: 'Goodbye,

Pyotr. Serve faithfully the one to whom you swear allegiance; obey your superiors; don't curry favour; don't volunteer for duty;* don't wriggle out of it; and remember the saying: take care of your clothes when they're new, but your honour from a tender age.' Mama tearfully exhorted me to take care of myself, and Savelich to look after her child. They wrapped me in a hare-lined jacket, with a fox-fur overcoat on top. I got into the cart with Savelich and set off along the road in floods of tears.

That same night I arrived in Simbirsk,* where I was supposed to spend a whole day buying in various necessary items, this being entrusted to Savelich. I stayed at an inn. Savelich set off round the shops in the morning. Tired of staring out of the window into a muddy alley, I went roaming round all the rooms of the inn. I entered the billiard saloon, where I saw a tall gentleman of about thirty-five, with long moustaches; he was wearing a dressing-gown and held a cue in his hand and a pipe between his teeth. He was playing against the marker, who sank a tot of vodka when he won, but had to crawl under the table when he lost. I began watching the game. The longer it went on, the more frequent became the crawling trips under the table, until finally the marker stayed under there. The gentleman pronounced a few choice expressions over him by way of a funeral service and offered to give me a game. I declined, not knowing how to play. This he evidently found strange. He looked almost pityingly at me; however, we got on talking. I learned that his name was Ivan Ivanovich Zurin, a captain of hussars who was recruiting in Simbirsk and staying at the inn. He proposed that we should dine together, taking pot luck, soldier-fashion. I readily agreed. We sat down to table. Zurin drank a great deal and regaled me too, saying I ought to get used to service life; he told me army stories that had me practically falling about with laughter, and we had became bosom pals by the time we got up from our seats. At this point he volunteered to teach me how to play billiards.

'It is', he said, 'an essential part of this man's army. On campaign, for example, you get to a township—what is there to do, I ask you? You can't be beating up the Jew-boys all the time. You end up at an inn, like it or not, and you get on playing billiards; and for that you have to know how to play!'

I was entirely persuaded, and began my course of instruction with great assiduity. Zurin was loud in his encouragement, marvelling at my speedy progress, and after several lessons, offered to play me for money, half-a-kopek a time, just so as not to play for no stakes at all—a most miserable way of going on, as he put it. I fell in with this also. Zurin ordered punch and talked me into trying it, repeating that I had to get used to army life, and what was army life without punch! I did what I was told. Meanwhile the game went on. The more I sipped at my glass, the bolder I became. The balls kept flying off the table; in my excitement I cursed the marker, who was keeping score, God alone knows how, and I kept putting up the stakes; in a nutshell, I behaved like some young whelp getting his first taste of liberty. Zurin glanced at his watch, laid down his cue, and announced that I had lost a hundred roubles. This embarrassed me somewhat. Savelich had my money. I started apologizing. Zurin cut me short: 'For goodness sake! Don't let that worry you. I can wait. And now let's be off to Arinushka's.'

What can I say? I ended the day in as dissipated a fashion as I had begun it. We had supper at Arinushka's. Zurin kept on filling my glass, repeating that I had to get used to army ways. When I got up from the table, I could hardly stand; Zurin drove me back to the inn at midnight.

Savelich met us on the porch. He sighed, seeing the unmistakeable signs of my zeal for army ways. 'What's happened to you, sir?' said he in a voice of woe. 'Where did you get as fuddled as that? Oh dear, oh lord! You've never done anything as bad as this in your life!'

'Shut up, you old grouch!' I stammered out. 'You're most likely drunk, get to bed . . . and put me to bed.'

Next morning I woke with a headache and only a dim recollection of the precious night's events. My reflections were interrupted by Savelich coming in with a cup of tea.

'Started early, Pyotr Andreich', he said, wagging his head. 'Soon started living it up. Who do you take after? I don't think your father or grandfather were drunkards; not to mention your dear mother: she's never touched anything but kvass since she was born. And who's to blame for it all? That blasted Monsieur. He was for ever running off to Antipovna: "Madam, je vous prie vodkoo." This is what comes of je vous prie! To be sure, he taught you some fine tricks, the son of a dog. Why did they have to hire a heathen as your tutor, as if the master didn't have enough of his own people!'

I felt ashamed of myself. I turned away and said: 'Go away, Savelich; I don't want any tea.' But it was hard to stop Savelich once he got started sermonizing. 'Now you see, Pyotr Andreich, what you get for drinking. A thick head and no appetite. A boozer is no good for anything . . . Drink off some pickle brine with honey, or best of all for a hangover is half a glass of home-brew. What do you say?'

At that moment a boy came in and gave me a note from Zurin. I unfolded it to read the following lines:

'Dear Pyotr Andreich, kindly send to me via the boy the hundred roubles you lost to me yesterday. I am in dire need of cash.

Ever at your service
Ivan Zurin.'

There was nothing for it. I assumed an indifferent expression and, turning to Savelich, who was 'zealous guardian of my money, clothing, and affairs', ordered him to give the boy a hundred roubles.

'What? Why?' asked the flabbergasted Savelich. 'I owe it,' I replied as stiffly as I could manage.

'Owe it!' protested Savelich, with mounting astonishment. 'But when, sir, did you manage to get into debt to him? There's something funny about that. Say what you will, sir, but I shan't give up the money.'

I thought that if at this decisive moment I did not get the better of the mulish old man, then later on it would be difficult for me to break free of his tutelage. With a haughty stare, I said: 'I am your master and you are my servant. The money is mine. I lost it in play because such was my pleasure. I felt like it. I advise you not to try to be clever and just do what you're told.'

Savelich was so taken aback by my words that he threw up his hands and froze on the spot. 'What are you standing there for?' I cried angrily. Savelich began to weep. 'Master Pyotr Andreich', he quavered. 'Don't break my heart. Light of my eyes! Listen to me, an old man: write to this brigand and tell him it was all in fun, that we haven't got that kind of money. A hundred roubles! Mercy on us! Say that your parents told you ever so sternly that you musn't gamble, except for nuts . . .'

'Enough of this nonsense', I broke in harshly. 'Bring the money or I'll throw you out by the scruff of the neck.'

Savelich stared at me with profound sorrow and went to fetch what I owed. I was sorry for the old man, but I wanted to break free and show I was no longer a child. The money was delivered to Zurin. Savelich hastened to get me out of that accursed inn. He appeared with the news that the horses were ready. With an uneasy conscience and silent remorse, I rode out of Simbirsk without saying goodbye to Zurin, or thinking I would ever see him again.

2

THE GUIDE*

> O land of mine, dear land,
> Land unknown!
> 'Twas not my will that I came here,
> My good horse did not bring me:
> What brought me, a bold young lad,
> Was youthful zest and vigour
> And tavern drinking bouts.
>
> (Old Song)*

My reflections as I travelled along were not particularly pleasant. My losses, by the standards of the time, were by no means insignificant. I could not help acknowledging in my heart that my conduct in the Simbirsk inn had been foolish, and I felt guilty towards Savelich. All these things were making me feel miserable. The old man was sitting glumly on the coach box, body averted, silent except for the occasional wheezing sigh. I wanted to make my peace with him without delay, but didn't know how to begin. At length I said:

'Come now, Savelich! Enough of this, let's make it up, I'm sorry; I can see myself that it was my fault. I misbehaved yesterday and I was wrong to offend you. I promise to be more sensible from now on and pay heed. Come, don't be angry; let's make it up.'

'Oh, master, Pyotr Andreich!' he replied with a heavy sigh. 'It's myself I'm angry with; it's me to blame all round. What was I thinking of, leaving you all by yourself in the inn! What can I say? My sins found me out: I thought to drop in on the sexton's wife, just to see my old friend. There you are: drop in on a friend and you're sat there for ever. Now I'm in trouble. What are the masters going to think of me? What are they going to say when they hear that their child is drinking and gambling?'

So as to comfort poor Savelich, I gave him my word not to lay out a kopek henceforth without his permission. He calmed down,

little by little, although he still wagged his head from time to
time, growling to himself: 'Hundred roubles! No laughing matter!'

I was nearing my appointed destination. All around stretched
a dismal wasteland, intersected by hills and gullies. Snow lay
everywhere. The sun was setting. The wagon was travelling
along a narrow road, or to be more accurate, a track made by
peasant sledges. Suddenly the driver started looking off to one
side and eventually doffed his cap and turned to me: 'Sir, wouldn't
you like to turn back?'

'What for?'

'The weather's tricky: the wind's getting up a bit; see it swirling the snow.'

'Well, fancy that!'

'But do you see that over there?' He pointed to the east with
his whip.

'I don't see anything, just the white steppe and a clear sky.'

'No, there, there: that cloud.'

I did indeed see a small white cloud on the horizon, which I
had taken at first for a distant hill. The driver explained to me
that the cloud presaged a blizzard.*

I had heard of the snowstorms hereabouts, that whole cara-
vans could be buried. Savelich shared the driver's view that we
should turn back. But the wind did not seem strong to me; I
trusted we could reach the next post-station in time and ordered
the driver to get a move on.

He got the horses galloping, but with a weather eye to the
east. The horses ran with a will. The wind increased in strength
as time went by. The cloud turned into a white cumulus which
rose up heavily and gradually extended across the sky. A pow-
dery snow began to fall, then suddenly started coming down in
flakes. The wind rose to a howl; the snowstorm was upon us. In
an instant the dark sky had merged with the sea of snow. The
world disappeared.

'Well, master,' yelled the driver, 'we're in trouble: it's a
blizzard!'

I peered out of the wagon: nothing but murk and swirling
snow. The wind howled with an intense ferocity that made it
seem alive; snow covered me and Savelich; the horses were
down to walking pace, and soon stopped altogether.

'Why have you stopped then?' I asked the driver.

'Why go on?' he responded, climbing down off his box. 'We don't know where we've got to as it is: there's no road and nothing but black all round.'

I began to upbraid him, but Savelich was on his side.

'That's what you get for not listening to him', he said angrily. 'We could have turned back to the coach-inn and filled up with tea and slept there till morning. The storm would have died down, and we could have gone on. And what's all the hurry? You'd think we were off to a wedding!'

Savelich was right. There was nothing we could do. The snow was coming down thick and fast, forming a drift by the wagon. The horses stood there, heads down, occasionally shuddering. The driver walked about adjusting the harness for something to do. Savelich went on grumbling, while I stared about in all directions, in hopes of glimpsing some sign of habitation or a track to follow, but I could make nothing out at all beyond the dense whirling of the storm . . . Suddenly I caught sight of something black. 'Hey, driver!' I shouted. 'Look there, what's that black thing?' The driver began peering. 'The lord only knows, sir,' said he, getting back into his seat. 'A cart, maybe, or a tree, but it looks to be moving. Must be either a wolf or a man.'

I ordered him to make for the unknown object, which immediately began to move towards us. We got up to him in two minutes. 'Hey, good man!' the driver shouted to him. 'D' you happen to know where the road is?'

'The road is here. I'm standing on the hard surface,' responded the traveller. 'What of it?'

'Listen, my good fellow,' I said to him, 'do you know the country hereabouts? Could you guide me to a night's lodging?'

'I know the country hereabouts,' replied the traveller. 'Lord be praised, I know it inside out, on foot or horseback. But you can see the weather: you'd lose your way. Better stay here and wait it out, maybe the storm will die down and the skies clear: then we'll find the direction by the stars.'

His calm demeanour heartened me. I had made up my mind to submit to God's will and spend the night in the middle of the steppe, when the traveller suddenly leapt nimbly on to the box and told the driver: 'Well, thank the lord, human habitation not far off; turn right and off you go.'

'Why should I turn right?' enquired the driver, displeased. 'Where can you see the road? Another man's horses, sting 'em up—and away, is that it?'

I thought the driver had the right of it.

'Yes, really,' I said, 'what makes you think there's a house nearby?'

'Because the wind gusted from that direction,' replied the traveller, 'and I smelt smoke; means there's a village not far off.'

His shrewdness and keen sense of smell took me aback. I ordered the driver to proceed. The horses stepped ponderously through the deep snow. The wagon slowly moved on, now heading into a snow-drift, now tumbling down into a gully and heeling over, first to one side, then to the other. It was like a ship sailing across a stormy sea. Savelich groaned as he kept lurching into my side. I let down the blind, wrapped myself in my fur coat, and fell into a doze, lulled by the singing of the storm and the rocking of the slow-moving wagon.

I dreamed a dream which I could never afterwards forget and in which I still see something prophetic when I relate it to the strange events of my life. The reader will forgive me: he probably knows from experience how prone man is to fall prey to superstition, whatever his contempt for such credulous beliefs might be.

I was in that mental and emotional state when reality gives way to day-dreaming, and merges with it to form the vague visions of approaching sleep. I fancied that the blizzard was still raging and that we were still wandering about that snowy desolation . . . All at once, I saw gates and drove into the yard of our manor-house. My first thought was fear that my father would be angry at my involuntary return to the nest and regard it as deliberate disobedience. I jumped down from the wagon and saw my mother coming out on to the porch to meet me with an expression of profound distress. 'Ssh,' she said, 'your father is mortally ill and wants to say farewell to you.' Fear-stricken, I follow her into the bedroom. I see that the room is dimly lit; people are standing near the bed with sorrowful faces. I quietly approach the bed; mother raises the bed-curtain slightly and

says: 'Andrey Petrovich, Petrusha has come after hearing of
your illness: bless him.' I kneel down and fix my gaze on the sick
man. What was this? . . . Instead of my father, there in the bed
lay a peasant with a black beard, gazing at me cheerfully. I
turned to my mother in bewilderment, saying: 'What does this
mean? That's not my father, and why should I ask a muzhik's
blessing?'

'Never mind Petrusha, it's your proxy father; kiss his hand
and let him bless you . . .'

I refused. Then the muzhik jumped up from the bed, seized
an axe from behind him, and began brandishing it in all directions. I wanted to run . . . and couldn't; the room filled up with
dead bodies; I stumbled over a body and slipped in pools of
blood . . . The terrible muzhik gently called to me, saying: 'Don't
be afraid, come and receive my blessing . . .' Horror and bewilderment overwhelmed me . . . And at that moment, I awoke; the
horses had come to a halt; Savelich was tugging me by the arm,
saying: 'Get out, sir: we've arrived.'

'Arrived where?' I asked, rubbing my eyes.

'A wayside inn. With God's help, we ran straight into the
fence. Out you get, master, and have quick warm-up.'

I got out of the wagon. The blizzard was still in progress,
though by now somewhat abated. It was pitch black. The innkeeper met us at the gate, holding a lantern under his cloak, and
led me into a room that was cramped but reasonably clean; it
was lit by a torch. A rifle and a tall Caucasian hat hung on the
wall.

The innkeeper, a Yaik Cossack* by nationality, proved to be
a peasant of about sixty, still hale and vigorous. Savelich carried
my trunk in after me and asked for a fire to make tea, of which
I had never before felt in such need. The host went off and
busied himself.

'Where's the guide, though?' I asked Savelich.

'Here, your honour,' answered a voice from up above. I looked
up at the bunk and saw two glittering eyes.

'What's the matter, friend, frozen?'

'I should think I am in just a thin coat! I had a sheepskin, but
why deny it, I pawned it at an inn last night: it didn't seem so
cold then.'

At that moment, the host entered with the boiling samovar; I offered our guide a cup of tea and the muzhik slid down from his bunk. His outward appearance struck me as remarkable:* he was about forty, of medium build, lean and broad-shouldered. Grey streaks were present in his beard; his large, lively eyes darted here and there. His face bore quite a pleasant, if roguish, expression. His hair was close-cropped in a ring; he was wearing a ragged coat and Tartar trousers. I handed him the cup of tea; he sipped at it and made a face.

'Your honour, be good enough to ask them to bring me a glass of vodka: we Cossacks don't drink tea.'

I willingly complied. The host took a quart bottle and glass from the cupboard and went over to him, looking him in the eye: 'Aha!' said he. 'You're in these parts again! Where've you sprung from?' My guide winked significantly and answered with a folk-saying: 'Flew into the garden, pecked at the hemp-seed: old girl threw a stone at me but missed. And how are your people?'

'What do you mean, our people!' our host replied, continuing the allegorical conversation. 'They were going to ring for the evening service, but the priest's wife wouldn't let them: the priest's away visiting, the devil's in the churchyard.'

'Be quiet, uncle', my wanderer broke in. 'When the rain falls, the mushrooms will spring up; and where there's mushrooms, there'll be a basket. But for now' (here another wink), 'hide your axe behind your back: the forester's about. Your good health, your honour!' So saying, he picked up the glass, crossed himself, and drank it off at a gulp. Then he bowed to me and got back into his bunk.

I couldn't understand anything of this thieves' cant; but afterwards I divined that the talk was of the Yaik forces, at that time recently pacified after the 1772 rising.* Savelich listened with an expression of great disapproval. He glanced suspiciously, now at the host, now at the guide. The inn, or in local parlance, the *umet*, lay off in the direction of the steppe, away from any inhabited spot and bore a considerable resemblance to a bandits' hideout. Still, there was nothing for it. Pressing on was out of the question. Savelich's anxiety amused me greatly. Meanwhile I made ready for the night and lay down on a bench. Savelich decided to get up on the stove; the host lay on the floor. Soon the whole hut was snoring and I dropped off and slept like a log.

Waking rather late in the morning, I saw that the storm had subsided. The sun was shining. Snow was lying in a blinding shroud on the boundless steppe. The horses were harnessed. I settled accounts with the innkeeper, who took such a modest sum from us that even Savelich didn't start up an argument or haggle, as was his wont. His suspicions of the day before were completely wiped from his mind. I called the guide, thanked him for his assistance, and gave him fifty kopeks for vodka. Savelich scowled.

'Fifty kopeks for vodka!' said he. 'What's that for? That you were pleased to give him a lift to the inn? As you wish, master, but we have no fifty kopeks to spare. If we give everybody vodka money, you'll soon be starving yourself.'

I couldn't quarrel with Savelich. I had promised that the money should be entirely at his disposal. I was vexed, however, that I could not thank the man who had rescued me, if not from disaster, then at least from a very unpleasant predicament.

'Very well,' I said coolly, 'if you don't want to give him fifty, then take something out of my clothes chest. He's not dressed warmly enough. Give him my hare-skin jacket.'

'Good heavens, master Pyotr Andreich!' said Savelich. 'Why give him your hare-skin jacket? He'll drink it away, the dog, in the first tavern.'

'It is not your worry, greybeard,' said my vagabond, 'whether I drink it away or not. His honour is gifting the fur from his shoulders: that is his noble will, and your servile business is to obey without arguing.'

'You fear not God, brigand!' retorted Savelich angrily. 'You can see the child hasn't reached years of discretion, yet you are ready to take advantage of his innocence by robbing him. Why do you need a squire's jacket? You won't even get it round your damned great shoulders.'

'Stop trying to be clever,' said I to my guardian. 'Bring the jacket here at once.'

'Good God almighty!' groaned my Savelich. 'A hare-skin, good as new! Not even to someone deserving—a confessed drunkard!'

However, the hare-skin jacket materialized. The muzhik at
once began trying it on. And so it proved, the jacket which even
I had outgrown was rather tight for him. However, he somehow
contrived to get it on, popping the seams. Savelich almost howled
as he heard the threads snap. The vagabond was extremely
pleased with my gift. He accompanied me to the wagon and
said, bowing low:

'Thank you, your honour! May God reward you for your
charity. I shall never forget your kindness.'

He went his way, and I set off on my journey, paying no heed
to Savelich's vexation, and soon forgot the previous day's blizzard, my guide, and the hare-skin jacket.

On arriving in Orenburg, I presented myself to the general at
once. I saw before me a man of considerable height, but by now
stooped with age. His long hair was quite white. His old, faded
uniform reminded me of a warrior of Anna Ioannovna's time,*
while his speech betrayed a strong German accent. I gave him
my father's letter. At the mention of his name, he shot a swift
glance at me: 'Goot Gott!' he said. 'It hardly seems yesterday
that Andrey Petrovich vos your age and now he's got a grand
boy like you! Ach, time, time!' He broke the seal on the letter
and started reading it under his breath, commenting as he went.
'"Dear Andrey Karlovich, I hope that your excellency"... Vot's
all this formality? Tfu, he should be ashamed! Of course: discipline above all, but is that the vay to write to an old kamrad? ...
"your excellency has not forgotten"... hmm ... "and ...
when ... the late Field Marshal Min ... campaign ... also I ...
Karolinka ... " Ech, bruder! So he remembers our old prank?
"Now to business ... my rascal to you"... mmm ... "hold
him with hedgehog gauntlets".* Vot is hedgehog gauntlets?
Must be a Russian proverb ... Vot is hedgehog gauntlets?' he
repeated, addressing me.

'It means,' I replied, with as innocent an expression as I could
manage, 'treat him gently, don't be too rough, a loose rein, hold
him with hedgehog gauntlets.'

'Hmm ... I understand, "and not let him have his head" ...
no, apparently hedgehog gauntlets must mean something else ...
"Enclose his identity card" ... Where is it, then? Ah, here is
is ... "notify Semyonoffsky Guards" ... Very well, very well,

all shall be done . . . "Allow me to set rank aside and embrace you as an old comrade and a friend". Ach! Got there at last . . . so on and so forth . . . Well, master,' he said, the letter now read and identity card put to one side, 'all shall be done: you vill be an officer and transferred to the *** regiment, and so as not to vaste time, you will go to the Belogorsk Fort, where you vill serve under Captain Mironov, a good-hearted and honourable man. You vill be in the real army there and learn vot discipline is. There's no point in you being in Orenburg; dissipation is bad for a young man. As for today, I invite you to dine with me.'

'Things get no better!' I thought to myself. 'What was the point of being a sergeant in the Semyonovsky Guards before I was born! Where has it got me? The *** regiment in some backwater fort on the edge of the Kirghiz–Kaisakh steppe!'

I dined with Andrey Karlovich and the old adjutant. Strict German economy ruled at his table, and I suspect that his fear at occasionally having to share his bachelor meal with another guest was one reasom for dispatching me to the garrison in such a hurry. Next day I said my goodbyes to the general and set out for my appointment.

3

THE FORT

We are sitting in our fort here,
Living off just bread and water;
If grim foemen come to call
Take our buns and scale the wall,
We'll arrange a feast they'll rue
Load our gun with grapeshot too.

(Soldier song)

Antique people, dear sir.

(*The Minor*)*

Belogorsk Fort* lay about twenty-five miles from Orenburg.
The road led along the steep bank of the Yaik. The river was not
yet frozen and its leaden waters were melancholy and dark between the dreary, snow-covered shores. Beyond them stretched
the Kirghiz steppe. I was absorbed in reflections, mostly of a
melancholy nature. Garrison life held few attractions for me. I
tried to picture Captain Mironov, my future commander, and
came up with a severe, irascible old man, knowing nothing beyond the army, and ready to put me under arrest on bread and
water for the most trifling dereliction. Meanwhile it was coming
in dark. We were travelling along quite swiftly.

'Is it far to the fort?' I asked my driver.

'Not far,' he responded. 'There, you can see it over yonder.'

I gazed round in all directions, expecting to see menacing
bastions, towers, and a moat; but I could make out nothing
except for a small village, surrounded by a log palisade. On one
side stood three or four hay-ricks, half-buried in snow; on the
other, a crooked windmill, its bast sails idly sagging.

'Where on earth is the fort?' I enquired in surprise.

'That's it there,' answered the driver, indicating the village,
and as he spoke we drove into it.

I caught sight of an ancient, cast-iron cannon by the gates; the
streets were cramped and winding; the huts were squat and

mostly straw-thatched. I gave orders to be taken to the commander, and a minute later the wagon halted outside a small wooden house, built on an eminence near a church, also of wood.

Nobody came out to meet me. I went into the passage and opened the door into the anteroom. An old veteran was sitting on the table, sewing a blue patch on the elbow of his green uniform. I ordered him to announce me. 'Just go in, master,' the veteran replied. 'Our folk are at home.' I entered a clean little room, with old-world furnishings. In the corner stood a dresser; an officer's diploma, framed and glazed, hung on the wall; nearby were some colourful folk-prints depicting the taking of Kustrin and Ochakov,* as well as *Choosing a Bride* and *The Cat's Funeral*.* An old woman, wearing a quilted jacket and a scarf over her head, sat by the window. She was unwinding some yarn which a one-eyed old man in the uniform of an officer held stretched across his hands.

'What can we do for you, master?' she said, going on with her work. I replied that I had arrived to serve in the fort and was presenting myself to the commander, as was my duty, and was about to address the one-eyed man, taking him for the commandant. The lady of the house cut short my prepared speech.

'Ivan Kuzmich is not at home,' said she. 'He's gone to visit Father Gerasimov; still, what's the odds master, I'm his wife. You are very welcome. Do sit down, master. She called the maid and asked her to summon the sergeant. The old man stared at me inquisitively with his one eye.

'If I may make so bold,' he said, 'in which regiment are you serving?' I satisfied his curiosity.

'And if I may be so bold,' he pursued, 'why did you transfer from the Guards to a garrison?'

I replied that such had been the will of my superior officers.

'No doubt for conduct unbecoming', continued the tireless interrogator.

'That's quite enough of your nonsense,' the captain's wife told him. 'You can see the young man is tired after his journey; he's not in the mood to bother with you (hold your arms straighter). And you, young master,' she went on, turning to me, 'don't be too downhearted that they've packed you off here to the back of beyond. You're not the first and you won't be the last. You'll like it once you get used to it. Alexey Ivanich Shvabrin's been here over four years for murder. Lord only knows what made him do it; you see, he rode out of town with a certain lieutenant, and they took swords with them, then they up and started jabbing away at each other; but Alexey Ivanich ran the lieutenant through, and in front of two witnesses, too! What can you do, I ask you? It's a good horse that never stumbles.'

At that point the NCO entered, a fine-looking young Cossack.

'Maximich!' said the captain's wife. 'Take the gentleman officer to some clean quarters.'

'Yes, Vasilisa Egorovna,' replied the NCO. 'Should I put his honour in Ivan Polezhaev's house?'

'Nonsense, Maximich,' said the captain's wife. 'He's full up as it is; I'm his child's godmother and he still remembers that we're his betters. Take the gentleman—what's your name and patronymic, my dear? Pyotr Andreich? ... Take Pyotr Andreich to Semyon Kuzov's place. The rascal has let his horse into my vegetable garden. Well then, Maximich, is everything under control?'

'All quiet, thanks be,' responded the Cossack, 'except that in the bath-house, Corporal Prokhorov had a fight with Ustinya Negulina over a pail of hot water.'

'Ivan Ignatich!' said the captain's wife to the one-eyed old man. 'Sort out this Prokhorov and Ustinya business and find out who's to blame. Then punish both of them. Well, Maximich, off you go and God be with you. Pyotr Andreich, Maximich will take you to your billet.'

I bowed myself out. The Cossack conducted me to a hut which stood on the high bank of the river, on the very edge of the fort. Semyon Kuzov's family occupied half of the hut, and the other half was mine. It consisted of one room, reasonably tidy, divided by a partition. Savelich started unpacking as I stared out of the narrow little window. The melancholy steppe stretched away in front of me. A handful of huts straggled across obliquely; a few hens wandered along the street. An old woman, standing on her porch with a trough, was calling her pigs who were answering with amiable grunts. And this was the place where I was condemned to pass my youth! Anguish seized me;

I turned away from the window and went to bed without supper, notwithstanding the exhortations of Savelich, who kept repeating in desolate fashion: 'Lord almighty! He won't eat anything! What will the mistress say if her child should fall ill?'

The following morning I had just started to get dressed when a young officer came in to see me. He was short in stature, with a swarthy face that was strikingly ugly, but full of animation.

'Excuse me', he said in French, 'for just coming in like that to make your acquaintance. I learned of your arrival yesterday; the urge to set eyes on a human face so overwhelmed me that I couldn't restrain myself. You'll understand that when you've lived here for a bit longer.'

I guessed that this was the officer discharged from the Guards for duelling. We introduced ourselves at once. Shvabrin was very far from being stupid. His conversation was witty and entertaining. He described the commandant's family and circle with high good humour, as well as the region where my fate had led me. I was laughing heartily when in came the same veteran who had been mending his uniform in the commandant's anteroom, with an dinner invitation from Vasilisa Egorovna. Shvabrin volunteered to accompany me.

Approaching the commandant's house, we could see a score of ancient veterans on the square, with tricorn hats covering their long plaits. They were drawn up at attention. The commandant stood facing them, a tall, vigorous old man, wearing a nightcap and a nankeen dressing-gown. On seeing us, he came over, said a few agreeable words to me, then resumed command. We stopped to watch the drill, but he asked us to go in to Vasilisa Egorovna, promising to follow us.

'There's nothing worth watching here,' he added.

Vasilisa Egorovna received us with informal cordiality, treating me as if we were old friends. The veteran and Palashka were laying the table.

'I don't know what's got into my Ivan Kuzmich with all this drilling!' said the commandant's wife. 'Palashka, call the master in to dinner. Now where's that Masha?'

At this, there entered a girl of about eighteen, with a round, rosy face and auburn hair smoothly combed behind her burning ears. At first glance, I was not taken with her. I was looking with prejudiced eyes: Shvabrin had described Maria Ivanovna, the captain's daughter, as a perfect ninny. She sat down in the corner and began sewing. Meanwhile, cabbage soup was served. Vasilisa Egorovna, not seeing her husband, sent Palashka after him a second time.

'Tell the master: his guests are waiting, the cabbage soup is getting cold; there's plenty of time for drill, God willing; he'll have his fill of shouting.'

The captain soon appeared, accompanied by the one-eyed old man.

'What's all this, my dear?' said his wife to him. 'Food served long ago, and no getting you in here.'

'Now then, Vasilisa Egorovna,' replied Ivan Kuzmich, 'I was on duty: I was drilling the old soldiers.'

'Let's hear no more of that!' retorted his wife. 'Drilling the old soldiers indeed! They don't grasp the first thing, and you know precious little about it either. You'd be better staying at home and praying to God; dear guests, come and be seated.'

We sat down to dinner. Vasilisa Egorovna didn't stop talking for an instant, fairly peppering me with questions: who were my parents, were they still alive, where did they live, and what were the family circumstances. On hearing that my father owned 300 serfs,* she said 'Fancy! There are indeed rich folk in the world! We only have one serf wench, Palashka; still, praise be, we get by. One misfortune though: Masha; she's of an age to marry, but what kind of dowry has she got? A fine-tooth comb, a besom broom, and a three-kopek bit (God forgive me) to take to the bath-house. Fine if a good man comes along, otherwise it's stay an old maid for ever.'

I glanced at Maria Ivanovna; she was blushing furiously and teardrops fell on to her plate. I began to feel sorry for her, and I hastened to change the subject.

'I've heard', I said rather aimlessly, 'that the Bashkirs* are getting ready to attack your fort.'

'From whom did you hear that, dear fellow?' enquired Ivan Kuzmich.

'That's what they told me in Orenburg.' I replied.

'That's all rubbish!' said the commandant. 'We've heard nothing for ages. The Bashkirs have been given a good fright, and the Kirghiz* have been taught a lesson as well. They won't be poking their noses in here, don't worry; and if they do, I'll give them a lesson that will keep them quiet for the next ten years.'

'Are you not frightened,' I continued, addressing the captain's wife, 'staying here in the fort, exposed to such dangers?'

'You get used to it, dear boy,' she answered, 'About twenty years ago, when we were transferred here from the regiment, heavens, I was really scared of these unbaptized wretches! As soon as I set eyes on their lynx-fur hats and heard their yelling, believe me, my dear, my heart would stand still! But now I'm so used to it that I wouldn't stir if they came to tell us that the scoundrels were prowling round the fort.'

'Vasilisa Egorovna is a most courageous lady', observed Shvabrin solemnly. 'Ivan Kuzmich can bear that out.'

'She's not the timid sort, believe you me.'

'What about Maria Ivanovna?' I asked. 'Is she as brave as you?'

'Masha brave?' answered her mother. 'No, Masha's a coward. Can't bear to hear a rifle-shot to this day without quaking. And a couple of years ago when Ivan Kuzmich got a notion to fire off our cannon for my name-day, my little bird nearly breathed her last, she was so frightened. Since then we haven't fired that blasted cannon.'

We got up from table. The captain and his wife went off to lie down, and I went to Shvabrin's place and spent the whole evening with him.

4

THE DUEL

Well then, take position if you must,
And see your person run through by my thrust!

(Knyazhnin)*

Several weeks went by, and my life in the Belogorsk Fort became not only bearable but positively agreeable. I was accepted as a son in the commandant's household. Husband and wife were the most estimable of people. Ivan Kuzmich, who had joined the army as a soldier's son, was a simple, uneducated man, but kind-hearted and honourable in the highest degree. He was under his wife's thumb, which suited his happy-go-lucky disposition. Vasilisa Egorovna looked on army affairs the way she regarded her domestic duties, and ran the fort exactly as she did her own little house. Maria Ivanovna soon ceased to be afraid of me. We got to know each other. I found her to be a sensible and sensitive girl. Imperceptibly I began to grow attached to the kindly household, even to Ivan Ignatich, the one-eyed garrison lieutenant, concerning whom Shvabrin invented an illicit connection with Vasilisa Egorovna. That this had not a shred of plausibility did not worry Shvabrin.

I was promoted to officer rank. Service life was not onerous. In our God-protected fortress there were neither inspections, drills, nor sentry-duty. It was the commandant's whim to drill his men occasionally, but he had not yet been able to get all of them to tell their right side from their left, although many would cross themselves at every turn in case they got it wrong. Shvabrin had a number of French books. I started reading them and developed a taste for literature. Of a morning I would read, do translation exercises, and sometimes even compose verses. I almost always had dinner with the commandant, where I usually spent the remainder of the day; in the evening, Father Gerasim and his wife, Akulina Pamfilovna, the premier newsmonger of the whole district, might put in an appearance. Naturally I saw

Shvabrin every day, but I found his conversation was gradually becoming less agreeable. His continual jokes at the expense of the commandant's family I found most distasteful, especially his caustic remarks about Maria Ivanovna. There was no other company in the fort, but I had no desire for any.

Despite the forecasts, the Bashkirs remained quiet. Tranquillity reigned around our fort. But the peace was broken by sudden hostilities within.

I have already spoken of my interest in literature. My efforts were passable, by the standards of those days, and came in for high praise from Alexander Petrovich Sumarokov* some years afterwards. One day I managed to write a little song which pleased me. Everyone knows that composers look for a sympathetic listener under the pretext of asking for advice. And so, I wrote out my song and took it to Shvabrin, who was the only one in the fort who could appreciate the productions of a versifier. After some brief prefatory remarks, I took my notebook from my pocket and read him the following verses:

> I banish thoughts of love's delight,
> Trying to forget that fairest she,
> And ah, in shunning Masha's sight,
> I think to gain my liberty!

> But her eyes that first attracted,
> Never give me my release;
> They still haunt my soul distracted,
> Have made an end to all my peace.

> Thou on learning of my anguish,
> Pity Masha, pity me,
> As my fate is yet to languish,
> Still a prisoner to thee.

'What do you think of it?' I asked Shvabrin, expecting praise, as my right and due. But to my great vexation, Shvabrin, usually indulgent, declared roundly that my song was no good.

'Why's that?' I asked, hiding my annoyance.

'Because', he replied, 'verses like that are worthy of my teacher Vasily Kirilich Tredyakovsky,* and remind me very much of his love couplets.'

Thereupon he took my notebook and began mercilessly

dissecting every line and every word, mocking me in the most caustic fashion. This was more than I could bear, and I snatched the book from his hand, saying that I would never again show him my compositions. Shvabrin laughed at that threat also.

'We shall see', he said, 'whether you can keep your word: poets need an audience, like Ivan Kuzmich does a carafe of vodka before dinner. And who is this Masha before whom you confess your tender passion and lovelorn sorrows? Not Maria Ivanovna is it?'

'None of your business', I scowled, 'what Masha it is. I'm not asking for your opinion, or your guesses either.'

'Oho! A touchy poet and a shy lover!' Shvabrin went on, irritating me more and more. 'But heed some friendly advice: if you want to succeed I would suggest trying something other than songs.'

'And just what does that mean, sir? Be good enough to explain.'

'By all means. It means that if you want Masha Mironova to come and visit you after dark, give her a pair of earrings, not tender verses.'

My blood was beginning to boil.

'And why do you have that opinion of her?' I asked, barely restraining my indignation.

'Because', he replied with a diabolical grin, 'I know her little ways from experience.'

'You lie, blackguard!' I cried in fury. 'That's an utterly shameless lie.'

Shvabrin's face altered. 'I shan't let that pass', he said, gripping my arm. 'You will give me satisfaction.'

'As you please; whenever you like!' I replied, overjoyed. At that moment I was ready to tear him to pieces.

I at once set off to Ivan Ignatich and found him with needle in hand: he had been delegated by the commandant's wife to string mushrooms for winter drying.

'Ah, Pyotr Andreich!' he said on seeing me. 'Greetings! To what do we owe the pleasure? What can we do for you, if I may make so bold?'

I explained in a few brief words that I had quarrelled with Alexey Ivanich and I had come to ask him, Ivan Ignatich, to be my second. He heard me out, all attention, fixing on me his solitary eye.

'You are pleased to say', he said, 'that you want to run Alexei Ivanich through and you want me to be a witness? Is that the case, I make bold to ask?'

'Just so.'

'Good lord, Pyotr Andreich! What's this you've got yourself into? You've had words with Alexey Ivanich? Not the end of the world, is it? Calling names won't hurt you. He said nasty things to you, so you do the same; he punches you in the face, you give him one on the ear, and another, and a third. Then you go your separate ways; we'll make peace between you. Whereas, killing your neighbour—is that a good thing to do, may I ask? Too bad if you run Alexey Ivanich through, I'm not so fond of him myself, but what if he makes a hole in you? Who has the last laugh then, may I presume to ask?'

The lieutenant's reasonable arguments did not sway me. I stuck to my intention.

'As you wish,' said Ivan Ignatich. 'Do as you think fit. But why on earth should I be a witness? What's the point of that? People fight, is that some kind of wonder, may I ask? Praise be, I've been in action against the Swede and the Turk and seen enough of all that.'

I made efforts to explain the duties of a second to him, but Ivan Ignatich couldn't make head or tail of it.

'Be it as you wish,' said he, 'but if I'm to get involved in this affair, it will only be to go to Ivan Kuzmich and report to him, in the line of duty, that a crime is being hatched in the fort against the state interest: would it not be prudent for the commandant to take appropriate measures . . .'

I took fright and began to beg Ivan Ignatich to say nothing to the commandant; I had a hard job of it; he gave me his word and I resolved to cease badgering him.

I spent the evening, as was my custom, at the commandant's. I strove to appear cheerful and nonchalant, so as not to excite suspicion, and avoid bothersome questions; I must admit, though, that I did not possess that coolness for which those in my position are almost always praised. That evening I was disposed to be tender and affectionate. Maria Ivanovna attracted me more than usual. The thought that I was seeing her perhaps for the last time endowed her with something touching in my eyes. Shvabrin also made his appearance that evening. I took him to one side and informed him of my conversation with Ivan Ignatich.

'Why do we need seconds?' he said coldly. 'We can make do without.'

We arranged to fight behind the hay-ricks not far from the fort, and to be there the next day at seven in the morning. We were talking so amicably that Ivan Ignatich let the cat out of the bag in his joy.

'High time too,' he told me with a pleased expression. 'A bad peace is better than a good quarrel; let your honour suffer, not your health.'

'What was that, Ivan Ignatich?' said the commandant's wife, who was consulting the cards in the corner. 'I didn't catch that.'

Ivan Ignatich, noticing the signs of my displeasure, and recalling his promise, grew flustered and was unable to reply. Shvabrin was quick to come to his rescue.

'Ivan Ignatich', he said, 'approves of our reconciliation.'

'And who did you quarrel with, my dear?'

'Pyotr Andreich and I had rather a serious falling-out.'

'Why was that?'

'Nothing really: over a song, Vasilisa Egorovna.'

'What a thing to quarrel over! A song! . . . how on earth did it happen?'

'Well, it was like this: Pyotr Andreich composed a song a little while ago and sang it today when I was there, and I struck up my favourite:

> Captain's daughter, hear me, flower,
> Don't go walking at the midnight hour.

We had words about it. Pyotr Andreich was inclined to be angry, but later on decided that everyone is free to sing whatever he likes. That was the end of the matter.'

Shvabrin's effrontery almost drove me to fury, but no one apart from me understood his coarse allusion; at least no one paid any attention. From songs, the talk turned to poets, and the commandant remarked that they were a dissipated lot of fearful drunkards, and gave me his friendly advice to leave off writing, as a business which was repugnant to the army and never led to any good.

I found Shvabrin's presence unbearable and soon said good-bye to the commandant and his household. On arriving home, I inspected my sword, tried the point, and went to bed, ordering Savelich to wake me up after six.

Next day, at the appointed time, I was standing behind the hay-ricks, awaiting my opponent. Soon he too appeared.

'We may be disturbed,' he told me, 'best get it over quickly.'

We took off our jackets and, waistcoat-clad, bared our swords. At that moment Ivan Ignatich suddenly appeared from behind the hay-rick, accompanied by five veterans. He summoned us to the commandant. We obeyed sullenly; the soldiers surrounded us and we set off for the fort after Ivan Ignatich, who led us along in triumph, striding out with amazing pomposity.

We went into the commandant's house. Ivan Ignatich opened the door, announced solemnly: 'delivered!' Vasilisa Egorovna came to meet us.

'Oh, my dears! Did you ever see the like? What? Eh? Planning murder in our fort! Ivan Kuzmich, arrest them at once! Pyotr Andreich! Alexey Ivanich! Hand over your swords, come on, come on! Palashka, take these swords to the store-room. Pyotr Andreich! I didn't expect this of you. You should be ashamed. It's all very well for Alexey Ivanich: he was discharged from the Guards for murder, and he doesn't believe in the Lord God; but what about you? What are you getting into?'

Ivan Kuzmich fully agreed with his spouse and kept putting in: 'Just you listen; what Vasilisa Egoronva says is right. Duels are expressly forbidden in military regulations.' Meanwhile Palashka had taken our swords and borne them off to the store-room. I couldn't help laughing. Shvabrin preserved his gravity. 'For all the respect I bear you,' he told her coolly, 'I cannot but remark that you are upsetting yourself for nothing in pronouncing judgement on us. Leave that to Ivan Kuzmich: it is his business.'

'Ah, my dear,' countered the commandant's wife, 'surely man and wife are one spirit and one flesh? Ivan Kuzmich! What are you gaping at? Lock them up now in different places on bread and water, till they get over this nonsense of theirs; and let

Father Gerasim impose a penance on them so that they pray to God for forgiveness and repent in the sight of all.'

Ivan Kuzmich did not know what decision to make. Maria Ivanovna had gone very pale. Little by little the storm abated; the commandant's wife calmed down and made us kiss one another. Palashka brought us our swords. We left the commandant's, to all appearances reconciled. Ivan Ignatich accompanied us.

'You should be ashamed,' I said to him angrily. 'Reporting us to the commandant, after giving me your word that you wouldn't!'

'As God's my judge I never told Ivan Kuzmich,' he replied, 'Vasilisa Egoronva wormed it all out of me. She organized everything without the commandant knowing. Anyway, thanks be to God that it's all ended the way it has.' With these words he turned off homewards, leaving Shvabrin and myself alone.

'Our business can't end this way', I told him.

'Of course not,' replied Shvabrin. 'You will answer to me with your blood for your insolence; still, they'll probably be keeping an eye on us. We'll have to pretend for a few days. *Au revoir*!' And we parted as if nothing was amiss.

On my return to the commandant's house I sat next to Maria Ivanovna, as usual. Ivan Kuzmich was out and Vasilisa Egorovna was busy about the house. We talked in an undertone. Maria Ivanovna reproached me gently for the anxiety I had caused them all by my quarrel with Shvabrin.

'I practically fainted when I heard that you were going to fight with swords. How strange men are! For a single word, which would likely be forgotten in a week, they're ready to kill one another and sacrifice not just their lives, but their conscience and the happiness of those who ... But I'm sure you didn't start the quarrel. Alexey Ivanich was bound to be to blame.'

'And why do you think that, Maria Ivanovna?'

'Oh it's just ... he's such a scoffer! I don't like Alexey Ivanich. I detest him; but it's an odd thing, not for the world would I want him to dislike me as much as that. That would upset me dreadfully.'

'And what do you think, Maria Ivanovna, does he like you or not?'

Maria Ivanovna stammered and blushed.

'I think so,' she said. 'I think he does.'

'What makes you think so?'

'Because he asked for my hand.'

'Your hand! He asked to marry you? When was that, then?'

'Last year. About two months before you came.'

'And you said no?'

'As you can see. Alexey Ivanich, of course, is a clever man, and comes from a good and wealthy family, but when I think of having to kiss him during the wedding in front of everyone . . . Not for anything! Not for all the riches in the world!'

Maria Ivanovna's words had opened my eyes and explained a good deal. I now understood his persistent denigration of her. Doubtless he had observed our mutual attraction and tried to alienate us from each other. The words which had provided a pretext for our quarrel seemed to me even more abhorrent now that, instead of a coarse and indecent sneer, I perceived a calculated slander. My desire to punish the insolent traducer grew even stronger, and I awaited a suitable opportunity with impatience.

I did not have to wait long. The following day, when I was working on an elegy and gnawing my pen as I tried to find a rhyme, Shvabrin came knocking at my window. I laid down my pen and took up my sword as I went out to him.

'Why drag matters out?' Shvabrin said to me. 'We're not being watched. Let's go down to the river. Nobody will interfere there.'

We set off in silence. After descending the steep path, we halted by the river and bared our blades. Shvabrin was more skilful than I was, but I was the stronger and bolder and Monsieur Beaupré, the former soldier, had given me a number of fencing lessons which I put to good use. Shvabrin had not expected to find in me such a dangerous antagonist. For a long time we were unable to do one another any damage; eventually, observing that Shvabrin was weakening, I began pressing him hard, almost driving him into the river. Suddenly I heard someone loudly calling my name. I turned to see Savelich running down the steep path towards me . . . At that same moment I felt a sharp stab in the chest just below the right shoulder; I fell senseless.

5

LOVE

Ah, you maiden, maiden so pretty!
Don't you get married so young,
Ask your mother and father first,
Mother and father and kinfolk;
Gather much wisdom, maiden,
Much wisdom and a dowry.

(Folk song)

If you find a better man, you'll forget me.
If you find a worse, you'll remember.

(The same)*

As I came to, I was for some time unable to recollect where I was and what had happened to me. I was lying on a bed in an unfamiliar room, feeling extremely weak. Savelich was standing before me holding a candle. Someone was carefully unwinding the bandages in which my chest and shoulder were swathed. Gradually my mind cleared. I remembered my duel and guessed that I had been wounded. At that moment the door creaked.

'Well, how is he?' whispered a voice that set me trembling.

'Just the same,' sighed Savelich. 'The fifth day now and still unconscious.'

I wanted to turn over but couldn't.

'Where am I? Who's there?' I brought out with a effort. Maria Ivanovna approached the bed and bent over me.

'Well, how do you feel?' she said.

'Thank heaven,' I answered weakly. 'Is it you, Maria Ivanovna? tell me . . .'

I hadn't the strength to go on and lapsed into silence. Savelich gave a sharp exclamation, his face a picture of joy.

'He's come round, he's come round!' he kept repeating. 'Praise to thee, O Lord! Well, master, Pyotr Andreich! You gave me a scare! Just fancy, the fifth day! . . .'

Maria Ivanovna interrupted him.

'Don't talk a lot to him, Savelich,' she said. 'He's still weak.'

She went out, closing the door quietly. My thoughts were in turmoil. So then, I was in the commandant's house. Maria Ivanovna had been coming in to me. I wanted to ask Savelich some questions but the old man shook his head and covered his ears. I closed my eyes in vexation and was soon fast asleep.

When I awoke, I summoned Savelich and instead found Maria Ivanovna before me; the angelic voice greeted me. I cannot describe the sweetness of the emotion that overwhelmed me at that moment. I seized her hand and drew it to me, bathing it with affectionate tears. Masha did not withdraw it . . . and suddenly her lips were brushing my cheek and I felt a hot, fresh kiss. Fire ran through me.

'Sweet, kind Maria Ivanovna,' I said, 'be my wife, consent to make me happy.'

She recovered herself.

'For goodness' sake calm yourself,' she said, removing her hand. 'You are still in danger: your wound could open up again. Take care of yourself if only for my sake.'

So saying, she went out, leaving me in rapturous delight. Happiness revived me. She was going to be mine! She loved me! This thought filled my entire being.

From that time forward, I got better by the hour. I was attended by the regimental barber-surgeon, as there was no other medical man in the fort. Thank the lord, he knew his limits. Youth and nature hastened my recovery. The commandant's whole household looked after me. Maria Ivanovna did not leave my side. Naturally enough, at the first suitable opportunity I renewed my interrupted declaration of love and Maria Ivanovna heard me out more patiently. She acknowledged her heartfelt attachment to me without the least affectation and said that her parents would of course be overjoyed at her happiness.

'But consider carefully,' she added, 'won't there be objections from your parents?'

I pondered this. I had no doubts concerning my mother's tenderness; but knowing my father's nature and way of thinking, I felt that my love would not move him to any extent and that he would regard it as a young man's foolishness. I candidly admitted as much to Maria Ivanovna and resolved to write to

my father as eloquently as I knew how, and ask for his parental
blessing. I showed the letter to Maria Ivanovna, who found it so
touching and convincing that she had no doubts of its success
and surrendered to the feelings of her tender heart with all the
trustfulness of youth and love.

I made it up with Shvabrin in the first days of my convales-
cence. Ivan Kuzmich had ticked me off about the duel, saying:
'Ah, Pyotr Andreich! I should place you under arrest, but you've
been punished enough. As for Alexey Ivanich, I've got him
shut up under guard in the granary, and Vasilisa Egorovna has
his sword under lock and key. Let him think things over and
repent.'

I was too happy to harbour feelings of hostility. I began to
plead for Shvabrin, and the kind-hearted commandant, with the
agreement of his wife, decided to release him. Shvabrin came to
see me and expressed his profound regret about what had taken
place between us; he admitted that it had all been his fault, and
begged me to forget what had happened. Not being by nature
rancorous, I genuinely forgave him both for the quarrel and the
wound he had inflicted on me. I saw in his slanderous remarks
the exasperation of wounded self-esteem and rejected love, and
magnanimously excused my luckless rival.

Soon I had made a complete recovery and moved back to my
quarters. I awaited the answer to my letter, not daring to hope,
while trying to suppress any grim forebodings. I had not yet
discussed the matter with Vasilisa Egorovna and her husband;
but my proposal could not have come as a surprise to them.
Neither Maria Ivanovna nor I had attempted to disguise our feelings for each other, and we were confident in advance of their
consent.

At long last, Savelich came in one morning with a letter in his
hand. I seized it, trembling. The address was written in my
father's hand. This prepared me for something important, because it was usually mama who wrote to me, with father adding
a few lines on the bottom. For a long time I refrained from
opening the package and kept rereading the formal superscrip-
tion, 'To my Son Pyotr Andreyevich Grinyov, Belogorsk Fort,
Orenburg Province'. I tried to guess from the writing what
frame of mind lay behind the letter. Eventually I nerved myself

to open it up and saw from the first lines that the whole business had foundered. The letter ran as follows:

'My son Pyotr!

We received on the 15th of this month your letter to me in which you ask for our parental blessing and consent to marriage with Maria Ivanovna, daughter of Mironov, and I am not disposed to give either my blessing or my consent. Moreover, I intend to get over there and teach you a lesson for your misbehaviour, like some urchin, for all your officer rank: you have shown that you are not yet worthy to bear the sword, presented to you for the defence of your country, not for duelling with other hare-brained scamps like yourself. I shall write to Andrey Karlovich immediately, requesting him to transfer you a long way from Belogorsk Fort, where you might get over your foolishness. Your mother took ill with worry when she heard about your duel and that you'd been wounded. She's taken to her bed. What's going to become of you? Pray God to help you mend your ways, though I dare not hope for his great mercy.

Your father A.G.'

It was with mixed feelings that I read this letter. The cruel expressions father made so free with deeply wounded me. The contempt with which he referred to Maria Ivanovna seemed to me as unseemly as it was unfair. The thought of transferring out of Belogorsk Fort horrified me, but the news of my mother's illness grieved me still more. I was incensed at Savelich, not doubting that it was through him that my parents had heard about the duel. Pacing back and forth in my room, I halted before him and said, with a menacing stare:

'It seems it's not enough that because of you I was wounded and spent all of a month at death's door: you want to kill my mother as well.'

Savelich was thunderstruck.

'Mercy on me, master,' he said, almost weeping. 'What are you saying? Me the reason you were wounded? God is my witness, I was running to place myself as a shield between your chest from Alexey Ivanich's sword! My accursed old age prevented me. But what have I done to your mother?'

'What have you done?' I answered. 'Who asked you to write reports about me? Were you attached to me as a spy?'

'I? Write reports on you?' replied Savelich in tears. 'Lord God in heaven! Then be good enough to read what the master writes to me: you'll see what reports I've done on you.'

He took out a letter and I read the following:

'You should be ashamed, old hound that you are, that in spite of my strict orders, you haven't reported to me about my son Pyotr Andreyevich, and that outsiders have been forced to inform me concerning his misdoings. Is that how you carry out your duty and the will of your master? I'll send you out to the fields to tend the pigs, old hound, for covering up the truth and pandering to the young man. On receipt of this I command you to write to me at once concerning his state of health, which I am told has improved; and where he was wounded and whether they made a good job of treating him.'

It was obvious that Savelich was in the right and that I had been wrong to insult him with my reproaches and suspicions. I begged his forgiveness, but the old man was inconsolable.

'To think I have lived to see the day,' he kept repeating. 'This is the thanks I get from my masters! I'm an old dog and a swineherd, and I'm the cause of your wound as well! No, master Pyotr Andreich! It's not me, it's that blasted monsieur's fault: he's the one who taught you to jab away with iron skewers and stamp your foot, as if jabbing and poking would keep an evil man away! That's what comes of hiring a monsieur and throwing away money for nothing.'

Who had gone to the bother of telling my father about my behaviour? The general? But he didn't seem to be too concerned about me; Ivan Kuzmich hadn't regarded it as his duty to report my duel. I was lost in conjecture. My suspicions alighted on Shvabrin. He was the only one to gain advantage from informing on me, possibly resulting in my removal from the fort and a break with the commandant's family. I went to inform Maria Ivanovna of all this. She met me on the porch.

'What's happened to you?' she said on seeing me. 'How pale you are!'

'It's all over!' I answered, and gave her my father's letter. It was her turn to grow pale. When she had read it she returned it to me with a trembling hand, and said in an unsteady voice:

'Evidently it is not my fate . . . Your relations don't want me in their family. Let the Lord's will be done in all things! God knows what is best for us. There is nothing for it, Pyotr Andreich; may you at least be happy.'

'That must not be!' I exclaimed, seizing her hand. 'You love me and I'm ready for anything. Let us go and throw ourselves at your parents' feet; they're simple folk, not hard-hearted and arrogant . . . They will bless us; we'll get married . . . and with time, I'm sure we we can mellow my father; mother will be on our side; she'll forgive me . . .'

'No, Pyotr Andreich,' Masha replied. 'I shan't marry you without the blessing of your parents. You would not be happy without their blessing. Let us submit to God's will. When you find the one destined for you, when you fall in love with another—God bless you, Pyotr Andreich; and I, for you both . . .'

At this she burst into tears and moved away from me; I thought to go into the room after her, but sensed that I would not be able to control myself, and so returned home.

I was sitting plunged in deep musings when Savelich broke my train of thought.

'There you are, sir,' he said, handing me a sheet of paper. 'Look and see if I am an informer on my master, and whether I'm trying to make trouble between father and son. I took the paper from his hand: it was Savelich's reply to the letter he had received. Word for word it read:

'Andrey Petrovich, Sir, our gracious father!

I have received your gracious letter, in which it pleased you to be angry with your serf, that I should feel shame at not carrying out my master's instructions: but I, not an old hound, but your faithful servant, do obey my master's instructions and have always served you with all my heart and grown grey in so doing. I wrote nothing to you concerning Pyotr Andreich's wound so as not to give needless alarm; I hear that the mistress Avdotya Vasilyevna was so anxious in any case that she has taken to her bed, and I shall pray to God for her health. Pyotr Andreich was wounded under the right shoulder, in the chest, just under the bone, about three inches deep, and lay at the commandant's house, where we carried him from the river-bank, and the barber here, Stepan Paramonov, took care of him; now Pyotr Andreich is well, thank God, and there is nothing but good to write about him. The word is that his superiors are pleased with him, and he is like an only son to Vasilisa Egorovna. What happened to him was not the lad's fault: a horse has four legs, and yet it stumbles. And as you are pleased to write that you will send me into the fields to herd pigs, let your lordly will be done in that also. Whereupon I make humble obeisance.

Your faithful serf
Arkhip Savelev'

I couldn't help laughing once or twice, reading the old man's epistle. I was in no mood to reply to my father, and Savelich's letter was enough, I thought, to reassure my mother.

From that time on my situation altered. Maria Ivanovna barely spoke to me and did her best to avoid me. The commandant's house became hateful to me. I gradually learned to sit at home by myself. Vasilisa Egorovna at first reproached me for it, but in the face of my obduracy left me in peace. I only saw Ivan Kuzmich when duty required it. I met Shvabrin seldom, and then reluctantly, the more so because I detected in him a concealed hostility which only went to confirm my suspicions. My life became intolerable to me. I lapsed into a cheerless brooding, which was fed by solitude and idleness. The flame of love grew stronger in my isolation and became more and more trying. I lost my taste for reading and verse-writing. I was afraid either of losing my mind or plunging into dissipation. However, certain startling developments, which were to have a profound effect on my entire life, suddenly delivered a powerful and salutary shock to my spirit.

6

THE PUGACHEV REBELLION

You, young lads, just listen,
To what we, the old men, have to tell.

Song*

Before I begin describing the strange events to which I was
witness, I must say a word or two about the position Orenburg
Province occupied in 1773.

This rich and extensive province was inhabited by a great
many semi-savage peoples, who had only recently acknowledged
the sway of Russian sovereigns. Their constant revolts, their
unfamiliarity with law and civil life, their irresponsibility and
cruel ways, demanded unceasing surveillance on the part of the
government if their allegiance was to be maintained. Forts were
built in places thought to be suitable, and garrisoned for the
most part by Cossacks, the ancient possessors of the banks of the
Yaik. But the Yaik Cossacks entrusted with the duty of preserv-
ing the peace and security of this territory had themselves been
restive and dangerous subjects for a time. In 1772 there had
been an insurrection in their chief settlement. This had been
prompted by the strong measures applied by Major-General
Traubenberg, in order to return them to their proper allegiance.
The upshot was the barbarous killing of Traubenberg, a wilful
change of their government, and the eventual crushing of the
rebellion by grapeshot and cruel punishments.

This had taken place some time before my arrival at Belogorsk
Fort. All was quiet, or so it seemed; the command had trusted
too easily in the supposed repentance of the crafty rebels, who
nurtured their hatred in secret and waited for a suitable opportunity to renew the troubles.

I return to my story.

One evening (it was at the beginning of October 1773), I was
sitting at home by myself, listening to the wailing of the autumn
wind, and staring at the clouds through the window as they

scudded past the moon. Someone came to summon me in the
commandant's name. I found Shvabrin there, Ivan Ignatich, and
the Cossack sergeant. Neither Vasilisa Egorovna nor Maria
Ivanovna were in the room. The commandant greeted me with
a preoccupied air. He locked the door, sat everybody down, took
a paper from his pocket, and said: 'Gentlemen officers, important news! Listen to what the general writes.' He then put on his
glasses and read the following:

'To the Gentleman Commandant of Belogorsk Fort, Captain
Mironov.

Secret.

I herewith inform you that the escaped prisoner and schismatic* Emelyan Pugachev, having with unpardonable insolence
taken upon himself the name of the late Emperor Peter III, has
assembled a gang of villains and incited unrest in the Yaik settlements and has already taken and destroyed several forts,
pillaging and murdering everywhere. For this reason, you are
ordered on receipt of this letter to take immediately all necessary
measures to repulse this villain and impostor, if possible de-
stroying him utterly, should he head towards the fort entrusted
to your care.'

'Take necessary measures!' said the commandant, removing
his glasses and folding the document. 'You heard that; easier
said than done. The villain is strong, that's clear enough. And
we've only got 130 men, not counting the Cossacks, who can't
be relied upon, no offence Maximich.' The sergeant grinned.
'However, there's nothing for it, gentlemen officers! Look to
your duty, post guards and send out night patrols; in case of
attack, lock the gates and get the men on parade. You, Maximich,
keep a close eye on your Cossacks. The cannon should be inspected and given a good clean. Above all, keep all this to your-
selves, so that nobody in the fort finds out anything before they
should.'

Having issued these orders, Ivan Kuzmich dismissed us. I
went out with Shvabrin, talking over what I had just heard.

'How do you think it will all end?' I asked him

'God alone knows,' he responded. 'Time will tell. I don't see anything of major importance on the horizon for the moment. That is, if . . .' At which he fell to thinking and began whistling a French aria.

In spite of all our precautions, news of Pugachev's appearance spread through the fort. Ivan Kuzmich, though he had the greatest respect for his wife, would not for the world have disclosed to her a military secret entrusted to him in the line of duty. On receipt of the general's letter, he quite artfully got Vasilisa Egorovna out of the way, telling her that Father Gerasim had received some wonderful news from Orenburg, which he was keeping a great secret. His wife immediately conceived a desire to go and see the priest's wife, and on Ivan Kuzmich's advice took Masha along with her, so that she wouldn't be bored on her own.

Ivan Kuzmich, now sole master, had immediately sent for us, and had locked Palashka in the store-room so that she might not eavesdrop on us.

Vasilisa Egorovna returned home without having elicited anything from the priest's wife, and learned that during her absence Ivan Kuzmich had held a conference and that Palashka had been under lock and key. She guessed that she had been hoodwinked by her husband and set about interrogating him. But Ivan Kuzmich had made his dispositions in preparation for the onslaught. He was no whit abashed and replied jauntily to his inquisitive consort:

'You see, my dear, our women have taken to using straw in their stoves and an accident could result from that, so I have issued strict orders that from now on the women are not to use straw in the stoves, but use instead brushwood and fallen branches.'

'And why did you have to lock Palashka up?' enquired his wife. 'Why did the poor girl have to stay in the store-room until we got back?'

Ivan Kuzmich was not ready for this question; he got mixed up and mumbled something fairly incoherent. Vasilisa Egorovna could perceive her husband's trickery, but knowing she would get nothing out of him, ceased her questioning, and started talking about the salted gherkins, which Akulina Pamfilovna had prepared in a most unusual way. Vasilisa Egorovna was unable to sleep the whole night, and simply couldn't guess what might have been in her husband's head that couldn't be divulged to her.

Next day, returning from mass, she caught sight of Ivan Ignatich pulling out of the cannon bits of rag, pebbles, pieces of wood, knuckle-bones, and all manner of rubbish stuffed into it by little boys.

'And what might these warlike preparations mean?' thought the commandant's wife. 'Are they expecting a Kirghiz attack? But surely Ivan Kuzmich wouldn't try to hide a little thing like that from me?'

She called to Ivan Ignatich, with the firm intention of worming out the secret which was torturing her feminine curiosity.

Vasilisa Egorovna made a few remarks connected with the household, in the manner of a judge beginning his investigation with a few questions off the point, questions to lull the defences of the defendant. Then after a few moments pause, she sighed deeply and said with a shake of the head: 'Lord above! What news! What's will be the end of it all?'

'Never fear, ma'am!', said Ivan Ignatich. 'God is merciful; we've plenty of soldiers, plenty of powder, and I've cleaned up the gun. No doubt we'll drive off Pugachev. With God on our side, no one can harm us!'

'And what sort of a man is this Pugachev?' asked the commandant's wife.

At this point, Ivan Ignatich realized that he had said too much and stopped abruptly. But it was too late now. Vasilisa Egorovna forced him to confess everything, after giving her word not to tell anyone.

Vasilisa kept her promise not to say a word to anyone, except the priest's wife, and that only because her cow was still wandering about on the steppe, and might be seized by the villains.

Soon everybody began talking about Pugachev. Rumours were various. The commandant sent the sergeant with instructions to get the full picture from the settlements and forts round about. The sergeant returned two days later and announced that he had seen a great many fires on the steppe about forty miles from the fort, and heard from the Bashkirs that an unheard-of force was approaching. However, he couldn't say anything positive about that because he had been afraid to go any further.

In the fort, an unusual agitation had become evident among the Cossacks; they gathered in knots on every street, talking quietly among themselves, and dispersed on seeing a dragoon or a garrison soldier. Spies were sent among them. Yulai, a baptized Kalmyk, gave a valuable piece of information to the commandant. The sergeant's report, according to Yulai, had been false: on his return, the crafty Cossack had told his comrades that he had been with the rebels, presented himself to their leader, who had permitted him to kiss his hand and had a long talk with him. The commandant immediately placed the sergeant under arrest, and appointed Yulai in his place. This news was received by the Cossacks with obvious dissatisfaction. They grumbled loudly and Ivan Ignatich, who carried out the commandant's order, heard them saying with his own ears:

'Just you wait, garrison rat!'

The commandant considered interrogating his prisoner that very day, but the sergeant had escaped, probably with the assistance of accomplices.

This new turn of events increased the commandant's nervousness. A Bashkir was captured with seditious literature upon him. On this occasion the commandant thought he would convene his officers again, and to this end proposed to get rid of Vasilisa Egorovna under a suitable pretext. But since Ivan Kuzmich was the most straightforward and truthful of men, he could find no other method beyond the one he had used once already.

'Listen, Vasilisa Egorovna', he said, clearing his throat, 'they say Father Gerasim has been sent from town . . .'

'That's enough of your fibbing, Ivan Kuzmich,' his wife interrupted. 'No doubt you want to call a meeting to talk about Emelyan Pugachev without me; well it won't wash!'

Ivan Kuzmich goggled at her.

'Well, mother,' he said. 'If you know everything already, then stay by all means; we'll talk about it even with you there.'

'That's better,' she replied. 'It's not like you to pull tricks; send for the officers then.'

We assembled once more. Ivan Kuzmich, in the presence of his wife, read to us Pugachev's appeal written down by some half-literate Cossack. The bandit announced his intention of marching at once against our fort; he invited the soldiers and

Cossacks to join his band, and exhorted the commanders not to resist, threatening execution otherwise. The appeal was expressed in crude but forceful language* and was bound to create a considerable impression on the minds of simple people.

'What a rogue!' cried the commandant's wife. 'Daring to make conditions! Go out to meet him and lay our colours at his feet! Son of a dog that he is! Does he not know that we've been in the service forty years and seen it all! Surely no commanders have done what he asks?'

'One wouldn't think so,' replied Ivan Kuzmich, 'but I hear the bandit has taken a good many forts.'

'He's obviously in considerable strength.'

'Well, now we'll find out just how strong he is,' said the commandant. 'Vasilisa Egorovna, give me the key to the barn. Ivan Ignatich, bring that Bashkir here and tell Yulai to fetch a whip.'

'Wait a moment, Ivan Kuzmich,' said his wife, rising from her chair. 'Let me take Masha somewhere out of the house, otherwise she'll hear the cries and get frightened. And I'm not too keen on torture either if truth be told. Good luck to you.'

In the old days, torture was so ingrained a part of the judicial process* that the beneficent order abolishing it remained a dead letter for a long time. It was thought that the accused's own confession was essential for the full exposure of his guilt, an idea not only without foundation but positively contrary to common juridical sense: for if a denial by the accused is not acceptable as proof of innocence, his confession is even less a proof of guilt. Even nowadays I occasionally hear old judges complaining of the abolition of the barbaric custom. At the time of which I write, nobody had any doubts as to the necessity for torture, neither judge nor accused. Therefore the commandant's order did not surprise or perturb any one of us. Ivan Ignatich went off to fetch the Bashkir who was locked in Vasilisa Egorovna's barn, and a few minutes later the prisoner was fetched into the anteroom. The commandant ordered that he be brought before him.

The Bashkir stepped across the threshold with difficulty (he was manacled) and, taking off his tall hat, halted in the doorway. I glanced at him and shuddered. I shall never forget that man. He looked over seventy. He had neither nose nor ears. His head was shaven and a few straggling grey hairs served him instead of a beard. He was small in stature, thin and bent, but his narrow little eyes still blazed.

'Ehe!' said the commandant, recognizing the terrible signs indicating that he had been one of the rebels punished in 1741.

'It's plain to see you're an old wolf who's been in our traps. It's not the first time you've been in arms against us since your noddle's been shaved so smooth. Come a bit closer and tell me who sent you?'

The old Bashkir said nothing and stared at the commandant with an expression of total vacancy.

'Why don't you say something?' Ivan Kuzmich pursued. 'Or don't you understand Russian? Yulai, go on ask him in your language, who sent him to our fort?'

Yulai repeated Ivan Kuzmich's question in the Tartar language. But the Bashkir looked at him in the same way and said not a word.

'*Yakshi*,'* said the commandant. 'You'll talk for me. Boys! Get that stupid striped robe off him and put a few stitches in his back. And, Yulai, mind you lay it on good and hard!'

Two veterans began stripping the Bashkir. The face of the wretched man registered alarm. He looked round in every direction, like some small animal cornered by children. When one of the veterans took his arms and twined them round his own neck, hoisting the old man on to his shoulders, while Yulai picked up the whip and brandished it, the Bashkir uttered a feeble, beseeching moan; with a shake of the head he opened his mouth where twitched a little stump in place of a tongue.

When I recall that this happened in my time and that I have lived to see the mild reign of the Emperor Alexander,* I cannot but be amazed at the swift progress of enlightenment and the spread of humane principles. Young man! If my notes should fall into your hands, remember that the best and most enduring changes are those which stem from an improvement in moral behaviour, without any violent upheaval.

Everyone was shocked.

'Well,' said the commandant, 'we'll plainly get nothing useful out of him. Yulai, take the Bashkir back to the barn. And we, gentlemen, have other things to discuss.'

We began talking over our situation, when suddenly a breathless Vasilisa Egorovna came in, with an air of extreme agitation.

'What's the matter with you?' asked the astonished commandant.

'Gentlemen, it's a calamity!' answered Vasilisa Egorovna. 'The Lower Lake fort was captured this morning. One of Father Gerasim's workers has got back from there. He saw it happen. They hanged the commandant and all the officers. All the soldiers were taken prisoner. The scoundrels will be here before we know it.'

This unexpected news stunned me. I knew the commandant of Lower Lake, a quiet and modest young man; two months or so before, he and his young wife had passed through on his way from Orenburg and stayed with Ivan Kuzmich. Lower Lake was about sixteen miles away. Pugachev's assault was to be expected hourly. I vividly imagined the fate of Maria Ivanovna, and my heart quailed within me.

'Listen Ivan Kuzmich!' I said to the commandant. 'Our duty is to defend the fort to the last breath; that goes without saying. But we must think about the safety of the women. Send them to Orenburg, if the road is still clear, or to a more secure fort a long way off, where the villains can't reach.'

Ivan Kuzmich turned to his wife and said:

'You hear, mother, shouldn't we be sending you off while we deal with the rebels?'

'Nonsense!' said his wife. 'Where's the fort bullets can't reach? What's the matter with Belogorsk? Praise be, we've lived over twenty-one years here. We've seen off Bashkirs and Kirghiz: we can sit out Pugachev as well!'

'Well, mother,' countered Ivan Kuzmich, 'stay if you think the fort is safe, but what are we going to do with Masha? It's all very well if we can sit tight or relief comes, but what if the villains take the fort?'

'Well, in that case . . .' Here Vasilisa Egorovna faltered and fell silent, with an expression of considerable anxiety.

'No, Vasilisa Egorovna,' the commandant went on, observing that his words had produced an effect, perhaps for the first time in his life. 'It's not good for Masha to stay here. Let's send her to Orenburg, to her godmother; they've got plenty of troops there and cannon too, and the walls are stone. And I would advise you to go off there as well; never mind if you're an old woman, just see what'll happen to you if they take the fort by storm.'

'All right,' said his wife. 'So be it, we'll send Masha away. But don't even ask me in your dreams: I shan't go. I'm not going to part with you in my old age and seek a lonely grave in some strange place. We've lived together, we'll die together.'

'Something in that,' said the commandant. 'Well, no sense in wasting time. Start getting Masha ready for the journey. We'll send her off at first light tomorrow, and we'll give her an escort, although we've got no spare men really. Where is Masha anyway?'

'With Akulina Pamfilovna,' replied his wife. 'She didn't feel well after she heard that Lower Lake had been captured; I hope she doesn't fall ill. Lord almighty, what times we've lived to see!'

Vasilisa Egorovna went off to superintend her daughter's departure. The talk at the commandant's continued; but I no longer intervened and heard nothing. Maria Ivanovna appeared at supper, pale and tearful. We ate in silence and rose from the table more quickly than usual; saying our good nights to the whole family, we dispersed to our quarters. But I deliberately forgot my sword and returned for it: I had a presentiment that I would find Masha alone. And indeed she met me in the doorway and handed me my sword.

'Goodbye, Pyotr Andreich,' she said to me, sobbing. 'They're sending me to Orenburg. Take care and be happy; it may be that the Lord will permit us to see one another again; but if not . . .' Here she burst into tears. I embraced her.

'Goodbye, my angel, goodbye my sweet, my heart's desire! Whatever happens to me, be assured my last thought and prayer will be for you.'

Masha wept, with her head pressed into my chest. I kissed her ardently and hurried from the room.

7

THE ASSAULT

My head, my little head,
Loyal head of mine!
My head has served
Three and thirty years.
Ah, this head never won
No profit, no joy,
No word of praise,
No high rank;
All this head ever earned
Are these two tall poles,
With cross-beam of maple,
And a silken noose.

(Folk song)*

That night I neither slept nor undressed. At dawn I intended to make for the fort gates, from which Maria Ivanovna was due to set out, and bid her goodbye for the last time. I sensed a great change in me: my inner agitation was a great deal less oppressive than the despondency in which I had recently been plunged. The sadness of parting was mingled with obscure but delicious hopes and an impatient anticipation of danger, as well as stirrings of noble ambition. The night passed imperceptibly. I was about to leave the house when my door opened and a corporal entered to inform me that our Cossacks had left the fort during the night, forcing Yulai to go with them; also that strangers were riding round the fort. The thought that Maria Ivanovna might not have time to leave terrified me; I issued hurried instructions to the corporal and rushed away at once to the commandant.

It was getting light by now. As I raced along the street, I heard someone calling. I halted.

'Where are you off to?' asked Ivan Ignatich, as he caught me up. 'Ivan Kuzmich is on the rampart and has sent me to fetch you. Pugachev has arrived.'

'Has Maria Ivanovna got away?' I asked, my heart quaking.

'No, she hasn't,' replied Ivan Ignatich. 'The Orenburg road has been cut; the fort is surrounded. Things look bad, Pyotr Andreich!'

We went up on to the rampart, an eminence formed by nature and reinforced by a palisade. All the fort's inhabitants were jostling together there. The garrison was standing to arms. The commandant was pacing before his sparse ranks. The cannon had been hauled there the day before. The proximity of danger had inspired the old warrior with unusual vigour. Some twenty horsemen were riding across the steppe not far from the fort. They appeared to be Cossacks, but there were Bashkirs among them, easily recognized by their lynx-fur hats and quivers. The commandant walked round his troops, telling the soldiers:

'Well, my lads, let us stand together for our Mother Empress and show the world that we are brave men and true!'

The soldiers loudly protested their zeal. Shvabrin was standing next to me, staring unwaveringly at the enemy. The men riding across the steppe, observing the bustle inside the fort, gathered together in a group and began talking among themselves. The commandant ordered Ivan Ignatich to aim the cannon at this group, and set the fuse himself. The ball whizzed over them without doing any damage. The horsemen scattered and immediately galloped out of sight, leaving the steppe deserted.

At this point Vasilisa Egorovna appeared on the rampart, accompanied by Masha, who did not want to leave her side.

'Well?' asked the commandant's wife. 'How goes the battle? And where on earth's the enemy?'

'The enemy is not far off,' responded Ivan Kuzmich. 'With God's help all will be well. What's the matter, Masha, frightened?'

'No, daddy,' answered Maria Ivanovna. 'I'm more frightened at home by myself.'

At this, she glanced at me and forced herself to smile. I involuntarily gripped my sword-hilt, recalling that I had received it from her hands, as a defence for my beloved, as it were. My heart was on fire. I imagined myself her own knight. I longed to show that I was worthy of her trust and impatiently awaited the moment of decision.

And now fresh mounted hordes appeared from behind a rise a quarter of a mile from the fort, and soon the steppe was

aswarm with a multitude of men, armed with spears and bows.
In their midst rode a man in a red caftan, mounted on a white
horse, with an unsheathed sabre in his hand. This was Pugachev
himself. He came to a halt. The rest surrounded him and, at his
command, as it appeared, four horsemen detached themselves
and galloped at full tilt right up to the fort. We recognized them
as renegades from our own troops. One of them was carrying a
sheet of paper under his hat; another had Yulai's head stuck on
the end of his spear, which he shook loose and hurled at us over
the palisade. The head of the poor Kalmyk fell at the commandant's feet. The renegades shouted:

'Don't shoot; come out to the sovereign. The sovereign is
here!'

'I'll teach you!' yelled Ivan Kuzmich. 'Lads! Fire!'

Our soldiers let fly with a volley. The Cossack with the paper
swayed and fell from his horse; the others galloped back. I
glanced at Maria Ivanovna. Aghast at the sight of Yulai's bloody
head and deafened by the volley, she seemed dazed. The commandant called for a corporal to take the paper from the hand of
the dead Cossack. The corporal went out into the steppe and
returned, leading the dead man's horse by the bridle. He handed
the document to the commandant. Ivan Kuzmich read it to
himself and then tore it into shreds. Meanwhile the rebels were
plainly getting ready for action. Soon bullets began whistling
about our ears, and several arrows struck the palisade and the
ground near us.

'Vasilisa Egorovna!' said the commandant. 'This isn't women's business; take Masha away; you can see she's in a terrible
state.'

Vasilisa Egorovna, subdued under fire, glanced out at the
steppe, which betrayed signs of considerable activity; then she
turned to her husband and said:

'Ivan Kuzmich, God's will be done in life and death. Bless
Masha. Masha go to your father.'

Masha, pale and trembling, sank to her knees and bowed to
the earth before him. The old commandant made the sign of the
cross three times over her, then raised her and, after kissing her,
said in an altered voice:

'Well, Masha, may you be happy. Pray to God: he will not

desert you. If you find a good man, God grant you love and concord. Live with him as Vasilisa Egorovna and I have done. Well, goodbye, Masha. Vasilisa Egorovna take her away, hurry.' (Masha threw her arms round his neck and burst into tears.)

'Let us kiss as well', said his weeping wife. 'Goodbye, my Ivan Kuzmich. Forgive me if I have ever vexed you!'

'Goodbye, goodbye, my dear!' said the commandant, embracing his old woman.

'Now, that's enough! Off home now, off you go; and if you have time, dress Masha in a sarafan.'

His wife and daughter went off. I glanced after Maria Ivanovna; she looked back and nodded. Then Ivan Kuzmich turned to us and all his attention was directed at the enemy. The rebels were forming up around their leader, and all at once began dismounting.

'Stand firm now', said the commandant. 'The attack's coming . . .'

At that moment there came a frightful shrieking and yelling as the rebels made for the fort at a run. Our cannon was loaded with grapeshot. The commandant let them get to the closest possible range before suddenly letting fly again. The shot found its mark in the very heart of the mob. The rebels scattered on both sides and fell back. Their leader was left alone at the front . . . He brandished his sabre and seemed to be vehemently exhorting them . . . The yelling and shrieking which had momentarily subsided was immediately renewed.

'Now, lads,' said the commandant. 'Open the gates, beat the drum. Lads! Forward, on the sortie. Follow me!'

The commandant, Ivan Ignatich, and I were instantly beyond the rampart, but the cowed garrison had not stirred.

'What are you standing there for, boys?' cried Ivan Kuzmich. 'Do or die—it's a soldier's duty!'

It was then that the rebels rushed upon us and burst into the fort. The drum fell silent; the garrison threw down their arms; I was nearly knocked off my feet, but I got up and entered the fort along with the rebels. The commandant, wounded in the head, was standing amid a group of villains who were demanding his keys. As I made to rush to his assistance, some brawny Cossacks seized me and tied me up with their belts, repeating:

'You're going to get it for disobeying the sovereign!'

We were dragged along the streets, as the people came out with bread and salt. The bells were pealing. Suddenly the crowd began shouting that the sovereign was in the square waiting for the prisoners and receiving oaths of allegiance. The folk were pouring into the square and we were hustled along in the same direction.

Pugachev was sitting in an armchair* on the porch of the commandant's house. He was wearing a red Cossack caftan, trimmed with gold. His tall sable cap with gold tassels was pulled down over his glittering eyes. I thought his face seemed familiar. Cossack elders surrounded him. Father Gerasim, pale and trembling, was standing by the porch, cross in hand, and appeared to be silently beseeching him to spare the imminent victims. A gallows was swiftly being erected in the square. As we approached, the Bashkirs drove the people back and we were brought before Pugachev. The bells stopped ringing; a profound silence ensued.

'Which one is the commandant?' asked the pretender.

Our sergeant stepped forward from the crowd and indicated Ivan Kuzmich. Pugachev gave the old man a menacing stare and said:

'How dare you oppose me, your sovereign?'

The commandant, fainting from his wound, summoned up his last reserves and replied in a steady voice:

'You are not my sovereign, you're a thief and an impostor, d'ye hear?'

Pugachev frowned grimly and waved a white handkerchief. Several Cossacks seized the old captain and dragged him to the gallows. The mutilated Bashkir whom we had interrogated on the previous day appeared on the cross-beam. He was holding a rope in his hands, and a moment later I saw poor Ivan Kuzmich hoisted into the air. Then Ivan Ignatich was brought forward.

'Swear,' said Pugachev to him. 'To your sovereign Pyotr Fyodorovich!'

'You are not our sovereign,' replied Ivan Ignatich, repeating the words of his captain. 'You, man, are a thief and an impostor!' Pugachev waved his handkerchief again and the good lieutenant was hanging next to his old chief.

My turn was next. I stared boldly at Pugachev, ready to

repeat the answer given by my great-hearted comrades. Then, to my indescribable amazement, I caught sight of Shvabrin among the rebel elders, wearing a Cossack caftan, his hair shaven close to a top-knot. He went up to Pugachev and said a few words in his ear.

'Hang him!' said Pugachev, without glancing at me. A noose was thrown round my neck. I began reciting a prayer to myself, repenting sincerely before God for all my transgressions, and beseeching him to preserve those near to my heart. I was dragged beneath the gallows.

'Don't be scared, don't be scared,' my executioners kept repeating, perhaps genuinely wanting to keep my spirits up. All at once, I heard a shout:

'Stop! Curse you! Wait on!'

The executioners stopped. I looked and saw Savelich lying at Pugachev's feet.

'Our Father,' the poor old man was saying. 'What good will the death of a noble child be to you? Let him go; they'll give a ransom for him; if you want to make an example and put fear in people, hang me, an old man!'

Pugachev gave a sign and I was instantly untied and set free.

'Our father has pardoned you,' they told me.

At that moment I cannot say that I was glad of my release, but I won't say I was sorry about it either. My feelings were in too much turmoil. I was again brought before the pretender and made to kneel before him. Pugachev extended a gnarled hand.

'Kiss his hand! Kiss his hand!' came the calls from round about. But I would have preferred the cruellest of deaths to such a vile humiliation.

'Master Pyotr Andreich!' whispered Savelich, who was standing behind me and pushing. 'Don't be stubborn! What's it matter to you! To hell, just kiss the vill . . . (blast!) kiss his hand.'

I made no move. Pugachev let his hand fall, saying with a grin:

'His honour, it seems, is dazed with joy. Lift him up!'

I was raised to my feet and let go. I was a spectator of the dreadful comedy as it proceeded.

The fort inhabitants began swearing allegiance. They approached one after the other, kissing the crucifix and then bowing to the pretender. The garrison soldiers stood by. The sweating tailor, equipped with his blunt scissors, cut off their plaits. They shook themselves and approached the hand of Pugachev, who pronounced them pardoned and accepted them into his band. This went on for nearly three hours. Finally Pugachev got up from his chair and left the porch, accompanied by his elders. A white horse, richly caparisoned, was led up to him. Two Cossacks raised him by the elbows and placed him in the saddle. He announced to Father Gerasim that he would be dining with him. At that moment a woman's cry rang out. Several bandits had dragged Vasilisa Egorovna, dishevelled and stripped naked, onto the steps. One of them had even managed to adorn himself with her padded jacket. Others were hauling out feather mattresses, chests, crockery, sheets, and all kinds of other bits and pieces.

'Please, my dear sirs!' the old woman was crying. 'Let me go in peace. Dear sirs, take me to Ivan Kuzmich.' Suddenly she glanced over at the gallows and recognized her husband.

'Blackguards!' she cried out in a frenzy. 'What have you done to him? Light of my life, Ivan Kuzmich, my brave soldier! Prussian bayonets and Turkish bullets couldn't touch you; you didn't lay down your life in honourable battle, you have perished at the hand of an escaped convict!'

'Shut the old witch up!' said Pugachev. At this, a young Cossack struck her across the head with his sabre, and she fell lifeless across the porch steps. Pugachev departed; the people swarmed after him.

8

AN UNINVITED GUEST*

An uninvited guest is worse than a Tartar

(Proverb)

The square emptied. I was still rooted to the spot, unable to collect my wits, thrown into confusion by so many dreadful emotions.

Uncertainty over the fate of Maria Ivanovna tormented me worst of all. Where was she? What had happened to her? Had she managed to hide? Was her refuge secure? . . . Filled with disquieting thoughts, I entered the commandant's house . . . It was quite desolate; the chairs, tables, and chests had been broken up; the crockery was smashed; everything had been dragged about. I ran up the little staircase that led to the bedrooms, and for the first time in my life stepped into Maria Ivanovna's room. I saw her bed, ripped to pieces by the marauders; the wardrobe had been broken open and ransacked; a lamp still glowed before the empty icon-case. A mirror hanging between the windows had also survived . . . Where on earth was the mistress of this humble, maidenly cell? A frightful thought flashed through my mind: I pictured her in the hands of the bandits . . . My heart shrank within me . . . I wept bitter, bitter tears and loudly called out the name of my beloved . . . At that moment I heard a slight noise and Palasha appeared from behind the wardrobe, pale and trembling.

'Oh, Pyotr Andreich!' she said, clasping her hands. 'What a day! The horrors! . . .'

'And Maria Ivanovna?' I asked impatiently. 'What about Maria Ivanovna?'

'The young lady is alive,' replied Palasha. 'She's hidden at Akulina Pamfilovna's.'

'The priest's house?' I cried, horror-struck. 'Good God! But that's where Pugachev is! . . .'

I dashed out of the room and was in the street a second later. I ran headlong for the priest's house, unseeing and unthinking.

I could hear shouts, singing, and laughter coming from it . . .
Pugachev was feasting with his companions. Palasha had run
after me. I sent her to call Akulina Pamfilovna without attracting
attention. A moment later, the priest's wife came out to me in
the passage with an empty bottle in her hands.

'For God's sake, where is Maria Ivanovna?' I asked, in a state
of unspeakable anxiety.

'She's lying here on the bed, my dear, behind the partition,'
replied the priest's wife. 'Well, we nearly had trouble, but, praise
be, it all passed off smoothly: the villain had just sat down to eat,
when my poor lamb wakes up and groans! . . . My heart stood
still. He heard it:

'"And who've you got there moaning, old woman?"

'I bowed low before the robber:

'"My niece, sire; took ill, she's been in bed a fortnight."

'"Is she young, this niece of yours?"

'"She is, sire."

'"So show me your niece, old woman."

'My heart was beating so, but there was nothing for it.

'"As you wish, sire; only the lass cannot get up and come to
your grace."

'"That's all right, old woman, I'll go myself and have a look."

'And the wretch actually went behind the partition and what
do you think! He pulled back the curtain and looked in with
those hawk's eyes of his! And nothing happened . . . The Lord
delivered us! And would you believe it, my man and I were all
ready for a martyr's death. Luckily, my dear, she didn't know
who he was. God almighty, what things we've lived to see! I
declare! Poor Ivan Kuzmich! Who'd have ever thought! . . . And
Vasilisa Egorovna? And Ivan Ignatich, of all people? Why him? . . .
How did they spare you? And what about Shvabrin, Alexey
Ivanich? He's has his hair cropped and he's here living it up
with them! He's a sharp one and no mistake! And when I mentioned my sick niece, he gave me such a look it went through me
like a knife, believe me; but he didn't give me away, I'll say that
for him.'

At this, there came drunken shouts and Father Gerasim's
voice. The visitors were demanding wine, the host was calling
for his spouse. The priest's wife began bustling about.

'Get yourself off home, Pyotr Andreich', she said. 'I haven't time for you now; the brigands are good and drunk, and you don't want any trouble with them in that state. Goodbye, Pyotr Andreich! What will be, will be; we trust God will not abandon us!'

The priest's wife went off. Somewhat reassured, I set off for my quarters. Passing the square, I saw several Bashkirs jostling round the gallows, dragging the boots from the hanged men; I suppressed with difficulty a surge of indignation, sensing that any intervention would be pointless. Bandits were running about the fort, plundering the officer's houses. The shouting of drunken rebels resounded everywhere. I arrived home and Savelich welcomed me on the threshold.

'Thanks be to God!' he cried out on seeing me. 'I was beginning to think the villains had taken hold of you again. Well, master Pyotr Andreich! Would you believe it? They've robbed us of everything, the rogues: clothes, sheets, belongings, crockery—they've left nothing! Well, what of that! Thank God, they've spared you! And, sir, did you did you recognize their *ataman*?'

'No, I didn't; who is he anyway?'

'What, master? You've forgotten that drunk who tricked you out of your jacket at the inn? The hare-skin jacket, new as new; and how the brute split the seams trying to get it on him!'

I was amazed. The resemblance between Pugachev and my guide was indeed astonishing. I was convinced that Pugachev and he were one and the same person, and now understood the reason for the pardon I had been granted. I could not help marvelling at the strange chain of circumstance: a boy's jacket, given to a tramp, had rescued me from the noose, and a drunk who staggered about tavern courtyards was besieging forts and shaking the empire!

'Wouldn't you like something to eat?' asked Savelich, a man of set habit. 'There's nothing in the house; I'll go and hunt something up and cook it for you.'

Left alone, I became a prey to reflection. What was I to do? To remain in the fort under the command of the ruffian or follow after his band, was not worthy of an officer. My duty demanded that I should present myself where my service would be of most use to my country in the present difficult circumstances

... But love strongly prompted me to stay near Maria Ivanovna and be her defender and protector. Although I foresaw an imminent and certain alteration in circumstances, I could not help shuddering when I pictured the peril of her situation.

My reflections were cut short by the entry of one of the Cossacks, who ran in with the announcement that 'the great sovereign requires you to see him'.

'Where is he, then?' I asked, preparing to obey.

'In the commandant's house', replied the Cossack. 'After dinner, our father went to the bath-house and is now taking his ease. Well, your honour, it's well seen that he's a person of distinction: he was pleased to eat two roast piglets for dinner, and steamed himself that hot, even Taras Kurochkin couldn't stand it, he gave the birch twigs to Fomka Bikbaev and they had a hard job to bring him round with cold water. Can't be denied: everything he does is on the grand scale ... And in the bath-house, they say, he showed the royal marks on his chest: on one side the two-headed eagle,* about the size of a five-rouble piece, and his own face on the other.

I did not deem it necessary to argue with the Cossack and went off with him to the commandant's house, picturing my audience with Pugachev and trying to divine what the outcome would be. The reader may well imagine that I was not altogether at my ease.

It was starting to get dark when I arrived at the commandant's house. The gallows with its two victims showed up ghastly black. The body of the commandant's poor wife still sprawled under the porch, near which two Cossacks stood on guard. The one conducting me went in to announce me, and returning at once, led me into the same room in which I had so tenderly bid Maria Ivanovna farewell on the previous day.

An extraordinary picture met my eyes: at the table, which was covered with a table-cloth and set about with bottles and glasses, Pugachev and some dozen Cossack elders sat in their caps and coloured shirts; they were flushed with wine, their eyes sparkling. Shvabrin and our sergeant, the recent renegades, were not among them.

'Ah, your honour!' said Pugachev, on seeing me. 'Welcome, welcome, honour and a place for you.'

His companions made room for me. I sat down in silence at the end of the table. My neighbour, a young Cossack, slender and handsome, poured a glass of ordinary wine for me, which I did not touch. I began to survey the gathering with curiosity. Pugachev sat in the place of honour, elbows on the table, propping his black beard on a broad fist. His facial features were regular and quite appealing, evincing nothing ferocious. He frequently turned to a man of about fifty, calling him either count or Timofeich, and sometimes honouring him as 'uncle'. They all treated one another as comrades and did not demonstrate any particular deference towards their leader. The conversation revolved about the morning's assault, the success of the rising, and future operations. Each of them boasted, put forward his opinion, and freely argued with Pugachev. And it was resolved at this odd war council to go on to Orenburg: a daring stroke, but one that almost achieved a disastrous success! The march was announced for the following day.

'Well, brothers,' said Pugachev. 'Let's have my favourite song to sing us to sleep. Chumakov, you start!'

My neighbour struck up a mournful barge-hauler's song* and everyone took it up in unison:

> Do not rustle your leaves, green mother oak-tree,
> Do not disturb me, bold young lad, as I think my thoughts.
> That tomorrow I, bold young lad, go to the questioning
> Before a stern judge, the Tsar himself.
> Then the sovereign-Tsar will question me.
> Tell me, tell me, lad, you peasant's son,
> With whom you went a-robbing and a-pillaging,
> Did you have many comrades with you?
> I will tell you, our hope, orthodox Tsar,
> I will tell the whole truth, nothing but the truth,
> That I had but four comrades:
> My first was the darkness of night,
> The second of my comrades was my trusty blade,
> The third of my comrades was my trusty steed,
> The fourth of my comrades was my bow so taut,
> My messengers, my arrows hot.
> At which our hope, the orthodox Tsar will say.
> Well done, my child, you peasant's son,
> You knew well how to rob and answer me!

> For you, my child, I will provide
> Amid the fields a lofty dwelling-place,
> With two tall posts and a beam across.

It is impossible to convey the effect this folk-song about the gallows produced in me, sung as it was by people destined for the gallows. Their grim faces, harmonious voices, the mournful expression they gave to their words, expressive enough in themselves—altogether it overwhelmed me with a kind of mystic awe.

The guests drank another glass apiece, then stood up and said their good-nights to Pugachev. I made to follow them, but Pugachev said:

'Stay there; I want to have a talk with you.'

We remained face to face.

For some time we observed a mutual silence. Pugachev was staring fixedly at me, occasionally narrowing his left eye with a startling expression of roguish mockery. At length he laughed with such unaffected gaiety that I, as I looked at him, unaccountably began laughing too.

'Well, your honour?' he said. 'Your knees started knocking didn't they, when my lads threw the rope round your neck? Scared stiff, I'll be bound . . . And you'd have been dangling there if it hadn't been for your serving-man. I recognized the old sod right away. Well, and did you imagine that the man who guided you to that inn was the supreme sovereign?' (Here he assumed a solemn and mysterious air.) 'You are gravely at fault in my sight,' he went on, 'but I pardoned you for your charity, in that you rendered me a service when I was obliged to hide from my enemies. But that is merely a beginning! You will see how I reward you when I come into my kingdom! Do you promise to serve me zealously?'

The scoundrel's question and his bold manner seemed so amusing, that I could not restrain a smile.

'Why the smile?' he asked, scowling. 'Or don't you believe that I am the supreme sovereign? Straight answer, now.'

I was flustered: to acknowledge a tramp as my sovereign was out of the question: that seemed unforgiveable cowardice. To call him an impostor to his face was to invite destruction; what

I had been ready to do under the gallows in the eyes of all, in the first blazing heat of indignation, now seemed pointless bravado. I hesitated. Pugachev grimly awaited my answer. At length (and I can recall that moment now with pride), my sense of duty triumphed over the human weakness within me. I answered Pugachev:

'Listen: I will tell you the honest truth. Think on, how can I acknowledge you as my sovereign? You are no fool, you would see yourself I was deceiving you.'

'Who am I then, in your opinion?'

'God alone, knows, but whoever you are, you're playing a dangerous game.'

Pugachev shot a glance at me.

'So you don't believe that I am Tsar Pyotr Fyodorovich? Very well. But doesn't fortune favour the brave? Didn't Grisha Otrepyev* reign as tsar? Think of me what you like, but don't desert me. Why should you worry who I might or might not be? Whoever the priest is, he's called father. Serve me in faith and truth, and I will make you a field marshal and a prince. What do you say?'

'No,' I replied firmly. 'I was born a nobleman; I swore my oath to the Empress. I can't serve you. If you really wish me well, let me go to Orenburg.'

Pugachev brooded on this.

'And if I do let you go,' he said, 'will you promise at least that you will not serve against me?'

'How can I promise you that?' I answered. 'You know yourself that's not up to me: if I'm ordered out against you, I'll go, there's nothing for it. You're a commander yourself now, and you demand obedience from your men. What would it be if I were to refuse to serve, when my service is required? My life is in your hands: if you set me free—I thank you; if you execute me, God will judge you; in any case I have told you the truth.'

My sincerity impressed Pugachev.

'So be it,' he said, clapping me on the shoulder. 'Hang him if you're going to, if not, spare him. Go where you will, and do as you like. Come and say goodbye to me tomorrow, but for now, off you go to bed, I'm getting sleepy myself.'

I left Pugachev and went out into the street. The night was

still and frosty. The moon and stars shone brightly, picking out the square and the gallows. All was dark and silent within the fort. Only in the tavern were there any lights and the echoing shouts of the last revellers. I glanced over at the priest's house. The shutters and gate were closed. All was quiet in there, it seemed.

I got back to my quarters and found Savelich, worrying over my absence. The news of my release brought him unspeakable gladness.

'Glory be to thee, O God!' he said, crossing himself.

'We'll leave the fort at first light tomorrow and just follow our noses. I've made you a little something; have a bite, master, and you sleep the sleep of the just till morning.'

I followed his advice and, after a hearty supper, fell asleep on the bare floor, mentally and physically exhausted.

9

PARTING

So sweet with you to be united;
So sad, so sad, that I must part
From one whose beauty so delighted,
As if I took leave of my heart.

(Kheraskov)*

Early next morning I was awakened by the sound of a drum. I
went off to the assembly area. Crowds of Pugachev's men were
drawn up near the gallows, where the victims of the previous
day still hung. The Cossacks sat on horseback, while the soldiers
sloped arms. Banners were fluttering. Several cannon, among
which I recognized our own, had been mounted on gun-
carriages. All the fort inhabitants were there, waiting for the pretender. By the porch of the commandant's house, a Cossack was
holding a splendid white Kirghiz horse. My eyes sought out the
corpse of the commandant's wife. It had been taken somewhat
to one side and covered with some bast matting. At last Pugachev
emerged from the passage. The people bared their heads.
Pugachev halted on the porch and greeted one and all. An elder
handed him a sack filled with copper coins, which he proceeded
to throw out in handfuls. The people rushed to pick them up,
amid much shouting and not without bodily harm. Pugachev
was surrounded by his chief confederates. Shvabrin stood among
them too. Our glances met. In mine he might have read contempt, and he turned away with an expression of genuine venom
and feigned derision. Pugachev, catching sight of me in the
crowd, gave a nod and called me over to him.

'Listen,' he said. 'Get yourself off to Orenburg straight away
and inform the governor and all his generals that he can expect
me within the week. Advise them to welcome me with filial love
and obedience; otherwise they will not escape a cruel death. A
pleasant journey, your honour!'

Then he addressed the people, indicating Shvabrin: 'Here,

my children, is your new commander: obey him in everything, he is responsible to me for you and the fort.'

I was horror-stricken at these words: Shvabrin was being appointed commander of the fort; Maria Ivanovna was being left in his power! Lord, what would happen to her? Pugachev descended from the porch. His horse was led up and he leapt nimbly into the saddle, without waiting for the Cossacks who had intended to assist him.

At this moment, I saw my Savelich make his way out of the throng, go up to Pugachev, and hand him a sheet of paper. I could not imagine what the upshot of this would be.

'What's this?' asked Pugachev heavily.

'Read and you will see,' replied Savelich. Pugachev took the paper and scrutinized it for a long time with a significant air.

'Why don't you write clearly?' he said at length. 'Our serene eyes can make nothing out. Where is my chief secretary?'

A young fellow in a corporal's uniform ran smartly up to Pugachev.

'Read it aloud,' said the pretender, giving him the paper. I was extremely curious to learn what my guardian had been minded to write to Pugachev. The chief secretary began to spell out the following, in a loud voice: 'Two gowns, one calico, one striped silk, to the value of six roubles.'

'What does this mean?' said Pugachev, frowning.

'Order him to read on,' answered Savelich, placidly.

The chief secretary continued.

'Uniform of fine green cloth, seven roubles. White cloth breeches, five roubles. Twelve Dutch linen shirts with ruffles, ten roubles. One chest containing tea service, two roubles and a half . . .'

'What's all this foolery?' Pugachev interrupted. 'What have chests and ruffled breeches to do with me?'

Savelich hawked and started explaining.

'This, father, you see, is the inventory of my master's goods, stolen by the villains . . .'

'What villains?' asked Pugachev menacingly.

'I beg pardon, a slip of the tongue,' replied Savelich. 'Not villains then, but your boys rummaging and pilfering. Don't be angry: a horse can stumble, and it's got four legs. Order him to read to the end.'

'Finish reading,' said Pugachev. The secretary went on:

'Bedspread, chintz, a second of taffeta, cotton-stuffed—four roubles. A scarlet rateen coat, lined with fox-fur, forty roubles. And there is the hare-skin jacket, given to your grace at the wayside lodging, fifteen roubles.'

'I never heard the like!' cried Pugachev, his eyes blazing.

I must confess, I was very much afraid for my poor mentor. He was about to launch into explanations once again, but Pugachev cut him short:

'How dare you approach me with such trifles?' he shouted, grabbing the paper from his secretary's hands and hurling it in Savelich's face.

'Stupid old man! So they've been stolen: is that a calamity? You should pray eternally for me, and my lads, old sod that you are, that you and your master aren't hanging alongside those disobedient ones . . . Hare-skin jacket! I'll give you hare-skin jacket! And you know what, I'll flay the hide off your living body and make a jacket out of that!'

'As you please', responded Savelich. 'But I am a servant and I have to answer for my master's property.'

Pugachev was evidently in an indulgent vein.

He turned away and rode off without another word. Shvabrin and the elders followed him. The rebel band marched out of the fort in orderly fashion. The people went along to see Pugachev on his way. I remained along on the square with Savelich. He was holding the inventory in his hands and scrutinizing it with a profoundly disconsolate air.

Seeing me on good terms with Pugachev, he had thought to put the situation to good use; but his cunning scheme had not met with success. I was minded to berate him for his inappropriate zeal, but couldn't help laughing.

'You can laugh, sir,' responded Savelich. 'Laugh away, but when it comes to getting all new stuff, we'll see if it's a laughing matter then.'

I hurried off to the priest's house to see Maria Ivanovna. The priest met me with grievous news. During the night, she had developed a high fever. She was unconscious and delirious. I quietly went up to her bed. I was struck by the alteration in her face. She did not recognize me. I stood before her for a long time, heeding neither Father Gerasim nor his good wife, who, it seemed, were trying to comfort me. I was a prey to grim imaginings. The situation of the poor defenceless orphan, abandoned alone among vicious rebels, and my own helplessness horrified me. Shvabrin, Shvabrin, tormented my imagination worst of all. Invested with power by the pretender, in charge of the fort where the unfortunate girl was—an innocent object of his hatred—he might do anything. What was I to do? How could I render her assistance? How rescue her from the hands of the villains? There was only one resource remaining: I decided to set out for Orenburg at once, so as to hasten the liberation of the Belogorsk Fort and do what I could in that enterprise. I bade farewell to the priest and Akulina Pamfilovna, fervently entrusting to her the one I already regarded as my wife. I took the hand of the poor girl and kissed it as I shed tears.

'Farewell,' said the priest's wife, as she saw me out. 'Goodbye, Pyotr Andreich. Perhaps we shall meet under happier circumstances. Don't forget us and write often. Poor Maria Ivanovna has no comfort or defender apart from you.'

I went out into the square and paused for a moment, gazing at the gallows, bowed towards it, walked out of the fort, and headed along the Orenburg road, accompanied by Savelich, who never left my side.

I was walking along, preoccupied with reflections, when I suddenly heard hoof-beats behind me. I glanced round and saw a Cossack galloping out from the fort, holding a Bashkir horse by the bridle and gesturing to me from afar. I stopped and soon made out our sergeant. As he galloped up, he slid down from his horse, saying as he gave me the reins of the other:

'Your honour! Our father is presenting you with a horse and the fur from his own shoulders' (a sheepskin was tied to the saddle). 'And in addition,' the sergeant faltered, 'he has also made you a gift of fifty kopeks . . . but I seem to have lost it along the road; please forgive me in your generosity.'

Savelich eyed him askance and growled:

'Lost it along the road! And what's that you've got clinking under your shirt? You should be ashamed!'

'What's clinking under my shirt?' countered the sergeant not a whit abashed. 'God save you, greybeard! It was the bridle that was clinking, not coins.'

'All right,' I said, curtailing the argument. 'Convey my thanks to the one who sent you; try to find the fifty you lost on the way back, and keep it for vodka.'

'Very grateful to your honour,' he replied, turning his horse. 'I will pray eternally for you.'

So saying, he galloped back, with one hand holding his shirt, and in a minute was lost to view.

I donned the sheepskin and mounted, placing Savelich behind me.

'There you see, sir,' said the old man. 'I didn't petition the rogue in vain. The thief's conscience troubled him, although a sheepskin and a leggy Bashkir nag aren't worth half what the rogues stole from us, and what you were pleased to give him yourself; still, they'll come in handy, mustn't look a gift horse in the mouth.'

10

A TOWN UNDER SIEGE

An eagle gazing down,
With plain and hill now his,
his eye turned on the town.
Behind the camp he bade
a thundercloud be wrought,
And, lightning-charged, at night,
against the city brought.

(Kheraskov)*

As we approached Orenburg, we saw a gang of convicts, with heads shaven and faces disfigured by the executioner's pincers. They were working near to the fortifications, under the supervision of the garrison veterans. Some were carting off the rubbish that had accumulated in the ditch; others were digging up the earth with spades; on the rampart, masons were carrying bricks and renovating the town wall. Sentries stopped us at the gates and requested identification. As soon as the sergeant heard that I had was travelling from Belogorsk, he took me straight to the general's house.

I found him in the garden. He was inspecting the apple trees, now denuded by the breath of autumn, and assisted by the old gardener was carefully wrapping them in warm straw. His face was a picture of serene good nature and health. He was glad to see me and began questioning me concerning the horrible events I had witnessed. I recounted it all to him. The old man listened attentively, snipping off dry twigs the while.

'Poor Mironov!' he said, when I had concluded my sad narration. 'I'm sorry about that: he was a good officer. And Madam Mironov was a good-hearted lady and a real expert at pickling mushrooms. But what about Masha, the captain's daughter?'*

I replied that she had remained in the fort, in the care of the priest's wife.

'Ai-ai-ai,' the general put in. 'That's bad, very bad. You can never rely on the discipline of bandits. What's going to happen to the poor girl?'

I replied that Belogorsk Fort was not far off and that, no doubt, his excellency would not delay sending forces to free the poor inhabitants. The general shook his head mistrustfully.

'We'll see about that, we'll see,' he said. 'There'll be time enough to talk about that. I would ask you to come and take a cup of tea with me: today I have a meeting of the military council. You can give us reliable information about this scoundrel Pugachev and his forces. In the meantime, go and get some rest.'

I went off to my allotted quarters, where Savelich had already set up house, and began the wait till the appointed hour. The reader will readily understand that I did not fail to appear at the council meeting, which was bound to play such a role in my fate. I was at the general's before time.

I found one of the town officials there, in charge of customs as I recall, a fat, florid-faced old man in a brocade caftan. He began bombarding me with questions about what had happened to Ivan Kuzmich, whom he called an old pal of his, and frequently interrupted me with supplementary questions and moralizing remarks which showed him to be, if not a man versed in the arts of war, then at least one possessed of shrewdness and native wit. Meanwhile, the rest of those invited had arrived. Apart from the general himself, there was not a single military man there. When all had taken their seats and everyone had got their cup of tea, the general spelled out in considerable clarity and detail how matters stood.

'And now, gentlemen,' he went on, 'it behoves us to decide how to proceed against the rebels: attack or defence? Either option has its advantages and disadvantages. Offensive action offers greater hope for the speedy destruction of the enemy; defence is safer and more reliable . . . So, therefore, let us put the matter to the vote in due and proper form, that is, starting with the most junior in rank. Mister Ensign!' he continued, turning to me, 'kindly give us your opinion.'

I rose, and having briefly described Pugachev and his band, said positively that the pretender could not withstand a properly armed force.

My opinion was greeted by the officials with obvious dissatisfaction. They saw in it the impetuosity and rashness of a
young man. A murmuring began, and I distinctly overheard the
word 'puppy'. The general addressed me, smiling, and said
'Mister Ensign! The first votes in military councils are usually
cast in favour of offensive operations; that is in the order of
things. Now let us continue the voting. Mister Collegiate Councillor!* Tell us your opinion.'

The old man in the brocade caftan hurriedly drained the last
third of his cup of tea, with its significant admixture of rum, and
replied to the general:

'I think, your excellency, that we should act neither offens-
ively nor defensively.'

'How can that be, Mister Collegiate Councillor?' protested
the general, much taken aback. 'Tactics can admit of no other
method—defensive manœuvres or attack . . .'

'Your excellency, proceed by bribery.'

'Heh-heh! Your opinion is a most sensible one. Tactics allow
for bribery, and we will make use of your advice. We can offer
for that good-for-nothing's head . . . 70 roubles or so, or even
100 . . . from the secret funds . . .'

'And in that case,' interrupted the customs chief, 'they'll
deliver up their *ataman* bound hand and foot, or I'm a Kirghiz
ram, and no collegiate councillor.'

'We will think and talk more on this later,' replied the general. 'However, military measures must be taken as well in any
case. Gentlemen, give your views in proper order.'

All opinions proved to be opposed to my own. Every official
spoke of the unreliability of the troops, the uncertainty of success, the need for caution, and the like. Everyone thought it
more prudent to remain under the protection of the guns, behind a stout stone wall, rather than trust to the fortune of arms
on the field of battle. At length the general, having listened to all
opinions, knocked the ash out of his pipe and made the following speech:

'My dear sirs, I have to declare to you that for my own part
I am absolutely in agreement with the gentleman ensign: that
opinion is founded on all the rules of sound tactics, which
almost always favours the offensive over defence.'

Here he paused and began to fill his pipe. My self-esteem was triumphant. I looked proudly at the officials, who were whispering among themselves with an air of annoyance and unease.

'However, dear sirs,' he continued, emitting, along with a deep sigh, a dense cloud of tobacco smoke, 'I do not dare to take upon myself such a great responsibility when the matter under discussion is the security of the provinces entrusted to my by my most gracious sovereign, Her Imperial Majesty. Therefore I concur with the majority opinion, which has come down in favour of the safest and most prudent course, to await a siege within the town and repulse enemy attacks with artillery and (as far as may be possible), sorties against them.'

It was now the officials' turn to glance derisively at me. The council broke up. I couldn't help regretting the weakness of the venerable warrior, who, against his own convictions, had decided to follow the advice of untrained and inexperienced people.

Some days after this memorable meeting of the council we learned that Pugachev, true to his word, had drawn near to Orenburg. I could see the rebel forces from the heights of the town wall. I fancied their numbers had increased tenfold since their last assault, the one I had witnessed. They were also equipped with the artillery which Pugachev had taken from the small forts he had already overrun. Recalling the decision of the council, I foresaw a lengthy period of confinement within the walls of Orenburg, and almost wept with exasperation.

I won't describe the Orenburg siege, which belongs to history rather than to a family record. I will only say briefly that the said siege, because of the carelessness of the local authorities, was disastrous for the inhabitants, who had to contend with famine and all manner of other calamities. It can easily be imagined that life in Orenburg was absolutely intolerable. Everyone despondently awaited their fate; everyone complained at the high prices, which were indeed fearful. The citizens became accustomed to cannonballs flying into their back-yards; even Pugachev's assaults were no longer a matter for curiosity. I was dying of boredom. Time was passing. I received no letters from the Belogorsk Fort. All the roads were cut. Separation from Maria Ivanovna became unbearable to me. I was tormented by the

uncertainty over what had become of her. My one distraction
was in raiding the enemy. By the grace of Pugachev, I had a
good horse with whom I shared my meagre ration and on which
I sallied beyond the walls every day to exchange fire with
Pugachev's cavalry. In these skirmishes, the advantage was
usually to the villains who were well-fed, well-horsed, and well-
liquored. The garrison's skinny cavalry could not cope with
them. Sometimes our starving infantry also took the field, but
the depth of the snow prevented them from operating successfully against scattered horsemen. The artillery thundered in vain
from the height of the rampart, and was unable to move in the
field because the horses were exhausted. So much for our military operations! This was what the Orenburg officials termed
caution and prudence!

One day, when we had managed to scatter and drive off a
fairly dense troop, I rode up to a Cossack who had lagged behind his comrades; I was preparing to strike him with my Turkish sabre, when he suddenly doffed his cap and shouted:

'Hallo! Pyotr Andreich! How is the world with you?'

I looked at him and recognized our sergeant. I was unspeak-
ably glad to see him.

'Hello, Maximich,' I said. 'Are you long out of Belogorsk?'

'Not long, master Pyotr Andreich; I came back here only
yesterday. I've got a little letter for you.'

'Where is it, then?' I cried, blushing all of a sudden.

'I've got it,' replied Maximich, putting his hand inside his
shirt. 'I promised Palasha I would get it to you somehow.'

At this, he handed me a folded piece of paper and immediately galloped off. I opened it and trembled as I read the following lines.

'It was God's will to deprive me of father and mother all at once:
I have no kin or protector on the earth. I am turning to you,
knowing that you always wished me well and that you are ready
to help anyone at all. I pray God that this letter reaches you
somehow! Maximich has promised to get it to you. Palasha has
also heard from Maximich that he often sees you in the distance
during sorties, and that you take no care for yourself at all, and
have no thought for those who pray to God in tears on your

behalf. I was ill for a long time, and when I recovered, Alexey Ivanovich, who is in command here in place of my late father, forced Father Gerasim to hand me over to him, threatening him with Pugachev. I am living in our house under guard. Alexey Ivanovich is forcing me to marry him. He says that he saved my life when he covered up Akulina Pamfilovna's deception, when she told the villains that I was her niece. I would sooner die than be the wife of someone like Alexey Ivanovich. He treats me very cruelly, and threatens that if I don't change my mind and agree, he will take me to the scoundrel's camp and the same thing will happen to me as to Lizaveta Kharlova. I begged him to give me time to think. He has agreed to wait another three days; if I won't marry him after three days, there will be no mercy shown. Master Pyotr Andreich! You are my sole protector; intercede for a poor girl. Beg the general and all the commanders to send a relief force to us quickly, and come yourself if you can. I remain your humble, poor orphan.

Maria Mironova'

On reading this letter, I almost went out of my mind. I set off for the town, spurring my poor horse mercilessly. On the way, I tried to devise one scheme after another to rescue the poor girl, and came up with nothing. Galloping into town, I went straight to the general's and burst in to see him.

The general was walking to and fro across the room, smoking his meerschaum pipe. On seeing me, he halted. No doubt struck by my appearance, he enquired solicitously as to the reason for my precipitate entrance.

'Your excellency,' I said, 'I am turning to you, as to my own father; in God's name do not refuse my request: the matter concerns my life's happiness.'

'What is it, my son?' asked the astonished old man. 'What can I do for you? Say on.'

'Your excellency, order me to take a company of soldiers and fifty Cossacks and send me to retake Belogorsk Fort.'

The general gave me a searching look, assuming, no doubt, that I had taken leave of my senses (which was not far from the mark).

'How do you mean, retake Belogorsk Fort?' he said at last.

'I guarantee success,' I replied fervently. 'Just let me go.'

'No, young man,' he said shaking his head. 'Over a distance like that, the enemy could easily cut your communications with headquarters and achieve a complete victory over you. Severed communications . . .'

I took fright, seeing him getting drawn into military considerations, and hastened to cut him short.

'The daughter of Captain Mironov', I told him, 'has written me a letter. She asks for help; Shvabrin is forcing her to marry him.'

'Really? Oh, this Shvabrin is a *Schelm** and a half! and if he falls into my hands, I'll have him tried in twenty-four hours and shot on the fort parapet! But meanwhile we must have patience . . .'

'Have patience!' I cried, fairly beside myself. 'Meanwhile he marries Maria Ivanovna! . . .'

'Oh!' countered the general. 'That's no great worry: better for her to be Shvabrin's wife for the time being: he can provide protection for her; and when we've shot him, then, God willing, there'll be suitors enough. Nice widows don't stay maids long; that is, I mean, a widow will find a husband quicker than an unmarried girl.'

'I'd sooner die,' I said in a frenzy, 'than give her up to Shvabrin!'

'Oh-ho-ho!' said the old man. 'Now I see: you, it seems, are in love with Maria Ivanovna. That's a different matter! Poor chap! But all the same, there is no way I can give you a company of soldiers and fifty Cossacks. Such an expedition would be imprudent: I cannot take responsibility for it.'

I hung my head; despair overwhelmed me. Suddenly an idea flashed across my mind: what it entailed the reader will see in the next chapter, as the old-fashioned novelists say.

11

THE REBEL ENCAMPMENT

> Although by nature fierce, the lion sated lay.
> 'Why deign to visit me within my den today?'
> He asked caressingly.
>
> (A. Sumarokov)*

I left the general and hurried off to my quarters. Savelich met me with his usual exhortations.

'Why have anything to do with drunken bandits? Is that a fit occupation for a nobleman? These are evil times: you'll perish for nothing. Might be all right if you were fighting the Turks or the Swedes, this lot aren't fit to be mentioned.'

I cut short his speech with a question: how much money did I have all told?

'All you need,' he replied with a smug expression. 'The rogues did plenty of rummaging, but I still managed to hide some away.' At this, he pulled out a long knitted purse from his pocket, filled with silver.

'Well, Savelich,' I told him. 'Give me half now; and keep the rest for yourself. I'm going to the Belogorsk Fort.'

'Master Pyotr Andreich!' quavered my good-hearted guardian. 'Don't tempt providence; how can you travel at this time when the bandits have blocked the way? Have pity for your parents at least, if not for yourself. How would you get there? And why? Wait a little while: when the troops arrive, they'll round up the rogues; then you can travel wherever in the world you like.'

But my resolve was not to be shaken.

'Too late to discuss that,' I answered the old man. 'I have to go, I can't do otherwise. Don't get upset Savelich: we shall see each other again, God willing! Now watch you don't start having scruples and stinting yourself. Buy what you need even if it's three times the normal price. I'm presenting the money to you. If I don't get back in three days . . .'

'What do you mean, sir?' Savelich interrupted. 'Me let you go on your own? Don't ask that even in your dreams. If you've really made your mind up to go, I'll follow you, on foot if need be. I shan't desert you. Sit behind a stone wall without you? I haven't lost my senses have I? Do as you please, sir, I shan't leave you.'

I knew there was no arguing with Savelich, and allowed him to get ready for the journey. Half an hour later I mounted my fine horse, while Savelich got on his lame old nag which a town resident had given him free, being no longer able to feed her. We approached the town gates; the guards let us pass and we rode out of Orenburg.

It was starting to get dark. My route led past Berda village, Pugachev's encampment. The direct road was covered with snow; but there were horses' tracks all over the steppe, made afresh every day. I was going at a full trot. Savelich could hardly keep in touch with me and kept calling out:

'Slow down, sir, for heaven's sake, slow down. This blasted nag of mine can't keep up with your long-legged devil. What's all the hurry? All right if it was a feast, but this'll be the death of us, shouldn't wonder ... Pyotr Andreich ... master Pyotr Andreich! ... Don't do it! ... God almighty, a noble child will be lost!'

Soon the Berda lights began twinkling. Savelich still hung on, without ceasing his plaintive prayers. I was hoping to round the village safely, when I suddenly glimpsed in the murk straight in front of me about five muzhiks armed with oak cudgels: they were the outlying guards of Pugachev's encampment. They called out to us. Not knowing the password, I wanted to ride by them in silence, but they at once surrounded me, and one of them seized my bridle. I drew my sabre and struck the muzhik across the head; his cap saved him; nevertheless, he staggered and let go the bridle. The rest ran off in confusion; I took advantage of the moment to put spurs to my mount and gallop away.

The darkness of the approaching night might have saved me from any danger, but I suddenly looked round and saw that Savelich was not with me. The poor old man with his lame horse couldn't have got away from the bandits. What was I to do? After waiting a few minutes and assuring myself that he had been detained, I wheeled my horse and set off to rescue him.

As I approached a gulley, I heard shouts in the distance and my Savelich's voice. I put on speed and soon found myself among the guardian muzhiks who had stopped me a few minutes earlier. Savelich was among them. They had dragged the old man from his horse, and were preparing to tie him up. My arrival pleased them considerably. They hurled themselves on me with a shout and in a trice I had been dragged from my horse. One of them, apparently their chief, informed us that he would take us before their sovereign at once.

'And our father's will', he added, 'may be to hang you straight away, or wait till God's dawn.'

I put up no resistance; Savelich followed my example, and the guards brought us in triumphantly.

We crossed a gulley and entered the encampment. Fires were burning in all the huts and there was hubbub and shouting everywhere. I met a good number of people out on the streets, but no one took any notice of us in the darkness or recognized me as an Orenburg officer. We were taken straight to a hut which stood on a corner of the main thoroughfare. A number of wine-barrels and two cannon stood by the entrance.

'This is the palace,' said one of the muzhiks. 'We'll announce you.'

He went into the hut, or palace, as the muzhiks called it. It was lit by two tallow candles, and the walls were covered in gold paper; for the rest, the benches, table, wash-basin on a string, towel on its nail, the oven-fork in the corner, the hearth set about with pots, everything was like an ordinary peasant's hut. Pugachov was sitting under the icons, dressed in a red caftan and tall hat, arms solemnly akimbo. A number of his chief comrades were standing near him, feigning an air of servility. It was evident that news of the arrival of an officer from Orenburg had aroused intense curiosity among the rebels and they were preparing to welcome me in formal style. Pugachev recognized me at first glance. His assumed solemnity vanished instantly.

'Ah, your honour!' he said briskly. 'How are you? Why has God brought you here?'

I replied that I was on personal business when his people had stopped me.

'And what business was that?' he enquired. I was lost for an answer. Pugachev, supposing that I was reluctant to explain before witnesses, turned to his comrades and bade them depart. They all obeyed, bar two, who did not stir from their places.

'You can speak out in front of them,' Pugachev told me, 'I hold no secrets from them.'

I stole a sidelong glance at the pretender's confidants. One of them, a thin, bent old man with a grizzled beard, had nothing remarkable about him apart from a blue ribbon worn across the shoulder of his grey coat. But I shall never forget his comrade. He was tall, stout, and broad-shouldered; he seemed about forty-five to me. A bushy red beard, grey sparkling eyes, a nose without nostrils, and reddish blotches on his brow and cheeks gave his broad, pock-marked face an indescribable expression. He was wearing a red shirt, a Kirghiz gown, and wide Caucasian trousers. The first, as I learned later, was the renegade Corporal Beloborodov;* the second, Afanasy Sokolov, nicknamed Khlopusha, an exiled criminal, who had escaped from the Siberian mines on three occasions. In spite of the seething turmoil of my emotions, the company in which I had unexpectedly found myself profoundly stirred my imagination. But Pugachev brought me to earth with his question: 'Speak: what business made you leave Orenburg?'

A strange notion came to me: it was as if providence, in bringing me to Pugachev a second time, was giving me an opportunity to achieve my ends. I resolved to use the opportunity, and without thinking over my decision further, I replied:

'I was on my way to Belogorsk Fort to release an orphan who is being ill-treated there.'

Pugachev's eyes glittered.

'Who of my people dares ill-treat an orphan?' he shouted. 'He may have the cunning of the devil, but he shan't escape my justice. Speak: who is the guilty man.'

'Shvabrin is the culprit,' I replied. 'The sick girl you saw at the priest's house is being held captive by him and he wants to marry her by force.'

'I'll teach Shvabrin a lesson,' said Pugachev menacingly. 'He'll find out what arbitrary ill-treatment of the people means. I'll hang him.'

'Permit me a word,' said Khlopusha in a hoarse voice. 'You were in a hurry to make Shvabrin commandant of the fort, and now you're in a hurry to hang him. You've already offended the Cossacks by putting a nobleman over them; don't frighten the nobles by executing them on the first denunciation.'

'There's no need to pity them or do them favours!' said the old man in the blue ribbon. 'There's no harm in hanging Shvabrin and no harm in questioning this officer properly either, as to why he's honoured us with a visit. If he doesn't acknowledge you as tsar, then he has no right to seek justice from you, and if he does so acknowledge, what has he been doing sitting in Orenburg all this time with your enemies? Will you not command me to take him into the office and apply a little heat: my feeling is that he has been sent to spy on us by the Orenburg commanders.'

The logic of the old villain seemed quite convincing to me. Ice ran through my body at the thought of whose hands I had fallen into. Pugachev noticed my perturbation.

'Well, your honour?' he said with a wink. 'My field marshal, it appears, is talking sense. What think you?'

Pugachev's taunt restored my spirits. I calmly replied that I was in his power and that he was at liberty to deal with me as he thought fit.

'Good', said Pugachev. 'First tell us what state the town is in.'

'Praise be, all is well,' I replied.

'All well?' repeated Pugachev. 'And the people dying of hunger?'

The pretender was speaking the truth; but it was my bounden duty to assure him that these were empty rumours and that Orenburg was plentifully supplied.

'You see,' put in the old man, 'he's lying to your face. All the fugitives agree that in Orenburg there is famine and death, they're eating carrion and glad of it; meanwhile his grace tells us that there's plenty of everything. If you want to hang Shvabrin, hang this young blood on the same gallows, so there's no cause for envy.'

The accursed old man's words obviously swayed Pugachev. Fortunately Khlopusha started contradicting his comrade.

'Enough of that Naumich,' he told him. 'You want everybody strangled or knifed. What makes you such a hero? Look at what your soul's got to hang on to. You've one foot in the grave yourself, and you want other people done in. Haven't you got enough blood on your conscience?'

'And since when have you played the saint? Why are you so merciful all of a sudden?'

'Of course, I'm a sinner too,' replied Khlopusha. 'And this arm' (here he clenched his bony fist, and rolling back his sleeve revealed a shaggy arm), 'this arm too is guilty of shedding Christian blood. But I killed enemies, not guests: at the open crossroads or in the dark forest, not at home sitting by the stove; club and axe were my weapons, not womanish slanders.'

The old man turned away, muttering 'slit nostrils!'

'What are you whispering, you old sod?' shouted Khlopusha. 'I'll give you slit nostrils: just you wait, your time will come, God willing, and you'll sniff the pincers . . . In the meantime, watch out I don't tear that straggly little beard off!'

'Gentlemen, *Yenerals*!' Pronounced Pugachev solemnly. 'Stop the squabbling. It would be no bad thing if all the Orenburg dogs dangled from the same beam; what is bad is if our own hounds start snarling at each other. Come now, be friends.'

Khlopusha and Beloborodov stared grimly at one another, without uttering a word. I saw the necessity of changing the tenor of this conversation, which might end very badly for me, and so, addressing Pugachev, I said with a cheery air:

'Ah, I was forgetting to thank you for the horse and sheepskin. But for you, I'd have frozen to death on the road and never reached town at all.'

My ruse worked. Pugachev glowed. 'One good turn deserves another', he said, with a narrow-eyed wink. 'Now tell me what business you have with that girl Shvabrin is ill-using? Touched the dashing young man's heart? Eh?'

'She is my fiancée,' I replied, noting a favourable change in the weather and seeing no need to conceal the truth.

'Your fiancée!' cried Pugachev. 'Why on earth didn't you say so before? Well, we shall marry you and celebrate at your wedding!' Then, turning to Beloborodov: 'Listen field marshal! His honour and I are old friends; let's sit down to supper; then we'll sleep on it and decide what we're going to do in the morning.'

I would gladly have refused the proposed honour but there was nothing for it. Two young Cossack girls, the daughters of the hut-owner, laid a white cloth on the table, then fetched bread, fish soup, and several bottles of wine and beer; once more I found myself sharing a meal with Pugachev and his terrifying companions.

The orgy of which I was an unwilling witness lasted until late at night. Eventually drink overcame the talkers. Pugachev fell into a doze as he sat in his chair; his comrades got up and indicated that I should leave him. I went outside with them. On Khlopusha's orders, the guard led me off to the hut which served as an office, where I found Savelich and where they left me with him under lock and key. My guardian was so amazed at what he had seen taking place that he did not question me at all. He lay down in the darkness, sighing and groaning for long enough; at length he began to snore, and I gave myself up to my reflections, which prevented me from dozing off for so much as a minute all night.

Next morning I was summoned in Pugachev's name. I went to him. A wagon stood near his gate, harnessed up with a troika of Tartar horses. People were thronging the streets. I met Pugachev in the passage: he was dressed for the road, in fur coat and Khirgiz cap. His companions of the previous day surrounded him, with an obsequious air, strongly at variance with what I had witnessed the previous evening. Pugachev greeted me genially and ordered me to sit next to him in the wagon.

We seated ourselves. 'To Belogorsk!' said Pugachev to the broad-shouldered Tartar, who was standing up to drive the troika. My heart began to pound. The horses set off, the bell began to ring, and the wagon shot forward . . .

'Stop, stop!' came a voice only too familiar, and I saw Savelich, running to meet us. Pugachev ordered the driver to halt.

'Master Pyotr Andreich!' cried my guardian. 'Don't abandon me in my old age among these rasc . . .'

'Ah, the old sod!' Pugachev said. 'Again God has allowed us to meet. Come on, you can sit with the driver.'

'Thank you, sire, thank you my father!' said Savelich, seating himself. 'May God grant you a hundred years of life, that you pitied and gave comfort to me, an old man. I will pray to God for you all my life and never mention the hare-skin jacket again.'

This hare-skin jacket might have finally angered Pugachev in real earnest. Fortunately, the pretender either failed to hear it or ignored the inapposite remark. The horses galloped on; people along the road halted and bowed from the waist. Pugachev nodded to either side. Within a minute we had left the encampment and were galloping along the smooth road.

What I was feeling at that moment can readily be imagined. Within a few hours I was going to see her whom I had previously considered lost to me. I pictured to myself the moment of our union. I thought also of the man in whose hands my fate lay and who, through a strange sequence of events, was secretly bound to me. I recalled the impulsive cruelty, the bloodthirsty ways of him who had volunteered to be the liberator of my beloved! Pugachev did not know that she was the daughter of Captain Mironov; the enraged Shvabrin might reveal all to him; Pugachev might find out in other ways ... Then what would happen to Maria Ivanovna? A shiver ran through me, and my hair rose on end ...

Suddenly Pugachev broke in on my reflections, turning to me with a question.

'What is making your honour so thoughtful?'

'How can I not be thoughtful,' I answered. 'I am an officer and a nobleman; yesterday I was fighting against you, and today I am riding along in the same carriage, and the happiness of my whole life depends on you.'

'What's the matter then, frightened?' asked Pugachev.

I answered that having been spared by him once before, I was relying not only on his mercy but also his aid.

'And you're right, so you are!' said the pretender. 'You saw my lads giving you looks; and the old man was insisting today that you should be tortured and hanged; but I didn't agree,' he added, lowering his voice, so that Savelich and the Tartar couldn't overhear, 'remembering your glass of wine and hare-skin jacket. You see, I'm not as bloodthirsty as your friends call me.'

I recalled the taking of Belogorsk Fort, but did not deem it necessary to contradict him, and said nothing.

'What do they say of me in Orenburg?' asked Pugachev, after a pause.

'Oh, they say that you're a difficult handful; you've certainly made your mark.'

The face of the pretender was a picture of smug content.

'Yes,' he said, genially. 'I'm a warrior all right. Do your lot in Orenburg know about the battle near Yuzeyeva?* Forty *yenerals* killed, four armies taken prisoner. What do you think—could the King of Prussia* stand up to me?'

The bandit's bragging amused me.

'What do you think, yourself?' I said to him. 'Could you deal with Frederick?'

'With Fyodor Fyodorovich? And why not indeed? I am coping with your *yenerals* already; and they've beaten him before now. Up to now, my arms have been triumphant. Give me time and you'll see more before I march on Moscow.'

'And you intend marching on Moscow?'

The pretender brooded for a while before saying in a low voice:

'God knows. My road is narrow; I've little room for manœuvre. My lads are getting above themselves. They're robbers. I've got to keep my ears pricked; at the first failure they'll try to save their own necks by offering up my head.'

'Just so!' I told Pugachev. 'Wouldn't it be better to detach yourself from them first, in good time, and throw yourself on the mercy of the Empress?'

Pugachev grinned bitterly.

'No,' he replied. 'It's too late for me to repent. There'll be no mercy for me. I shall carry on the way I began. Who knows. Perhaps I'll win. Grishka Otrepyev did rule over Moscow as tsar, didn't he?'

'And do you know what became of him? He was thrown out of a window, murdered, burnt, and his ashes fired from a cannon!'

'Listen,' said Pugachev, with a kind of savage inspiration. 'I'll tell you a story that was told to me as a boy by an old Kalmyk woman. Once, the eagle asked the raven: tell me, raven-bird, how is it you live 300 years in the wide world, when I have only thirty-three years? Because, sir, the raven replied, you drink living blood whereas I feed on carrion. The eagle thought: why don't I do the same and feed likewise? Good. The eagle and the raven flew along and spied a fallen horse; they flew down and alighted. The raven began pecking and praising its taste the while. The eagle pecked once, then again, and then he flapped a wing and told the raven: no, friend raven, rather than feed for 300 years on carrion, I'll drink my fill of fresh blood, then let come what will! What do you think of my Kalmyk tale?'

'Clever,' I answered him. 'But living by murder and banditry is the same as eating carrion in my opinion.'

Pugachev looked at me with astonishment and made no reply. We both sat on in silence, each plunged in his reflections. The Tartar struck up a dismal song; Savelich swayed as he dozed on the box. The wagon flew along the smooth winter road . . . Suddenly I saw a little village on the steep bank of the Yaik, a palisade and belfry. Within a quarter of an hour we were driving into Belogorsk Fort.

12

THE ORPHAN

Like our little apple-tree,
No top or leafy branches;
Like our little princess,
No father and no mother.
No one to dress her,
No one to bless her.

(Wedding song)*

The wagon rolled up to the porch of the commandant's house.
The people had recognized Pugachev's bell and were running
after us in crowds. Shvabrin met the pretender on the porch.
He was dressed as a Cossack and had let his beard grow. The
renegade helped Pugachev to alight from the wagon, expressing
his joy and zeal for service in ignoble phrases. When he caught
sight of me he was taken aback, but swiftly recovered himself
and stretched out a hand, saying:

'You've come over too? High time!'

I turned away from him without a word.

My heart sank within me once we were inside the long-
familiar room where the late commandant's diploma still hung
on the wall, like a melancholy epitaph to times gone by. Pugachev
sat down on the sofa where Ivan Kuzmich used to doze, lulled
by his wife's grumbling. Shvabrin himself brought him vodka.
Pugachev drank a glass and told him, indicating me: 'Some for
his honour as well.' Shvabrin approached me with his tray, but
I recoiled from him a second time. He seemed to have lost his
self-command. With his usual quick-wittedness, he had of course
guessed that Pugachev was displeased with him. He was cowed
by him, but at me he kept glancing mistrustfully. Pugachev
asked him about the state of the fort, rumours of enemy troop
movements, and things of that sort, then abruptly asked him:

'Tell me, friend, who's the girl you've got locked up here?
Show her to me.'

Shvabrin went as white as death.

'Sire,' he faltered . . . 'Sire, she isn't locked up . . . she's ill . . . she's lying in the bedroom.'

'Take me to her,' said the pretender, rising from his chair. There was no getting out of it. Shvabrin conducted Pugachev into Maria Ivanovna's room. I followed after them.

Shvabrin halted on the staircase.

'Sire!' he said. 'You are empowered to demand anything you wish of me, but do not order an outsider to enter my wife's bedroom.'

I shook. 'So, you're married!' I said to Shvabrin, ready to tear him apart.

'Silence!' Pugachev cut me short. 'Leave this to me. As for you,' he went on, addressing Shvabrin. 'Stop trying to be clever and wriggle out of things: whether she's your wife or not, I'll take anyone I wish to see her. Follow me, your honour.'

At the door of the bedroom Shvabrin again halted and said falteringly:

'Sire, I warn you she's delirious, she's been raving incessantly for more than two days.'

'Open up!' said Pugachev.

Shvabrin began searching his pockets and said he hadn't brought the key. Pugachev kicked the door; the lock flew off; the door opened and we went in.

One look and I froze. Maria Ivanovna was sitting on the floor, in a tattered peasant dress, pale, thin, and with hair dishevelled. A pitcher of water stood before her, covered with a slice of bread. On seeing me, she started and cried out. I cannot describe my emotions at that moment.

Pugachev looked at Shvabrin and said with a bitter smile: 'It's a nice hospital you have here!' Then he went up to Maria Ivanovna: 'Tell me, my dear, what is your husband punishing you for? How have you earned his displeasure?'

'My husband?' she repeated. 'He's no husband of mine. I will never be his wife! I would rather die, and I will die if I am not released.'

Pugachev threw a threatening glance at Shvabrin:

'And you dared to deceive me! You know, scoundrel, what you deserve.'

Shvabrin fell to his knees ... At that moment contempt outweighed all feelings of hate and anger in me. I looked with loathing at a nobleman grovelling at the feet of a renegade Cossack. Pugachev was appeased.

'I pardon you this time,' he told Shvabrin, 'but know that if you transgress again, this will be remembered.'

He then turned to Maria Ivanovna and said tenderly:

'Go fair maiden; I grant you your freedom. I am the sovereign.'

Maria Ivanovna shot a quick glance at me and realized that before her stood the murderer of her parents. She covered her face with both hands and fell back senseless. I rushed to her; but at that moment my old acquaintance Palasha burst courageously into the room and began to see to her young lady. Pugachev left the bedroom, and all three of us went down to the sitting-room.

'Well, your honour?' said Pugachev, laughing. 'We've rescued your fair maiden! What say we send for the priest, and make him marry his niece? I could give her away, Shvabrin can be best man; we'll eat, drink, and drown our sorrows.'

What happened next was what I had been afraid of. Shvabrin, hearing Pugachev's suggestion, lost his self-control.

'Sire!' he cried out in a frenzy. 'I'm in the wrong, I told you lies; but Grinyov is deceiving you as well. This girl isn't the niece of the local priest: she's the daughter of Ivan Mironov, who was executed when this fort was captured.'

Pugachev fixed his blazing eyes on me.

'What's this?' he asked me in bewilderment.

'Shvabrin has told you the truth,' I replied steadily.

'You didn't tell me this,' observed Pugachev, whose face had darkened.

'Just think,' I replied, 'could I have mentioned in front of your men that the daughter of Mironov was alive? They would have torn her to pieces. Nothing could have saved her!'

'True enough,' said Pugachev. 'My drunkards wouldn't have spared the poor girl. The priest's wife did well to deceive them.'

'Listen,' I pursued, seeing the good mood he was in. 'I don't know who you are, and I don't want to know ... But as God is my witness, I would be glad to pay with my life for what you have done for me. Just as long as you don't demand anything that is against my honour and Christian conscience. You are my benefactor. Finish the way you have begun: release me and this poor orphan to go wherever God commands. And wherever you are, and whatever happens to you, we will pray God every day for the salvation of your sinful soul . . .'

It appeared that Pugachev's grim heart was touched.

'Let it be even as you say!' he said. 'Hang him or spare him, one or the other: that's my way. Take your pretty miss and take her wherever you wish, and may God grant you love and concord.'

He then turned to Shvabrin and ordered him to make out a pass valid for all the outposts and forts under his control. Shvabrin, utterly crushed, stood as if transfixed. Pugachev went off to inspect the fort. Shvabrin accompanied him; I remained behind under the pretext of getting ready for the journey.

I ran to the bedroom. The door was closed. I knocked.

'Who's there?' asked Palasha.

I identified myself. Maria Ivanovna's sweet little voice came out from behind the door.

'Wait a moment, Pyotr Andreich, I'm getting changed. Go over to Akulina Pamfilovna's: I'll be there presently.'

I obeyed and went to Father Gerasim's house. Both he and his wife came running out to meet me. Savelich had already alerted them.

'Greetings, Pyotr Andreich,' said the priest's wife. 'God has permitted us to meet again. How are you? We've talked of you every day. And Maria Ivanovna has borne up under it all without you, the little lamb! . . . So tell me, master, how's it you're on such good terms with Pugachev? How's it he didn't make away with you? At least the villain's to be thanked for that.'

'That's enough, old woman,' Father Gerasim broke in. 'No need to go babbling all you know. Salvation is not gained by much talking. Dear Pyotr Andreich! In you come, if you please. It's been a long, long time.'

The priest's wife put before me what there was, and kept up a non-stop stream of talk. She related to me how Shvabrin had forced them to give up Maria Ivanovna; how Maria Ivanovna had wept and hadn't wished to part with them; how Maria Ivanovna kept up communication with her through Palasha (a spirited lass who made the sergeant dance to her tune as well); how she had advised Maria Ivanovna to write to me, and much else. I in turn gave them a brief account of my own story. The priest and his wife crossed themselves on hearing that Pugachev knew of their deception. 'The power of the cross is with us!' said Akulina Pamfilovna. 'May God avert this storm-cloud. And that Shvabrin; I declare; a fine one I must say!' At that very moment, the door opened and Maria Ivanovna came in with a smile on her pale face. She had left off her peasant garment and was dressed as before, simply and sweetly.

I seized her hand and for a long time could not utter a word. We were both silent because of the fullness of our hearts. Our hosts realized that they were in the way, and left us. We were alone together. All was forgotten. We talked and talked and could not say enough. Maria Ivanovna told me everything that had happened to her from the capture of the fort; she described to me the full horror of her situation, all the trials inflicted upon her by the odious Shvabrin. We also recalled our happy former times ... We both wept ... At length I began to reveal my plans. For her to stay in the fort, in the power of Pugachev and commanded by Shvabrin was impossible. Nor could Orenburg be thought of, since it was undergoing all the miseries of the siege. She had not a single living relative. I suggested she go to the country, to my parents. At first she hesitated, fearing the known antipathy of my father. I reassured her. I knew that father would be glad and consider it a duty to welcome the daughter of a worthy soldier who had perished for his country.

'Sweet Maria Ivanovna!' I said finally. 'I look upon you as my wife. A miracle has united us indissolubly: nothing in the world can part us.'

Maria Ivanovna heard me out without feigned coyness or elaborate evasions. She felt that her fate was united with mine. But she repeated that she would not be my wife without the blessing of my parents. I didn't contradict her. We kissed with genuine passion, and thus all was resolved between us.

An hour later the sergeant brought me my pass, signed in Pugachev's scribbles, and summoned me to him. I found him ready to take to the road. I cannot convey how I felt, parting from that terrible man, a monster, a villain to all but me. Why not speak the truth? At that moment a strong feeling of sympathy drew me to him. I had a burning desire to tear him out of this company of scoundrels he led, while there was still time. Shvabrin and the crowd jostling near us prevented me from saying all that filled my heart.

We parted amicably. Pugachev, catching sight of Akulina Pamfilovna in the crowd, wagged an admonitory finger and gave her a meaning wink; then he boarded his wagon, gave orders for Berda, and when the horses had moved off, once more leaned out and called to me:

'Goodbye, your honour! Perhaps we'll meet again some day.'

We did indeed meet again, but in what circumstances! . . .

Pugachev had gone. I gazed for a long time at the white steppe, across which his troika was skimming. The people dispersed. Shvabrin had vanished. Everything was prepared for our departure; I had no wish for further delay. Our things had all been loaded aboard the old commandant's carriage. The coachmen had the horses harnessed in a flash. Maria Ivanovna went to say farewell to the graves of her parents, who had been buried behind the church. I wanted to go with her but she asked to be left alone. She returned in a few minutes, brushing away her silent tears. The carriage was brought round. Father Gerasim and his wife came out on to the porch. The three of us got into the wagon, Maria Ivanovna, Palasha, and myself. Savelich scrambled up on to the box.

'Goodbye, Maria Ivanovna, my lamb! Goodbye Pyotr Andreich, our bright falcon!'* said the priest's good-hearted wife. 'A safe journey, and may God grant you both happiness!'

We drove off. I caught a glimpse of Shvabrin at the window of the commandant's house. His face was a picture of grim malevolence. I did not wish to gloat over a crushed enemy and turned my eyes the other way. At last we drove out of the gates and left Belogorsk Fort for ever.

13

ARREST

> Don't be angry, dear sir, but duty bids me say
> That you must go to jail at once, without delay.
> By all means, I'm prepared; but in our conversation
> I hope I am allowed to give an explanation.
>
> (Knyazhnin)*

United so unexpectedly with the dear girl, over whom only that morning I had been so tortured with anxiety, I could not believe it, and kept imagining that everything that had happened to me had been but an empty dream. Maria Ivanovna gazed pensively, now at me, now at the road, and, so it seemed, had not yet come round or recovered herself. We sat in silence. Our hearts were too exhausted. About two hours later, in some unperceived fashion, we found ourselves at a neighbouring fort, also under Pugachev's control. Here we changed horses. Judging by the speed with which they were harnessed up and the helpful eagerness of the bearded Cossack, placed by Pugachev as commandant here, I saw that, thanks to the loquacity of our driver, they took me for one of the pretender's courtiers.

We proceeded on our way. It began to get dark. We approached a small town where, according to the bearded commandant, there was a strong detachment on its way to join the pretender. We were halted by the guards. To the question, 'Who goes there?' the coachman roared out:

'The sovereign's friend and his lady wife.' Suddenly a crowd of hussars surrounded us with a torrent of foul language.

'Out you get, devil's pal,' said a moustachioed sergeant-major. There'll be a hot time for you and your lady wife!'

I got out and asked to be taken to their commander. Seeing an officer, the soldiers ceased their abuse and took me to their major. Savelich stuck close by me muttering to himself:

'So much for the sovereign's friend! Out of the frying-pan into the fire. Lord almighty, how's it all going to end?' The wagon followed after us at walking pace.

Inside five minutes we came up to a little house, brightly lit. The sergeant-major left me under guard and went in to report. He returned at once, announcing that his excellency had no time to receive me and had ordered that I was to be taken to the jail and the lady brought before him.

'What does this mean?' I cried frantically. 'Has he lost his senses?'

'I do not know, your honour,' replied the sergeant-major. 'His excellency has ordered your honour to be taken to the jail, and her honour to be brought before his excellency, your honour!'

I rushed up on to the porch. The guards did not think to restrain me, and I burst straight into the room, where about six hussar officers were playing bank. The major was dealing. To my amazement, I recognized him as Ivan Ivanovich Zurin, who had fleeced me at the Simbirsk inn!

'Is it possible?' I cried. 'Ivan Ivanich! Is it you?'

'Egad, Pyotr Andreich! Such is fate, eh? Where have you come from? Wonderful, friend. Care for a hand?'

'Thank you. I'd prefer lodgings to be found for me.'

'What lodgings? Stay with me.'

'I can't; I'm not alone.'

'Well, bring your pal as well.'

'I'm not with a pal; I'm with a lady.'

'A lady! Where on earth did you get hold of her? Oho, friend!' At these words, Zurin whistled so significantly that everyone burst out laughing, and I was thoroughly embarrassed.

'Well,' Zurin went on, 'so be it. You shall have your lodging. A pity . . . We might have lived it up a bit, like the old days . . . Hey! Boy! Why aren't they bringing that girl-friend of Pugachev's in here? Or is she being stubborn? Tell her not to be frightened: say the gentleman's very handsome and won't do her any harm, then give her a good slap.'

'What are you saying?' I said to Zurin. 'What Pugachev girl-friend? It's the daughter of the late Captain Mironov. I've brought her out of captivity and I'm now escorting her to my father's village and leaving her there.'

'What! You mean it was you they were reporting just now? Good lord! What on earth's this about?'

'I'll tell you all about it later. Now, for heaven's sake, reassure the poor girl; your hussars have frightened her to death.'

Zurin at once gave the necessary orders. He went out himself into the street to apologize to Maria Ivanovna for the unwitting misunderstanding and ordered the sergeant-major to conduct her to the best lodgings in town. I stayed the night with him.

We had supper and, when we were alone, I told him of my wanderings. Zurin heard me out with great attention. When I had finished, Zurin shook his head and said:

'All this is very good, friend, except for one thing: why the hell do you want to get married? I, an honourable officer, would not wish to deceive you: believe you me, marriage is folly. What do you want to go messing about with a wife for, and dandling babies? Eh, to blazes with that. Take a tip from me: get rid of this captain's daughter. I've cleared the Simbirsk road and it's safe. Send her off tomorrow by herself to your parents; you stay here with my detachment. There's no point in going back to Orenburg. If you fall into rebel hands, you'll hardly get out of them again. That way all this love nonsense will pass off by itself, and everything will be all right.'

Although I was not quite in accord with him, I felt that duty and honour required my presence in the army of the Empress. I resolved to follow Zurin's advice, to send Maria Ivanovna on to the village, and remain with his detachment.

Savelich arrived to help me undress. I announced that next day he was to be ready to travel on with Maria Ivanovna. He was disposed to dig his heels in.

'What do you mean, sir? How can I desert you? Who will look after you? What will your parents say?'

Knowing my guardian's obstinacy, I resolved to try and convince him with gentleness and candour.

'My friend Arkhip Savelich!' I said. 'Do not refuse. Be my benefactor; I am not in need of a servant here, and I won't be easy if Maria Ivanovna travels on without you. In serving her, you will be serving me, because I have definitely decided to marry her as soon as circumstances permit.'

Here Savelich threw up his arms with a look of indescribable astonishment.

'Marry!' he repeated. 'The child wants to marry! And what will your father say, and what will your dear mother think?'

'They will consent, I'm sure of it, when they get to know Maria Ivanovna. I am also relying on you. Father and Mother trust you: you will speak up for us won't you?'

The old man was touched.

'Ah, Pyotr Andreich, my dear young master!' he replied. 'Though it's early for you to be thinking of marriage, Maria Ivanovna is such a good young lady, it would be a sin to miss the chance. Let it be as you say! I will go with her, angel of God that she is, and humbly tell your parents that a bride such as her has no need of a dowry.'

I thanked Savelich and lay down to sleep in the same room as Zurin. Overwrought and excited, I talked away. Zurin at first responded readily, but little by little his words became fewer and less coherent; eventually, instead of a reply to one of my queries, he began snoring and whistling. I stopped talking and soon followed his example.

The following day I came to Maria Ivanovna. I informed her of my plans. She recognized their sense and concurred with me at once. Zurin's troops were due to quit the town that day. There was no time to lose. I parted with Maria Ivanovna, entrusting her to Savelich and giving her a letter to my parents. She began to cry.

'Goodbye Pyotr Andreich!' she said in a soft voice. 'Whether we see one another again or not, God alone knows; but I shall never forget you; only you will remain in my heart as long as I live.' I could not reply. People were all around us. I didn't want to give way in front of them to the feelings that agitated me. At last she drove away. I returned to Zurin, sorrowful and silent. He tried to cheer me up. I wanted distraction. We spent the day in wild and noisy fashion and in the evening set out on campaign.

This was at the end of February. The winter, which had prevented military operations, was passing and our generals were preparing for joint action. Pugachev was still camped in front of Orenburg. Meanwhile the various detachments near him were joining up and nearing the villains' nest. Rebel villages, on seeing our forces, were returning to their allegiance; the bands of brigands were flying from us and everything pointed to a speedy and happy conclusion.

Soon Prince Golitsyn routed Pugachev in front of the Tatishchev Fort* and scattered his forces, relieved Orenburg, and, it appeared, had dealt the rebellion a final and decisive blow. Zurin was at that time deployed against a band of rebellious Bashkirs, who dispersed before we got a glimpse of them. Spring caught us in a Tartar village. The streams overflowed and the roads became impassable. We consoled ourselves in our inactivity with thoughts of the imminent end of these dull and petty hostilities against brigands and savages.

But Pugachev had not been apprehended. He appeared among the Siberian mines, gathered fresh bands there, and resumed his vile doings. Rumours of his success spread once more. We heard of the destruction of Siberian forts. Soon, news of the capture of Kazan and the march of the pretender on Moscow roused our army commanders, who had been carelessly idling, trusting in the impotence of the despised rebel. Zurin received orders to cross the Volga.

I won't describe our campaign and the conclusion of the war. I will just say that the misery was extreme. We passed through villages ravaged by the rebels, and had perforce to deprive the poor inhabitants of what they had contrived to save. The rule of law had broken down everywhere: landowners hid out in the woods. Robber bands plundered far and wide; the commanders of independent detachments punished and pardoned as they pleased; the state of the whole vast territory where the conflagration had raged, was horrifying . . . May the Lord save us from seeing a Russian rebellion, senseless and merciless!

Pugachev was in flight, pursued by Ivan Ivanovich Mikhelson.* Soon we learned of his total defeat. At length Zurin received news of the pretender's capture, along with orders to halt. The war was over. At last I would be able to go to my parents! The thought of embracing them, of seeing Maria Ivanovna, of whom I had had no news whatever, inspired me with rapture. I skipped like a child. Zurin laughed and said with a shrug:

'No good will come of this! If you get married, you'll be done for—and for no good reason.'

But meanwhile a strange feeling was poisoning my joy: the

thought of the scoundrel spattered with the blood of so many innocent victims, and of the execution which awaited him, troubled me against my will: 'Emelya, Emelya!' I thought in vexation, 'why didn't you fall on a bayonet or get in the way of the grapeshot? It was the best thing you could have devised.' How could it be otherwise? The thought of him was inseparable from the mercy he had shown me during one of the grimmest episodes of his career, and the release of my bride from the hands of the detested Shvabrin.

Zurin gave me leave. In a few days I would again be in the midst of my family, see my Maria Ivanovna again . . . all at once an unexpected storm burst upon me.

On the day appointed for my departure, at the very moment when I was preparing to set off, Zurin came into my hut, holding a paper and looking extremely concerned. A pang went through my heart. I felt unaccountably fearful. He sent my orderly outside and announced that he had some business with me.

'What is it?' I enquired anxiously.

'A minor inconvenience,' he responded, handing me the paper. 'Read what I've just received.'

I began to read: it was a secret order to all detachment commanders to place me under arrest, wherever I was, and send me at once under guard to Kazan, to the Commission of Inquiry set up with regard to the Pugachev rising.

The paper almost dropped from my hands.

'Nothing I can do,' said Zurin. 'My duty is to carry out the order. I expect rumours of your friendly trips with Pugachev have somehow reached the authorities. I hope the business doesn't have any serious consequences and that you will clear yourself before the commission. Keep your chin up, and off you go.'

My conscience was clear; I didn't fear a tribunal, but the thought of postponing my sweet tryst, perhaps for months horrified me. The cart was ready. Zurin parted amicably with me. I was seated in the cart. Alongside me were two hussars with drawn swords as I set out along the highway.

14

THE TRIBUNAL

Wild rumour runs free
Like the waves of the sea.

(Saying)*

I was certain that it was my unauthorized absence from Orenburg
that lay at the root of everything. I could easily vindicate myself:
raiding had not only never been forbidden, but was actively
encouraged. I might be accused of excessive rashness, but not of
disobeying orders. My friendly relationship with Pugachev, however, could be attested by many witnesses and was bound to
appear at least suspicious. Throughout the journey I pondered
over the interrogation awaiting me, rehearsing my answers before the tribunal, and made up my mind to state the honest
truth, thinking this to be the simplest as well as the most reliable
way of proceeding.

I arrived in Kazan to find the city burned down and laid
waste. Along the streets, instead of houses lay piles of charred
wood, smoke-blackened walls stood without roofs or windows.
Such were the traces left by Pugachev! I was taken to the fort,
which had survived intact amid the burned-down city. The
hussars handed me over to the officer of the guard. He ordered
a blacksmith to be brought. My legs were shackled and fitted
tightly. Then I was taken to the prison and left there alone in a
cramped and dark kennel of a cell, with only bare walls and a
tiny window barred by an iron grille.

Such a beginning presaged nothing good. However, I lost
neither courage nor hope. I turned to the consolation of all those
in distress, and for the first time tasted the sweetness of prayer,
poured forth from a pure but riven heart. I fell asleep serenely,
unworried as to what was to become of me.

On the following day the prison guard woke me, explaining
that I was wanted at the commission. Two soldiers conducted

me across the courtyard into the commandant's house, halted in the anteroom, and sent me in alone to the inner rooms.

I entered a fairly large hall. At a table covered in papers sat two men: an elderly general of stern and forbidding appearance, and a young Guards captain, of about twenty-eight, very agreeable of aspect, deft and easy in his manner. At a separate table by the window sat a secretary with a pen behind his ear, bent over a paper, poised to write down my evidence. The interrogation began. I was asked my name and rank. The general inquired whether I was the son of Andrey Petrovich Grinyov. My answer elicited a harsh:

'A pity such a worthy man should have so unworthy a son!'

I replied calmly that whatever the charges laid against me, I hoped to dispel them with an honest statement of the truth. My confidence was not to his liking.

'You, friend, are sharp enough,' he said, frowning, 'but we've dealt with sharper!'

Then the young man asked me when and for what reason I had entered Pugachev's service, and what missions I had carried out for him.

I replied indignantly that I, as an officer and nobleman, could not have taken service with Pugachev or undertaken any commissions from him.

'How is it then,' countered my interrogator, 'that a nobleman and officer was spared by the pretender when all his comrades were foully slain? How did this same officer and nobleman carouse on friendly terms with the rebels, accept gifts from the chief villain, a fur coat, a horse, and fifty kopeks? Whence this strange friendship, on what was it based if not on treason, or at the least on odious and culpable cowardice?'

I was deeply offended by the words of the Guards captain, and began my defence with some vehemence. I recounted how my acquaintance with Pugachev had begun on the steppe, during the blizzard, and how he had recognized me and spared me; I had not scrupled to accept a sheepskin and horse from the pretender, but on the storming of Belogorsk Fort I had engaged in the defence till the last possible moment. Finally I quoted my general who could testify to my fighting spirit during the terrible siege of Orenburg.

The stern old man picked up an opened letter from the table and began reading it aloud:

'To your excellency's question regarding Ensign Grinyov, allegedly involved in the present troubles and trafficking with the enemy amounting to a breach of duty and breaking his oath, I have the honour to report: the aforementioned Ensign Grinyov served in Orenburg from the beginning of October of last year, 1773, to the 24th of February of this year, on which date he absented himself and did not report for duty again under my command. I heard from fugitives that he was in Pugachev's camp and drove with him to Belogorsk Fort, where he had been serving earlier; as regards his conduct, I can . . .'

At this point he stopped reading and said severely:

'What will you say in your own defence now?'

I was minded to go on, as I had begun, and explain my connection with Maria Ivanovna as honestly as all the rest. But I suddenly felt an overwhelming sense of revulsion. It occurred to me that if I were to name her, the commission would call her to account; and the thought of involving her name with the vile denunciation of malefactors and bringing her to confront the villain in person—that fearful thought left me so shaken that I began to stammer and flounder.

My judges, who were beginning, it seemed, to listen to my answers somewhat more favourably, were once more prejudiced against me at the sight of my embarrassment. The Guards officer demanded that I face the chief informer face to face. The general ordered *yesterday's villain* to be called. I looked keenly at the door, expecting the advent of my accuser, when in came Shvabrin. I was amazed at the change in him. He was dreadfully pale and thin. His hair, recently jet-black, had gone completely grey: his long beard was matted. He repeated his accusations in a weak but determined voice. According to him, I had been sent by Pugachev to Orenburg as a spy; every day I had ventured out to skirmish in order to pass over written news of how things were going in the town; that I had eventually gone over to the pretender openly, travelling with him from fort to fort, trying in every way to undermine my fellow renegades, in order to supplant them and benefit from the rewards handed out by the pretender. I heard him out in silence and was thankful for one thing: the name of Maria Ivanovna had not been uttered by the vile scoundrel, perhaps because his pride was hurt at the thought of her who had rejected him with scorn; or because in his heart there remained a spark of the same feeling that had compelled me to remain silent—however that may have been, the name of the daughter of the Belogorsk commandant was not pronounced in the presence of the commission. I was confirmed even more in my intention, and when the judges asked how I could over-turn Shvabrin's testimony, I replied that I held to my original explanation and could say nothing more in vindication. The general ordered us to be taken away. We left together. I glanced calmly at Shvabrin, but said no word to him. He grinned venom-ously and, picking up his chains, overtook me and quickened his pace. I was led off to prison again, and was not called for ques-tioning after that.

I was not a witness to everything it remains for me to impart to the reader, but I have heard stories about it so often that the smallest details are etched on my memory and I feel as if I had been invisibly present.

Maria Ivanovna was received by my parents with that genuine cordiality so typical of people of the old century. They saw the grace of God in having the opportunity to shelter and cherish a poor orphan. Soon they became genuinely attached to her, because it was impossible to know her and not fall in love with her. My love no longer seemed mere folly to my father; while mother's only wish was that her Petrusha should wed the sweet captain's daughter.

Rumours of my arrest shocked the entire household. Maria had told the story of my strange acquaintance with Pugachev so unaffectedly that, so far from being alarmed, they had even laughed heartily about it. Father would not believe that I could be involved in a vile rebellion, whose aim had been the over-throw of the throne and the destruction of the nobility. He questioned Savelich sternly. My guardian did not conceal that the young master had been the guest of Emelka Pugachev and that the villain had pardoned him, but swore that he had heard nothing of any treachery. The old folk were reassured and awaited favourable news with impatience. Maria Ivanovna was extremely anxious, but kept her own council, being in the highest degree unassuming and prudent.

Several weeks passed . . . Suddenly my father received from Petersburg a letter from our relative Prince B. The prince was writing to him about me. After the usual introduction, he announced that suspicions about my involvement in the designs of the rebels had apparently proved only too well-founded; that exemplary punishment must await me, but that the Empress, out of respect for the services and declining years of my father, had decided to pardon his son and, in reprieving me from ignominious execution, had ordered only that I be exiled to a remote part of Siberia in perpetuity.

This unexpected blow almost killed my father. He lost his accustomed firmness and his grief (normally silent) found vent in bitter complaints.

'What!' he kept repeating, fairly beside himself. 'My son involved in Pugachev's plans! God of righteousness! That I should live to see it! The Empress spares him from execution! Does that make it any easier for me? It's not a matter of the death penalty. An ancestor of mine went to the block standing up for what he saw as his sacred conscience; my father suffered alongside Volynsky and Khruschev.* But for a nobleman to betray his oath, consort with bandits, murderers and runaway serfs! . . . Shame and dishonour to our family name! . . .'

Frightened by his despair, mother didn't dare weep in front of him, and tried to rally his spirits by talking of the unreliability of rumour and the fickleness of public opinion. My father was inconsolable.

Maria Ivanovna suffered more than anyone. Being certain that I could vindicate myself whenever I chose, she guessed the truth and regarded herself as guilty of my miserable situation. She concealed from everyone her tears and distress, meanwhile constantly thinking of ways to save me.

One evening my father was sitting on the sofa, leafing through the *Court Calendar*, but his thoughts were far away and his reading did not have its usual effect on him. He was whistling an old march tune. Mother was silently knitting a woollen jumper, while the occasional tear fell on her work. Suddenly Maria

Ivanovna, who was also sitting at her work, announced that necessity obliged her to go to Petersburg and she begged to be given the means to do so. Mother was very upset.

'Why do you have to go to Petersburg?' she said. 'You don't mean to say, Maria Ivanovna, you too wish to leave us?'

Maria Ivanovna replied that her entire future depended on this journey and that she was going to seek out patronage and assistance from powerfully placed people, as the daughter of a man who had suffered for his loyalty.

My father bent his head: any word touching his son's supposed crime was painful to him and seemed a biting reproach.

'Go then, my dear!' he sighed. 'We don't want to stand in the way of your happiness. May God grant you find a good man for a husband, not a publicly shamed traitor.' He rose and went out of the room.

Maria Ivanovna, left alone with mother, gave a partial explanation of her plans. Mother embraced her tearfully and prayed to God for the safe accomplishment of the proposed course of action. Maria Ivanovna was furnished with all necessities, and a few days later she set off with the loyal Palasha and Savelich, who, though forcibly parted from me, consoled himself at least with the idea that he was serving my betrothed bride.

Maria Ivanovna arrived safely in Sofia and, having found out at the posting-station that the imperial court was at Tsarskoye Selo,* decided to stop there. She was given a cubby-hole behind a partition. The stationmaster's wife at once engaged her in conversation, announcing that she was the niece of one of the court stokers, and proceeded to let her into all the secrets of court life. She told her at what hour the Empress usually awoke, had her coffee, took her walk; what great lords attended her at that time; what she had been pleased to say at table the previous day, whom she received in the evening—in short, Anna Vlasevna's talk was worth several pages of historical notes, and would have been precious to posterity. Maria Ivanovna paid close attention to all this. They went out into the park, where Anna Vlasevna told her the story of every walk and every little bridge, and having strolled to their heart's content, they returned to the post-house much pleased with one another.

Early the following morning Maria Ivanovna awoke, got

dressed, and went quietly out into the park. It was a lovely morning, the sun was lighting up the tops of the lime trees, turning yellow now beneath the cool breath of autumn. The broad lake glittered motionless. Awakening swans came swimming majestically out from behind the bushes that overhung the banks. Maria Ivanovna walked near a beautiful lawn where a monument had just been erected to Count Pyotr Alexandrovich Rumyantsev. All at once, a little white English dog began barking as it ran towards her. Maria Ivanovna took fright and halted. At that very moment a pleasant female voice was heard:

'Don't be afraid, she won't bite you.'

And Maria Ivanovna saw a lady sitting on a bench opposite the monument.* Maria Ivanovna sat down at the other end of the bench. The lady gave her a searching glance; Maria Ivanovna, from her side, with the help of several sidelong glances, contrived to examine her from head to foot. She was wearing a white morning dress, a nightcap, and sleeveless jacket. She appeared to be about forty years old. Her face, full and rosy, radiated composed dignity, while her blue eyes and slight smile had an ineffable charm. The lady was the first to break the silence.

'You are not from these parts?' she enquired.

'No indeed, ma'am, I arrived only yesterday from the provinces.'

'You came with your parents?'

'Oh no, ma'am, I came alone.'

'Alone! But you are so young.'

'I have no father or mother.'

'You're here on business of some sort?'

'Just so, ma'am. I have come to petition the Empress.'

'You're an orphan: you're probably complaining of some injustice or wrong done you?'

'Oh no, ma'am. I have come to ask for mercy, not justice.'

'Who are you, may I enquire?'

'I am the daughter of Captain Mironov.'

'Captain Mironov! The one who was commandant of one of the Orenburg forts?'

'Just so, ma'am.'

The lady seemed moved.

'Forgive me', she said, her voice even gentler, 'for prying into your affairs; but I am often at court; explain to me the nature of your petition, and perhaps I might be able to help you.'

Maria Ivanovna stood up and thanked her respectfully. Everything about the unknown lady instinctively attracted her and inspired her confidence. Maria Ivanovna took a folded piece of paper from her pocket and gave it to her unknown benefactress, who began reading it to herself.

At first she read with an attentive and benevolent air, but all at once her face altered—and Maria Ivanovna, who was following her every movement, became alarmed at the stern expression which had been a moment ago so pleasant and serene.

'You're petitioning for Grinyov?' said the lady icily. The Empress cannot pardon him. He went over to the pretender not through ignorance or credulity, but as an unprincipled and dangerous scoundrel.'

'Oh, that's not true!' cried Maria Ivanovna

'What do you mean, not true?' retorted the lady, flushing.

'It's not true, before God, it's not true! I know the whole story. I will tell you everything. It was for me alone that he underwent everything that has befallen him. And if he did not exonerate himself before the tribunal, it was because he did not wish to involve me.' She then warmly recounted everything the reader already knows.

The lady heard her out attentively.

'Where are you staying?' she asked, and on hearing that it was at Anna Vlasevna's, she added with a smile:

'Ah! I know it. Goodbye, and tell no one of our meeting. I hope you will not have long to wait for an answer to your letter.'

With these words, she rose and went off into a covered walk, and Maria Ivanovna returned to Anna Vlasevna, filled with the joy of hope.

The postmistress upbraided her for walking so early of an autumn day, injurious, in her opinion, to a young girl's health. She brought the samovar, and over a cup of tea was just about to get started on her endless stories about the court when, all at once, a court carriage drew up by the porch and a chamberlain entered to announce that the Empress had deigned to invite the maiden Mironova.

Anna Vlasevna was astounded and fell into a flutter.

'Good heavens!' she cried. 'The Empress requires you at court. How on earth did she find out about you? And how will you present yourself before her? I don't suppose you know how to . . . shouldn't I go with you? I can at least forwarn you to some extent. And how can you go in your travelling things? Oughtn't I to send to the midwife for her yellow hooped gown?'

The chamberlain announced that the Empress wished Maria Ivanovna to go alone in the clothes she was wearing. There was nothing for it: Maria Ivanovna got into the carriage and went to the palace, armed with the advice and good wishes of Anna Vlasevna.

Maria Ivanovna sensed that our fate was to be decided; her pounding heart fairly quailed within her. A few minutes later the carriage stopped at the palace. Maria Ivanovna ascended the staircase, trembling. The doors before her opened wide. She passed through a long series of sumptuous vacant rooms; the chamberlain pointed the way. At length, after they had come to a set of closed doors, he stated that she would be announced, and left her by herself.

The thought of seeing the Empress face to face so terrified her that she could barely keep her feet. A moment later the doors opened, and she entered the Empress's boudoir.

The Empress was seated at her toilette. Several courtiers surrounded her and respectfully allowed Maria Ivanovna through. The Empress turned benignly towards her and Maria Ivanovna recognized the lady she had spoken so freely to but a short while before. The Empress beckoned her closer and said, with a smile:

'I am glad I could keep my word and grant your petition. Your case has been attended to. I am convinced of the innocence of your fiancé. Here is a letter which you will take to your future father-in-law.'

Maria Ivanovna took the letter with a trembling hand, fell to the Empress's knees, who raised her and kissed her. The Empress talked with her.

'I know that you are not rich,' she said, 'but I am in the debt to the daughter of Captain Mironov. Have no anxiety for the future. I will undertake to see to your fortune.'

After making much of the poor orphan, the Empress allowed

her to go. Maria Ivanovna left in the same court carriage in which she had arrived. Anna Vlasevna, who had been eagerly awaiting her return, showered her with questions to which Maria Ivanovna made some sort of answer. Anna Vlasevna was exasperated at her feeble memory but put it down to provincial shyness, and graciously forgave her. That same day Maria Ivanovna went back to the country, without being curious enough to give Petersburg a glance . . .

The memoirs of Pyotr Andreyevich Grinyov come to an end at this point. Family history tells us that he was released from imprisonment at the end of 1774 by express order of the Empress; that he was present at the execution of Pugachev,* who recognized him in the crowd and gave him a nod of the head that a moment later, dead and bloodied, was displayed to the people. Soon after that, Pyotr Andreich married Maria Ivanovna. Their descendants flourish in Simbirsk province. About twenty miles from *** lies a village belonging to ten owners. In one of the manor-house wings they display, glazed and framed, a handwritten letter from Catherine II. It is addressed to Pyotr Andreich's father and contains the exoneration of his son and praise for the intelligence and heart of Captain Mironov's daughter. The manuscript of Pyotr Andreyevich Grinyov was supplied to us by one of his grandsons, who had found out that we were producing a work dealing with the period described by his grandfather. We decided, with the permission of the relatives, to publish it separately, seeking out an appropriate epigraph for each chapter and taking the liberty of altering some proper names.

The publishers

19 October 1836

PETER THE GREAT'S BLACKAMOOR*

By Peter's iron will
Russia is transformed.

(N. Yazykov)*

1

I am in Paris:
I have begun to live, not just breathe.

(Dmitriev, *A Traveller's Journal*)*

Among the young men whom Peter the Great sent into foreign parts to acquire knowledge essential to the transformed Russian state was his godson, the blackamoor Ibrahim.* He studied at the Paris military academy and passed out a captain of artillery; he then distinguished himself in the Spanish War,* before returning to Paris after being badly wounded. The Emperor, amid his vast labours, never failed to inquire after his favourite and always received the most flattering reports as to his progress and conduct. Peter was greatly pleased with him and more than once summoned him back to Russia: Ibrahim, however, was in no hurry. He pleaded various excuses: his wound, a desire to complete his studies, lack of money. Peter indulged his requests, urging him to look after his health, thanking him for his zeal in acquiring knowledge, and, though extremely careful when it came to his own expenditure, did not stint the treasury where Ibrahim was concerned, accompanying the money he provided with fatherly advice and cautionary instruction.

All the historical records testify to the unprecedented folly, luxury, and unconstrained frivolity of the French at that period. The last years of Louis XIV's reign, marked as they were by the strict piety, formality, and decorum of the court, had left no trace. The Duke of Orleans,* who combined a great many brilliant qualities with a whole assortment of vices, possessed, alas, not a shred of discretion. The orgies at the Palais-Royal were no secret in Paris; the example was contagious. It was at that time that John Law* made his appearance; greed for money was combined with an appetite for enjoyment and dissipation; estates were ruined; moral standards collapsed; Frenchmen laughed and calculated, and the state declined to the skittish sound of satirical vaudeville refrains.

Meanwhile, society presented a most diverting spectacle. Culture and the demand for entertainment had brought all the classes closer together. Wealth, civility, fame, talent, mere eccentricity, anything that provided food for curiosity or gave promise of pleasure was received with equal approbation. Literature, learning, and philosophy abandoned their quiet retreats and appeared in high society, both to comply with the fashion and to direct it through their opinions. Women ruled, but no longer demanded adoration. Superficial courtesy replaced profound respect. The pranks of the Duke de Richelieu,* the Alcibiades of the modern Athens, belong to history and give us some inkling of the moral climate of the age.

> Temps fortuné, marqué par la licence,
> Où la folie, agitant son grelot,
> D'un pied léger parcourt toute la France,
> Où nul mortel ne daigne être dévot,
> Où l'on fait tout excepté pénitence.*

Ibrahim's arrival, his looks, cultivation, and native wit attracted wide attention in Paris. All the ladies wanted to see *le Nègre du Czar* at their houses, and vied with one another to capture him. The Regent frequently invited him to his gay parties; he attended suppers enlivened by the presence of the young Arouet and the old Chaulieu, the talk of Montesquieu and Fontenelle;* he never missed a single ball, not one festive gathering, not one first night, and gave himself up to the social whirl with all the ardour of his youth and race. But the thought of exchanging this dissipation, these brilliant amusements, for the austere simplicity of the Petersburg court was not the only thing that dismayed Ibrahim. Other powerful attachments bound him to Paris. The young African was in love.

The Countess D., no longer in the first flush of youth, was still renowned for her beauty. At seventeen, on her emergence from the convent, she had been married off to a man she had not had time to love, and who had not troubled about the matter since. Rumour ascribed various lovers to her, but in the indulgent estimation of society she enjoyed a good name, since she could not be reproached with any ridiculous or titillating escapades. Her house was the most fashionable in town and attracted the best Parisian society. Ibrahim was presented to her by young Merville,* by common account her latest lover—an impression he strove might and main to bear out.

The Countess received Ibrahim respectfully, but without particular fuss: this flattered him. Usually people regarded the young blackamoor as something of a wonder, clustering round him and showering him with greetings and questions. Dissembled though it was under a cloak of good will, this curiosity wounded his self-esteem. The delightful attentions of women, almost the sole end of our strivings, far from rejoicing his heart, actually filled it with bitterness and resentment. He sensed that for them he was a kind of exotic animal, a special creation, something alien, a chance apparition in a world with which he had nothing in common. He positively envied people who went about unnoticed, and looked upon their insignificance as a happy state indeed.

The notion that nature had not fashioned him for reciprocal passion saved him from conceit and any claim to vanity, a fact which lent a rare charm to his attitude to women. His conversation was unaffected and dignified; this was to the liking of Countess D., who had grown weary of the relentless jesting and subtle insinuations of Gallic wit. Ibrahim was a frequent visitor. Little by little, she grew used to the outward appearance of the young blackamoor and began to find that black curly head positively agreeable, as it moved about among the powdered wigs in her drawing-room. (Ibrahim had sustained a head-wound and wore a bandage instead of a wig.) He was twenty-seven years of age; he was tall and slim, and more than one beauty glanced at him with a somewhat more flattering sentiment than mere curiosity. The prejudiced Ibrahim, however, either noticed nothing or took it for mere flirtation. When his eyes met those of the Countess, on the other hand, his mistrustfulness would vanish. Her gaze conveyed such sweet good nature, her manner towards him was so unaffected and spontaneous, that it was impossible to detect the faintest trace of flirtation or mockery.

Thoughts of love never entered his head, but it had now become imperative for him to see the Countess every day. He was forever seeking out ways to meet her, and every time he did so it seemed to him an unlooked-for grace from heaven. The

Countess divined his feelings before he did so himself. There is no denying that a love without hope or demand touches the female heart more surely than all the wiles of seduction. When Ibrahim was present the Countess followed his every movement and listened intently to whatever he said; without him she would become pensive, or lapse into her habitual mood of abstraction . . . Merville was the first to become aware of their mutual attraction and congratulated Ibrahim. Nothing so fans the flames of love as encouragement from a disinterested party. Love is blind and, lacking confidence in itself, is quick to grasp at any support. Merville's words awakened Ibrahim. The notion of possessing a beloved woman had never entered his thoughts till now; all at once, hope lit up his soul; he fell head over heels in love. Alarmed by the frenzy of his passion, the Countess attempted in vain to resist with friendly admonitions and counsels of prudence. She herself was starting to weaken. Incautious favours followed swiftly one after another. At length, carried away by the power of the passion she had herself inspired, she succumbed to its pressure and gave herself to the rapturous Ibrahim . . .

Nothing can be concealed from the watchful eyes of society. The Countess's new liaison soon became common knowledge. Certain ladies were astonished at her choice, many others regarded it as perfectly natural. Some laughed, others thought it an unpardonable indiscretion on her part. In the first transports of passion, Ibrahim and the Countess were oblivious, but soon enough they became aware of the *doubles entendres* of the men and the barbed remarks of the women. Ibrahim's formal and aloof manner had preserved him until now from assaults of this kind; he fretted under them and did not know how to repel them. The Countess, accustomed as she had been to the respect of society, could not bear to see herself as the subject of gossip and witticisms. She would complain tearfully to Ibrahim, now bitterly reproaching him, now imploring him not to defend her lest, by pointlessly fanning the scandal, he ruin her completely.

A new circumstance arose to complicate her position still further. The consequence of imprudent love became apparent. All reassurances, advice, and suggestions were considered and rejected. The Countess saw nothing beyond her inescapable ruin and awaited it in despair.

As soon as the Countess's condition became known, gossip started up with renewed vigour. Ladies of sensibility exclaimed in horror; the men laid wagers as to whether the Countess would give birth to a white or a black child. Epigrams proliferated at the expense of her husband, who alone in all Paris knew and suspected nothing.

The fateful moment drew nearer. The Countess was in a dreadful state. Ibrahim was with her every day. He saw her mental and physical powers gradually waning. Her tears, her horror never left her for long. At length she felt the first pains. Measures were swiftly taken. A way was found of getting the Count out of the way. The doctor arrived. Two days previously a poor woman had been persuaded to consign her new-born baby to the hands of strangers; a trustworthy person was sent to fetch it now. Ibrahim was in the study next to the bedroom where the wretched Countess lay. With baited breath he heard her muffled groans, the maid's whispering, and the doctor's instructions. Her labour was protracted. Every groan lacerated his heart; every interval of silence filled him with dread ... All at once he heard the feeble wail of an infant and, unable to restrain his joy, he rushed into the bedroom. A black baby lay on the bed at her feet. Ibrahim approached it, his heart pounding. He blessed his son with a trembling hand. The Countess smiled weakly and stretched out a feeble arm ... but the doctor, fearing the effect of too much excitement for his patient, drew Ibrahim away from the bed. The new-born baby was placed in a covered basket and conveyed out of the house by way of a secret stair-case. The other baby was fetched and the cradle placed in the Countess's bedroom. Ibrahim took his departure, somewhat re-assured. The Count was expected. He returned late, and learned of his wife's safe delivery with great satisfaction. In this way the public, which had been expecting a titillating scandal, was cheated, and had perforce to seek consolation in mere backbiting.

The normal tenor of existence was resumed. Ibrahim, however, sensed that his destiny was bound to change, and that his association with the Countess was certain, sooner or later, to come to the notice of Count D. In that case, whatever happened, the Countess's ruin was inevitable. He loved passionately and was loved as passionately in return, but the Countess was headstrong and flighty. This was not her first affair. Revulsion, hatred might replace even the fondest feelings in her heart. Ibrahim pictured the moment of her cooling; up till now he had not experienced jealousy, but now sensed its horrors; he imagined that the pains of parting must be less intense, and now contemplated breaking off his ill-starred liaison, quitting Paris and setting out for Russia, whither both Peter and an obscure sense of personal duty had long been calling him.

2

No more does beauty captivate,
No more has joy its former rapture,
Nor is my fancy quite so free,
Nor spirit quite so well contented . . .
By lust for honour now tormented:
The sound of glory summons me!

(Derzhavin)*

The days and months went by and the infatuated Ibrahim could not steel himself to leave the woman he had seduced. The Countess was growing more attached to him by the day. Their son was being brought up in a distant province. Society gossip was starting to subside, and the lovers began to enjoy more tranquillity, recalling in silence the turmoil of the past and trying not to think of the future.

One day Ibrahim found himself at the levée of the Duke of Orleans. The Duke, as he passed by, came to a halt and handed him a letter, instructing him to read it at his leisure. It was a missive from Peter I. The sovereign, guessing the real reason for his absence, had written to the Duke that he had no intention of imposing his will on Ibrahim, and was leaving it to him whether to return to Russia or not, but that in any event he would never abandon his former protégé. This letter touched Ibrahim to the bottom of his heart. From that moment his destiny was decided. On the following day he announced to the Regent his intention of setting out at once for Russia.

'Think of what you are about,' said the Duke to him. 'Russia is not your fatherland; I do not think you will ever see your tropical homeland again; but your lengthy sojourn in France has made you as much a foreigner to the climate and semi-barbarous ways of Russia. You were not born a subject of Peter. Believe me: take advantage of his magnanimous permission. Remain in France, for which you have already shed your blood, and be assured that here too your services and talents will not go without suitable reward.'

Ibrahim thanked the Duke sincerely, but remained firm in his intentions.

'I am sorry for it,' the Regent said, 'but still, you are right.'

He promised to release Ibrahim from the army, and wrote of all this to the Russian Tsar.

Ibrahim swiftly made his travel arrangements. On the eve of his departure he spent the evening with the Countess, as usual. She knew nothing; Ibrahim had not had the courage to be open with her. The Countess was serene and in good spirits. She had called him over several times to make fun of his preoccupied mood. After supper everyone dispersed. There remained in the drawing-room only the Countess, her husband, and Ibrahim. The wretched man would have given anything in the world to have been alone with her, but the Count, it appeared, had settled himself so comfortably by the fire that there was no prospect of getting him out of the room. All three stayed silent.

'*Bonne nuit,*' said the Countess at length. Ibrahim's heart shrank as it suddenly sensed all the pangs of parting. He stood motionless.

'*Bonne nuit, messieurs,*' repeated the Countess. He still made no move . . . At length his eyes dimmed and he began to feel giddy; he could barely make his way out of the room. When he got home, he wrote the following letter, almost automatically:

'Sweet Leonora, I am going away and leaving you for ever. I am writing because I have not the strength to explain matters otherwise.

My happiness could not continue. I have enjoyed it in despite of fate and nature. You were bound to cease loving me; the enchantment had to fade. That thought has always haunted me even in those moments when, or so it seemed, I was oblivious to everything, when at your feet I was drunk with your passionate self-sacrifice, your infinite tenderness . . . The frivolous world mercilessly persecutes in practice what it permits in theory: its icy mockery would have overcome you, sooner or later, humbled your ardent soul, and in the end you would come to be ashamed of your passion . . . what would have become of me then? No! Better to die, better to leave you before that dreadful moment arrives . . .

'Your peace of mind is my paramount concern: you could not enjoy that with the eyes of the world fixed upon you. Remember everything that you had to endure, all the insults to your self-esteem, all the torments of fear; remember the terrible birth of our son. Think: should I subject you any longer to such anxieties and dangers? Why try to unite the destiny of so frail and beautiful a creature with the wretched lot of a blackamoor, a pitiful creation, scarce worthy to be called a man?

'Forgive me, Leonora, forgive me my sweet, my only friend. In leaving you, I am leaving the first and last joys of my life. I have neither homeland nor kindred. I am going to dreary Russia where complete solitude will be my only consolation. The exacting work to which I am dedicating myself henceforth, if it does not suppress, will at least divert me from the tormenting recollections of days of ecstasy and bliss . . . Forgive me, Leonora, I tear myself away from this letter as if from your embrace; forgive me and be happy—and give a thought sometimes to the poor blackamoor, your faithful Ibrahim.'

That very night he set out for Russia.

The journey did not seem as terrible as he had expected. His imagination triumphed over reality. The further he got from Paris, the closer and more vividly he pictured the things he was abandoning for ever. Without being aware of it, he found himself on the Russian frontier. Autumn was setting in by now. The coachmen, however, despite the poor state of the roads, carried him like the wind, and on the seventeenth morning of his journey he arrived in Krasnoye Selo,* which in those days lay on the main road.

There remained eighteen miles to Petersburg. While the horses were being harnessed, Ibrahim went into the coachmens' hut. In the corner a tall man in a green caftan, smoking a clay pipe, was reading the Hamburg papers, his elbows resting on the table. Hearing someone come in, he raised his head.

'Ba! Ibrahim?' he cried, getting up from the bench. 'Grand to see you godson!'

Ibrahim, recognizing Peter, was on the point of rushing towards him, but came to a respectful halt. The sovereign approached him, embraced him, and kissed him on the head.

'I was forewarned about your arrival,' said Peter, 'and came out to meet you. I've been waiting here since yesterday.'

Ibrahim was lost for words to express his gratitude.

'Order them to bring your wagon on behind us,' said the Tsar. 'You get in with me and we'll go on home.'

The sovereign's carriage was brought round. He got in with Ibrahim and they galloped off. In an hour and a half they were in Petersburg. Ibrahim gazed about him curiously at the new-born capital,* which was rising out of the swamps at the bidding of the autocrat. Rough dams, canals without embankments, wooden bridges everywhere proclaimed the recent victory of human will over the resistance of the elements. The houses looked as though they had been built in a hurry. In the entire city there was nothing of magnificence, apart from the Neva,* not yet adorned with its granite frame but already covered with warships and merchant vessels. The sovereign's carriage came to a halt at the palace called the Tsaritsyn Garden. On the porch, Peter was greeted by a woman of about thirty-five, very beautiful and dressed in the latest Paris fashion. After kissing her, Peter took Ibrahim's hand and said:

'Do you recognize my godson, Katenka? I would like you to love him and be kind to him as you used to.' Ekaterina turned her dark, piercing eyes upon him and extended an amiable hand. Two handsome young girls,* tall and slender, fresh as roses, stood behind her and approached Peter respectfully.

'Liza,' he said to one of them, 'do you remember the little black boy who used to steal my apples for you in Oranienbaum? Well, this is him: let me introduce him.' The Grand Duchess laughed, blushing. They went into the dining-room. The table had been laid in expectation of the Tsar. Peter sat down to the meal along with his entire family, and invited Ibrahim to join them. During dinner the sovereign chatted with him on various topics, quizzing him about the Spanish War, the internal affairs of France, and the Regent, whom he liked despite finding much in him to disapprove. Ibrahim had a precise and observant mind. Peter was much pleased with his responses; he recalled certain aspects of Ibrahim's infancy and retailed them with such good-natured gaiety that no one would have taken the courteous and hospitable host for the hero of Poltava,* the mighty and dread transformer of Russia.

After dinner the Tsar, as was the Russian custom, went off to rest. Ibrahim was left alone with the Empress and the Grand Duchesses. He attempted to satisfy their curiosity, describing the Parisian way of life, the festivals there, and the vagaries of fashion. Meanwhile a number of personages close to the sovereign were assembling at the palace. Ibrahim recognized the splendid Prince Menshikov,* who on seeing a negro talking to Ekaterina, looked at him haughtily askance; Prince Yakov Dolgoruky,* Peter's brusque adviser; the scholar Brus,* whom the people called the Russian Faust; the young Raguzinsky, his former comrade; and others who had come to report to the Tsar and receive instructions.

The Tsar returned in about two hours.

'Let's see whether you've forgotten your old duties,' he said to Ibrahim. 'Take a slate and follow me.'

Peter shut himself up in his workshop and busied himself with state affairs. In turn he worked with Brus, Prince Dolgoruky, Chief of Police Devier,* dictating to Ibrahim a number of decrees and decisions. Ibrahim was staggered by the speed and firm resolve of his judgement, the power and flexibility of his attention, and the sheer range of his activities. At the conclusion of his labours, Peter took out a notebook to check whether he had dealt with everything planned for that day. Then, as they left the workshop, he said to Ibrahim.

'It's getting late; you're tired, I expect: spend the night here, like in the old days. I'll wake you tomorrow.'

Ibrahim, left on his own, had difficulty in collecting himself. He was in Petersburg, he had seen once again the remarkable man with whom he had spent his infancy, all unaware of his greatness. It was almost with remorse that he admitted in his heart of hearts that Countess D., for the first time since their parting, had not been his sole preoccupation all day. He saw that the new way of life which awaited him, the work and constant activity, might revive his soul, wearied as it was by passion, idleness, and secret melancholy. The thought of being the colleague of a great man and, alongside him, influencing the destiny of a great people evoked in him for the first time a noble sense of ambition. It was in this frame of mind that he lay down on the camp-bed prepared for him, only for his usual dream to transport him to far-off Paris and the arms of his sweet Countess.

3

Like clouds that cross the sky,
The thoughts within us change their airy shapes,
We hate tomorrow what we love today.

                              (W. Küchelbeker)*

On the following day, as promised, Peter woke Ibrahim and
congratulated him on his appointment as first lieutenant in the
Grenadier company of the Preobrazhensky regiment, in which
he himself was a captain. The courtiers clustered round Ibrahim,
each trying to ingratiate himself with the new favourite. The
haughty Prince Menshikov clasped his hand cordially. Sheremetyev* enquired about his Parisian acquaintances, while Golovin*
invited him to dinner. The rest followed this last example, so that
Ibrahim received enough invitations to last him a good month.

   Ibrahim's days had a sameness about them, but were filled
with activity; consequently, he never felt bored. Day by day he
grew more and more attached to the Tsar, gaining ever-more
insight into his lofty purposes. Following a great man's thoughts
is the most absorbing of studies. Ibrahim saw Peter in the Senate, debating with Buturlin* and Dolgoruky as they analysed
important questions of legislation; at the Admiralty,* establishing the maritime might of Russia; saw him in the company of
Feofan, Gavriil Buzhinsky and Kopievich;* and in his leisure
hours examining translated foreign publications, or visiting some
merchant's manufactory, craftsman's yard, or scholar's study.
To Ibrahim, Russia seemed to be one vast workshop, where only
machines moved, where every workman, a cog in an established
process, was busy about his task. He regarded himself too, as
obliged to toil at his own bench and regret the diversions of
Parisian life as little as possible. It was more difficult for him to
dismiss another fond memory: he often thought about Countess
D., picturing her justified indignation, her tears and misery
... but sometimes a dreadful notion oppressed his heart: the
dissipations of high society, a new liaison, another fortunate

lover—he shuddered; jealousy began to seethe in his African blood, and hot tears threatened to course down his dusky face.

He was sitting one morning in his study, surrounded by official papers, when all of a sudden he heard a loud greeting in the French language; Ibrahim turned round excitedly and young Korsakov,* whom he had left in Paris in the midst of the social whirl, embraced him with joyful exclamations.

'I've only just arrived,' said Korsakov, 'and rushed straight over to see you. All our Parisian friends miss you and send their greetings; Countess D. ordered me to tell you to come back at all costs; here's a letter from her.'

Ibrahim seized it, trembling, and stared at the familiar handwriting of the address, not daring to believe his eyes.

'I'm very glad to see you haven't died of boredom yet in this barbarous Petersburg!' Korsakov went on. 'What do people find to do here? How do they spend their time? Who's your tailor? Have you got an opera at least?'

Ibrahim replied absently that the Tsar was presently working in the dockyard. Korsakov burst out laughing.

'I can see you have no time for me at the moment,' he said. 'We'll have our talk out another time; I'm off to present myself to the Tsar.'

With this he spun on his heel and trotted out of the room.

Ibrahim, left on his own, hastily unsealed the letter. The Countess reproached him tenderly, complaining of his dissembling and lack of trust.

'You say', she wrote, 'that my peace of mind is more precious to you than anything in the world: Ibrahim! If that were true, could you have reduced me to this state with the sudden news of your departure? You were afraid that I might hold you back; rest assured that, despite my love, I would have known how to sacrifice it for the sake of your advantage and what you consider to be your duty.' The Countess ended her letter with passionate avowals of her love and implored him to at least write to her now and then, if there was now no hope of their ever meeting again.

Ibrahim reread this letter twenty times, rapturously kissing the precious lines. He burned with impatience to hear something about the Countess, and got ready to go to the Admiralty, hoping to catch Korsakov there, but the door opened and Korsakov himself reappeared; he had already presented himself to the Tsar—and was, as usual, very pleased with himself.

'*Entre nous*,' he told Ibrahim, 'the Tsar is a passing strange individual; imagine, I found him wearing some sort of sackcloth jerkin, on the mast of a new ship, up which I had perforce to clamber with my dispatches. I stood on a rope ladder and had no room to make a proper bow. I was completely flustered, something that has never happened to me before. The Tsar, however, after reading the documents, looked me up and down and was no doubt favourably struck by the taste and elegance of my attire; at any rate he smiled and invited me to this evening's Assembly. I'm a complete foreigner in Petersburg though; in the six years I've been away I've completely forgotten how things are done here. Please, could you be my Mentor,* come and fetch me and introduce me around?' Ibrahim assented and hastened to turn the talk to a topic which interested him rather more.

'Well, what about Countess D.?'

'The Countess? Of course at first she was very upset about your departure; then little by little she recovered and found herself a new lover; guess who—that lanky Marquis R.; why the goggle eyes? Or do you really thing it so odd? Don't you know that it's not in human nature to be sad for long, especially female nature? Just you think about that, while I go and rest after the journey; don't forget to call for me, though.'

What were the emotions which crowded Ibrahim's heart? Jealousy? Fury? Despair? No: it was a profound, oppressive bleakness. He kept repeating to himself: I was the one to see this coming, it was bound to happen. Then he opened the letter and read it over again, hung his head, and wept bitterly. He cried for a long time. The tears eased his heart. Glancing at the clock, he saw that it was time to be off. Ibrahim would have been glad to miss the function, but the Assembly was obligatory and the Tsar made a point of insisting on the attendance of his entourage. Ibrahim got ready and drove round for Korsakov.

Korsakov was sitting in his dressing-gown, reading a French book.

'So early?' he said, on seeing Ibrahim.

'For goodness sake,' Ibrahim responded, 'it's already half-past five; we'll be late; be quick and get dressed and let's be off.'

Korsakov began bustling about and ringing his bell for all he was worth; servants came running in; he hurriedly began dressing. A French valet handed him a pair of shoes with red heels, blue velvet trousers, a spangled pink caftan; his wig was swiftly powdered in the anteroom and brought in to him. Korsakov thrust his shorn head into it, ordered his sword and gloves, twirled before the mirror some dozen times, and announced to Ibrahim that he was ready. The footmen brought them bearskin cloaks and off they drove to the Winter Palace.*

Korsakov showered Ibrahim with questions. Who was the foremost beauty in Petersburg? Who was the best dancer, what dance was the rage at present? Ibrahim was extremely reluctant to gratify his curiosity. Meanwhile they had arrived at the palace. A good many long sleighs, ancient carriages, and gilded coaches were already standing on the lawn. Moustachioed, liveried coachmen jostled by the stairs, runners, resplendent in gold braid and plumes, carried their maces; hussars, pages, clumsy footmen, loaded with their masters furs and muffs: a retinue was essential according to the boyars of that time. Upon the arrival of Ibrahim a general whispering broke out: 'The blackamoor, the blackamoor, the Tsar's blackamoor!' He hurriedly conducted Korsakov through the motley crowd. A palace servant opened the doors wide for them. Korsakov froze . . . In a sizeable room, lit by tallow candles which burned dimly in the clouds of tobacco smoke, lords with blue sashes across their shoulders, envoys, foreign merchants, Guards officers in green uniforms, ship's captains in short jackets and striped trousers swayed back and forth to the incessant noise of a brass band. The ladies sat near the wall, the younger set glittering in all the lavishness of fashion. Gold and silver glistened on their robes; their slender waists rose like flower stems out of gorgeous hooped skirts; diamonds sparkled in their ears, in their long tresses, and about their necks. They glanced gaily right and left, awaiting their cavaliers and the start of the dancing. The middle-aged ladies had artfully attempted to combine the new style of dress with the prohibited old one:* their bonnets resembled the sable cap worn by the Tsaritsa Natalya Kirilovna,* while their gowns and mantillas somehow recalled the sarafan and the padded jacket. They attended these newly instituted festivities with more astonishment than pleasure, it seemed, and looked askance at the wives and daughters of the Dutch skippers, in their calico skirts and red blouses, who went on knitting their stockings, laughing and chatting among themselves just as if they were at home. Korsakov simply couldn't get over it. A servant, noticing the new arrivals, came up to them with beer and glasses on a tray.

'*Que diable est-ce que tout cela?*' Korsakov whispered to Ibrahim in an undertone. Ibrahim could not help smiling. The Empress and the Grand Duchesses, resplendent in their beauty and finery, moved between the rows of guests, talking hospitably with them. The Tsar was in another room. Korsakov, wishing to be seen by him, had a hard time pushing his way through the ceaselessly surging crowd. The next room was occupied for the most part by foreigners, solemnly puffing on their clay pipes and draining earthenware tankards. The tables were set about with bottles of wine and beer, leather tobacco pouches, glasses of punch, and chess-boards. Peter was playing draughts at one of these tables with a broad-shouldered English sea-captain. They zealously saluted one another with salvos of tobacco smoke, and the Tsar was so disconcerted by an unexpected move of his opponent's that he failed to notice Korsakov, fidgeting close by. At that moment, a stout gentleman with a sizeable nosegay on his chest came in to announce, in a stentorian voice, that the dancing had commenced—and at once went out again; a great many guests trooped out after him, among them Korsakov.

The unexpected scene took him aback. Along the entire length of the ballroom ladies and their cavaliers stood in two rows opposite one another, while the most dirge-like music was played; the gentlemen bowed low, the ladies curtsied even lower, first to the front, then to the right, then to the left, then again to the front, then to the right and so on. Korsakov bit his lip and stared wide-eyed at this convoluted way of passing the time. The bowing and curtseying went on for nearly half an hour; eventually they gave over and the stout man with the nosegay proclaimed that the ceremonial dances were finished, and commanded the musicians to play a minuet. Korsakov rejoiced and prepared to shine. Among the young lady guests, one in particular had caught his eye. She was about 16 years of age and dressed richly, though with taste. She was sitting next to a middle-aged man of imposing and forbidding aspect. Korsakov flew over to her and asked her to do him the honour of dancing with him. The young beauty looked at him in bewilderment and seemed not to know what to say in reply. The frown of the man sitting next to her deepened. Korsakov waited for her answer, but the gentleman with the nosegay came up to him, led him to one side of the hall, and said solemnly:

'My dear sir, you have breached etiquette, in the first place by approaching the young person without the three requisite bows; in the second, by taking it upon yourself to invite her, when during minuets it is the lady who has that right, not the gentlemen; on this account you must be severely punished, namely by drinking the *Goblet of the Great Eagle.*' Korsakov was becoming more and more bewildered. In a trice the guests had surrounded him, noisily demanding that the law be immediately carried out. Peter, a great one for personally superintending punishments of this sort, overheard the laughter and all the shouting, and emerged from his room. The crowd gave way before him and he entered the circle where stood the condemned man and the marshal of the Assembly holding an enormous goblet filled with Malmsey. He was vainly trying to persuade the transgressor to obey the law voluntarily.

'Aha,' said Peter, on seeing Korsakov. 'You're in it now, my lad. Be good enough, monsieur, to drink without flinching.'

There was nothing for it. The poor dandy drained the whole goblet without drawing breath, then handed it to the marshal.

'Listen, Korsakov,' said Peter. 'Those pants of yours are made of a kind of velvet even I don't wear, and I'm a lot richer than you. That is extravagance; see that you and I don't have a falling out.'

On receiving his admonishment, Korsakov tried to leave the circle, but staggered and almost fell over, to the indescribable delight of the Tsar and the whole jolly company. This episode, far from dampening the harmony and entertainment of the main business of the evening, made it even livelier. The gentlemen began scraping and bowing, the ladies curtsied and clicked their heels with increased vigour, by now ignoring the rhythm of the music. Korsakov was unable to participate in the general gaiety. The lady he had selected, at the command of her father, Gavrila Afanasievich, came over to Ibrahim, and with blue eyes lowered, demurely proffered her hand. Ibrahim danced the minuet with her and led her to her seat; then, hunting out Korsakov, conducted him out of the ballroom, sat him in the carriage, and took him home. On the way, Korsakov started babbling incoherently: 'Damn the Assembly! ... Damn the Goblet of the Great Eagle! ...' But he soon fell sound asleep, and was oblivious as he was undressed and put to bed; he woke next day with an aching head and only a vague recollection of the scraping and curtseying, the tobacco smoke, and the gentleman with the nosegay and the Goblet of the Great Eagle.

4

Our forbears took their meals at leisure,
Full slowly then you would have found
The pitchers, silver cups, full measure
With foaming wine and ale go round.

*(Ruslan and Lyudmila)**

Now I must acquaint the gentle reader with Gavrila Afanasievich Rzhevsky. He came of an ancient boyar lineage and possessed an immense estate; he was hospitable and loved falconry; his retinue of servants was numerous indeed. In short, he was a thoroughgoing Russian gentleman; he could not abide what he called the German spirit, and in his domestic arrangements tried to preserve the customs of the good old days he cherished.

His daughter was seventeen years old. She had lost her mother while still a child. She had been brought up in the old-fashioned way, that is, surrounded by nurses and nannies, playmates and serving-maids, could embroider in gold, and couldn't read or write; her father, despite his detestation of all things foreign, had been unable to resist her desire to learn the German dances from a captive Swedish officer domiciled with them. This worthy dancing-master was some fifty years of age; his right leg had been shot through at Narva* and was not, therefore, overagile when it came to minuets and courants, but the left could execute the most exacting *pas* with astonishing ease and accomplishment. His pupil did honour to his efforts. Natalia Gavrilovna was renowned at the assemblies for being the best dancer, which was part of the reason for Korsakov's misdemeanour. He came round the next day to make his excuses to Gavrila Afanasievich, but the smooth and dapper address of the young dandy made a poor impression on the proud old nobleman, who promptly gave him the witty nickname of the French monkey.

It was a holiday. Gavrila Afanasievich was expecting several guests and relations. The table was being laid in the ancient hall. The guests were arriving with their wives and daughters, at last released from seclusion by the domestic edicts of the Tsar and his own personal example. Natalya brought every guest a silver tray set about with gold cups, and every one of them, as he drank, regretted that the custom of a kiss bestowed on such an occasion in days of yore was now in abeyance. They sat up to the table.

In the place of honour, next to the host, sat his father-in-law, Prince Boris Alexeyevich Lykov, a seventy-year-old boyar; the other guests observed family seniority, recalling the happy days when order of precedence ruled.* They sat down with the men on one side of the table and the women on the other. At the far end of the table sat the usual people: the housekeeper in her jerkin and head-dress; the dwarf, a thirty-year-old child, wrinkled and prim; and the captive Swede in his faded blue uniform. The table, piled high with dishes, was surrounded by a numerous and bustling throng of servants, among whom the butler was conspicuous with his stern expression, large paunch, and majestic immobility. During the first few minutes of the dinner, attention was devoted exclusively to the products of our traditional cuisine; only the clatter of plates and busy spoons disturbed the general silence. At length the host, seeing that the time had come to entertain his guests with agreeable conversation, turned round and enquired: 'Where on earth's Ekimovna? Fetch her here.' Several servants made to rush away in various directions, when at that very moment an old woman, rouged and powdered, adorned with flowers and oddments, and wearing a low-cut brocade dress, came in dancing and humming a tune. Her arrival was greeted with pleasurable anticipation.

'Good evening, Ekimovna,' said Prince Lykov, 'how are you getting along?'

'Well and nicely, man: singing and dancing and waiting for a suitor.'

'Where on earth have you been, old fool?' asked the host.

'I've been dolling myself up, man, for the honoured guests, for God's holiday, just as the Tsar and the boyars commanded, to give the whole world a laugh, German-style.'

These words evoked loud laughter, and the fool stayed in her place behind the host's chair.

'A fool may tell lies, but the truth slips out,' said Tatyana Afanasievna, the host's elder sister, and held by him in great respect. 'Really, today's fashions make the whole world laugh. Since you gentlemen have shaved your beards off* and dressed up in skimpy jackets, you can hardly talk about women's clothes of course: still, it's a pity about the sarafan, the girls' ribbons, and the woman's head-dress. When you look at today's beauties, you don't know whether to laugh or cry: hair frizzed up like tow, greased and powdered with French flour, their tummies laced so tight it's a wonder they don't snap in half—and with their petticoats hooped so they have to get into carriages sideways and bend down to get in a door. They can't stand, can't sit, and can't breathe—they're proper martyrs, the poor darlings.'

'Ah, my dear Tatyana Afanasievna,' said Kirila Petrovich T. He had been a governor in Ryazan, where he had contrived in some underhand way to acquire 3,000 serfs and a young wife. 'In my view a wife can dress as she pleases. She can look like a scarecrow or the Emperor of China, just as long as she doesn't order new gowns every month and throw perfectly good ones out. It used to be that the grandmother's sarafan formed part of the granddaughter's dowry, but dresses nowadays—what do you see? What the mistress wears today, the maid wears tomorrow. What's to be done? It's the ruination of the Russian gentry! A disaster, and that's all about it.'

At these words, he sighed and looked at his own Maria Ilinichna, who, it appeared, took a poor view both of this praise of the old days and the disparagement of the new order. The other beauties shared her displeasure, but held their peace, for in those days self-effacement was regarded as an essential attribute of a young woman.

'And whose fault is it?' asked Gavrila Afanasievich, frothing up his mug of kvass. 'Is it not we ourselves? The young lasses act the fool and we encourage them.'

'But what can we do if the matter is out of our hands?' retorted Kirila Petrovich. 'Many a one would be glad to keep his wife shut away in the *terem*,* but they come round beating drums and summoning them to the Assembly; the husband goes for his whip and the wife dolls herself up. Oh, these dratted Assemblies! The Lord has visited them upon us for our sins.'

Maria Ilinichna was on tenterhooks; her tongue fairly itched; at length she could not contain herself, and turning to her husband, asked him with an acid smile what was wrong with the Assemblies.

'What's wrong with them', responded her spouse heatedly, 'is that since they were introduced, husbands have been at odds with their wives. Wives have forgotten the apostolic word: *the wife should venerate her husband*; it's new clothes they worry about now, not household affairs; they don't think of how to please their husbands but of how to attract the attention of giddy officers. And is it decent, madam, for a Russian noble-woman to be associating with tobacco-smoking Germans and their maidservants? Dancing and talking to young men at all hours—it's unheard of. It would be bad enough with relatives, but these are outsiders, strangers.'

'I should like to put in a word, but walls have ears,' said Gavrila Afanasievich, frowning. 'Still, I have to confess the As-semblies aren't to my taste either: if you're not careful, you're knocking up against some drunk or they make you drunk your-self, just for a joke. You have to watch that some scamp isn't up to mischief with your daughter; nowadays the young people are so spoilt, it passes belief. Take the son of the late Evgraf Sergeyevich Korsakov; at the last Assembly he made such a commotion over Natasha, I fairly blushed. Next day I look and here's a carriage, rolling right into my courtyard; I thought who in heaven's name could it be—Prince Alexander Danilovich, perhaps? Not at all: it was young Korsakov! Couldn't stop at the gate and put himself out by coming to the porch on foot—not he! In he flew! Bowing and scraping and gabbling away! . . . The fool Ekimovna can take him off to a T; come on now fool: show us the foreign monkey.'

The fool Ekimovna seized the lid of one of the dishes, tucked it under her arm as if it were a hat, and began cringing, scraping and bowing to all sides, murmuring: 'Monsieur . . . Mamzelle . . . Assembly . . . *pardon*.' Universal and prolonged laughter attested to the general delight.

'It's Korsakov to the life,' said old Prince Lykov, wiping away the tears of laughter when calm had more or less been restored. 'Still, we have to face it. He's not the first and he won't be the last to come back from foreign parts as a clown to holy Russia. What do our children learn abroad? To bow and scrape, babble in double-Dutch, have no respect for their elders, and chase after other men's wives. Out of all the young fellows educated abroad (God forgive me) the Tsar's blackamoor is the nearest thing to a man.'

'Of course,' put in Gavrila Afanasievich, 'he's a solid and decent fellow, not like that feather-headed . . . Now who's that driving through the gates? Not that foreign monkey again? What are you gaping at, idiots?' he went on, addressing his servants: 'Run and turn him away; and tell him that in future . . .'

'Old greybeard, are you in your right mind?' the fool Ekimovna broke in. 'Or are you blind: that's the sovereign's sleigh, the Tsar has arrived.'

Gavrila Afansievich rose hastily from the table; everyone rushed to the windows; and they did indeed see the Tsar, who was mounting the front steps, leaning on his aide-de-camp's shoulder. Turmoil broke out. The host rushed out to welcome the sovereign; servants ran hither and yon like mad things, the guests were terrified, some even contemplating a swift departure homeward. Suddenly Peter's booming voice could be heard out in the passage. All went quiet and the Tsar entered, accompanied by the host, who was dumbstruck with joy. 'Greetings, gentlefolk,' said Peter, his expression genial. They all bowed low. The Tsar's swift glance picked out the host's young daughter among the crowd; he called her to him. Natalya Gavrilovna approached quite boldly, but was blushing to her shoulders as well as her ears. 'You get prettier by the day,' said the sovereign, kissing her on the head as was his wont; then turning to the guests, he said:

'Now what's this? I've disturbed you. You were dining; I would ask you to resume your seats, and for me some anise vodka, Gavrila Afanasievich, if you please.' The host dashed over to his stately butler, snatched the tray from his hands, and filling a golden goblet, proffered it to the Tsar with a bow. Peter drank and bit into a pretzel before again asking the guests to go on with their meal. Everyone resumed their places, except for the dwarf and the housekeeper, who dared not remain at a table honoured by the Tsar's presence. Peter sat himself down next to the host and asked for some cabbage soup. The sovereign's orderly handed him a wooden spoon mounted in ivory, and a little knife and fork with green bone handles; Peter never used any implements but his own. The meal which a moment before had been full of high spirits and chatter, proceeded in silence and constraint. The host, out of respect and pleasure, ate nothing; the guests were all formality and listened in reverence as the sovereign conversed in German with the Swede about the 1701 campaign.* Ekimovna, the fool, questioned several times by the Tsar, answered with a kind of timid stiffness which (I might say in passing) was not indicative of any innate stupidity. Finally the dinner came to an end. The sovereign rose, followed by the other guests.

'Gavrila Afanasievich!' said Peter. 'I need to have a word with you in private,' and taking him by the arm, led him off to the drawing-room and shut the door. The guests remained in the dining-room, discussing in whispers the significance of this unexpected visitation. Fearing to presume, they quickly left, one by one, without thanking the host for his hospitality. His father-in-law, daughter, and sister saw them off at the threshold and remained alone in the dining-room, awaiting the sovereign's departure.

5

I will find a wife for you
As I am a miller true.

(Ablesimov's opera
The Miller)*

After half an hour the door opened and Peter emerged. With a grave inclination of the head he acknowledged the threefold obeisance of Prince Lykov, Tatyana Afanasievna, and Natasha, and went straight through to the hallway. The host passed him his red sheepskin coat, saw him to his sleigh, and while on the steps, thanked him for the honour conferred upon him. Peter departed.

Returning to the dining-room, Gavrila Afanasievich seemed to have much on his mind. He testily ordered the servants to be quick and clear the table, sent Natasha to her room, and having announced to his sister and brother-in-law that he needed to talk to them, led them into the bedroom where he usually took his rest after dinner. The old prince lay down on the oak bedstead, Tatyana Afanasievna sat down on an ancient brocaded armchair, and drew up a footstool. Gavrila Afanasievich locked all the doors, sat down on the bed at Prince Lykov's feet, and began in a low voice:

'The sovereign had a reason for paying me a visit; guess what he was pleased to talk to me about?'

'How can we know, dear brother of mine,' said Tatyana Afanasievna.

'The Tsar hasn't asked you to be a *voivode** has he?' enquired his brother-in-law. 'High time too. Or has he offered you an ambassadorship? Why not? It's not just government secretaries who get sent to foreign countries, prominent people do as well.'

'No,' replied his son-in-law, scowling. 'I'm a man of the old school, our services aren't needed these days, though an Orthodox Russian gentleman may well be worth as much as these modern upstarts, pancake-vendors, and heathens. Still, that's another story.'

'So what was he pleased to talk about for such a long time, brother?' asked Tatyana Afanasievna. 'You're not in some kind of trouble are you? God save and defend us!'

'It's not trouble exactly, but I must confess, I was taken by surprise.'

'What is it brother, what's it all about?'

'It's about Natasha: the Tsar came to propose a match for her.'

'Thank heavens,' said Tatyana Afanasievna, crossing herself. 'The girl's of an age, and like matchmaker like bridegroom. Lord grant them love and harmony, honour is there in plenty in any case. For whom does the Tsar seek her hand?'

'Hmm,' Gavrila Afanasievich cleared his throat. 'For whom? That's just it, for whom.'

'Who is it then?' repeated Prince Lykov, by now beginning to doze off.

'Guess,' said Gavrila Afanasievich.

'My dear brother,' responded the old lady, 'how are we supposed to guess? There are plenty of young men at court: any one of them would be glad to have your Natasha as a wife. Is it Dolgoruky?'

'No, not Dolgoruky.'

'Just as well: far too high and mighty. Shein, Troekurov?'*

'Neither one.'

'I don't much like them either: featherbrains, too much of the German spirit about them. Well then, Miloslavsky?'

'No, not him.'

'Just as well too: rich but stupid. Who then? Eletsky? Lvov? No? Not Raguzinsky, is it? All right, I can't think. Who does the Tsar propose for Natasha?'

'The blackamoor Ibrahim.'

The old lady exclaimed and clasped her hands. Prince Lykov raised his head from the pillow and repeated in astonishment: 'The blackamoor Ibrahim!'

'Dear brother of mine,' said the old lady tearfully, 'don't condemn your own child, don't deliver her into the clutches of this black devil.'

'But how can I oppose the sovereign's will,' rejoined Gavrila Afanasievich, 'when he has promised to show us favour, myself and all our family?'

'What's this,' cried the old prince, sleep now banished, 'marry my own grandchild Natasha to a bought blackamoor?'

'He's not of the common stock', said Gavrila Afanasievich. 'He's the son of a blackamoor sultan. The Turks captured him and sold him in Constantinople, where our envoy rescued him and presented him to the Tsar. The blackamoor's elder brother came to Russia with a considerable ransom and . . .'

'Dear Gavrila Afanasievich,' his sister broke in, 'we've heard that fairy-tale about Prince Bova and Eruslan Lazarevich.* Just tell us what your reply was to the Tsar's matchmaking.'

'I told him that he had power over us, and our duty as his servants was to obey him in all things.'

At that moment there came a noise from behind the door. Gavrila Afanasievich went to open it, but feeling resistance, had to push hard. The door opened—and they saw Natasha stretched out unconscious on the blood-stained floor.

Her heart had stood still when the sovereign shut himself in with her father. A kind of foreboding had whispered to her that the matter concerned her, and when Gavrila Afanasievich sent her out, announcing that he had to talk with her aunt and grandfather, she had not been able to resist the impulse of feminine curiosity and had quietly stolen through the inner rooms to the bedroom door. She had not missed a word of the whole dreadful conversation: when she heard her father's final words, the poor girl had fainted and, in falling, struck her head against the iron-bound chest which held her dowry.

The servants came running; they picked up Natasha and carried her to her bedroom and laid her on the bed. After a while she revived and opened her eyes, but recognized neither her father nor her aunt. A high fever set in and she kept on talking in her delirium of the Tsar's blackamoor and her wedding—then all of a sudden she called out in a piercing voice: 'Valerian, sweet Valerian, my life! Save me: here they come, here they come! . . .' Tatyana Afanasievna shot an anxious look at her brother, who turned pale, bit his lip, and left the room. He went back to the old prince, who, unable to climb the stairs, had remained below.

'How's Natasha?' he enquired.

'Bad', responded the distressed father. 'Worse than I thought: she's raving about Valerian.'

'Which Valerian is this?' asked the old man, alarmed. 'Not that *Streltsy** orphan you brought up in your household?'

'That's the one,' replied Gavrila Afanasievich. 'It was my bad luck that his father saved my life during the *Streltsy* revolt and the devil prompted me to take the blasted wolf-cub into my own house. Two years ago, when I got him into the army at his own request, Natasha burst into tears as she said goodbye, and he looked petrified. I thought that was suspicious—and told my sister as much. But since then Natasha hasn't mentioned him, and nothing's been heard of him since. I thought she'd forgotten about him, but it seems not. It's settled: she'll marry the blackamoor.'

Prince Lykov did not contradict him: that would have been fruitless. He went home; Tatyana Afanasievna remained by Natasha's bedside; Gavrila Afanasievich, having sent for the doctor, shut himself up in his room, and a mournful silence reigned within his house.

The unexpected matchmaking had surprised Ibrahim at least as much as Gavrila Afanasievich. This is how it happened: Peter, while working with Ibrahim, had said to him:

'I can see that you're depressed, my friend; tell me frankly: is there anything you need?'

Ibrahim assured the Tsar that he was content with his lot and wished for nothing better.

'Good,' said the Tsar. 'If you're miserable for no reason, then I know how to brighten you up.'

When work had finished, Peter asked Ibrahim:

'Did you like the girl you danced the minuet with at the last Assembly?'

'She's very nice, sire, and seems a modest, sweet-natured girl.'

'Then I'll get you better acquainted. Would you like to marry her?'

'I, sire?'

'Listen Ibrahim, you're a fellow on his own, no kith and kin, a stranger to everybody but me. If I were to die today, what would become of you tomorrow, my poor blackamoor? You have to get yourself settled while there's still time; find a support in new ties, make an alliance with the Russian boyar class.'

'Sire, I am happy to enjoy the protection and favour of your majesty. God grant I do not survive my Tsar and benefactor, that is all I wish for; but if I did have a mind to marry, would the young lady and her relations consent? My appearance . . .'

'Your appearance! Stuff and nonsense! You're a fine fellow, are you not? The young lady has to obey the will of her parents, and we'll see what old Gavrila Rzhevsky has to say when I am your matchmaker.'

So saying, the sovereign ordered his sleigh to be brought, leaving Ibrahim plunged in profound contemplation.

'Marry!' thought the African. 'Why on earth not? Surely I'm not doomed to spend my life in solitude, without knowing the joys and most sacred obligations of man just because of having been born in a hot climate? I can't depend on being loved: a childish objection! Can love be trusted anyway? Does it exist in the fickle female heart? Having renounced those sweet delusions for ever, I have chosen other, more practical attractions instead. The Tsar is right: I must guarantee my future. Marriage with the young Rzhevskaya will unite me to the proud Russian nobility, and I will cease to be an alien in my new homeland. I shan't demand love from my wife, I will be content with her loyalty, and I will win her friendship by my constant tenderness, trust, and indulgence.'

Ibrahim wanted to get down to work as usual, but his imagination was too much beguiled. He abandoned his papers and went for a stroll along the Neva Embankment. Suddenly he heard Peter's voice; he turned to see the sovereign dismiss his sleigh and come after him with an expression of high good-humour.

'It's all settled, my friend,' said Peter, taking his arm. 'I've arranged your marriage for you. Tomorrow go and see your father-in-law; see you humour his boyar pride; leave your sleigh at his gate, cross the courtyard on foot; talk to him about his services and his noble pedigree, and you'll have him eating out of your hand. And now,' he continued, with a shake of his oak cudgel, 'walk with me to that rogue Danilych's house, I need to have words with him about his latest pranks.'

Ibrahim, warmly thanking Peter for his fatherly solicitude, saw him as far as Prince Menshikov's magnificent palace and then returned home.

6

A sanctuary lamp burned dimly before the glass case which held
the old family icons in their glittering mounts of gold and silver.
Its guttering flame cast a weak light over the curtained bed and
a small table set about with labelled medicine bottles. Near the
stove, a maid sat at her spinning-wheel, and the faint whirring of
the spindle was the only sound that disturbed the silence of the
bedroom.

'Who's there?' asked a feeble voice.

The maid at once rose, went over to the bed, and raised the
curtain slightly.

'Will it be getting light soon?' Natasha asked.

'It's noon already,' replied the maid.

'Good heavens, why is it so dark then?'

'The shutters are closed, Miss.'

'Help me to get dressed, quickly.'

'I mustn't, Miss, doctor's orders.'

'Am I ill, then? Has it been long?'

'Two weeks now.'

'Really? I feel as if I'd just lain down yesterday . . .'

Natasha fell silent; she began to collect her scattered thoughts.
Something had happened to her, but what was it exactly? She
couldn't bring it to mind. The maid was still standing before
her, waiting for orders. At that moment a muffled sound came
from below.

'What's that?' enquired the sick girl.

'The ladies and gentlemen have finished their dinner and are
leaving the table,' answered the maid. 'Your aunt will be coming
here presently.'

Natasha seemed glad to hear this; she made a feeble gesture.
The maid drew the bed-curtain and seated herself at the spinning-
wheel once more.

A few minutes later a head in a broad white mob-cap with
dark ribbons appeared in the doorway and asked in an undertone:

'How is Natasha?'

'Hello, auntie,' said the invalid softly; Tatyana Afanasievna
hurried over.

'The young lady has come round,' said the maid, carefully pulling up an armchair to the side of the bed. The old woman tearfully kissed her niece's wan, drowsy face, and seated herself beside her. In her wake came the German doctor in black caftan and scholar's wig; he felt Natasha's pulse and announced in Latin and then in Russian that she was out of danger. He asked for paper and an ink-well, wrote out a new prescription, and left. The old lady rose, kissed Natalya once more, and went off downstairs to give the good news to her brother.

In the drawing-room, the Tsar's blackamoor, uniformed and wearing his sword, was sitting and talking respectfully with Gavrila Afanasievich. Korsakov was stretched on the down sofa, listening to their conversation and teasing a venerable hound; tiring of this occupation, he went over to the mirror, his usual refuge from boredom, and in it caught sight of Tatyana Afanasievna who, all unnoticed, was gesturing to her brother from the doorway. 'You're wanted, Gavrila Afanasievich,' said Korsakov, turning towards him and interrupting Ibrahim. Gavrila Afanasievich at once went to his sister and closed the door to behind him.

'I wonder at your patience,' Korsakov said to Ibrahim. 'You've spent a good hour listening to nonsense about the ancient lineage of the Lykovs and the Rzhevskys, and putting in your own moral comments as well! In your shoes *j'aurais planté là* the old humbug and all his line, and that includes Natalya Gavrilovna, all coy and pretending to be ill, *une petite santé*. Tell me honestly, you're not really in love with that little *mijaurée?** Listen to me Ibrahim, take my advice this once; really, I'm more sensible than I may seem. Drop this foolish notion. Don't get married. I get the impression that this bride of yours has no particular liking for you. Who knows what may happen? Take me, I'm not bad-looking of course, but I have had occasion to deceive husbands who were no worse than me, honestly. You yourself . . . recall our Parisian friend Count D.? You just can't rely on a woman being faithful; he's a happy man who can be indifferent to it! But you! . . . With that passionate, brooding, and suspicious nature of yours, your flattened nose, your thick lips, your curly wool, to throw yourself into all the dangers of matrimony? . . .'

'Thank you for the friendly advice,' interrupted Ibrahim coldly, 'but you know the saying: you don't have to worry about rocking other people's babies.'

'Just watch out, Ibrahim,' responded Korsakov, laughing, 'that you don't have to illustrate that saying in the literal sense later on.'

The conversation in the other room, however, was becoming heated.

'You'll kill her,' the old woman was saying. 'She won't survive the sight of him.'

'But just think,' countered her brother stubbornly. 'It's two weeks now he's been visiting as her bridegroom, and so far he hasn't set eyes on the bride. He might start thinking her illness is a sham, and we're just trying to gain time to wriggle out of it somehow. And what will the Tsar say? He's already sent three times to enquire after Natalya's health. Say what you like, but I don't intend to quarrel with him.'

'Merciful heavens,' said Tatyana Afanasievna, 'what's to become of the poor girl? At least let me prepare her for the visit.'

Gavrila Afanasievich assented and returned to the drawing-room.

'Thank heavens,' he said to Ibrahim. 'The crisis has passed. Natalya is much better; if I weren't embarrassed at leaving our dear guest Ivan Evgrafovich all by himself, I'd take you upstairs to have a peep at your bride.'

Korsakov congratulated Gavrila Afanasievich on the news and begged him not to feel uneasy on his account, assuring him that he had to go anyway, and dashed out into the hall, giving his host no chance to see him off.

Meanwhile Tatyana Afanasievna had hastened to prepare the invalid for the appearance of her alarming visitor. Entering the bedroom, she sat down panting by the bed. She took Natasha's hand, but had not had time to utter a word when the door opened. Natasha asked who had come: the old woman was horror-struck and remained mute. Gavrila Afanasievich drew back the curtain, looked bleakly at the invalid, and asked how she was. The girl tried to smile at him, but was unable to do so. Her father's stern gaze was dismaying, and a feeling of anxiety overwhelmed her. At that moment she sensed someone standing by the head of the bed. She raised herself with an effort and suddenly recognized the Tsar's blackamoor. At this she recalled the full horror of the future awaiting her. But her exhausted mind did not register any noticeable shock. Natasha lowered her head on to the pillow once more and closed her eyes. Her heart beat painfully. Tatyana Afanasievna gave her brother a sign that the patient wanted to sleep, and they all quietly left the bedroom, apart from the maid, who sat down at her spinning-wheel once more.

The miserable invalid opened her eyes and, no longer seeing anyone at her bedside, called the maid and told her to fetch the dwarf. But at that very moment the rotund, aged child rolled up to her bed. Swallow (as they called the dwarf) had come upstairs after Gavrila Afanasievich and Ibrahim as fast as her little legs could carry her, and concealed herself behind the door in keeping with that curiosity inborn in the fair sex. Natasha had caught sight of her and dismissed the maid; the dwarf sat down on a footstool by the bed.

Never did such a small body contain so much in the way of mental activity. She was involved in everything, was privy to everything, and always busy about some affair or other. In her artful and ingratiating way she had contrived to secure the love of her masters and the hatred of the rest of the household, which she ruled like a tyrant. Gavrila Afanasievich listened to her reports, her complaints, and her petty requests; Tatyana Afanasievna was forever consulting her opinion and being guided by her advice. For her part, Natasha nurtured a boundless affection for her and confided all the thoughts and stirrings of her sixteen-year-old heart.

'You know, Swallow,' she said, 'my father is giving me in marriage to the blackamoor?'

The dwarf gave a deep sigh, and her wrinkled face grew even more so.

'Is there no hope?' Natasha pursued. 'Surely father will take pity on me.'

The dwarf shook her cap.

'Won't grandfather and auntie stand up for me?'

'No, mistress. The blackamoor has managed to charm everybody while you've been ill. The master think's he's wonderful and the prince just raves about him. Tatyana Afanasievna says:

"Such a pity he's a blackamoor, otherwise we couldn't wish for a better bridegroom."'

'Oh, good heavens, good heavens!' groaned poor Natasha.

'Don't be depressed, our beauty,' said the dwarf, kissing the feeble hand. 'If you have to marry the blackamoor, you still have your freedom. It's not like the old days; husbands don't lock their wives up: I hear the blackamoor's a rich man; your house will be like the cup that runneth over, you'll be in clover . . .'

'Poor Valerian!' said Natasha, but so quietly that the dwarf could only guess the words, rather than hear them.

'That's just it, mistress,' she said, lowering her voice mysteriously. 'If you thought less about the *Streltsy* orphan, you wouldn't have raved about him when the fever was on you, and your father wouldn't be angry with you.'

'What?' said Natasha, alarmed. 'I raved about Valerian, father heard, and was angry!'

'That's it, that's the trouble,' replied the dwarf. 'Now if you ask him not to give you to the negro, he'll think Valerian is the reason. There's nothing for it: just submit to your father's will, and what will be, will be.'

Natasha uttered no word of protest. The thought that her heart's secret was known to her father had shaken her imagination. One hope remained to her: to die before the hateful wedding took place. This thought comforted her. Weak and miserable as she was, she resigned herself to her fate.

7

In Gavrila Afanasievich's house, to the right of the entrance hall, lay a small room with one tiny window. Inside was a simple bedstead covered with a flannel blanket. In front of the bed stood a pine table on which burned a tallow candle. Some sheet music lay open. On the wall hung an old blue uniform and a tricorn hat of the same age; above it, three nails held a folk-print of Charles XII* on horseback. The sound of a flute could be heard in this humble habitation. The captive dancing-master, its solitary occupant, in night-cap and nankeen dressing-gown, was beguiling the boredom of a winter evening by playing some old Swedish marches to remind him of his gay young days. After keeping this exercise up for a good two hours, the Swede dismantled his flute, laid it in its case, and began to undress.

At that moment the latch on his door was lifted and a tall, handsome young man in uniform came into the room.

The astonished Swede rose to his feet in alarm.

'You don't recognize me, Gustav Adamich,' said the young visitor, evidently touched. 'You don't remember the boy you taught Swedish musketry, with whom you nearly started a fire in this very room by shooting off a toy cannon?'

Gustav Adamich peered at his visitor intently . . .

'Eh-eh-eh,' he cried at length, embracing him. 'Marvellous, jost that you here. Sit down, your old rascal. Let's tok.'

[The fragment breaks off at this point.]

EXPLANATORY NOTES

Tales of the Late Ivan Petrovich Belkin

3 [*epigraph*]: from Denis Fonvizin's comedy *The Minor* (1782).

quit-rent: depending on the conditions set by their masters, Russian serfs were required to pay quit rent (*obrok*) as assessed on the property they worked; the alternative system was payment in kind (*barshchina*).

The Shot

7 [*epigraphs*]: the first epigraph is drawn from the long narrative poem *The Ball* by Evgeny Abramovich Baratynsky (1800–44), a contemporary of Pushkin, highly esteemed for his philosophical poetry and the harmony of his style. In this work a cold Muscovite beauty, Princess Nina, falls in love with the Byronic hero Arseny. His old inamorata Olga reappears after a long absence and Arseny is forced to tell Nina that he cannot love her. Nina sees the happy couple at a ball and returns home to take poison. Pushkin esteemed the poem for its realistic portrayal of the conflict between the powerful hero and heroine, and its psychological insight. In an essay of 1828 he called it a work filled with uncommon charm and praised the humorous and playful tone of its swift narrative. The second is from 'An Evening on Bivouac' (1822), a story by A. Bestuzhev-Marlinsky, who was much read at the time for his colourful and exotic descriptions of Eastern locations and his sensational plots.

8 *turned down . . . card*: bending down a corner of the card meant the player wished to bet all his money; the act was called *paroli*. As Paul Debreczeny comments, the practice was 'a bit tricky, for a player might "absentmindedly" bend his card unintentionally or when he was not entitled to; this was the cause of Silvio's quarrel with the young officer in "The Shot"' (*The Other Pushkin*, 198).

11 *Burtsov . . . Davydov's poems*: Alexander Petrovich Burtsov, hussar and bon vivant made famous by the poet and soldier Denis Davydov in three poems (two entitled 'To Burtsov' and the 'Hussar Feast'). Denis Vasilievich Davydov (1784–1839), swashbuckling hero of the 1812 campaign—the model for the character Denisov in Tolstoy's *War and Peace*—is also remembered as the 'hussar poet' whose exciting lyrics celebrate drink, women, and heroism.

18 *Alexander Ypsilanti's rebellion*: Ypsilanti (1792–1828) was the magnetic leader of the secret Greek organization called the Hetairists whose battle to liberate Greece from Turkish rule galvanized Lord Byron. They were defeated at the Battle of Skulyani on 17 June 1821.

The Snowstorm

19 [*epigraph*]: the lines are from Vasily Zhukovsky's famous ballad *Svetlana* (1813), vv. 113–16 and 127–34.

game of Boston: a type of whist that probably developed in France and became popular in America in the late eighteenth century. For a technical description, see David Parlett, *The Oxford Guide to Card Games* (Oxford, 1990), 206–8.

assessor: a bureaucratic rank without specified duties. On the civilian hierarchy of the Table of Ranks devised in 1722 to regulate the promotion of civil servants and entrance into the nobility, the assessor (initially called 'collegiate assessor' when the post carried some function in the administrative colleges or Senate) was in the eighth of the fourteen possible classes. To be eligible for membership of the nobility one had to advance to the eighth class.

21 *Masha*: the diminutive for 'Maria'.

25 *Borodino*: Napoleon's victory over the defending Russian army on 7 September 1812 at Borodino, seventy-five miles from Moscow, was the highpoint of his ill-fated Russian campaign and led to the retreat of the Russians under General Kutuzov and the capture and burning of Moscow a week later. Over 40,000 Russians and nearly 60,000 French soldiers perished in the single day of battle.

26 *'Vive Henri Quatre'*: from Charles Collé's (1709–83) comedy, *La Partie de chasse de Henri IV*, evidently popular after the restoration of the monarchy in 1814.

arias from 'Gioconda': that is, *Joconde, ou les coureurs d'aventures* (1814), opera by Nicolas Isouard (1773–1818), a Maltese composer of French origin.

And threw their bonnets in the air: the citation is from Alexander Griboedov's enormously popular classic comedy *Woe from Wit* (performed first in 1831 and published in 1833), II. v.

27 *S' amor non è, che dunque?*: Pushkin's narrator quotes a truncated line from Petrarch, Sonnet cxxxii. In full, the line means 'If it is not love, what then is it that I feel?'

28 *St Preux's first letter*: the reference is to J.-J. Rousseau's epistolary novel, *Julie, ou la Nouvelle Héloïse* (1761), whose main hero, the young plebeian tutor Saint Preux, falls in love with his aristocratic pupil; the discourse

and manner that Rousseau gave his characters had was a major influence in the relations between the sexes as represented by writers of the Sentimentalist movement.

The Undertaker

31 [*epigraph*]: from Derzhavin's gigantic ode *The Waterfall*, ll. 66–7, which was written in commemoration of Prince Grigory Potemkin Catherine II's general and sometime lover, in 1791. The central image of the waterfall is a metaphor for human life.

33 *Pogorelsky's postman*: the reference is to a story by Anton Pogorelsky, 'The Lefertov District Poppyseed-cake Vendor' (1825), one of the first Hoffmanesque stories in Russia. The vendor in question is an elderly female baker who moonlights as a witch. Upon inheriting her home the postman Onufrich and his family experience supernatural incidents. The story was very popular, but reference to it here is ironical since the Gothic and supernatural events of 'The Undertaker' take place in a dream.

with pole-axe . . . cloth: quotation from 'Foolish Pakhomovna' by A. E. Izmailov (1779–1831).

34 *unserer Kundleute*: (German) 'our customers'.

The Stationmaster

38 [*epigraph*]: Prince Pyotr Andreevich Vyazemsky (1792–1878), poet and trusted friend to Pushkin; he was the author of numerous essays and notebooks that show him to have been the most trenchant literary critic of his day.

Murom brigands: the city of Murom, on the middle reaches of the Oka River, about 200 miles east of Moscow, was of ancient foundation; in the medieval period it flourished as a trading centre to the east and was famed for its forests.

martyr of the fourteenth grade: the narrator's Sentimentalism does not dull his attention to status, as made clear by this reference to the Stationmaster's place on the final rung of the Table of Ranks. For more on this Table, see note on *The Captain's Daughter*, p. 172.

40 *the story of the prodigal son*: Luke 15: 11–32. Pushkin may have based his story of a prodigal daughter on two French works he clearly knew, the abbé Prévost's 'Aventure d'une jeune fille de la campagne' (1739; republished in 1816), and Jean-François Marmontel's story 'Lauretta'.

45 *Demuth's Hotel*: according to J. Bastin, *La Russie: guide du voyageur à St Petersburg* (St Petersburg–Leipzig, 1866), this was one of the principal hotels located in the centre just off the main thoroughfare, Nevsky Prospect; it had been receiving guests since the second half of the eighteenth century and was recommended for its modest cost and spacious rooms. Pushkin lived there intermittently.

46 *Liteinaya*: the Liteinaya Quarter is located in the centre of St Petersburg and takes its name from its main street, Liteiny Prospect, which is the first street after the Anichkov Bridge and runs perpendicular to Nevksy Prospect. In Pushkin's time the area was home to a large group of charitable institutions and gardens, including the St Catherine Institute for Girls, the Mari Hospital, and the Alexandra Hospital for women.

47 *the loyal Terentich in Dmitriev's beautiful ballad*: Dmitriev's ballad 'The Caricature' (1797) narrates the story of an army man who returns home after a twenty-year gap only to find his house boarded-up and the garden overgrown. His loyal servant Terentych recognizes him and sadly tells him of his wife's infidelity. She and her lover abandoned their home five years earlier. While she is never heard from again, the soldier eventually remarries.

The Lady Peasant

50 *[epigraph]*: from *Dushenka* (1783) by Ippolit Fyodorovich Bogdanovich (1744–1803). His version of the myth of Amor and Psyche might be called the Russian equivalent of Pope's *The Rape of the Lock*. A mock-epic full of baroque grace, wit, and erotic charm, Bogdanovich's work seems to have influenced Pushkin when he was writing *Ruslan and Lyudmila*.

'Senate Record': this reference is almost certainly to the *St Petersburg News*; it appeared weekly in Russian and German, and was virtually an official publication, containing news of wars, laws, and decrees. While published by the Academy of Sciences, from 1742 each issue was submitted to the Senate Press for approval.

English garden: a landscape garden favouring the natural look typified in England by the work of Capability Brown in contrast to the artificial and formal style of the French Garden.

But Russian grain won't grow in foreign ways: this is a line from A. A. Shakhovskoy's play *Satire*. A prolific dramatist, Shakhovskoy (1777–1848) was a literary reactionary who defied the changing fashions of Romanticism and continued to write dramas and comedies in the neoclassical style. Despite their literary differences, Pushkin and Shakhovskoy were on good terms.

50 *Board of Trustees*: this body was one of a series of institutions founded in the reign of Catherine II. While the the the chief duty of the *opekunskii soviet* concerned the welfare of orphanages and widows, it also undertook financial transactions like mortgages.

52 *Jean Paul*: Jean Paul Richter (1763–1825), German novelist. Pushkin read him in an 1829 French translation.

nota nostra manet: 'let our observation stand.'

Pamela: This first novel of Samuel Richardson (1689–1761) was published to acclaim in 1740 and enjoyed a great vogue on the continent. It consists of letters and journals, and describes the attempted seduction of Pamela Andrews by her employer. Eventually, after a tortured sequence of imprisonment and attempted rape, the protagonists conceive a genuine affection for one-another. The novel attracted a strong following among female and clerical readers, who regarded the heroine as a model specimen of feminine virtue. Pushkin's heroines have it on their reading-lists: Tatyana from *Eugene Onegin* interprets Onegin's character through the lens of eighteenth-century fiction.

54 *sarafan*: sleeveless peasant dress usually worn in the summertime over a long-sleeved blouse.

62 *sleeves, à l'imbécile*: sleeves that are padded at the top and taper to a slender wrist.

64 *our study is going better than the Lancaster system*: pedagogical method aimed at creating mass education that was devised by the Englishman Joseph Lancaster (1778–1838). The Lancaster system advocated the use of more advanced young adults in the education of the very young, and enjoyed popularity in Europe, England, and North America during the early nineteenth century.

Natalya, the Boyar's Daughter: Nicholas Karamzin's 1792 tale of a young woman who displays outstanding bravery in defending the medieval republic of Novgorod.

66 *Alyosha*: the diminutive for 'Alexey'.

67 *Mais . . . êtes-vous fou?*: 'But leave me be then, Sir. Are you mad?'

The Queen of Spades

71 *If rain . . . going*: the verses are by Pushkin.

sacrifice the necessary in the hope of acquiring the superfluous: Hermann's rule seems to derive from a line in Voltaire: 'Le superflu, chose très necessaire', *Le Mondain* (1736), v. 22.

72 *faro*: faro, also known as *stoss*, was one of the most popular card games in the eighteenth and nineteenth centuries. As Neil Cornwell notes in

his commentary, 'it was a game, to all intents and purposes, of pure chance, with virtually no element of skill'. Two packs of cards were involved in this duel between a banker and one or more players. Drawing from one pack, the punter would place one card face down on the table and then stake a sum on it. Drawing from the second pack, the banker then placed cards face up on alternating sides of the marked card. If the card that fell to the right matched the exposed card the stake went to the banker. If the match occured with a card on the left, then the victory went to the punter.

73 *Casanova . . . memoirs*: Giacomo Casanova (1725–98), Italian memoirist and notorious womanizer whose major work is his *Memoires*, first published in German in 1822, then in a censored French edition in 1826. His memoirs give a lively if somewhat exaggerated portrait of eighteen-century social and sexual behaviour.

au jeu de la Reine: that is, the card games played at the queen's table in her apartments.

75 [*epigraph*]: 'It appears that Sir has a decided preferance for servant girls?' 'What do you expect, Madam? They are newer at the game.'

82 [*epigraph*]: 'You, my angel, write me four-page letters faster than I can read them.' Pushkin is the author of the epigraph.

85 *Madame Lebrun*: the French artist Louise-Élisabeth Vigée-Lebrun (1755–1842) was famous for painting aristocratic figures (mainly women rather than men), and was well known in Russia where she lived for five years (1795–1800), as she recounts in her memoirs.

Leroy . . . Montgolfier balloon . . . Mesmer's magnetism: Julien Leroy (1686–1759) was a famous watchmaker and craftsman. The hot-air balloon was invented by the brothers Jacques-Etienne and Joseph-Michel Montgolfier in the early 1780s. Friedrich Anton Mesmer (1733–1815), originator of 'mesmerism', or 'animal magnetism', which caused a great stir in fashionable French society—see Robert Darnton, *Mesmerism and the End of the Enlightenment in France* (Harvard, 1968).

89 [*epigraph*]: 'A man without values and without religion.' The source is Voltaire's 'Dialogue d'un Parisien et d'un Russe' (1760).

90 *'oubli ou regret'*: before approaching a potential partner for the mazurka a pair of young women would draw straws by each taking a password like *oubli* or *regret* and then offering him a blind choice. He would then partner the bearer of whichever password he chose.

92 *coiffeured à l'oiseau royale*: as defined by the *Trésor de la langage française*, a coiffure with bird-feathers arranged in the hair.

93 *Swedenborg*: the misattribution to the Swedish mystic Emanuel Swedenborg (1688–1772) is deliberate and part of Pushkin's strategy of mystification.

93 ... *in expectation of the midnight bridegroom*: allusion to the New Testament Parable of the Wise Virgins, Matthew 25.

96 [*epigraph*]: a technical term. 'Normally several people would punt against the banker ... In between actions each player was allowed to change his bet; if he wished to do so he would call out *attendez!* ("wait"). This exlamation, especially if pronounced with excited emphasis, could sound like a rather rude command, offensive to the banker if he was a man of mature years or high rank. Vyazemsky records in his *Old Notebook* that a certain Count Gudovich, having attained the rank of colonel, stopped taking the role of banker in faro, explaining that "it is undignified to subject yourself to the demands of some greenhorn of a sublieutenant who, punting against you, almost peremptorily yells out: *attendez!*" This anecdote ... may have inspired Pushkin's epigraph to Chapter Six.' (Paul Debreczeny, *The Other Pushkin* (Stanford, 1983), 199).

100 *Obukhov Hospital*: in his *St. Petersburgh, a Journal of Travels To and From that Capital* (London, 1829), Dr A. B. Granville provides a description of value to the reader in imagining Hermann's eventual fate. Of the four important hospitals in St Petersburg: 'That of Obouchoff [*sic*] is the largest civil hospital and contains 625 beds in all, including about 120 for lunatic patients treated at the charge of the city. It is situated on the quay of the Fontanka. It has an open ground railed in before it, and a very extensive front, with a large garden behind. The system of internal arrangement differs in every respect from that of the Military hospitals, and is by no means so good. Wards, a quarter of a mile in length on the ground and first stories, are not calculated to insure that quiet, comfort, and silence, which are so essential in the treatment of disease' (ii. 279). Pushkin's intention in having Hermann incarcerated here is implicitly ironical: not only has he failed to secure a great fortune, but the would-be Napoleon cannot even pay for his own care.

The Captain's Daughter

101 [*title*]: the title was affixed by Pushkin in late 1836 before the work was sent for review by the censor; hitherto in correspondence he referred to the work simply as 'the novel'. In imitation of the beginning of Scott's *Rob Roy*, the draft version strengthened the element of the family chronicle with a preface from Peter Grinyov to his grandson. Pushkin deleted it at a late stage in his work on the novel. In naming Grinyov's memoir after Masha Mironova, Pushkin shifts the balance between the work's two poles as a historical novel and a family chronicle. It must also be allowed that while the author assigned the title, it seems to

reflect Grinyov's point of view. For him history represents the set of challenges through which he came of age, and its outcome is the happy chain of occurrences that brought him and Masha together.

101 [*epigraph*]: a truncated version of the proverb 'Take care of your clothes when they're new, but your honour from a tender age.' The full version is quoted by the elder Grinyov as part of his valedictory to his son. The theme of honour as a function of individual behaviour and one's class becomes a central part of the plot when Grinyov is accused of treason. The pardon that Catherine II grants him through Masha Mironova's efforts not only restores his honour and status in his family, but also brings the account full circle symbolically: having satisfied his father's injunction to preserve his honour, he has undergone a rite of passage and is now free to marry and begin his own family.

103 [*epigraph*]: Yakov Borisovich Knyazhnin (1742–91), poet, playwright, and bureaucrat; adapted Metastasio and Voltaire for the Russian stage. Best known for his comic opera *Misfortune From a Coach* (1739) and for his historical tragedy *Vadim of Novgorod* (1789), the republican tone of which so displeased Catherine the Great that she banned it from the stage. The epigraph is taken from his comedy *The Braggart* (1786), III. vi.

Minikh: Russianized name of Count Burckhardt-Christof Münnich (1683–1767) was recruited for service in the Russian army by Peter the Great. Minikh became the president of the Military College in 1732 and instituted a series of reforms in the military. For his political intriguing he was exiled by the Empress Elizabeth Petrovna in 1741 and returned to favour by Peter III in 1762. He remained loyal to the Emperor when he was overthrown by his wife, but Catherine II showed him no animus. Pushkin mentions him for two reasons: first, to explain that his loyalty to Peter III cost the elder Grinyov a place at court; and secondly, as a means of dating him. Originally Pushkin had planned to link Grinyov to Minikh's first period of disgrace in 1741, but then changed his mind and marked the year 1762 in the manuscript. However, the new date was problematic since Peter Grinyov is said to be 17 in 1773, which contradicts the account given of his childhood years in the country. In the end Pushkin, without resolving the contradiction, suppressed the date from the final version of the novel.

entered as a sergeant in the Semyonovsky regiment: the formation of the two élite Guard regiments dates to the reign of Peter the Great. The Preobrazhensky and Semenovsky were initially the preserve of the gentry. A stint in the Guards became a prerequisite to service in the army. Before 1714 young men of good family beginning service at the age of 15 had entered the army as officers despite their total lack of experience and ability to lead. In his effort to upgrade the army Peter the Great required scions of the gentry to serve in the rank and file of the Guards before attaining officer-rank in the army.

103 *Monsieur Beaupré*: the emigration to Russia of figures with biographies similar to that of Beaupré helped to create a fixture of Russian comedy of the eighteenth century. Like Grinyov's hapless Beaupré, the teachers in Denis Fonvizins's great comedies *Brigadir* (1769) and *The Minor* (1782), and in I. A. Krylov's *The Fashionable Shop*, are lampooned for their incompetence and laziness, while their employers are mocked for their ignorance and gullibility. After the French Revolution numerous fugitives found positions in Russian homes and in schools, including Marat's brother La Harpe, who served as tutor to Alexander I. 'To My Italian Uncle' (1844), a magnificent poetic tribute to his tutor by E. A. Baratynsky, the most important poet of the period after Pushkin, makes it clear that there were exceptions in life and literature to the stereotype.

104 *outchitel*: Russian for 'teacher.'

105 *Court Calendar*: an annual publication since 1745 listing courtiers, official postings, and honours.

106 *Orenburg*: capital city of Orenburg province, 1,680 versts from Moscow in the Urals. Founded originally in 1735 as a defence town against Bashkir tribesmen, it was also an important market town at the crossroads of Eastern trade-routes.

107 *Serve faithfully the one to whom you swear allegiance ... don't volunteer for duty*: Grinyov's injunction is an approximate quotation from the historian V. N. Tatishchev's account of his parting from his father: 'In 1704 my parent, when sending me and my brother off to the forces, sternly instructed us thus: that we should never refuse any service that was laid upon us and never put ourselves forward for anything.' In 1836 Pushkin devoted an essay to Tatishchev, and it is likely that he came across the exchange as printed in Tatishchev's 'Last will' during his research. The characterization of the elder Grinyov in the farewell episode owes a clear debt to an analogous scene in *Waverley*, ch. 6, 'The Adieus of Waverley', where Edward Waverley bids his family farewell and sets out for Scotland.

Simbirsk: in south-eastern Russia, founded as Sinbirsk in 1648 by order of Tsar Aleksei Mikhailovich (father of Peter I) as a fortress against incursion by the Tartars and Turks. In the eighteenth century the city also became an important trading centre in the Volga basin.

111 *The Guide*: Pushkin closely follows Scott's practice of adding chapter titles. His choice here directly echoes *Quentin Durward*, ch. 15, 'The Guide'.

111 [*epigraph*]: the epigraph is a slightly altered quotation from a soldier's song about recruitment. Early in their meeting Grinyov asks Pugachev whether he knows the region, using the word *storona* (side) that occurs in the song. Pugachev, unlike Grinyov, can contradict the song because he belongs to the world of the steppe.

112 *presaged a blizzard*: it has been pointed out that the description of the storm derives from a passage in S. T. Aksakov's story *The Blizzard* (1834). Comparison provides an excellent example of the usual prose style of the period and, by contrast, of Pushkin's habitual inclination to create drama by paring down description to the bare essentials as a setting for his characters reactions. Here is Aksakov's setting:

> A small cart extended along the narrow, like the track of peasant sleds, country path, or to put it better—along a trace recently laid down along the immense snowy wastes . . . A white cloud quickly rose and grew from the East, and when the final pale rays of the setting sun disappeared behind the mountain the enormous snow-cloud had already obscured the better half of the sky and shaken out of itself fine snowy powder; already in the usual noise of the wind one could hear from time to time something like the distant weeping of a child, and sometimes the howl of a hungry wolf . . . The white snow-cloud, enormous as the sky, encompassed the entire horizon and quickly covered with its thick curtain the final light of the red, burnt, evening sun. Suddenly night descended . . . the blizzard approached in all its fury, in all its terrors. The wasteland wind went wild at liberty, tore up the snowy steppes, and like swan-down threw them up to the heavens . . . A white gloom covered everything, impenetrable like the gloom of the darkest autumn night! Everything blended together, everything became confused: the earth, air, sky turned into a cauldron of boiling snowy earth which blinded eyes, arrested breathing, howled, whistled, howled, groaned, beat, shuddered, scuddered from all sides, upwards and downwards, winding round like a snake, and suffocated everything that fell in its path . . . The blizzard grew more savage by the hour. It howled all night and the entire next day so that no travelling was possible. Deep ravines became high drifts . . . Finally, the turbulence of the snowy ocean began to grow quiet, still continuing even when the sky had begun to shine with cloudless blue. Another night passed. The wild wind quieted down, the snow settled. The steppe looked like a stormy sea that had suddenly turned to ice . . .

115 *Yaik Cossack*: a group of Cossacks who were named after the River Yaik along which they were settled. After the Pugachev rebellion the river was renamed the Ural.

116　*His outward appearance struck me as remarkable*: as D. Yakubovich noted
　　　in an excellent article on borrowings from Scott in Pushkin's novel, the
　　　first appearance of Pugachev echoes Scott's device of introducing the
　　　heroes of his historical fiction anonymously. In an unpublished work,
　　　Stephanie Sandler has pointed out that Pushkin also took over from the
　　　Waverley novels the pretender figure who challenges the loyalties of the
　　　hero and teaches him unexpected lessons.

　　　In *History of Pugachev*, ch. 4, Pushkin gives the following description
　　　of Pugachev: 'Emelyan Pugachev, a Cossack of the service class from the
　　　Zimoveisk stanitsa, was the son of Ivan Mikhailov who had died long
　　　earlier. He was about 40 years of age, of medium height, swarthy and
　　　lean; his hair was dark auburn in colour, his beard black, small, and
　　　wedge-shaped. His upper lip had been split in childhood during a fist-
　　　fight. On his left temple he had a white spot and on both sides of his
　　　chest spots that remained after the so-called black illness. He was il-
　　　literate and made the sign of the cross in the manner of the Old Believers.'

　　　1772 rising: from 1744 the Cossacks were placed under the administra-
　　　tion of the governor of Orenburg, who withdrew their traditional right
　　　to elect their own leader (*ataman*) and placed them under the jurisdic-
　　　tion of the state, thus making them liable to corporal punishment. In
　　　the late 1760s heavy conscription of the Cossacks into the army at low
　　　wages led to complaints. In 1772 General Traubenberg led an inquiry
　　　into the matter; he found against the Cossacks. In January 1772 he was
　　　murdered in a riot that was only put down at the end of June, when the
　　　government inflicted harsh punishment on the rebels. In his *History of
　　　Pugachev* Pushkin saw the episode as a harbinger of impending popular
　　　unrest: 'Secret consultations occurred throughout the steppe camps
　　　and distant settlements. Everything foretold a new rebellion. A leader
　　　was lacking. A leader was sought.'

118　*Anna Ioannovna's time*: the death of Peter II in 1730 brought to an end
　　　the male line of the Romanovs and caused a crisis in the succession.
　　　Anna, daughter of Ivan V and widow of the Duke of Courland, was
　　　appointed by a Secret Council, which intended to rule through Anna.
　　　But the new Empress turned the tables on this clique and abolished it.
　　　Thereafter her reign was highly autocratic and infamously corrupt.
　　　Much of the blame was said to lie with a group of Germans elevated to
　　　high office by the Empress, including Count Ostermann in the foreign
　　　office, Münnich in the army, and most notoriously Ernst-Johann Biron,
　　　the empress's lover, whose name became a byword for political perse-
　　　cution, graft, and corruption, the so-called *Bironovshchina*. Anna's reign
　　　was marked by religious intolerance and undisguised contempt for Peter's
　　　vision of a new Russia. She died in 1740.

118 *hold him with hedgehog gauntlets*: a usual Russian idiom applied to authoritative figures.

120 *[epigraphs]*: 'Soldier song', probably a pastiche by Pushkin. The quotation is from Fonvizin's play *The Minor*, III. v. The figure of the 'minor' harks back to allusions in the first chapter, reinforcing the historical setting of the novel while also placing the Grinyov family in its cultural and social milieu.

Belogorsk Fort: Pushkin's invented name for the Orenburg Fortress which was erected in 1734 at the intersection of the Ora and Ural rivers. Its location changed two further times until it reached its present position in 1744 when it became the provincial capital. The Orenburg line of fortresses were built in the 1730s along the Yaik and Ui rivers.

121 *taking of Kustrin and Ochakov*: the Turkish fortress Ochakov was captured by Marshal Minikh in 1737. The unsuccessful seige of Kustrin occured in 1758.

'*The Cat's Funeral*': this *lubok*, a billboard illustration, enjoyed wide popularity, and dates to the period of Peter the Great. Initially, the meaning of the painting appears to have been a satirical reaction to the pomp and circumstance of Peter's funeral in 1724. Eventually the composition was interpreted as an anti-Petrine allegory in which a number of opponents (the mice) to Peter's reforms bury him (the cat).

124 *my father owned 300 serfs*: this is a substantial number. According to the historian Michael Confino, *Domaines et seigneurs en Rusie vers la fin du XVIIIe siècle* (Paris, 1963), in the late eighteenth century the vast majority of landowners in European Russia owned fewer than sixty serfs.

Bashkirs: Muslim tribes of Turkic origin settled mainly on the Western range and hills of the Urals. The Bashkirs had become subjects of the Russian state in the sixteenth century following Ivan IV's conquest of Kazan, but resistance to colonization was chronic. Peter I had reinforced Orenburg and encouraged settlement along the Ural fortresses as a deterrent to the Bashkirs. From 1735 to 1741 the Bashkirs went on the rampage, causing tens of thousands of deaths. As a concession the Russian government relieved their tax burden in 1754. Peace was precarious, and in 1763 a rumour that Peter III was still alive fired hopes for release from the stringent conditions that Catherine II had imposed.

125 *Kirghiz*: central Asian tribal peoples scattered across Mongolia, Turkestan, and parts of southern Russia.

126 *[epigraph]*: from Knyazhnin's 1790 comedy *The Eccentrics*, IV. xii, where two servants are preparing to duel with short knives. The epigraph echoes the story of the Captain's wife concerning Shvabrin's duel.

127 *Alexander Petrovich Sumarokov*: often called the Russian Boileau, Sumarokov (1718–77) was the author of influential works in verse concerning neoclassical literary doctrine. In addition to a large poetic output distinguished by its formal range and smoothness of style, he is remembered for his tragedies, a number of which treated the sensitive political question of absolutism. For a time Catherine II was his patroness.

Vasily Kirilovich Tredyakovsky: author of a seminal treatise on Russian versification. Although his poems were derided for their complex syntax and vocabulary, Tredyakovsky (1703–69) made his mark in a wide range of poetic forms, including the song and ode. His philological works and translations made a vital contribution to the development of the Russian literary language.

134 *[epigraphs]*: Pushkin took the lines 'Ah, you maiden . . .' from a folk-song published in the *Collection of Russian Folk Songs* (St Petersburg, 1790). They first occur in his notebooks in 1830. 'If you find a better man, you'll forget me' comes from a song in the same collection, 'My heart was prophesying, was prophesying.'

141 *[epigraph]*: the ending of the song 'Akh, you, Volga, Volga, little Mother', published by N. Novikov in his *Collection of Russian Folk-Songs* (Moscow, 1780).

142 *schismatic*: i.e. an 'Old Believer', member of the religious sect whose adherence to the traditional church ritual and opposition to ecclesiastical reforms caused a schism in the church from the late 1650s. While Old Believers were persecuted and outlawed, they survived in small communities throughout the Tsarist and Soviet regimes. Apart from their religious convictions, they were known for their talents at commerce.

146 *The appeal was expressed in crude but forceful language*: although he was illiterate Pugachev was a commanding orator who made good use of the scribes in his band when producing propaganda. In the documents Pushkin compiled for his history there is a splendid example of the forceful, if chaotic, rhetoric that roused so many to rebel:

> To whomever dwells on this earth in cities and fortresses that are benevolent tributary to me, and to the most brave folk and their households, that is with children and wife, such are my commands that are announced, to wit: . . . those who are oppressed, who find themselves in sadness, having pined for me, when my name has been heard, those of you who thus desire without any doubt, come to me, come into my service and under my command; and since before this time your fathers and grandfathers in service to my fathers and grandfathers ventured on campaigns against villains, shed blood, but with our friends were friends, thus too are you to me faithful, soulfully

and spiritually, undoubting toward my shining self, to your sweet-tongued sovereign, with no faltering in your campaign, with no fickleness of hearts and without hypocrisy in your subjection to me and toward my commands . . . Hearken and when you enter into my service, then for this in the manner in which formerly you asked God for me, thus shall I take pity on you. And that I am your true merciful sovereign, confess and believe. Now have I thus welcomed you for the first time, even to the very last one of you, with lands, waters, fields, dwellings, grasses, rivers, fish, grains, laws, tilled fields, bodies, pay, land and powder, and as you have wished, so have I welcomed each and every life. Come then like beasts of the field: I free all of you who dwell upon this earth in your good and rash deeds and give eternal freedom to your children and grandchildren. Heed and fulfill my command . . .

146 *torture was so ingrained . . . process*: Grinyov's attack on torture as a traditional prerogative of the state echoes an important theme of Enlightenment thought. It had been a particular concern of the enlightened Milanese thinkers, like Cesare Beccaria (1738–94) and Alessandro Veri (1741–1816). Beccaria's *Dei delitte e delle pene* (*On Crimes and Punishments*) appeared anonymously in 1764 and in French translation in 1766, in which year Voltaire also wrote a celebrated commentary on the work. Beccaria advocated greater leniency in penalties and the abolition of torture, abolition of the death penalty, and reform of the legal system to make it equally fair to all social classes. Punishment must be appropriate to the crime and applied mainly as deterrent; thus, the pain of the punishment must just barely exceed the crime. The tract was placed on the Index in 1766. His ideas aroused the interest of such European monarchs as Frederick the Great, Maria Theresa of Austria, and the Grand Duke of Tuscany. In Russia this treatise exercised an important influence on the work of the Legislative Commission of 1766 convened by Catherine the Great. In its Great Instruction of 1767 the Commission formalized the rights of, among others, the nobility and for the first time made them immune from corporal punishment. In the chapters on crime and punishment Catherine declared views that were new for Russia. Proceeding from Beccaria and Montesquieu, she declared that guilt must be established by a court before a subject could be punished lawfully; in addition, she condemned torture, saying in Article 123 that 'The Usage of torture is contrary to all the Dictates of Nature and Reason; even Mankind itself cries out against it, and demands loudly the total Abolition of it.' For a thorough discussion of the Great Instruction, see Isabel de Madariaga, *Russia in the Age of Catherine the Great* (London, 1981), ch. 10.

The passage is interesting from both a sociological and literary point of view. With respect to the first, it shows that the younger Grinyov, like his father, regards the status of the nobility as a question of moment. In a series of steps culminating in the Manifesto of 1785, Catherine freed the gentry from compulsory service to the Crown. Her pronouncements encouraged more abstract thinking about the status and honour of the nobility; and while a number of writers, like Denis Fonvizin, wished the gentry, and especially members of the Senate, to act as a check on absolutism, in practice Catherine's policies led to consolidation of power in the monarch's hands. These are issues that the young Grinyov might have pondered as they were occurring during the 1770s, and in this respect the passage may have a contemporary ring about it. From a literary perspective, this is a moment where the older narrator steps to the fore. This is a good example of how in *The Captain's Daughter* the narrative splices together the double perspective of the youthful, even *faux-naif*, narrator, and that of the mature retrospective narrator who writes an account of his life for his grandchildren. The technique is common to the memoir-novel, a genre that may have contributed tangentially to Pushkin's creation of *The Captain's Daughter*.

147 *'Yakshi'*: a Tartar word, meaning 'all right' or 'good'.

mild reign of the Emperor Alexander: Alexander I ascended to the throne after the murder of his father Paul I in 1801. Under the guidance of his minister, Speransky, the first years of his reign gave hope for political reform and the establishment of a constitution; this period was traditionally known as the 'beautiful beginning' of his reign. After the defeat of Napoleon, Alexander's internal policies betrayed hopes for a more parliamentary-style monarchy fully engaging the political energies of the upper classes. Eventually Speransky was replaced by the reactionary Count Arakcheev whose name became a byword for oppression. Once lionized across Europe for his military conquests, Alexander I became increasingly prey in the latter years of his regime to mystical tendencies. He makes one last appearance in Pushkin's œuvre in his narrative *The Bronze Horseman*, recounting the catastrophic flood of 7 November 1824; it was less than a year after this natural catastrophe, during which the Emperor gesticulated emptily from the Winter Palace to the stricken populace, that he died.

150 *[epigraph]*: Pushkin reproduces the opening lines of a song on Ivan the Terrible's conquest of Kazan. Viktor Shklovsky brilliantly observed that all of the epigraphs relating to Pugachev are taken from songs that mention the Russian tsar either one line before the quotation begins or a line after its truncation. In this particular case the theme of the conquest of Kazan looks ahead to the epigraph to Chapter 10.

154 *Pugachev was sitting in an armchair*: although it is clear from Pushkin's *History* that the other rebels manipulated Pugachev, in the novel he dominates his followers. The trappings in this scene are distinctly regal, and are meant to remind the reader that whether or not anyone believed Pugachev's claim to be Peter III—murdered by his wife who took the throne as Catherine II in 1762—was less important than the pretender's ability to project his identity. Pushkin's fascination with the figure of the Pretender begins with the character of the the False Dmitry in *Boris Godunov* (see below).

157 *An Uninvited Guest*: cf. Scott, *Quentin Durward*, ch. 25, 'The Unbidden Guest'.

160 *the royal marks . . . the two-headed eagle*: the two-sided eagle was a part of the crest of the Russian empire since the fifteenth century. From the reign of Tsar Aleksei Mikhailovich (1645–76) the eagle was depicted with wings extended upwards, a sceptre and orb in its talons.

161 *barge-hauler's song*: the song 'Do not rustle your leaves, green mother oak-tree' was popular across a wide section of the Russian peasantry, including the Cossacks surrounding Pugachev.

163 *Grisha Otrepyev*: real name of the Polish impostor, known as the Pretender or False Dmitry, who claimed to be the Tsarevich Dmitry, son of Ivan the Terrible, during the Time of Troubles in 1610 that followed the death of Boris Godunov. Otrepyev held the throne briefly before being overthrown and executed in 1613, which marks the foundation of the Romanov dynasty.

165 *[epigraph]*: from a poem that begins: 'Charming view, tender glances! You hide from my eyes | Rivers and forests and mountains | will separate us for long.' Mikhail Matveevich Kheraskov (1733–1807) was the author of the first major Russian epic, the *Rossiada* (1778), several neoclassical novels, and a distinguished body of poetry that shows clear evidence of his Freemasonry.

170 *[epigraph]*: from Kheraskov's epic poem *Rossiada*, Book XI, which recounts Ivan IV's conquest of Kazan.

Poor Mironov . . . daughter?: as in the original, the Commander has lost the strong German accent he possessed in Chapter 2.

172 *Mister Collegiate Councillor*: in the Table of Ranks this position was the sixth of the fourteen grades and equivalent to a colonel in military rank. The Table of Ranks, devised by Peter the Great, organized civil and military officials according to fourteen classes as part of the Emperor's determination to formalize service to the state. To receive noble status one was required to advance to the eighth class. Thus the old nobility were obliged to serve the state (a rule that was relaxed under Catherine

II), and a new class of officials were enticed into service by the possibility of ennoblement.

176 *Schelm*: (German) 'knave, rogue'.

177 [*epigraph*]: despite the attribution the lines belong to Pushkin and are stylized in the manner of Sumarokov's fables.

180 *Corporal Beloborodov*: Ivan Naumovich Beloborodov (1740–74) from January 1774 joined the rebellion of Cossacks at Ekaterinburg. Pushkin's account in his novel departs from the historical record, for Beloborodov met Pugachev for the first time in May of that year. He was captured in July and executed in Moscow on 5 September 1774. In folklore his name came to represent reckless bravery.

185 *Yuzeyeva*: the forces of Pugachev were victorious here against General Carr on 8 November 1773.

King of Prussia: Frederick II (1712–86), king of Prussia since 1740. In 1759 he had been defeated by Russian forces in a battle at Kunersdorf.

187 [*epigraph*]: this is Pushkin's reworking of a wedding song that he had transcribed when he was in the Urals investigating oral sources for the Pugachev revolt. It runs as follows: 'Many, many are the branches, | many so many on the grey oak | But the grey oak does not have a golden little crown; | Many, many are the relations, the tribe | many so many of the princess soul, | But the princess soul lacks her native mother: there is someone to thank, | But no one to arm.'

According to Victor Shklovsky, a song like the one cited in the epigraph is sung when the bride is an orphan whose hand is given in marriage by her surrogate father and mother. In this instance Pugachev, as it were, is the surrogate father, a fact that accentuates the tragedy of this chapter since Pugachev executed Masha Mironova's parents.

192 *our bright falcon*: stock phrase from folkloric songs and poetry.

193 [*epigraph*]: despite Pushkin's attribution, these lines do not appear in any of Knyazhnin's works, and are likely to be pastiche.

197 *Prince Golitsyn . . . Tatischev Fort*: General Major Prince P. M. Golitsyn began his reconquest on 22 March 1774. Pushkin gave this account in the *History of the Pugachev Rebellion*: 'Golitsyn divided his troops into two columns, began his approach and opened fire, which was returned with equal strength from the fortress. The cannon fire continued for three hours. Golitsyn saw that it would be impossible to prevail with cannons alone and ordered General Freiman to lay siege using his left column. Pugachev aimed seven guns against him. Freiman took them out and assaulted the frozen rampart. The rebels defended themselves desperately, but were forced to yield to the might of proper weaponry and fled in all directions. Inactive until that point, the cavalry followed

them by all roads. The bloodshed was horrible. In one fortress up to 1,300 rebels perished. Their bodies were scattered across a space of 20 versts around Tatishchev. Golitsyn lost up to 400 dead and wounded and more than 20 officers. The victory was decisive.'

197 *Ivan Ivanovich Mikhelson*: (1740–1807), army major and veteran of Catherine the Great's Turkish campaign of 1770. His successes against Pugachev's supporters in Kazan and along the Volga were instrumental in Pugachev's defeat, leading to his promotion to the rank of general.

199 [*epigraph*]: slightly modified version of a saying published in the *Complete Collection of Russian Proverbs and Sayings* (St Petersburg, 1822); Pushkin had a copy of this book in his library.

203 *Volynsky and Khruschev*: Artem Petrovich Volynsky (1689–1740) began his career of public service in the military before Peter the Great assigned him to a diplomatic posting in Persia, where his brief was also to explore the possibility of acquiring control of the silk trade for Russia. In 1722 he married the Tsar's cousin, a Naryshkin, but fell into Peter's disfavour. Under subsequent regimes he regained favour, serving as Governor of Kazan and in various diplomatic capacities before moving closer to the court of the Empress Anna Ioannovna, where he was brought down by the enmity of her chief supporters, Biron and Count Osterman, on charges of corruption and accused of conspiring with Khrushchev to overthrow Anna and place Elizabeth on the throne. He was tortured and executed in June 1740. Among his papers there was found a treatise entitled a 'Project for the Correction of State Affairs'. His confidant and co-conspirator, Andrei Fedorovich Khrushchev (1691–1740), an expert on naval affairs, was loyal to the Petrine vision of a more modern Russia, having been educated in Holland as one of a large number of students sent abroad by Peter.

204 *Tsarskoye Selo*: small town outside St Petersburg, famous for the Summer Palace and the distinguished Lyceum that counted Pushkin among its graduates. Sofia is named after the Cathedral of St Sofia in the town.

205 *And Maria Ivanovna saw a lady sitting on a bench opposite the monument*: the details of this verbal description of the Empress famously reproduce a painting by one of Russia's finest portraitists, Vladimir Borovikovsky (1757–1852)—see cover illustration. In this small canvas the monarch is depicted in the park of the Summer Palace at Tsarskoye Selo; she is wearing a plain turquoise overcoat and bonnet and carries a walking-stick; at her side is a whippet or greyhound that looks up at his mistress affectionately. Catherine II gesticulates to a column in the background, erected to commemorate a victory at Chesme over the Turks, a symbol of her power, but also a signal that affairs of state are far from the

subject. Her kind face and open demeanour—she looks out at the viewer—suggest that power has not corrupted a soul naturally inclined to virtue. Pushkin's treatment of this adventitious meeting is a deliberate reworking of the incident in chapter 37 of Scott's *Heart of Midlothian*, where Jeanie Deans pleads for a pardon for her sister from Queen Caroline.

208 *execution of Pugachev*: on 10 January 1775. It is interesting to compare Grinyov's memory of this event with the documentary account Pushkin provided in his *History of the Pugachev Rebellion*:

> The execution of Pugachev and his co-conspirators took place in Moscow on 10 January 1775. In the morning an innumerable mass of people crowded around Boloto where a tall platform had been erected. On it there were seated the executioners, who were drinking wine as they waited for the victims. Around the platforms there were three gallows. Nearby infantry were stationed. The officers were in fur coats owing to the fierce, harsh frost. The roofs of the homes and shops were covered with people; the low square and nearby streets were crowded with coaches and carriages. Suddenly everything began to shake and rumble; there were shouts, 'they're bringing him, they're bringing him!' Following a division of cuirassiers there came a sled with a high railing. On it, with an uncovered head, sat Pugachev. Alongside there was a functionary of the Secret Expedition. While he was being transported Pugachev bowed in both directions. His sleigh was followed by the cavalry and a further crowd of condemned. An eyewitness . . . described the bloody spectacle in the following manner:
>
> 'The sleighs stopped opposite one end of the place of execution. Pugachev and his right-hand man Perfilyev, in the company of a priest and two functionaries, had hardly mounted the gallows when an order rang out to the guards and one of the functionaries began to read a manifesto. Practically each word reached me.
>
> 'Whenever the reader pronounced the name and nicknames of the chief villain, similarly the Cossack village where he was born, the superintending chief of police asked him loudly: "Are you the Don Cossack, Emelka Pugachev?" He answered with equal force: "Yes, my lord, I am the Don Cossack of the Zimoveisky village, Emelka Pugachev." Then throughout the entire reading of the manifesto, while looking at the church, Pugachev often crossed himself while his accomplice Perfilyev, tall, bent, pock-marked, and beast-like, stood unmovingly, looking downwards into the ground. Having finished the manifesto the priest said a few words to him, blessed him, and left the scaffold. The reader of the manifesto followed him. Then

Pugachev, making the sign of the cross, bowed several times to the ground, turning to the churches, then with a harried expression began to bid farewell to the people. As he bowed in all directions he said in a broken voice: "Farewell, Orthodox people; forgive me for offending before you; forgive, Orthodox people!" At this word the sign was given: the executioners hurried to undress him; they ripped off the white sheepskin coat, began to tear the sleeves of the red silk half-caftan. Then he clapped his hands, fell to the ground, and in a second his bloodied head hung in the air . . . The arms and legs were severed from the corpse and were distributed by the executioners to the four corners of the scaffold; his head was then displayed and stuck on a tall stake.

Peter the Great's Blackamoor

209 Pushkin wrote six chapters in 1827 and the beginning of a seventh in early 1828, whereupon he abandoned the project. The entire fragment was published for the first time in 1837, after Pushkin's death. The publisher gave the work its title, and assigned the epigraphs from a list of them that Pushkin had made on a separate sheet. Only two parts of the work were published in his lifetime, the first in 1828 and the second in 1830, both of which he republished in his journal *The Contemporary* in 1834.

In a letter to P. A. Vyazemsky of 1835 or 1836, Pushkin discussed the problematic terminology of words available in Russian for people of African heritage. In Russian the appropriate words are *negr* for 'negro' or 'black', *arap* for 'blackamoor', and *mulat* for 'mulatto'. The title of this sketch of his ancestor is in Russian *Arap Petra Velikogo*. From the same letter it is clear that the distinctions Pushkin draws do not stand in exact parallel to the semantic nuances available in English. While Pushkin draws no racial distinction between *negr* and *arap* (any black African can be referred to by either term), in English the word 'blackamoor' often meant a black African of Ethiopian origin. For Pushkin, however, while *negr* can mean any black African, the term *arap* has two usages to designate either: (i) a black person (not necessarily from Ethiopia), or (ii) a black African who lives in the service of a noble or the emperor, a customary usage in eighteenth-century English. In so far as Pushkin does not use the term *negr* to refer to his great-grandfather Hannibal, but rather calls him *arap* since he was in Peter the Great's service, 'blackamoor' has been preferred here as a way of suggesting the distinction that Pushkin makes.

[*epigraph*]: from the incomplete narrative poem *Ala: A Livonian Tale* (1824), ll. 30–1, by Nikolai Mikhailovich Yazykov (1803–47). Yazykov was one of a younger generation of Romantics often known as the 'Pushkin Pléiade'. He was the author of amorous verse and elegies, and a cycle of poems called the Pushkin cycle. The plot of the incomplete poem is only rudimentary, but the general subject is Peter the Great's expansion into the Baltic and the co-operation he received from nobles eager to shake off Swedish domination. The precise context of these lines is the mention of the Livonian nobleman Johann-Reinhold Patkul (1660–1707), who fled to Russia in 1702 to serve Peter the Great.

211 [*epigraph*]: Ivan Dmitriev (1760–1837) was a gifted poet of the Sentimental school, and an elegant stylist. Pushkin admired his poems and was galled when Dmitriev greeted *Ruslan and Lyudmila* critically in 1820. The epigraph is the truncated first line of the poem *The Journey of N. N. to Paris and London* (1803), the full version of which reads 'Friends! Sisters! I am going to Paris! I've begun to live, and not just breathe!' The anonymous traveller lampooned in the poem for his excessive enthusiasm about visiting Paris and London is Pushkin's uncle, Vasily L'vovich Pushkin (1770–1830), a minor poet and member of Karamzin's circle. With its light mockery of the ardour for things Western, the epigraph anticipates the satirical portrait of Korsakov.

the blackamoor Ibrahim: Pushkin referred to his own African ancestry in a number of works: during the period of exile mention of his African descent is associated with the poet's exoticism and his sense of personal freedom. In a note written in 1825 to accompany *Eugene Onegin*, ch. 1, stanza 50, Pushkin glossed a reference to Africa as follows:

> The author is of African descent on his mother's side. His great-grandfather Abrah Petrovich Annibal [*sic*] at the age of 8 was kidnapped from the shores of Africa and transported to Constantinople. The Russian ambassador, having rescued him, sent him as a gift to Peter the Great who had him baptized in Vilno. Consequently his brother arrived, first in Constantinople and then in Petersburg, and offered to buy him back; but Peter I did not agree to return his godson. Into his great old age Annibal continued to remember Africa, the luxurious life of his father, his nineteen brothers, of whom he was the youngest; he recollected how they were led before his father, hands bound behind their back, while he alone was free and used to swim under the fountains of his father's house; he remembered also his beloved sister Lagan, who swam far out after the ship on which he departed.
>
> At the age of 18 he was sent by the Tsar to France, where he began his service in the army of the Regent. He returned to Russia with a fractured head and the rank of a French lieutenant. Since then he was inseparable from the person of the Emperor. During the

reign of Anna, Annibal, a personal enemy of Biron, was exiled to Siberia on some ostensibly beneficent excuse. Bored by the solitude and the cruelty of the climate, he returned to Petersburg without permission and appeared before his friend Münich. Münich was amazed and advised him to hide as quickly as possible. Annibal retired to his estates, where he lived for the remainder of Anna's reign although he was thought to be serving in Siberia. When Elizabeth ascended the throne she showered him with kindness. A. P. Annibal died only during the reign of Catherine, having been relieved of the important duties of service with the rank of full general at the age of 92. . . . In Russia where the memory of remarkable people soon perishes owing to a paucity of historical records, the odd life of Annibal is known only according to family legends. In time we shall hope to publish his full biography.

For further details see the Introduction, pp. xxxiv–xxxv.

211 *the Spanish War*: Spain's failure to keep the terms of the Peace of Utrecht of 1713 brought on war with France and England from the spring of 1719 until January of 1720, when the Spanish accepted the accord.

Duke of Orleans: Philip, who ruled as regent of France after the death of Louis XIV in 1715 until the maturity of Louix XV in 1723.

John Law: Scottish banker (1671–1729) who worked as the comptroller-general for the French government and founded the India Company. He backed the development of the lower Mississippi Valley and helped to finance the settlement of New Orleans. His schemes almost bankrupted France. For a discussion of Law's symbolic importance as a gambler who tried to outwit chance, see Thomas Kavanagh, *Enlightenment and the Shadow of Chance: The Novel and the Culture of Gambling in Eighteenth-Century France* (London, 1993), ch. 3.

212 *Richelieu*: Armand, Duc de Richelieu (1696–1788), grand-nephew of the great Cardinal. His memoirs depict the depraved court-life of the time.

Temps fortuné . . . pénitence: from Voltaire's burlesque epic *La Pucelle*, canto xiii. The lines, characterizing the Regency, describe the relaxation of morals that followed upon the death of Louis XIV in 1715: 'Happy time, distinguished by licence, where Folly, jingling his bells, tripped lightly through the whole of France, where no mortal deigned to be pious, where people did everything but repent.'

young Arouet . . . Fontenelle: François Marie Arouet was the given name of Voltaire, who adopted an anagram of 'Voltaire le Jeune' in 1718; *old Chaulieu* (1639–1720): clergyman, French poet known for his free-thinking and embrace of hedonism; *Montesquieu*: Charles-Louis (1689–1755). French political philosopher famed for his treatise *De l'esprit des lois* (1748). In this context his name must be intended to recall his *Lettres persanes* (1721), a satire on French and Parisian society as seen through the eyes of two Persian travellers; *Fontenelle*: Bernard le Bovier, sieur de Fontenelle (1657–1757), important French writer and thinker who anticipated the Enlightenment. His *Nouveaux dialogues des morts* revived the Lucianic dialogue as a form of philosophic investigation. His most famous work was the *Entretiens sur la pluralité des mondes*, in defence of the Copernican system. Prince Antiokh Kantemir, the Russian ambassador to France and England in the 1730s, and prominent supporter of the Petrine reforms, produced a translation of the *Entretiens*, the publication of which was blocked by the Church. In his *Satires* Kantemir had mocked the Orthodox Church for its opposition to the Copernican revolution.

213 *Merville*: probably Pierre Biarnoy de Merville, a French jurist and legal theorist from Normandy who made his career in Paris. He died in 1740.

217 [*epigraph*]: by Gavriil Petrovich Derzhavin, one of the greatest Russian poets (1743–1816), who played Horace to Catherine the Great's Emperor Augustus by engaging the Empress in a literary exchange that combined flattery with council. The epigraph is from one of his magnificent solemn odes, 'On the Death of Prince Meshchersky', ll. 67–72, which contain a meditation on the omnipotence and ubiquity of death.

219 *Krasnoye Selo*: during the summer this small town in the vicinity of St Petersburg garrisoned the military forces usually stationed in the capital.

220 *new-born capital*: St Petersburg was founded by Peter the Great in 1703. The capital was moved from Moscow to St Petersburg in 1712. The new capital had a population of about 40,000, and was second only to Moscow.

Neva: rising in Lake Ladoga north of the city, the river runs through St Petersburg and drains in the Gulf of Finland. St Petersburg is located on the river delta at the head of the Gulf of Finland. In 1777 and 1824 the river flooded the city and caused severe destruction: the latter occasion became the subject of Pushkin's final great poem, *The Bronze Horseman* (1835).

Ekaterina . . . handsome young girls: the reference is to Peter the Great's second wife and her daughters. Born to a peasant family in Lithuania, and once married to a Swedish officer, baptized Martha in the Catholic Church, mistress to Count Sheremetyev, Prince Menshikov, and then Peter the Great, she was accepted in 1708 into the Orthodox faith as Ekaterina Alekseevna. Her marriage to the Tsar, who had repudiated his first wife, Evodkia Lopukhina, was celebrated in 1712 and lasted until his death. Intrigue and the confused succession brought her to the thone in 1725. She reigned until her death in 1727, but her grasp of government was perfunctory and she was in fact no more than a stooge for Menshikov and his party. She was succeeded by Peter Alekseevich, the Tsar's grandson, but his rule was cut short when he died of small-pox on his wedding day at the age of 14 in 1730. Her two daughters, Anna and Elizabeth, were born out of wedlock, but Peter legally adopted his daughters after his marriage.

220 *Poltava*: site in Southern Russia of Peter the Great's stunning victory over Charlex XII of Sweden in 1709. The event formed the subject of Pushkin's epic poem *Poltava* (1827).

221 *Prince Menshikov*: the quintessential new man of Petrine Russia, Alexander Danilovich Menshikov (?1673–1729) rose from humble rank to become one of the emperor's most important aids. Little is known about his origins. According to one legend, he was said to have worked in his youth as an urchin selling pasties on the street in Moscow. He participated in the major campaigns of the Northern War and distinguished himself at Poltava. Although from 1714 he was constantly under investigation for financial improprieties, this 'child of Peter's heart', as Pushkin called him, never forfeited the Emperor's support and continued to exercise a key role in domestic affairs. He was said to have played a part in the murder of the Tsarevich Aleksei Petrovich. In 1719 he was made president of the Military College. After Peter's death he engineered the accession of Catherine I and for all intents and purposes ran the government. In 1727 his opponents succeeded in turning Peter II, her successor, against Menshikov. He was stripped of all his wealth and exiled. Menshikov died in 1729.

Prince Yakov Dolgoruky: Yakov Fedorovich (1659–1720), scion of a distinguished ancient family. A Westernizer and early supporter of Prince Peter. He was taken prisoner at the Battle of Poltava and held captive in Sweden for ten years. He was famous for his unswerving loyalty and rectitude.

the scholar Brus: Jacob Bruce (1670–1735) was descended from a noble Scottish family, his immediate ancestors having lived in Russia from 1647. Although he participated in numerous military campaigns and joined Peter's Grand Embassy to Europe in 1687 and 1689, he was renowned for his learning in mathematics, astronomy, and physics, and promoted the work of Copernicus. From 1706 he was director of the Civil Printing Press in Moscow.

Chief of Police Devier: the historian Vasily Klyuchevsky gives his real name as Anthony De Vière. According to the historian Konstantin Waliszewski, he was a Portugese Jew whom Peter recruited off a merchant ship in 1697. In 1718 he became the first general chief of police in St Petersburg. Legend has it that once, while accompanying Peter on an inspection of the capital, the party was forced to stop at a broken bridge. Peter descended from his carriage and participated in repairing the bridge, and then proceeded to thrash his chief of police before quietly resuming the conversation. Devier forced Menshikov into giving his daughter's hand in marriage to his son. Menshikov extracted his revenge after Peter's death by exiling him.

222 [*epigraph*]: Wilhelm Karlovich Küchelbeker (1797–1846), a lifelong friend of his schoolmate Pushkin, wrote tales, novels, criticism, several plays, and a large body of interesting but finally undistinguished verse. For his part in the Decembrist rebellion of 1825 he was exiled to Siberia, where he perished. The epigraph is from his neoclassical play *The Men of Argos* (*Argivane*), III. iii. Based on Plutarch's *Life of Timoleon*, it treats the theme of the leader who sacrifices his personal happiness in order to restore the liberty of Corinth, and expresses the civic-minded author's view of good kingship.

Sheremetyev: Boris Petrovich Sheremetyev (1652–1719) enjoyed a distinguished military career in the Great Northern War against Sweden, helping Peter to advance after the defeat at Narva. In 1704 he took Derpt, in 1705 quelled an uprising in Astrakhan, and after upsets in Courland redeemed himself with Peter at Poltava.

Golovin: Fedor Alekseevich (1650–1706), diplomat and general from 1700. He was attached to Peter's embassy to Western Europe and was a key player in Peter's domestic and military reforms of the army. In 1700 he was made head of the Foreign Office.

Buturlin: this is most likely to be Ivan Ivanovich (1661–1738), a professional soldier from a distinguished family who spent a decade in a Swedish prison after Peter's defeat at Narva in 1700. He visited Paris with Peter in 1716 and thereafter served him in various capacities. He ended his life in exile and disgrace, having been implicated in a plot against Catherine I, Peter's widow and successor.

Admiralty: originally a shipyard on the riverside opposite the Peter–Paul Fortress. The current structure was built by Andrei Zakharov from 1806 to 1823 and was based on the original plans drawn up in 1704. The three principal avenues of St Petersburg converge on to this splendid building with its great Admiralty arch, adorned with nymphs and allegories of Fame, and crowned by a golden spire which is the symbol of St Petersburg.

Feofan Prokopovich . . . Kopievich: Prokopovich (1681–1736) was a Kievan clergyman and key supporter and propagandist of Peter the Great's reforms. His orations, sermons and his treatise in justification of the

autocracy remain key sources on the period. *Gavriil Buzhinsky*: (?–
1731), an original member of the Holy Synod that placed the Church
under the Emperor's control. In 1726 he was appointed Bishop of
Ryazan and Murom. At the request of Peter, who admired his learning,
he translated Pufendorf's *Introduction to European History*, and his *De
officiis hominis et civis juxta legem naturalem*, published respectively in St
Petersburg in 1718 and 1726. Both projects reflected Peter's interest in
the theory of the state and the duties of citizenship. *Kopievich*: some
sources put I. F. Kopievich's death in 1707, which would make his
appearance anachronistic. Publisher and printer of Russian books, he
operated primarily out of Amsterdam where he produced textbooks on
navigation, arithmetic, and Latin grammar for use in Russia.

223 *Korsakov*: Boris Yakovlevich Korsakov (1702–57) spent the years from
1716 to 1724 studying naval matters in France.

224 *be my Mentor*: the expression derives from the efforts of the wise Mentor
to guide Ulysses' son in Fénelon's epic *Télémaque* (1699). On the place of
Fénelon in the education of aristocrats in Russia, see Richard Wortman,
Scenarios of Power: Myth and Ceremony in Russian Monarchy, vol. 1
(Princeton, 1995), 147–168; and Andrew Kahn, 'Introduction' to M. N.
Murav'ev, *Institutiones Rhetoricae: The Treatise of a Russian Sentimental-
ist*, ed. Andrew Kahn (Oxford, 1995), pp. l–liii.

225 *Winter Palace*: the Winter Palace, also known as the Hermitage, is the
fifth building to have been erected on this site on the Neva Embankment. The museum is the work of Bartoleomeo Rastrelli, who began it
in the reign of Elizabeth and was dismissed twenty years later by
Catherine II. In this context the name must refer to the first, Dutch-
style house built for Peter the Great by the Italian Trezzini in 1711–12;
it was destroyed in 1726.

new style of dress . . . prohibited old one: as part of his statist vision of a
Western-oriented Russia, Peter the Great understood the need for (and
difficulty of) changing everyday custom and supplanting everything
associated with the Russia of old with a new image. In 1698 he began
to compel courtiers to appear at court in clothing of a European cut,
prohibiting the old style caftan that was the standard garb of boyars and
merchants. A formal change in dress-code was promulgated in a decree
of 1700, reinforced by a second decree of 1705, requiring all servitors,
merchants, and townsmen 'to shave beards and moustaches'; failure to
comply was at the threat of considerable fines.

Tsaritsa Natalya Kirilovna: Natalya Kirilovna Naryshkina (1651–96),
last wife of Tsar Aleksei Mikhailovich and mother of Peter the Great.

229 [*epigraph*]: from Pushkin's delightful *Ruslan and Lyudmila* (1820), a poem in six cantos that combined Russian folklore and the rococo beauty of French mock-epic.

Narva: in November 1700 the Swedish king Charles XII, at the head of inferior forces, defeated Peter the Great's superior numbers who were besieging the fortress at Narva and dealt an early blow to the Russian Emperor's ambitions in the Baltic. The debacle gave Peter the incentive to reform his military forces and regularize conscription. This first battle was the beginning of the Great Northern War in which the Swedish and Russian empires vied for dominance in the region until the Treaty of Nystadt in 1721 granted Livonia, Estonia, and part of Karelia to Russia, and thus secured her access to the Baltic.

230 *when order of precedence ruled*: the hierarchy of political power and family status at the court among the boyar class was enshrined in the institution of *mestnichestvo*, which strictly determined etiquette and precedence at feasts and on ceremonial occasions. The Table of Ranks made service to the state the decisive criterion in Petrine Russia and supplanted the old system.

231 *shaved your beards off*: Peter the Great's programme of Westernization encompassed all aspects of Russian life, including the appearance of courtiers and gentry. An edict of 1689 compelled all men in attendance at court to wear European clothing and to shave their beards, regarded by Peter as a symbol of the old ways and pious obscurantism. The affront to Orthodoxy helped to secure Peter the reputation of the antichrist among certain religious sects, who viewed his secularization of the state with great alarm.

terem: women's quarters in the aristocratic dwellings of Old Russia.

234 *1701 campaign*: emboldened by their earlier victory at the port city of Narva, the Swedes moved against Peter the Great in the Baltic in the autumn of 1701. This time, however, their plans were thwarted by substantial Russian victories.

235 [*epigraph*]: the lines are from Ablesimov's comic opera *The Miller* (1779). Ablesimov wrote the libretto to music of N. M. Sokolovsky; its popularity endured throughout the nineteenth century. It tells of a miller who, posing as a fortune-teller and conjurer, tricks the parents of the clever peasant-girl Aniuta into consenting to her choice of a suitor. The plot owes something to J. J. Rousseau's *Le Devin du village* (1752), which had enjoyed a success in Moscow the year before. Like that work, Ablesimov's piece celebrates rustic virtue. The opera contains the first theatrical representation of a peasant bride's party.

voivode: the Russian term *voevodstvo* refers to an administrative and military unit.

236 *Shein, Troekurov*: early supporters of Peter. Alexander Semonovich Shein had a distinguished military career during the reign of the regent Sophia (1682–89) and helped Peter defeat the *streltsy* (on whom see below) and gain power. Fedor Troekurov's official duties included service as the monarch's table attendant and chamberlain.

237 *Prince Bova and Eruslan Lazarevich*: Prince Bova Korolevich is the hero of a popular Russian chivalric tale of the seventeenth century that was based on a French romance. Although of written provenance, it uses features of the oral folk-tale and the Russian epic song. After succeeding in many trials, Bova prevails against his evil stepmother and meets his beloved princess Druzhevna. The work was popular among the upper classes; indeed, the Tsarevich Aleksei Petrovich was known to have enjoyed reading it. The *Tale of Eruslan Lazarevich* is far more complex and colourful; it is based on episodes from the tenth-century Persian epic *Shah-nama*. The Russian version is given a Cossack setting for the victories of the brave hero. Pushkin drew on this work of Russian folklore for episodes of his *Ruslan and Lyudmila*.

238 *Streltsy*: originally formed in the sixteenth century by Ivan the Terrible as crack-troops, these dreaded musketeers sided with the Regent Sophia against the young Peter during the contest for the throne in 1689. In the aftermath of Peter's victory, the *Streltsy* were ruthlessly suppressed.

241 *j'aurais . . . mijavrée*: *j'aurais planté là*: 'I would just have chucked it; *une petite santé*: 'such delicate health'; *mijaurée*: 'affected, pretentious young girl.'

245 *Charles XII*: king of Sweden (1682–1718). From 1697 to 1718 he was a formidable opponent of Peter the Great's attempts to expand Russian naval power in the Baltic. Their continual clashes culminated with Charles's defeat at the Battle of Poltava in 1707. The decisive victory enhanced Peter's prestige among the European powers.

American Literature

British and Irish Literature

Children's Literature

Classics and Ancient Literature

Colonial Literature

Eastern Literature

European Literature

Gothic Literature

History

Medieval Literature

Oxford English Drama

Poetry

Philosophy

Politics

Religion

The Oxford Shakespeare

A complete list of Oxford World's Classics, including Authors in Context, Oxford English Drama, and the Oxford Shakespeare, is available in the UK from the Marketing Services Department, Oxford University Press, Great Clarendon Street, Oxford OX2 6DP, or visit the website at www.oup.com/uk/worldsclassics.

In the USA, visit www.oup.com/us/owc for a complete title list.

Oxford World's Classics are available from all good bookshops. In case of difficulty, customers in the UK should contact Oxford University Press Bookshop, 116 High Street, Oxford OX1 4BR.

A SELECTION OF   OXFORD WORLD'S CLASSICS

ANTON CHEKHOV   Early Stories
                     Five Plays
                     The Princess and Other Stories
                     The Russian Master and Other Stories
                     The Steppe and Other Stories
                     Twelve Plays
                     Ward Number Six and Other Stories

FYODOR DOSTOEVSKY   Crime and Punishment
                     Devils
                     A Gentle Creature and Other Stories
                     The Idiot
                     The Karamazov Brothers
                     Memoirs from the House of the Dead
                     Notes from the Underground and
                         The Gambler

NIKOLAI GOGOL   Dead Souls
                     Plays and Petersburg Tales

ALEXANDER PUSHKIN   Eugene Onegin
                     The Queen of Spades and Other Stories

LEO TOLSTOY   Anna Karenina
                     The Kreutzer Sonata and Other Stories
                     The Raid and Other Stories
                     Resurrection
                     War and Peace

IVAN TURGENEV   Fathers and Sons
                     First Love and Other Stories
                     A Month in the Country

A SELECTION OF OXFORD WORLD'S CLASSICS

	Six French Poets of the Nineteenth Century
HONORÉ DE BALZAC	Cousin Bette
	Eugénie Grandet
	Père Goriot
CHARLES BAUDELAIRE	The Flowers of Evil
	The Prose Poems and Fanfarlo
BENJAMIN CONSTANT	Adolphe
DENIS DIDEROT	Jacques the Fatalist
	The Nun
ALEXANDRE DUMAS (PÈRE)	The Black Tulip
	The Count of Monte Cristo
	Louise de la Vallière
	The Man in the Iron Mask
	La Reine Margot
	The Three Musketeers
	Twenty Years After
	The Vicomte de Bragelonne
ALEXANDRE DUMAS (FILS)	La Dame aux Camélias
GUSTAVE FLAUBERT	Madame Bovary
	A Sentimental Education
	Three Tales
VICTOR HUGO	The Essential Victor Hugo
	Notre-Dame de Paris
J.-K. HUYSMANS	Against Nature
PIERRE CHODERLOS DE LACLOS	Les Liaisons dangereuses
MME DE LAFAYETTE	The Princesse de Clèves
GUILLAUME DU LORRIS and JEAN DE MEUN	The Romance of the Rose

A SELECTION OF   OXFORD WORLD'S CLASSICS

GUY DE MAUPASSANT   A Day in the Country and Other Stories
    A Life
    Bel-Ami
    Mademoiselle Fifi and Other Stories
    Pierre et Jean

PROSPER MÉRIMÉE   Carmen and Other Stories

MOLIÈRE   Don Juan and Other Plays
    The Misanthrope, Tartuffe, and Other
      Plays

BLAISE PASCAL   Pensées and Other Writings

ABBÉ PRÉVOST   Manon Lescaut

JEAN RACINE   Britannicus, Phaedra, and Athaliah

ARTHUR RIMBAUD   Collected Poems

EDMOND ROSTAND   Cyrano de Bergerac

MARQUIS DE SADE   The Crimes of Love
    The Misfortunes of Virtue and Other Early
      Tales

GEORGE SAND   Indiana

MME DE STAËL   Corinne

STENDHAL   The Red and the Black
    The Charterhouse of Parma

PAUL VERLAINE   Selected Poems

JULES VERNE   Around the World in Eighty Days
    Captain Hatteras
    Journey to the Centre of the Earth
    Twenty Thousand Leagues under the Seas

VOLTAIRE   Candide and Other Stories
    Letters concerning the English Nation

A SELECTION OF   **OXFORD WORLD'S CLASSICS**

ÉMILE ZOLA   **L'Assommoir**
                      The Attack on the Mill
                      La Bête humaine
                      La Débâcle
                      Germinal
                      The Kill
                      The Ladies' Paradise
                      The Masterpiece
                      Nana
                      Pot Luck
                      Thérèse Raquin